CONFLUENCE

ALLIES AND ENEMIES

BOOK THREE IN THE SPACE FLEET SAGAS

DON FOXE

CABALLUS
PRESS™

Copyright © 2 0 1 7 donfoxe

This is a work of fiction. Names, characters, businesses, places, events and incidents are either the products of the author's imagination or used in a fictitious manner. Any resemblance to actual persons, living or dead, or actual events is purely coincidental.

Written by Don Foxe. donfoxe.com

Produced by Caballus Press, USA Division
www.caballuspress.com

Stock images are used for illustrative purposes only.
Some stock imagery from Pixabay.com and Unsplach.com.

ISBN: 9780998804453

Library of Congress Control Number: 2017949973

Acknowledgments

Nancy Thurmond for editing. In those places you find the grammar questionable, those are my decisions to add *style* over substance. She shakes her head, but allows me artistic license.

Author's back cover photograph courtesy of *Abri Kruger Photography*, South Africa.

Cover graphics are mine, for better or worse. I do listen to others with more experience and talent, but I have a vision, so I go with it.

A welcome to his new home to Daegen. Dae, was adopted from the Hilton Head Human Association. Risky thinks her new brother is a pain (puppy-zoomies galore), but loves him.

Finally, my love and appreciation to Sarah. This year has been one of incredible learning. The time necessary to produce books, as well as traverse the minefields of marketing, while trying to maintain a business and a life, would not be available without her.

THE SPACE FLEET SAGAS

CONTACT AND CONFLICT
Aliens and Humans.
Book One in the Space Fleet Sagas.
The Launch of the PT-109, John F. Kennedy

CONFRONTATION
Aliens and Humans. Allies and Enemies
Book Two in the Space Fleet Sagas.

SPACE FLEET SAGAS
A Collection of Adventures.
Backstories Prior to the Launch of PT-109
Four Short Stories and Two Novelettes

CONFLUENCE
Book Three in the Space Fleet Sagas.

CONNEXIONS
Book Four in the Space Fleet Sagas.
(Due Spring, 2018)

Contents

Previously in Space Fleet Sagas -

In **CONTACT & CONFLICT** . . .

First contact is made by Captain Daniel Cooper, commanding officer of the SFPT-109, John F. Kennedy; Earth's first space-worthy battleship of the newly sanctioned Space Fleet.

Refugees from a galactic war seek asylum. Cooper remains with the aliens while the JFK goes for supplies.

Zenge, the aliens invading peaceful trading alliance worlds, arrive. Cooper, with the help of two attractive aliens holds them at bay until the arrival of reinforcements.

Earth forces, demonstrating superior technology and tactical skills, destroy or drive off the invaders.

Along the way we discover Daniel Cooper is one of twelve survivors of an experiment to reengineer humans for life in space.

In **CONFRONTATION** . . .

A trip to the planet Rys is needed to acquire power crystals to maintain and build more ships based on the Martian technology. During the visit, Coop and the JFK once more encounter Zenge invaders, this time saving Rys.

We discover the Zenge are pawns of a race called the Mischene. Mischene supremacists are convinced they should rule the galaxy. A confrontation with the Mischene, and their Zenge army is inevitable.

Earth barters for communication advancements by scientists from Fell in return for Earth's help freeing their planet and removing the Zenge.

While these events occur in space, a secret society of influential and powerful people conspire to dissolve the UEC on Earth, returning our planet to regional rule.

A Mischene religious zealot gains control of the Mischene and Zenge forces and places Earth in the cross-hairs for elimination.

CHAPTER 1

"Casalobos," the Admiral called over his com.

"109 targeting incoming enemy torpedoes in support of your gunners, Admiral," she replied and cut off further distractions.

"Tal," he called next.

"First three Spirit fighters set to launch in less than one minute," replied the Squadron Leader. No tension detectable in her tone. "Next three will follow as soon as the rear blast deflectors retract. We'll take out as many targets as we can before they reach the carrier." She cut him off as well.

"OPERATIONS, update" he demanded, swiveling to face the twenty-something operator who would not dare cut him off.

"Incoming torpedoes within range of our laser defenses. Automatic fire commencing," he replied. "The third enemy destroyer fired their pulse cannon and plasma cannon at the Fairchild, Admiral. The loads will arrive at the same time as the torpedo swarm."

Switching his attention from the Admiral, the OPS controller informed fighter command, "Captain Tal, you now have fifty-three-seconds before the first wave of torpedoes impact."

Spirits 2, 5, and 6 fired rear thrusters against the deflectors for an emergency launch. Instead of a normal controlled departure, they screamed out of the hangar, passed through the force-screen that prevented atmosphere from escaping into open space, and exited above the carrier's flight deck.

The three light fighters immediately encountered intense cross-gravity waves unique to the vortex. Flamer, piloting 2, rode the strongest wave, allowing it to push his ship sideways. Spirit 2 slipped over the side of the Fairchild. Like a swimmer allowing an undertow to pull him out to sea, Flamer went with the wave until he could pull the ship out of its grip.

The other two pilots, Wild Bill and Yassin, both made the mistake of fighting the gravity distortions crossing over the battle carrier. The small ships attempted to push forward against forces capable of moving small planets. For a moment the fighters appeared to hang still in space, caught in swirls and eddies similar to gravity whirlpools around black holes. The ships and crews pinned between the carrier and incoming enemy fire.

Realizing the futility of fighting the headwind, Wild Bill yanked on his collective. The keel thrusters fired, sending Spirit 5 straight up the chute. The incoming pulse beam from the third enemy destroyer passed beneath them.

Yassin and the crew of Spirit 6 disappeared within the following plasma load. The fighter vaporized in the super-heated projectile's path toward the Space Fleet carrier's bridge.

The PT-109 removed incoming torpedoes as Kennedy, the ship's AI, acquired, determined speed and course, and fired. The ship employed railgun, lasers, and the plasma cannon, selecting the defense with the best odds of reaching a target in time to prevent an impact.

Sindy Kebede at Tac-Ops monitored the action while keeping watch on the reset-timer for the tachyon weapon, waiting for the system to recycle so she could take out the third destroyer.

"Comeon, comeon, comeon." She spoke the prayer-plea aloud, but it did not speed the process.

Genna controlled the Patrol Boat's back-up electro-magnetic generated force field. This allowed her to pad impact zones and minimize damage when missed torpedoes made contact. Instead of trusting untested software, she relied on reflexes enhanced by genetic engineering. The AI's avatar concentrated on the incoming torpedoes, dismissing those most likely to be hit by Kennedy, and projecting flight-lines for the ones getting through. Her calculations provided only seconds to increase the force field's strength at the points of impact. Her inhuman eye-hand coordination the last available opportunity to save the ship from lethal damage. All other systems operated at max, and Kennedy engaged with battling the gravity-distortions within the vortex, while defending the ship from enemy fire, and covering the battle carrier.

Elie piloted the battle-tested space boat. In spite of the distortions, she forced the 109 to move. With safety limits disconnected, she taxed the power plants. The Spaniard played a deadly game of shuttling power between maneuvering the ship, and shunting as much energy to the shields as possible. She kept an eye on Genna, trying to anticipate when the avatar would shift the field in order to slide power from performance to protection.

Her re-engineered strength nearly crushed the manual flight control yoke in her right hand when coms called out, "Spirit 6 is gone."

The coms officer continued to provide bad news. "Enemy pulse and plasma rounds exploded against the Fairchild's aft deck. Upper Flight Hangar force-screen disabled. The hangar entrance collapsed. Three Spirit fighters are trapped inside. Carrier's bridge hit, but remains operational."

Coms continued to voice data-reports displayed on his terminal, as well as communications incoming from the other three ships in the beleaguered battle group.

"The 99 continues to cover the Pegasus. The 99 has taken four torpedo hits. Top, front starboard section is open to space . . . section sealed. Upper deck plasma cannon is gone. Hit amidship on port side. Section sealed. Fourth torpedo was a dud."

From the pilot station, Elie could see Sindy's Tac-Ops halo-display. She knew they were doing an incredible job taking out torpedoes headed for them and the Fairchild. The loss of sonic force-field protection, no communications beyond immediate vicinity, the constant strain placed on the BCVG by the anomalies within the vortex, and more rounds incoming from enemy ships meant the odds of survival continued to stack up against them.

Genna successfully redirected forcefield depths and prevented more than minimal damage by five high-explosive torpedoes that evaded the ship's defenses. The Fairchild, a bigger, more important target, received more attention, and more damage.

Coms confirmed Casalobos' concerns.

"Four torpedoes were blunted by the Fairchild's force field, but one connected at the bridge. Captain, the damaged bridge could not withstand the concussion. Fairchild reporting bridge and combat control room, including main communications and telemetry consoles, destroyed. Operational control of the ship has been moved to Engineering."

In spite of the intense concentration required to pilot the ship, oversee command, and distribute energy, the Captain of the 109 could not ignore the call when she heard her name weakly through the Fellen trans-com bracelet she always wore.

"Noa, copy. It's Elie," she answered through gritted teeth, hoping her personal communications bracelet had the power to reach the twin Tal wore.

Kennedy, unrequested, boosted the signal while maintaining fire on incoming torpedoes.

"Hey, Loba. We're in pretty bad shape over here," came the reply. "My fighters are trapped behind the blast-deflection barriers. That probably saved us when the ceiling and walls came down. Hangar is venting atmosphere. Any crew not already dead escaped. They sealed the area. Spirits 3 and 4 are safe, functional, and stuck with me. We have environment inside the ships, but no way off the hangar. Hawks is not answering hails, and I'm unable to take command. Master Chief is running the show from engineering, but he's blind down there, Loba. He could use your help."

Elie smiled. One: relieved Noa, and the other fighter crews were alive. Two: The Israeli more concerned about the Master Chief than herself. Before she could respond to the gritty pilot, Sindy announced:

"Tachyon cannon ready. Firing. Hope you burn in hell," she added as the super-charged beam hurled towards the enemy destroyer. "Kennedy, light that mother-fucker up."

Coms called the action: "Third destroyer hit by our tachyon beam. The space-frame is crumpling. Multiple hits of kinetic and plasma loads from the 109 are on the way to finish the job."

With the distance to travel, and the vortex playing havoc with anything moving, it would take time and luck for the rods and plasma loads to reach the crippled destroyer.

Cons finally called out, "Two rods made contact. Implosion imminent (hesitation -- pause -- deep breath). There she blows. Implosion. Concussive reaction, amplified by the gravity distortions, completely taking out the disabled destroyer."

"Pegasus reports a hit to her starboard forward quarter. Casualties, but the section has been sealed. The ship remains operational. The 99 did one hell of a job keeping her safe," the LTJG added, not realizing the sting it gave Elie, who had not kept the Fairchild as well protected.

"Sorry, Noa," Elie said, releasing the yoke, and returning pilot control of the 109 to Kennedy. "I should have done more to protect the Fairchild."

"Stow it, Elie," Noa responded over the com. "The enemy ships targeted two-thirds of their armaments at us, not the Pegasus. The 109, the Fairchild crew, Flamer, and Wild Bill did everything possible. There were just too many incoming. If the Prophet and his other battlecruiser decide to join the fight now, I'm not sure we'll survive. Keep an eye on them, and get the group out of this kelba vortex."

"Any word on Hawks?" Elie asked.

"No, but until we know for sure if he survived or not I'm sure Rachelle and Sam will agree you should have flag. I'll call them. Noa, out."

Elie was not sure what to do, then Sindy's hand took hers. Casalobos released a long, slow breath. Whatever she faced, she had friends, an able crew, and a strong ship.

BEFORE THESE EVENTS - - -

PART 1

Conspiracy

Connections

Rivers begin from many different sources. Streams, lakes, underground springs, and glacial melting can form the headwaters that will eventually flow into a mighty river.

Something as simple as rainfall on a mountain, or melting snow can start the momentum that grows until a river eventually forms.

CHAPTER 2

Mississippi, US - Six Years Past

The jump across the small creek brought him into brush. The moonless night worked to his advantage; concealing him. A good thing since he tripped as much as walked through the overgrown thicket. His reengineered improvements, unfortunately, did not include enhanced night-vision. He had not packed special optical gear since his original plans did not include sneaking around in the dark.

His earlier examination of area maps surprised him with the number of shuttered old United States Navy facilities within a mile of his position.

Besides the old NASA propulsion testing center he intended to recon, to his south sat an outdated and abandoned Data Buoy Center once used to keep tabs on ocean waves and currents around the planet. To his north, the Navy once conducted research within a short walk of a Naval Oceanographic Office. These centers ceased operations before the global pandemic, but after sea-creep made the Gulf Highway, once Interstate 10, the new edge of the Gulf of Mexico.

It required effort to work through the overgrown brush, but reward arrived with a view of his objective. The propulsion testing center consisted of four building on the far side of an open field. Security lamps around the four buildings cast circles of yellow glow on the ground. Ambient light filtered onto the field. It would make getting across the field easier. It would also make it more dangerous.

No need to check his timepiece to know one-hundred-hour already passed. This late, or early, the lights operated as passive security, and not for workers to move between buildings.

He pulled small, high-def zoom binoculars from the pack around his waist. The exterior lights allowed him to see the double wire fences surrounding the compound. The outer ring twelve to fifteen-feet high, with a push-out of barbed sensor-wire mounted to the top, adding another two or three-feet. The inner fence looked eight-feet high with a double strand of sensor-wire running its length along the top.

"They will have motion detectors, or something similar, outside the fences," he said aloud. Bad habit; talking to one's self. Old habit he no longer worried about. Though he did whisper.

"Drainage ditches running east and west." He pulled the binoculars down. "Animals will use those for water. Can't be chasing possums every night. Less likely they set motion detection along the ditch," he surmised, returning the binoculars to his pack. "If I run along the ditch, good chance I get to the first fence without setting off an alarm. I should be able to jump the first one. Don't hesitate between them. Get over the inside fence, and into the shadowed side of that first building."

He pushed his way back through the thicket, then slowly moved along the creek bank, occasionally stepping into shallow water to pass a natural obstruction too tall, thorny, or thick for any other choice. A brief unwanted thought given to omnipresent alligators each time his feet entered the slow-moving water.

He soon noticed the depression allowing runoff from the field to merge with the stream. He crouched and followed it through the overgrowth.

Earlier in the evening he reconnoitered research buildings on the campus of the University of Southern Mississippi in Hattiesburg. He did not get inside, and did not learn anything of value, but sneaking around manicured bushes and flat parking lots did have its perks. No alligators and no nasty security fences topping the list.

He dropped to one knee at the edge of the open field. The dark clothing he wore blended with the scrub. Watching for movement. Waiting for guards to make a circuit. Patient.

Nothing happened. No obvious security patrols. No people moving between buildings. No transportation, ground or air, active. The lack of life pricked a momentary concern. If evil labored within the compound, there should be more security. If this was an honest research facility attempting to provide energy-independence for the United Earth, they might not consider it important.

One way to find out.

"Go." The word escaped with a breath. He churned across the field at an inhuman pace. The reengineering may not have given him night vision, but it sure as hell gave him speed.

He timed his leap, going up and over the twelve-foot (plus extra) obstacle, landing between the two security fences on two feet. No hesitation, and a couple of long strides followed by another leap.

The stun rounds hit him at the apex of the jump. Four of eight fired from compressed air rifles made contact and discharged. The high voltage ammo did not interfere with his momentum, but did interfere with his brain's ability to communicate with his muscles. Instead of landing on his feet, he plowed into the hard-packed dirt inside the second fence. His body convulsed. His body also fought the attack, allowing him to recover quicker than a normal human.

He pushed up in time for a stun prod to press into the back of his skull, just above the neck. When the juice hit, he went down.

The man holding the rod waved to the shooters on the roof. He addressed the team converging on the unconscious Space Ranger. "Find his transport. Sat-image shows it parked off the old access road leading to the wilderness. Disconnect the systems and trackers before you bring it in."

As that team departed, the team from the roof arrived.

"Bind him, hood him, and stick him in the secure cell on the second floor," he ordered. "If he twitches, hit him with the stunner."

"Which will make him twitch," a shooter quipped.

"Then stun him again. You do not take chances with this man."

"Why not just kill him now?"

"Information, leverage, and anything else the people in charge can think of," the one in command replied. "Get him into lockdown. We have a busy couple of days ahead making sure we're covered."

Space Fleet HQ. Toronto, CA - <u>Now</u>

"Admiral Singletary." The feminine voice sounded strained and excited. "A wormhole gate opened inside the Kuiper Belt. An alien ship entered the solar system."

Fleet Admiral Terrance Singletary's concentration on reassignment and redeployment of personnel interrupted by his Aide's news. Operation Counterstrike's expeditionary force, deployed to the planet Fell more than a year previously, would return to Earth within the coming month. The successful liberation of the planet from Zenge invaders would count as his first major win as Commander of the United Earth Council's Space Fleet. That he had little to do with the decision to launch the mission, the operational planning, or the actual fighting would not impact his acceptance of accolades.

Reassigning a quarter-million people involved advanced planning. The data-dumpers in Staffing required final approval on where they believed personnel should be allocated. He did not care what they believed. Where he wanted them mattered. Important decisions, but not to the level of the unexpected arrival of an alien ship.

"Where is the Kennedy? Did the aliens attempt contact?" he demanded, responding to the voice emanating from an embedded inter-office speaker.

"Captain Sligh is moving to intercept," his Aide, LTJG Krista Stewart, replied. She occupied the reception area, the final barrier before his sanctuary. Her responsibilities included filtering all incoming communications, as well as monitoring Fleet activity. "If the ship is broadcasting, there will be a lag of approximately five hours."

"How long for the Kennedy to reach the area?"

"Three-days, eighteen-hours. However, the 109 will receive communications before us. They can retransmit to Earth via STORM-HATCH. We should know more within three hours."

Not one to value patience, three hours awaiting news did not sit well. Nor was he a proponent of the changes within Space Fleet during the preceding five years. He called the SFPT-109, John F. Kennedy, 'the Kennedy,' and not '109.' Most Fleet personnel spoke of the ship as the 109 and the Artificial Intelligence operating the ship's systems as Kennedy. Giving the AI a de facto name seemed wrong to the Admiral.

As a youngster he saw the stories about Lethal Autonomous Weapons Systems (LAWS) driven by artificial intelligence devastating areas and killing people following the Pandemic. As a result, AI-operated systems took a set-back for decades. He foresaw nothing but problems resulting from their reemergence on Space Fleet ships.

"Is the Roosevelt still at Fell?" he asked.

"Yes, sir. Delivering the last load of supplies before Counter-strike personnel begin returning to Earth," Stewart answered.

"Forward Captain Harrington an update and order the SFPT-99's immediate return," he said. "With the convoluted way space-fold works, Captain Harrington might reach the alien ship before Captain Sligh."

"Actually, sir," Stewart's tone hesitant. Correcting the Admiral never a pleasant experience. "The 99 needs to exit the Fell system before reentering space-fold for the trip to our solar system. Captain Harrington will arrive in our system in four-days, twelve-hours."

"Order them back anyway, Lieutenant," Singletary replied, biting off each word. "Inform me immediately when we receive word on why that ship is here."

He shut down the inter-office coms, not waiting for a reply. He pushed the data pad with reassignment orders away. The recent forced retirement of Admiral Pamela Patterson, and his subsequent promotion, meant this would be his first actual test as Fleet Admiral in charge of providing security for the solar system.

He should be issuing orders. He should be considering different scenarios to handle whatever might come his way, but he did not want to overreact. He preferred people think of him as calm and in control of the situation. Best not to make moves others could criticize later.

The knock on the door interrupted his thoughts. It opened slowly. Krista Stewart looked around the edge.

"Should I inform the UEC?" she asked.

The UEC represented the central governing body for the planet. Space Fleet acted as a military force under their auspices.

"Inform Governor Arcand," Singletary said. "Tell him I have everything under control. And tell him I will keep him apprised."

The Aide's head disappeared. The Admiral's fingers tapped nervously atop his desk while he wondered if he overlooked anything else.

He turned the coms back on, in case Stewart thought of something else he should do.

Space - Between Jupiter and Saturn

"Captain, it's an Osperantue freighter," ENS Michael Cuthbert reported. The officer at the 109's communication console continued, "The ship is emitting an open hail across several channels. I can stream video and audio."

Faulkner Sligh, former commanding officer for Space Fleet shuttles and temporary Captain of the SFPT-109, wanted nothing more than for nothing more to happen before his impending retirement.

"Put it up, Ensign," he replied. "Everyone remains on battle stations. ENS Perrelli, monitor all scans. Let me know if that ship acts peculiar in any way."

Tony Perrelli nearly asked how he would recognize anything peculiar from an alien ship, but caught himself. "Yes, sir," he replied.

An image materialize on the forward Super High Definition (SHD). Humanoid with pale pink skin, wide-set doe eyes, wide nose, and thin lips. A Bosine; apparently female.

The com-trans converted Osperantue to English.

"I am Commander Sella Vasch of the Osperantue Freighter, Northern Sky. We are a civilian freight hauler and trader. We have no weapons. We come to meet with the humans who freed Fell to inform you Osperantue has also been liberated from the Zenge."

"What's the delay?" Sligh asked.

"Two-hours, forty-one minutes," Cuthbert answered.

The captain ordered the pilot to drop out of space-fold. Because the aliens did not possess tachyon-based communications equipment, his ship needed to reenter natural space to reply. He would use their older coms-system to broadcast a message the Osperantue could receive.

"Commander Vasch, this is Captain Faulkner Sligh of the United Earth Space Fleet vessel John F. Kennedy. We are making way for your location. Please come to a halt and hold. We will arrive in seventy-five hours."

Seventy-five hours passed with a combination of fear, trepidation, expectations, and excitement aboard the 109, at Space Fleet headquarters on Earth, and among the United Earth Council representatives informed of the alien ship's arrival. Mars Shipyard and Docks (MSD) and the Earth Moon Space Station (EMS2) maintained constant scans and visual surveillance of the Osperantue freighter.

The PT-109 entered natural space 50,000-miles from the Osperantue ship. With the two ships sharing proximal space, relying on older communications tech did not present a lag-problem.

"Commander Vasch, this is Captain Sligh. We scanned your vessel. I see no indication of weapons, however, I must be careful. I would like permission to access your systems to make sure you are who, and what, you profess."

"I am happy to oblige all requests," the Bosine replied. "Is there anything I must do to provide access?"

Kennedy, the ship's AI, answered. "I have systems entry already, Commander Vasch. It appears you are exactly what you say."

"Welcome to our solar system, Commander," Sligh said. He accepted Kennedy's assessment without comment. "We were under the impression Osperantue had been invaded and overrun by Zenge, following the orders of the Mischene."

"Yes, Captain. I was dispatched to inform Earth a grave misunderstanding has occurred. Six months ago, Mischene battlecruisers and troops loyal to the Aster Farum 3 government arrived in our system. They destroyed the Zenge space ships in orbit. They battled the Zenge and Mischene traitors on Osperantue. They freed my planet."

"Commander Vasch. Earth has an expeditionary force currently on the planet Fell. They defeated the Zenge presence on that world. The Zenge were led by Mischene officers and protected by Mischene battle ships. Can you be a bit more clear for me? You say Mischene forces liberated Osperantue from Zenge and Mischene traitors?"

"Exactly, Captain Sligh," the officer responded. The earnest timbre of her voice not lost in the communication or the translation. "The Zenge operate under the direction of a Mischene traitor who calls himself the Prophet. He radicalized a segment of the Mischene population, including several powerful people on Aster Farum 3. This Prophet, and Mischene converts to his religion, indoctrinated and trained the Zenge warriors. He is responsible for the attacks on Trading Alliance Worlds."

"Commander, a moment, please," Sligh said, and signaled the Coms officer to disconnect sound. "Counselor Bouvier, opinion?"

Genna Bouvier, Ship's Counselor, sat at the Operations and Tactical Console. The attractive strawberry blonde, with deep blue eyes and freckles, appeared young for the role of Counselor aboard a Fleet battle ship. Bio-electronics embedded in her brain before birth connected her directly to the ship's AI, creating a human-machine bond. The first viable human avatar to an artificial intelligence, created to prevent a sentient technology from insanity. She and Captain Daniel Cooper made first contact with extraterrestrials, and she possessed more experience than anyone else on board with Zenge, Mischene, and aliens in general.

"I cannot honestly say," she replied. "Commander Vasch believes what she says. Kennedy's bio-scans indicate no attempt at deceit. We knew about the Prophet, but intelligence considered him a pawn of the Mischene government. I suggest you try to learn more."

Sligh signaled for audio to resume.

"Sorry for the interruption, Commander," he said to the image on the bulkhead. "How did the Mischene come to the aid of Osperantue?"

"The Mischene loyalists, under Governor General Soren, removed the Prophet's people from influence in the Aster system. My understanding is the Mischene extremists supporting the

Prophet represented a small segment of their race. When the Prophet sent his commandeered fleet, officers, and Zenge terrorists to attack other worlds, his assets became spread thin. This allowed the Mischene loyalists under Governor Soren to retake control of the Aster system. Six months ago, the Mischene loyalists arrived at Osperantue to confront the Prophet's forces. They eradicated the invaders." Commander Vasch took a moment to calm herself, excited by the retelling of the story.

"Governor General Soren, himself, came to Osperantue to apologize for the actions of the Mischene traitors. He promised all the aid the Aster system could provide. They delivered supplies at no trade cost, and provided help to rebuild infrastructures destroyed by the Zenge. He promised Mischene loyalists will offer the same assistance to every world the Prophet's cult attacked and plundered."

The doe-eyed freighter captain looked away. She reached for something off-screen before returning to her narrative.

"The Governor received reports the Trade Alliance Worlds believe the Mischene supported the Zenge attacks in the galaxy." Vasch gave Sligh an intense look as she continued. "The Mischene loyalist want to make this right, Captain Sligh. They want the galaxy to understand a few Mischene extremist do not represent Aster Farum 3. That is why I volunteered to bring you this message."

The freighter commander read aloud from a hand-held flexsheet.

"I, Governor General Soren, and the honest and honorable citizens of Aster system, especially the Mischene race, feel morally responsible for the death and destruction the Prophet unleashed upon members of the Trading Alliance. The Prophet is insane and misguided. He and his core supporters do not represent the average Mischene.

"I am aware of planet Earth's actions to repel the traitors from the Quentle system, and the heroic efforts of humans to defeat the invaders on Fell. I offer to provide any and all support requested by Earth's forces in their efforts against the Prophet and the Zenge fanatics. Aster Farum 3 wishes to extend aid, supplies, or assistance required by the Fellen to speed their planet's recovery."

The Commander looked up from her note to address the human. "On board, I carry medical supplies for the people of Fell, provided by the Mischene loyalists. This small gesture is a first step in repairing the harm done by the Prophet."

"Why bring them to our solar system?" Sligh asked.

"Fear that when I arrived in the Fell system, under the current situation, your people might fire first," Vasch admitted. "The Mischene are aware Earth ships use space-fold technology to travel between star systems. They recommended I deliver the supplies here, along with an explanation, and ask you to pass both along to Fell."

"Captain Sligh," the ensign on coms interrupted. "You have a priority call from Fleet Admiral Singletary. The Admiral has been monitoring your conversation."

Captain Sligh turned to the monitor. "Commander, I appreciate your volunteering your ship to bring us this news. As you know, our forces have been through a protracted battle and we are all a bit on edge. I would appreciate it if you would allow a security team to board and inspect your vessel."

"Of course, Captain," the Bosine agreed. "I fully understand and extend a welcome to you. My ship is yours to command."

"Thank you, Commander Vasch. My security chief will contact you in a couple of minutes to determine the best way for our people to transfer to your ship."

Sligh ordered his coms officer to close current communications, instruct Space Fleet Marine Major Duval to contact Vasch, and put Admiral Singletary through.

The face on the SHD changed from the Bosine captain to the dark scowl of Space Fleet Admiral Terrance Singletary.

"I suppose it was necessary to keep me waiting, Captain," the Admiral started. "Make sure everything you download from the ship's computers is sent directly to Fleet Intelligence in Toronto. Keep your weapons up and your people alert. Wait for the arrival of the Roosevelt. By the time Captain Harrington is on site, I will have had the opportunity to parse the information. I will decide, at that time, what to do with the aliens and their ship. Singletary, out."

The image of the thin black man in his grey uniform disappeared, replaced by a virtual representation of the Osperantue freighter floating in the void.

Genna swiveled to face her commanding officer. "You did well, Captain."

Sligh nodded his appreciation. Further decisions would fall on Harrington, who held seniority. He silently asked the space fates to not let anything happen before the arrival of the 99.

CHAPTER 3

Space Port Harmony - Planet FELL

Elena Casalobos, Air Commander for Operation Crossroads, waited in the central command hut. The first building constructed by Earth forces at Harmony, formerly the Fellen space port of CHangoria 2. It became the OAT - Office for All Things. The structure, framed in metal alloys and clad in wood from local trees, blended with the older Fellen buildings. It housed the most advanced communications array ever created.

A Solid-State Tachyon Operations and Retrieval Monitor (STORM) display sat on a wooden table. More than a simple monitor, it could contain a captured tachyon particle in order to imprint information for transmission. It could also download and display distortion-free data.

Transmission or retrieval of communications and data happened through the Hernandez - ASparquila Tachyon Communications Housing (HATCH). The HATCH resembled a laser rifle surrounded by wire mesh. One rested on a swivel attached to the roof of the building.

STORM-HATCH or SH allowed real-time interstellar communications. The tachyon-based system enabled ships traveling is space-fold to send and receive communications. Until the breakthrough, ships in space-fold remained out-of-touch, forced to drop into natural space to send or receive messages.

A beefy, muscled Russian, legs stretched out in front of him, rested on a chair beside the Spanish Casalobos. Colonel Anton Gregory commanded ground forces for Operation Crossroads. The two commanders were Space Rangers, genetically reengineered humans, and friends for over thirty years.

A holographic mini-version of Admiral Singletary appeared above the STORM console. Their images would similarly appear atop the unit in an office adjacent to Singletary's.

"An Osperantue freighter arrived in our solar system." The conversation begun without introductions or pleasantries offered by Space Fleet's highest ranking officer.

"We know this," Gregory said. "It is why you recalled Captain Harrison and the 99."

"Yes, but what you do not know, Colonel Gregory, is the Osperantue claim their planet has been freed of Zenge invaders by what they describe as loyal Mischene military units," Singletary said.

"We know that, too," Casalobos replied. "We heard the conversation between Captain Sligh and Commander Vasch. We received copies of the data files downloaded by Kennedy."

"Who, exactly, authorized your access to any of this?" Singletary demanded.

"Space Fleet," Casalobos replied. "Communications' standing orders include keeping us informed of anything with the potential to impact our mission. I'd say an alien vessel showing up with news about Mischene and Zenge fits the bill."

"I assume Patterson set those orders before retiring," the angry little holo-image said. "Someone should have informed me following my promotion."

The Spaniard and the Russian said nothing to agree or disagree. Only one month away from returning to Earth, rocking a space boat this far from home made little sense.

"Fine," the Admiral finally said. "Captain Casalobos, task one of your fighters to recon Osperantue. I want to know if what the freighter captain says is true. Have them report directly to me. To me first, Captain. I'll decide if they should inform you of what they find, and whether they should return to Fell or proceed directly to EMS2."

Elena sat forward, about to rock the boat violently, when Anton placed a restraining hand on her arm.

"Yes, sir," she responded.

"Colonel Gregory, I'm ordering you to speed up the departure of personnel and equipment. I need all of my assets on hand. I intend to prepare Space Fleet for a sneak attack."

"Yes, Admiral. But there is one little thing."

"What little thing?"

"Not everyone wishes to return," Gregory informed his commander. "A few thousand people have decided they like Fell. They handed in resignation papers."

"How many exactly?" Singletary demanded. Holo-images do not always display colors and tones well, but the new tachyon system apparently did a better job. The Admiral's face grew darker.

"Twelve-thousand six-hundred and forty-one," Gregory replied. "Not counting Dr. Hiro Kimura. He is actually a civilian, and does not require a resignation."

"Tell them all no, Colonel," Singletary replied. "We are at war. I will not allow mass desertions. Anyone refusing the order to return will be courtmartialed and placed in prison."

"We can't do that, Admiral," Elena spoke up. "The people who joined the mission are all volunteers. None signed oaths to UEC or Space Fleet, unless they were already members of UEC military branches. Even then, when you declared Operation Crossroads as complete last month, it released them from service. Anyone serving UEC military branches, and having served their allotted time, have the right to resign."

If an image could explode, the interior of the hut would be charred.

"Captain Casalobos. Colonel Gregory. You will not leave one piece of equipment or one iota of supplies behind. If those deserters wish to remain, then we are better off without them. But I will not leave them anything UEC-owned. Is that clear?"

"Yes, sir," from both.

"You will not leave any part of our technology behind. Every space-fold crystal and array, as well as all components for the tachyon communication systems are to be packed up and shipped back to Earth. You have your orders, Singletary out."

Gregory looked at Elena. "Too bad so much equipment and supplies were lost or destroyed during all the battles. Many more things with too much damage to bother taking back. I do not think we can be held accountable if some of those who remain on Fell are smart enough to repair such useless items."

Elena smiled, realizing they were going to do whatever they could for the ones staying. She said, "I understand being protective of space-fold, but does the Admiral not remember the people who created the communications system are from Fell?"

"I think he prefers not to think about it," Gregory replied.

The two separated after leaving the OAT.

Casalobos ordered Noa Tal and the crew of Demon 2 to Osperantue. She informed Noa of the Admiral's orders. She told her long-time friend, and fellow Space Ranger, to obey those orders. Singletary was a pain and a prick, but he was also the boss.

Gregory amended the inventory lists by updating the equipment lost, destroyed, or too badly damaged to salvage. He recalculated the amount of supplies used during the operation. As it turned out, following his final accounting, they had few supplies remaining to transport back to Earth.

One thing Elena and Anton agreed about; the special METS (Multi-Environmental Tactical Skin-Suits) issued to everyone would be returned. It was one thing to tweak the Admiral's nose. The advanced suits protected the soldiers, modified environmental conditions, provided communications, and data. They were too valuable to leave. Space Fleet would mount a return force to recoup them.

Elena returned to the command hut and ordered the two specialists on station to take a five-minute break. She linked her communication-translator bracelet to the STORM-HATCH. With the added power, she could use the bracelet's private channel capability to contact Earth. "Nathan, it's Elie. Do you copy?"

More than a parsec away, but in less than four-seconds, she received a response.

"Elie. Nathan here. How you doing?"

"Everyone is fine. Are you aware of the Osperantue ship in the solar system?"

"I'm still Head of Sciences, Elie," he replied. "Singletary may not like it, but I'm too important to ignore, and too connected to ditch. I'm aware. We're waiting on Sam to arrive with the 99 before we decide what to do with them. I heard Singletary order your people to Osperantue."

"I thought he used a classified channel."

"He did. I have resources," Earth's most famous scientist and engineer said. His snicker came across the clear channel.

"Okay. Now for the real reason I called."

"Coop is still unconscious," Trent replied before she could ask. "He is physically fine. Physio is helping maintain muscle and joint mobility. All the wounds, even the head wound, are completely healed. Brain telemetry reads normal. We're just waiting for him to wake up."

"Thanks, Nathan. If anything changes . . ."

"You'll know when I know, Elie. Nathan, out."

Trent made sure the channel closed before addressing the man standing before a panoramic window, staring at a winter storm lashing the rocks along the shore of the island.

"That was tough," he said. "I hate lying to her."

Daniel Cooper turned from the view to face his friend. He nodded, then turned back to watch the storm.

CHAPTER 4

"The planet faces a religious crisis. The arrival of extraterrestrials opened the question of God, and the relationship between God and humans. From the Vatican, to Mecca, to Jerusalem, and all around the world, religious leaders are trying to maintain order. Is there a God? Do aliens believe in God? Do they know things we do not? Fear is a difficult enemy to fight. Religious groups who have sniped at each other for centuries, now combine to ask if aliens represent God, the devil, or something worse."

The man called Hadritak - the Presence, and the leader of the secret Camarilla Devolution - gloated.

The middle easterner devoted his life to terminating the concept of a centralized government able to tell his people the best way to apply laws. A man whose resolve multiplied with the reemergence of the Mufti in his home nation, and their promise to follow his leadership. Decades of deals, plans, and conspiracies ready to culminate. Their climax ending the short reign of the United Earth Council.

The other man in the room wore a business suit instead of a uniform. Known within the group as Cancer, his motivation to end the UEC revolved around gaining more personal power. When the UEC crumbled, he would step forward to provide security, leadership, and accept a role in controlling and commanding the military.

"It isn't just religion," Cancer added. "The UEC is reacting to the general population's discomfort with galactic politics. More than half of the Board of Governors are recent selectees. The new governors want Space Fleet to become primarily a military force and concentrate on system defense. While there are not enough to demand a complete shift in direction, Space Fleet is moving that way. New screening methods have been enacted for non-humans who apply for government positions, especially within the Fleet."

"We cannot allow extraterrestrials to become sympathetic figures," Hadritak said. "We must insure they remain separated from humans in order to maintain the narrative aliens are different, and potentially destructive to our ideals."

"We're keeping the refugees in New Zealand from traveling under the excuse they need protection," Cancer replied. "We are reassigning aliens off Space Fleet ships and onto platforms, or placed in positions on Mars or Earth to keep them out of the limelight."

"The world is experiencing distaste for a galactic war," Hadritak said. "Our media people constantly question the UEC's decision to send Earth into a war on a distant planet where humans die while fighting aliens there to kill other aliens. The mob mentality infecting newscasters has most of them following our lead. Doubt over the Earth's involvement weakens the UEC."

"The disinformation campaign designed by our partners is the keystone to our success," Cancer agreed.

"There are special broadcasts produced to question alien lifestyles, and how they may intend to spread their beliefs to our world. These documentaries will amplify people's natural fear of the unknown. Apprehension will soon lead to demands on the UEC representatives to restrict all alien movement. The UEC will have no choice but to act to calm a population stupid enough to believe the rumors and innuendo we create," the Arab said.

"The UEC will be held accountable for humans dying on distant planets for no reason, and allowing dangerous aliens safe haven. Representatives already hear the grumbles. We will soon have the momentum to call for disbanding the Council." Hadritak made his prediction looking out across the city of Toronto.

He turned his back on the view to face Cancer.

"What are the plans for Space Fleet's secondary mission, the exploration of new systems and attempts to make contact with alien lifeforms?" he asked.

"Delayed," Cancer replied. "The Board of Governors, as you well know, are moving toward Earth re-isolating from the galaxy. A growing number of civilian leaders believe we entered into galactic politics before proper preparation. First contact occurred long before anyone expected to encounter alien lifeforms. Discovering we have hundreds of neighbors, and they are embroiled in a major war makes people wonder which aliens are right and which are wrong. Those same doubts are spoken openly inside Space Fleet corridors, except . . ."

The Westerner moved to the window. Forty-four floors above mid-town Toronto. The cloudless sky ran to the horizon, and he could see the chop on Lake Ontario.

"Except what?"

"Our military forces have been kicking alien butt. Earth may be the newest planet to discover interstellar travel, but we appear to own the most sophisticated technology. We also have thousands of years of military history. Tactically, we held the advantage in every encounter with aliens."

"You think we should not isolate ourselves?" the Arab asked.

"We cannot ignore the lessons learned by Daniel Cooper's actions before the Bosine tried to kill him," Cancer said. "His successes in fighting the Zenge and out-maneuvering the Mischene, coupled with the current mission which freed Fell, have people within Space Fleet, and others in positions of influence, considering Earth as a potential power-broker in the galaxy. Our superiority with space-fold travel, weapons, tactical planning, and, now, communications could make us the big dog in the universe. In spite of our late arrival, we've arrived with the biggest, baddest stick."

"Many of those advantages resulted from the help of aliens," Hadritak reminded his co-conspirator. "Fairchild found space-fold in a hidden alien hangar. Communications technology bartered from Fellen engineers, and energy-producing crystals through an alliance with Rys. We must take care aliens do not receive too much credit for our superiority. I have enough votes to begin making changes to distance us from them."

"What will the UEC do about alien alliances?" Cancer asked.

"Place them on administrative hold. All agreements, alliances, treaties, and compacts are scheduled for reevaluation. Earth will not maintain a military force on Fell. All personnel will be recalled. Once the Star Gazer is no longer needed to haul Fleet personnel and supplies, refugees who wish to return to Osperantue can board. The ship will use space-fold to reach the nearest wormhole gate, where the arrays will be removed. They will be given a warm good-bye and good luck," he said, somewhat sarcastically.

"Osperantue freed by Mischene," Cancer said, turning his back on the view. "Osperantue reports claim the Mischene are not the power behind the Zenge invasions. There is actually another player directing the attacks. A Prophet. Is that not ironic? We have churned up the religions on Earth to question the beliefs of aliens, and an alien Prophet presents himself. It is perfect."

Hadritak sank into a chair. His dark eyes, hooded by bushy eyebrows, looked to a future as intoxicating as an oasis in a desert sandstorm.

"We have worked decades to dissolve the UEC in order to regain regional autonomy," he mused. "Now, on the verge of success, we are presented an opportunity to take control of more than a few regions on our one small world. We may have the ability to take the galaxy."

"A juggler's feat," Cancer said. "Do away with the UEC, keep Space Fleet in the hands of humans, and make sure those humans are loyal to the Camarilla. When the UEC disbands, Can-Am will be the logical one to maintain the military forces."

"I believe you are right," Hadritak agreed. "I have that under control. The potential snake in our garden is Nathan Trent. With Daniel Cooper gone Trent no longer has his most important piece, but we will need to watch the remaining Space Rangers. That is your responsibility, dear Cancer. I am sure you can arrange assignments that appear rewarding, but keep them at a reasonable distance until we have everything in place. We may even find uses for their talents."

"What about the threat represented by the Zenge and the Mischene, be it the loyalists, or the Prophet, or both? Do we wait for them to attack?"

"We will prepare to defend our solar system from an attack. The UEC intends to open a dialog with the Mischene. We must determine who is telling the truth. We must also decide who to send to peace talks to represent Earth. I will argue for the military, not diplomats. If there is to be an attack, I think Earth should be the one to strike first."

"There is no question Space Fleet must take the lead," Cancer agreed. "It makes the most sense. We insert our people to control the parlay and, ultimately, do what is best for the Camarilla. If

Space Fleet needs to strike first, whether the target is the Prophet, the Zenge, or the Mischene, it will be at a time of our choosing."

The attack on the Aster system came at a time chosen by Atticus Soren, the Sacred Prophet of the Tahbita.

When the wormhole nearest Aster Farum 3 opened, twelve Mischene battlecruisers came through the gate. Six stationed as support vessels in the Zenge system, taken by General Trewellan's troops, with the help of mutinous true believers on each ship. The other six commandeered following their arrival as scheduled replacements. Taken by surprise, crews were given an option to convert or die.

After entering the system, their weapons acquired unprepared Mischene ships orbiting Aster Farum 3, including the Governor General's new Super Battlecruiser. They fired on the unprotected ships until debris rained down through the atmosphere.

Communications and technical specialists loyal to the Prophet took control of all automated systems on the planet in the exact way the elder Soren did to the other worlds in the system when he launched his attack to control the system.

One-half-dozen Class One Carriers followed the twelve battlecruisers. Each carried 60,000 Zenge warriors. Nothing prevented them landing near major metropolitan areas and military bases on the planet.

Over 350,000 cold-blooded Zenge loosened a barrage of laser fire on military installations and personnel. While most attacked military target, others hacked through civilians with blades and finger-talons.

Amos Soren stood in his office screaming at Admiral Lexton, locked away in a bunker at the capital's space port.

"You can scream all you want, Amos. We had no warning, and we have no defenses available," the Admiral said from the screen. "I suggest you find a place to hide with plenty of food and water."

"Why don't you kill them with the shock collars?" Soren demanded.

"Because I had the collar codes changed," Atticus Soren said, his image overriding the Admiral's. "Hello, Father. I thought I would visit you for a change."

"Atticus, what have you done?" Amos pleaded. "You are Mischene. We have a destiny to fulfill. What you are doing today will destroy our future."

"It will destroy your future, Father. It will destroy the future of those who do not accept the word of the Creator, or his Voice," Atticus said, his image transmitted from the last battlecruiser to enter the system. "Those who accept and follow the truth of the Tahbita will rise, and together we will conquer the universe."

Soren started as a woman's scream penetrated through the solid doors of his private chamber.

"That would be Wandi Eskil," Atticus said. "I have video feeds from all around Aster Farum 3, including your offices, Father."

"Atticus, I surrender," the Governor of the entire system said to the image. "I can have all Mischene lay down their weapons. I will accept you as the Sacred Prophet. I can make the conquest of the Aster system simple for you."

"Thank you, Father, but I prefer ultimate defeat and humiliation to surrender. It makes it easier to convert survivors to the one true way after they witness the alternative. Before I order the Zenge outside your door to enter, I thought you should know. . . "

"Know what? You bastard. Your mother was a whore. You are no Prophet. You are left-over semen from a bad night. I made you the Prophet." Soren screamed at the monitor, spittle flying from his mouth.

"I thought you might like to know, as soon as I complete the conversion of the Aster system, I intend to do the same against your new enemy."

Atticus watched from two points of view as the doors to his father's private chambers blew inward. A half-dozen blood-covered Zenge attacked the white-haired man cowering behind his desk. Blood splattered, spraying Soren's portrait before it was ripped down in the melee.

The Prophet watched calmly as his father died.

"That's right, Father. Once I eliminate the Earthers, nothing will stand against us. Prophesy states the Mischene shall rule the universe, and follow the will of the Prophet. Earth will be eliminated from the galaxy . . . my will be done.

CHAPTER 5

"It's politics," Mara Trent said. Sixty, her hair black and wavy, eyes bright, and as smart as the day she discovered the key to unlocking the Martian codes four decades earlier.

"It's bullshit," Daniel Cooper replied.

The two held the discussion in the medical wing of Elliott Fairchild's mansion on Fin Island, Vancouver, Canada. Coop reclined on a comfortable leather chair any dentist would take pride in owning. Neurotrodes, affixed to his forehead and temples, monitored brain activity and transmitted the information to a holographic displayer. A 3d hologram of his brain hovered in the air, three-feet from where he sat.

"Spike." The one-word comment from Dr. Sonja Juri, Swiss clinical neurologist.

Sonja Juri arrived within the first forty-eight hours. She placed the neurotrodes on Coop's head and booted her holo-display before introducing herself to Mara, the medical staff, or Coop.

Coop's floating brain emitted small red sparks near the right frontal lobe.

Nathan Trent hired Dr. Juri in preparation for Coop's awakening. He provided her over fifty-years of reports detailing Daniel Marcel Cooper's behavior under every possible situation.

Clinical neuropsychology is a specialty in professional psychology that applies principles of assessment and intervention. Dr. Juri wrote extensively on her scientific studies of human behavior as they related to normal and abnormal functioning of the central nervous system. Her research dedicated to better understanding of brain activity and behavior relationships. She applied her findings to correcting behavioral problems.

Fifteen days passed since Coop awoke. Two weeks spent in physical rehabilitation.

While awake and able to follow directions, he never spoke, causing a great deal of concern. Mara Trent, an exolinguist, told everyone to shut up, keep their concerns to themselves, and treat him as normally. She spent every minute with him she could.

Talking. She maintained a monologue that included everything from current events, events on Fell, to memories and stories from the previous forty years.

Two days previously Coop spoke for the first time.

"Mara, could you not talk all the time?" he asked. "I need to think."

Afterward, Mara and Nathan brought Coop up to speed on events during his convalescence.

"Pam has been head of Space Fleet during the most incredible time in Earth's history," the tall, brown-haired, dark-eyed man said. His hair, always a bit shaggy, had grown longer. His stubble was now a full beard. His skin pale from months under artificial lights.

"From developing the ability to explore deep space, to encountering alien life. She was at the helm while Earth went into a battle against extraordinary odds. Odds Space Fleet overcame. Two planets and billions of lives saved. We've discovered alien technology able to advance ours by hundreds of years. We've made alliances with worlds trillions of miles away. We've gone from discovering the secrets of space travel to having partners from other worlds in less than fifty years. Pam's been in charge for every major victory. How the fuck could they ask her to resign?"

"Profanity," Juri remarked in her slightly-French, almost-German Swiss accent. "A good sign."

Mara ignored Juri. She looked down at her long-time friend. She had aged well, while he never aged because the Space Ranger Project activated his Methuselah genome pairs. Cooper regenerated every day.

"Those changes, happening one atop the other, created the problem, Coop," she said. "Earth is still humans acting like humans."

"Amen," Juri said. Her face hovered within inches of the floating brain, absorbed in whatever she saw occurring. Oblivious to the fact she commented aloud.

Mara continued. "Humans with centuries of basic hopes and fears unchanged, regardless of the changes happening around them."

She turned to look at the greying day sky outside the window. Fall barely arrived to western Canada, and winter already trying to push it aside.

"When conditions move so quickly they appear out of control, people demand more control. They watched a battle on the edge of our solar system between you with a couple of Earth's new space ships against a dozen intergalactic battleships. The people of Earth were given a taste of space. It came with death and destruction. It was exciting and it was frightening. You won. You saved a quarter of a million alien refugees. But what if you had lost?"

"We didn't lose," Coop reminded her. "Those refugees are now a part of our planet. They've settled into New Zealand and the people there accept their new neighbors."

"And with them, the people of Earth have to deal with the fact we are not alone in the universe," she replied. "Our religions and our belief systems are in question. Faith that helped many people through the pandemic which wiped out half the population is shaken. Everyone knew this was a possibility when Elliott discovered the spaceship and storage hanger on Mars fifty years ago. It's been thrown in their faces in high definition."

"They need strong leaders now more than ever," Coop countered. "Pushing the most experienced officer in Fleet out the door is stupid and dangerous."

"The new members of the Board of Governors for the United Earth Council are responding to fear, I grant you that," she said. "They were elected by a growing concern Earth is moving too quickly to engage in galactic politics. We were right to defend Rys from the Zenge attack. That alliance means we have the potential for an unlimited supply of crystals to power vital technologies, but the UEC acted without a mandate from the population. From the people they are supposed to represent."

Coop argued from his reclined position.

"The UEC agreed to send troops and ships to recover the planet of Fell in order to gain more advanced alien technology. The trade, tachyon-based FTL communications for our assistance in repelling the Mischene and Zenge invading their planet. Earth acted in the same way all of the Trading Alliance worlds interacted. We bartered for something we wanted by offering something of value in return. We now have the ability to communicate instantly from within space-fold travel and across trillions of miles of space." As the discussion between the two extended, he became less agitated.

Prior to entering the room, Dr. Juri instructed Mara to banter with her patient. She asked Mara to push him intellectually. Nearly forty-years married to Nathan Trent, considered Earth's greatest living scientist, made her the perfect candidate for such an assignment.

"We also suffered thousands of casualties in the battle," she said. "When the media on Earth reported on the war, they emphasize our losses. Thousands dead, and many more wounded to save an alien planet."

"Fell appreciates what we did," Cooper responded.

"Spike," Juri said.

"Other worlds in the galaxy will be looking to Earth as a leader against Zenge and Mischene aggression," he added.

"Earth isn't ready to lead," Mara answered, then sighed. "That is the crux of the problem, Coop. The memory of a pandemic that killed five billion people remains fresh. The anarchy, the brutality that followed for many of those who survived is still an open wound. The fight to bring all of Earth under one governing body was bloody, horrible, and necessary. People still live who remember borders, and the safety engendered through insulation from others."

"I was in that fight," Coop reminded his friend. "I was on the ground. I lost a lot of friends. It was worth every life spent."

"Agreed," the half-Jewish, half-Catholic woman nodded. "It still doesn't change the fact it was painful for every person on the planet. They are not ready to take on more pain. They are especially not ready to take on the pain of an entire galaxy of people they don't even know."

"The majority of those species and races they do not know are kind, friendly, and worth the risk," Coop said.

"You have a small sampling, Coop. Your experiences are also unique. You lived with two aliens. The Zenge and the Mischene are also out there. The Zenge the enemy we thought we knew. Then you discover the Mischene behind the curtain. Next, an Osperantue space ship arrives to tell us the Mischene are really good, but there is an extremist faction of Mischene behind the invasions. And now we are given another curveball. Atticus Soren's repudiations of these accusations are under analysis."

Coop sat straight up, his hands, super-strong, crushed the arms of the recliner as he asked, "How? What are you analyzing?"

"Oh, my word," Dr. Juri exclaimed.

Mara ignored her, concentrating on Coop. "Relax. He sent a drone through a wormhole. The 99 collected it and brought it to Earth. That Mischene are pointing the finger at each other is not the issue. How many more worlds in the galaxy are ruled by evil? How many wars are we expected to wage?" she asked.

"You think we should turn our backs on what we now know exists in the galaxy, just because we don't know everything?"

"I do not agree with what is happening," she answered. "I want us to move boldly into space. I want the Earth to stand as a shining beacon of safety and justice. I want Space Fleet to be the force to win over hearts and minds, and stand against tyranny. But I understand the politics as well."

"Politicians, driven by a media afraid of confrontation, and people afraid of change, decides to replace the current leadership with isolationists," Cooper responded through clenched teeth. "Pam forced into retirement. Aliens removed from all Space Fleet ships until they complete Fleet Training Schools. The troops on Fell recalled to Earth."

"Yes," Mara said. She looked outside once more. The grey day more somber. Raindrops pelted the window's glass pane. "The alliances and trade agreements between Earth, Rys, and Fell will be renegotiated by the new Board of Governors. All Space Fleet ships are required to remain within the solar system. The aliens in New Zealand have the option of boarding the Star Gazer and returning to Osperantue after it returns from Fell."

"We can't trust the Mischene," Coop said. He was reclining again, his eyes watching the play of rain on glass.

"The UEC is evaluating all of the information, from all sources. Except from you. As far as the world is concerned, you have disappeared, presumably still in a coma. Possibly dead. Even if you had their attention, you are not unbiased. You fought the Zenge and the Mischene, but even you did not know who directed their attacks. The pieces keep changing, Coop. Even on Earth. Some-one, or group is working incredibly hard to force Earth to step back from the other worlds. The United Earth teeters on dissolv-ing."

"When will our people head back to Earth?" Coop asked.

"They've already been recalled," she replied. "The UEC wants the troops back quickly. News outlets have been showing wounded and caskets coming off of our ships for months. The Governors want live heroes walking off and waving to the crowds. And they want it soon. They should all be back on Earth in three weeks."

Daniel Cooper closed his eyes. Mara, concerned he might fall back into the void he only recently climbed out of, stared at Juri. The doctor shook her head, and lifted a thumb.

"I just think it sucks they kicked Pam out," he said.

"If you think this sucks," Mara said, watching his face and lis-tening for Dr. Juri's 'spike,' as she tells him, "Pam's replacement is Terrance Singletary."

CHAPTER 6

Dr. Sophia Juri achieved the mantel of the leading expert on clinical neuropsychology before turning thirty-five. With smooth light skin, and cornsilk blonde hair, the woman still looked mid-twenties. Her somber grey eyes the one trait making her appear older.

Seated in a leather wingback chair facing Nathan Trent, who sat behind Elliott Fairchild's massive wooden desk, she appeared calm and assured. She earned her reputation, and did not feel overwhelmed by the presence of Space Fleet's Head of Sciences, or his wife, the famous exolinguist, Mara Trent. Mara, seated in a matching chair to her left, had already spent time with the Swiss researcher. From the first meeting, she and Mara established an easy rapport.

"Dr. Juri," Trent opened, "any determinations regarding Coop's recovery and current health?"

Juri crossed her right leg over her left knee, exposing rather creamy skin and a lot of thigh in the short dark-blue dress as it rose. The chic designer dress a vivid contrast to the white lab coat she also wore.

"I cannot tell you why he remained unconscious for ten months, and I cannot tell you what instigated his awakening, but I can tell you his remarkable regenerative powers heeled the damage to his brain. In fact, the new sections function at a significantly higher degree of efficiency than before his injuries."

"How so?" Trent asked.

"The laser which hit Captain Cooper seared across the left side of his head. It penetrated the skull, causing massive damage to the frontal lobe, brain tissue, both white and grey matter, and limited trauma to the rear brain. The areas damaged control motor functions on the right side of his body, as well as language and writing skills. Speech, hearing, logical reasoning, and mathematic thinking are more predominant in these areas."

"Coop is able to communicate with no apparent problems," Mara said.

"He has no problems with any of his higher functions," Juri responded. "His new brain, and, therefore, Captain Cooper function perfectly well."

"You said significantly more efficient," Trent interrupted.

"Incredibly more efficient would be more correct," Juri replied. "While Mara engaged him in conversation, attempting to cause emotional, reasoning, and argumentative responses, I monitored his brain functions. He was performing complex mathematical equations while carrying on their discussion."

"Any ideas what he was calculating?" Trent asked.

"Based on previous research data, I would say determining distances and times to travel to locations on Earth, and around the galaxy using different types of ships, factoring variable speeds. Conversation threads created a desire to take action. He made these calculations in nano-seconds."

"He's a space ship pilot," Trent said. "Those types of calculations are ones he makes subconsciously all the time."

"Not at the speed, and not with as many variables as he currently can," Juri answered. "He weighed and evaluated everything Mara told him, sifting everything through a reasoning and logic filter while maintaining a healthy emotional response."

"Is that why he regained his composure, his calm, so quickly after every outburst?" Mara asked.

"Yes. He continues to have emotions, feelings if you will. Most generated from the older left brain side. He accepts this, but also analyzes everything from the source to a huge number of potential responses before making a decision what to say, how to word it, and how to deliver the reply."

"His undamaged brain cells cooperate with the regenerated cells without rejection?" Mara, the linguist, found the information regarding Coop's new skills enlightening. She was well aware language and writing originated from the left brain. Coop's revivification of brain tissue represented the first such occurrence in human history. Brain injuries never fully healed. And damaged tissue never recovered better than the original.

"Actually, the regeneration of the white matter destroyed by the laser has created a faster, more streamlined communications transference between the new brain components and the old components." She plowed ahead, not waiting for another request for clarification.

"The brain utilizes grey and white matter. Grey matter contains most of the brain's neuronal cell bodies. The grey matter includes regions of the brain involved in muscle control and sensory perception such as seeing and hearing. Grey matter is home for memory, emotions, speech, decision making, and self-control. White matter is composed of bundles of myelinated nerve cell projections called axons, which connect various grey matter areas of the brain to each other. These bundles carry nerve impulses between neurons. Myelin acts as an insulator, increasing the speed of transmission of all nerve signals."

Juri uncrossed her legs, and leaned forward. The open lab coat and scoop neck on the dress exposed the swell of her breasts. Her excitement over explaining Cooper's new neurology increasing her breathing, raising and lower her chest.

"His revivified grey matter is now much more dense with neuronal cell bodies, and he appears to have more control over their functions. The myelin in the new white matter has increased the transmission time of the axons. He simply thinks faster than other humans. Faster than any artificial intelligence ever created."

"But he acts, talks, and seems the same Coop I've known for twenty-five years," Mara said.

"He is the same," the Swiss scientist replied. "Further along the evolutionary trail, but his personality is the same. Much of that originates from the right brain, the side not damaged when he was attacked."

"Anything more?" Trent asked.

"Two more tests I want to try before I remove the neurotrodes," Juri replied. "One to test motor function, and one to test emotional-physical responses to stimuli. If he performs as I suspect, he will be perfectly capable of resuming his life."

Fin Island - Outside

November winds criss-crossed the island. Fin Island, nestled between several larger islands on the northern coast of British Columbia, still felt the effects of Pacific weather fronts. Dark clouds sailed in from the Ocean, bringing sheets of cold rain, followed by periods of mist.

The staff erected a tent on a flat spot near a beach created by a finger of the sea jutting into the island from the East. One-hundred yards away, five targets flapped on metal poles driven into the sand.

Coop stood facing the targets, his back taking the brunt of the chill wind. He wore black BDU over a METS. The Multi-Environmental Tactical Skin-Suit developed by Trent industries provided warmth. Black baseball cap kept his longish hair out of the way and the rain out of his eyes.

Dr. Juri, also protected by a METS, dressed in rain-proof jacket, pants, and boots, had a more difficult time standing upright against the wind.

A lab tech emerged from the tent, gave Juri a thumbs up (telemetry recording operational), and handed Coop a laser pistol.

"Left hand," Juri said. "Look at me, Captain."

Cooper turned his head to look at the scientist. Her cornsilk hair plastered against her head.

"Without hesitation, when I say 'fire,' take a shot at the target furthest left."

He nodded, and she called, "FIRE!"

The pistol rose and a laser burst released before his head completely turned back to the beach. The lower left corner of the target was singed.

"Now, left to right, take a shot at each target. Take your time," she said.

He raised the weapon, taking a breath, letting it partially out, and fired. He repeated the process five times. He hit a target each time, with the last burst coming closest to center. The others cutting holes around the perimeters.

"Look at me again," she said. "This time, right hand." He switched the pistol. "Without hesitation, take a shot at each target as quickly as you can. Fire!"

The pistol crossed his body, coming up under his raised left arm. Five shots. Five center hits.

Coop followed Juri inside the tent. With the flaps closed, the reinforced material made the small area comfortable and relatively quiet.

"What did we just prove?" he asked.

Juri hesitated to answer while she reviewed the brain scans. "The left-handed shot simply set the target in your mind. When your brain's left side was given time to calculate all of the variables, from wind to rain, distance, the weapon's characteristics, it educated your right brain, and improved the muscle responses on your left side. With each shot fired, more information resulted in your aim improving."

"The analytical left side is strong enough to improve the responsibilities of the older right side of my brain," Coop surmised.

Engrossed in the holo-information, she nodded. "The left side was allowed free rein during the second test," she said. "Using the data obtained when you fired left handed, you made each minor adjustment necessary to compensate for environmental or mechanical variants. You hit dead center five of five in less than three-seconds."

"I'm officially freaky," he said.

"You're officially enhanced," Juri corrected. "I suppose, clinically, more enhanced since you already received physical improvements. We need to return to the compound. I have one last neuron-physical trial. I can remove those neuroprobes afterward."

Fin Island - Inside

Coop held his head beneath the hot spray of water. The shower removed the chill from the return trip to the compound, but could not wash away the doubts swirling about his own new self. Logically, he understood everything that occurred. Emotionally, he was fighting the fear he had changed into something not entirely human.

He did not startle, but was surprised when the particle-field keeping the water inside the shower parted and a nude Sophia Juri joined him.

The shower's oversized design allowed the steam to rise, giving a clear view of the woman. Five-six, creamy white skin, and toned muscles. The cornsilk pubic hair so light, it was barely there. Her breasts round, and firm, with long pink nipples and dark red areola. She wore a neuroprobe at each temple. Her hand found his arousal, and her tongue explored his mouth.

Coop lay on the damp sheets, watching the still-naked scientist as she hovered over a portable telemetry pad. They had sex in the shower, and moved to the bed without bothering to dry off in between. That had been two hours earlier.

"This your final trial?" He asked.

In response, she closed down the pad, and joined him on the bed. Gently she removed the four neuroprobes, pulled the two she wore off, and placed all six on a bedside table. "Trials all done," she said. "You are a perfectly healthy human male."

"Normal?" He asked.

"Oh, God, no," she replied, straddling him. "You, Daniel Cooper, are much better than anything normal."

Over the next three days Dr. Juri completed her reports for Nathan Trent. She spent her nights in Cooper's private rooms.

On the fourth day she signed a tedious promise to let no one know of Coop's existence, and a promise in return for her personal wealth, she would make none of her findings public until and unless released from the contract by either Nathan Trent or Daniel Cooper.

Coop did not come to the hover-port to see her off, and she had not expected his appearance.

"Now what?" Coop asked.

He sat in the same leather chair Dr. Juri used earlier in the week. Nathan leaned against the desk.

"I have to return to Toronto, and then EMS2," Trent answered. "I can't stay away too long, especially with all of the changes happening. You will continue your physical recovery. You also need time to adjust to how your brain processes information. Dr. Juri believes you should assimilate and begin to accept your new normal within two months."

"Space Fleet?"

"You need to consider your association with Space Fleet as over, Coop. The changes forced on us by the UEC and Admiral Singletary are not the kind of things you would quietly concede. For now, you remain MIA, possibly dead, definitely vanished. The staff on this island swore oaths to privacy, including remaining away from the mainland until you are ready to leave. Mara and Elliott are not telling anyone. That leaves Pam, Henry Brown, Heidi McCormack and Genna as the only other people who know about Fin Island. Pam is the only one who knows you're awake."

"Sky, Storm, Elie and the rest?" He asked.

"What do you think?" Trent asked. Partially because Coop's opinion mattered, and partly to see how his reasoning skills operated versus his emotional desires.

"I know I want to see them. I miss them. But everyone is safer if they continue to believe I'm out of action," he replied. "Like you said, I need the time to get one-hundred percent physically, and come to terms with my mental upgrades. I also have a year of global changes to catch up on and investigate." He held up a hand to stop his friend's objection.

"Investigate from here, Nathan," he said. "Elliott is the most wired-in person on the planet. Someone is trying to demolish everything we helped build over the past thirty-plus years. I want to discover who, and why, and what they plan on as a replacement for a United Earth. I can do that from here."

"Mara can help," Trent said. "She has a gift for seeing hidden meanings in words, spoken or written." Trent pushed away from the desk. "The troops who elected to return will arrive at MSD in a couple of weeks. I have final checks on the new Destroyer, Carrier, and the latest squadron of fighters to complete."

"I've seen the specs on the Destroyer, and the revisions to convert the second one to a Carrier Class vessel, but nothing on the new fighters," Coop said.

"On purpose," Trent replied. He smiled at someone he had know for decades, and someone he knew was still the same man. "If you saw the new Spirit fighter, there's no way in hell I could keep you away from the yoke."

CHAPTER 7

Access to the second sub-basement of the building housing the administration offices for the United Earth Council required the highest clearance. Agents strictly enforced Technical Surveillance Counter Measures (TSCM) used to secure the space and the corridors surrounding the meeting rooms located on that level.

The meeting room included a holo-wall screen accessed by a non-connected data pad. Non-connected to any system other than the display wall. The possibility of information intercepted beyond the four walls, short of a human leak, impossible.

The data pad belonged to Dr. Nathan Trent, Head of Sciences. It fell to him to provide the briefing to the others present.

A image of a grey and black torpedo-shaped cylinder without fins or tail hovered before the six people seated in front of Trent.

"I'll keep the science simple," he said. "The message and data are what we need to discuss, but you should have a basic understanding of the delivery system."

The cylinder began to slowly rotate. Impossible to determine a true size without a reference.

"This is a marvelous piece of technology," Trent explained. "A communication drone with a miniaturized wormhole engine. It's the same power and navigation system found in galaxy-class vessels used by the Trading Alliance worlds to access and travel via the wormhole channels between solar systems."

"Weapons capable?" General Karin Spross asked. General Spross, Chief of Joint Military Operations, represented the military branches of the United Earth Council. The Swiss-born military professional's career garnered four stars and a Doctorate in Military Science.

"This particular drone carried nothing remotely capable of offensive or defensive acts," Trent answered. "It consisted of the power system, navigational computer, the housing, venting, simple communications array, and a remarkable gas-based data file storage system."

The cylinder disappeared and a small glass tube filled with a smoky cloud replaced the image.

"The drone's design allows it to travel through a wormhole approximately four-times faster than a normal ship," Trent said. "It is designed to speed communications between systems. According to the information retrieved, it was created by scientists in the Aster System, and utilizes a special gas mined on one of the moons located there."

"Did you confirm the Mischene sent this drone?" Admiral Terrence Singletary asked. Singletary, current commander for UEC's Space Fleet, represented the para-military branch responsible for initial contact and security involving anything or anyone not from Earth.

"Not exactly," Trent answered. "This was sent to Earth by Atticus Soren, the Prophet."

Aya Ishihara, Japanese, and a great legal mind, represented UEC's newest division, the Exo-Legal Affairs Department (ELA). With the advent of alien contact, understanding alliances, trade agreements, and the rules and regulations of extraterrestrial societies, now came under her jurisdiction. ELA tasked to build the foundations for legal standing for when Earth negotiated with aliens the UEC understood the ground (space) rules.

The young (late twenties), attractive legal expert interjected, "The Prophet, as in the Mischene holy man responsible for the Zenge?"

"Again, yes and no, and the reason for this meeting," Trent replied. "According to the communication, Atticus Soren claims his father, Amos Soren, the Supreme Governor of a trading guild that dominates the Aster system, is the man responsible for the attacks on planets around the galaxy. I will make sure everyone receives classified copies of the translated communications. You will need to consider a response."

"Do you trust the information?" Paris Cassel, Director of UEC's Security Agency, espionage and counter-espionage, asked.

"I don't trust anything, but I cannot discount anything, either. I can only tell you what he tells us."

"Please get on with it, Dr. Trent," Guy Arcand, representing the UEC's Board of Governors (Directors), said. "You can save all the tech-talk for notes to the final transcripts. What does the Prophet want?"

The holo-wall displayed a star system. Trent brushed away the star and outlying planets, asteroids, planetoids, and non-relative debris. It left three planets, several moons, and twelve small green spirals twirling in the air.

"Aster system contains three inhabited planets in proximal orbits around a yellow-giant star called Resa Asteri Major. From nearest the star, outward, you see Aster Farum One, [AF1], Aster Farum Two [AF2], and Aster Farum Three [AF3]. The Mischene are indigenous to AF3.

"The system contains five inhabited moons, including the one orbiting AF2 where the data gas is mined. There are three other uninhabitable planets, and dozens of moons and planetoids. The system is circled by twelve wormhole gates."

"Twelve? Isn't that a lot?" The question came from the final person involved in the secret and secure briefing. Saleh Abd al-Rashid represented the elected members of the United Earth Council.

"It is and the reason Aster system is considered a major player in galactic trade," Trent replied. "The ability to access the system constantly by wormhole travel due to the number of gates, and the incredible amount of goods and services created by the eight inhabited planets and moons, make the system wealthy and influential. According to research made using the Osperantue and Fellen data shared with Earth, the Mischene trading guilds run the system, operating for over 5,000 years."

Trent brushed away everything except AF3, which he expanded.

"The Prophet claims his father's guild became greedy on a maniacal level. Governor Soren discovered the Zenge and decided to harvest the species to train as warriors. His planned to advance the Mischene dominance from AF3 to the known galaxy. Using religious laws and prophecies, his guild justified the invasion of other worlds as the next step in Mischene manifest destiny."

"Religion as interpreted by this Prophet?" al-Rashid asked.

"Religion used by Governor Soren to support racial supremacy of the Mischene," Trent answered. "According to the Prophet, his original responsibility was to act as a spiritual leader for the Zenge. He was sent to convert the species into fanatics driven to support the Mischene overlords. Again, this is coming from Atticus Soren. He claims he actually experienced a spiritual conversion. He came to believe his father's ambitions morally corrupt, the forced takeover of the Aster system wrong, and invading planets, murdering or enslaving the populations as evil."

"I have read of similar occurrences of politics and religion causing such actions among civilizations in Earth's own history," al-Rashid said. "Though on a much smaller scale. It is not unusual for religious leaders to recognize the corruption of their beliefs, and turn on the politicians."

"The Prophet, sorry, if I keep using the term," Trent said. "It is simpler to call him the Prophet, so we do not confuse him with his father. Whether he is or is not a prophet is not for me to judge."

"We get it, Trent," Arcand said. "Can we move this along?"

"The communication sent to us includes supporting data for the Prophet's claims," Trent continued. "The gas-delivery system provides an incredible amount of storage and no resistance. It is fast, efficient, and compact. Because of the amount of data, we needed two weeks to translate and analyze everything contained.

"We estimate the drone traveled thirteen days from Aster to our solar system. A wormhole-capable ship carrying people would take at least two months to make the same trip. You need to understand the information is at least one month old."

A second gas tube appeared.

"The information is supported by data we collected from a second drone," the scientist added. "While PT-109 and PT-99 retrieved the Prophet's drone, a second one arrived. This one sent by the Mischene loyalists on AF3."

Until now, Trent and Singletary the only ones present aware two drones arrived from the Aster system.

"The Prophet, Mischene military units loyal to him, and the Zenge commandeered several Mischene battlecruisers patrolling the Zenge system. They launched an invasion of the Aster system, specifically AF3, the Mischene home world. They also took control of inhabited moons, but did not attack AF1 or AF2. The moon Flare orbits AF2 and is the location of the gas mines and the research center where the message drones originated. Ship building and repair facilities are located on the other moons. "

The display produced images of battlecruisers, placing four around AF3, and twelve spread between AF3 and the two other inhabited planets, with two more, displayed in red, orbiting AF2.

"There are more than a dozen ships displayed," Trent said. "The green ones controlled by the Prophet, and the red are Mischene loyalists. As you can see, the green outnumber the red by eight-to-one. Some of the green ships are vessels located within the system when the Prophet attacked. These converted or were taken by the Prophet's forces."

The holo-image of AF3 replaced the gas tubes.

"Governor Amos Soren is dead. Mischene loyalist military units are under siege. The military commanders dispatched a drone of their own to ask for our help in repelling the Prophet and saving their civilian population."

Trent allowed a moment for those present to grasp the implication. Both sides in the struggle for Aster system were asking Earth to intercede.

"The Prophet claims no intention of invading the Aster system beyond stopping the Mischene loyalists, the influence of his father's guild, and releasing the Zenge from bondage," Trent said.

"He has the forces available to pull this off?" General Spross asked.

"He does," Trent replied. "He controls the assets assigned to Zenge activities in the Zenge system. He took control of over ninety-percent of the Mischene assets in the Aster system. He now commands the Zenge and Mischene handlers invading other worlds."

"That could add up to hundreds of ships, and millions of troops," Singletary said. As the head of Space Fleet, he had access to intelligence collected over the preceding year, including the estimates on enemy forces invading developed and undeveloped worlds.

"What does he want?" Arcand asked.

"A truce and a treaty with Earth," Trent answered.

"Explain," Ishihara said.

"The communication is a request that Earth send representatives to the Aster system for the purpose of peace," Trent said. "To keep it simple, the Prophet claims to have no desire to expand his influence beyond the Zenge system. He wants to return there, with all of the Zenge and those Mischene who believe in his interpretation of the Tahbita, the Mischene holy book. He intends to demilitarize the Zenge, and create a system of peace and harmony.

"He requests we act as a mediator between him, the Aster system residents, and the Trading Alliance worlds. He wants us to provide a peacekeeping force on AF3 while the loyalists remove all military and offensive capabilities. He suggests we can help establish laws designed to end subjugation of the other indigenous races."

"Doesn't want too much, does he?" Spross commented.

"He wants Earth to establish relationships with AF1, AF3, the moon habitats, and help return the system to a confederation," Trent added. "Also, to inform the other worlds in the galaxy of the truth, and request time for Aster to recover its footing, without fear of reprisals. Finally, he will supply aid and assistance, administered by Earth and other members of the Trading Alliance, to the worlds harmed by the Mischene loyalists."

"He suggests Earth should become the major player in ending the conflict that has disrupted the known galaxy," Ishihara said. "Why Earth?"

"We represent a superior force," Trent said.

"He's right," Singletary added. "We might be new on the stage, but we already proved Earth's technology and military skills are better than anything the aliens can throw at us. While they have spent thousands of year becoming merchants, we became leaders."

"The overwhelming sentiment of the population is they do not want the UEC expanding into galactic politics and entanglements," Arcand said. "We have removed our forces from Fell and suspended agreements, treaties, and even curtailed communications with the two planets we are most familiar with because of those opinions."

"And we must honor the wishes of our people," al-Rashid said. "But we must also lead our people. We must consider these requests seriously. One requests a military intervention. One asks for a diplomatic solution. Sending a delegation to speak with the Prophet could be done without fanfare. If we do not like what we see or hear, we can return and continue our isolation as we develop a better understanding of the worlds around us."

"If we do like what we hear, are we prepared to intervene?" Arcand asks.

"We do not need to make a decision regarding intervention at this time," al-Rashid countered. "It appears we only need to make a recommendation to the UEC representatives as to whether it would be in Earth's best interest to send ships to Aster system and meet with The Prophet. To discover the truth."

"At his choice of location? In Aster system?" Spross asked.

"Better there than here," Singletary replied. "If we send a delegation, I vote we send it with a battle group able to make them think long and hard about trying anything stupid. If we need to defend our ships, should any of the players there make the mistake of attacking, the collateral damage will occur in their system. They already know we can kick their butts with a PT boat and a couple of three-person fighters. Imagine what the Prophet will think when he sees a Destroyer and a Carrier filled with fighters pop into the Aster system without using one of those wormholes."

"Overconfidence is a dangerous thing," Spross warned.

"We will take the information, look over everything, and meet again in twenty-four hours," Arcand said. He stood, signaling an end to the meeting. "The data sticks Dr. Trent provides are to be kept classified and secure. They are eyes-only, and that means no sharing with anyone. Reach your own decision. When we come to a consensus, we'll present it to a secure meeting of the UEC representatives. They will have the data and our suggestion. They can all vote on what Earth's role will or will not be."

Nevada Desert

"The UEC voted to send representatives to meet with the Prophet in the Aster system," Trent said. He held up a METS suit, shaking the material, and inspecting it from different angles.

"It's a trap," Coop said. "What's special about this new suit?"

The two talked in Trent's personal, private, extremely secure research and development lab in the middle of the Nevada desert. Near the secure research and training base used by Space Fleet, but separate and separated by several miles of open terrain. No one allowed within ten miles of the lab, and nothing could fly overhead, including satellites.

"It's heavier," Trent replied. "I was a dumb-ass when I sacrificed additional force-deflection for weight on the suits for you and the other Space Rangers. I sometimes forget you are six-times stronger than before. You look so damn normal. If I had done this right the first time, the laser would have been deflected. Why do you think it's a trap?"

"The laser hit me in the head," Coop said. "Even if the body wounds were prevented, I would have taken the head shot. The Prophet is a religious zealot. He isn't going to negotiate."

"True. But if you did not have to recover from the body wounds, you might have recovered faster from the brain damage. Maybe he's just religious, and not a zealot. Maybe he actually wants a private nirvana in his own system."

"This new suit weighs twelve-ounces instead of six. It deflects lasers, where before it only prevented penetration by blades and projectiles. It isn't as silky, and will be more difficult to put on and take off. Anything else?"

"The full-body suits designed for Space Rangers include full head cover and integrated boots designed to use a new and improved spectrophotometer woven into the material. The new hybrid-material will match the exterior of the immediate surrounding area. It takes a couple of minutes to accomplish. If the background changes rapidly, you would be pretty obvious. To activate or deactivate the camouflage option, you have to rub a strip along the back of the sleeve's forearms. It deactivates immediately. They still use a system to either heat or cool the wearer based on need, but I added a rebreather hooked directly into the head-cover. In cold weather, foggy breath will not give you away. You can go into non-oxygenated areas, or toxic situations for hours. Hell, you could probably survive in outer space for an hour."

"Extremely cool," Coop said. "You could have brought this to Fin Island. Why did you send for me?"

Trent delivered a devilish smile. The inventor, engineer, scientist never truly grew out of the boy who loved new toys and surprising his friends. Without a word, he headed for the door, motioning Coop to follow.

Amused by the brilliant man's impish nature, Coop followed, his curiosity rising with the storage lift taking them toward the surface.

The doors opened, and they stepped into a hangar. Sensors turned on lights.

A ship sat center of the hangar. It looked ready to leap, and angry enough to bite your head off.

"Meet Wraith. A brand new class of ship. A one and only prototype. My baby," he said to Coop. "Built her as R&D, but also as a private personal transport if I felt the need to visit other worlds."

"This is the drone you sent to recon Fell before Operation Crossroads," Coop said. His eyes scanned the forward exterior of the ship, his brain running calculation and figuring aerodynamic qualities in the time between breaths. "You showed her to me on a video feed in the back of your hover-car."

"Yep. This is her, in the Martian-alloy composite flesh."

Angel and Demon class fighters were built similar to Stealth jets. The Wraith owed its heritage to the historic F-22 Raptor. The ship's design consisted of clipped delta wings with a reverse sweep on the rear. It employed four empennage surfaces and currently rested on retractable tricycle landing gear. Surfaces included canted vertical stabilizers and horizontal tails. His practiced eye and new analytical powers determined the set up allowed the tails to move.

The wide cockpit sat forward center, above a rectangular grill with the appearance it could scoop space from in front and blast it out the back. Side-mounted double-barrel small-bore railguns placed on either side of the cockpit. Coop spotted the SH communications catch and send tube running along the bottom of the craft. The ship's underbelly appeared seamed for bomb-bay doors.

"Wingspan of fifty-six feet," Trent said."Length is seventy-two feet, and height is only twenty-four feet. Two power plants. One provides in-atmosphere and simple space travel. Don't have a top end on the speed inside the troposphere, but she has hit Mach 10.

We estimate up to 300,000mph in natural space. The space-fold is .12SL [twelve-percent of the speed of light] inside a system and 1KPCd [1,000 parsecs per twenty-four hours] in open space."

Trent folded his arms, looking and sounding like a proud new dad.

"She's equipped with advanced gravotonics," he informed the former test pilot. "You can make a ninety-degree turn at Mach 8 and the gravotonics will prevent your organs from recoiling and splattering the inside of the ship. No matter what you try, there will be negligible g-force effect on your body."

Trent walked under the extended wing and pointed to the rear edge.

"The fixed wings and stabilizers allow her to move in and out of atmospheres. The same design reduces the effect of gravity wells during space flight near large objects. She is made of advanced materials. The airframe is light, but sturdy inside an atmosphere. The combination of low profile, materials, and special synthetic coating make her nearly invisible to surface or non-surface generated scans."

He returned to the front of the ship.

"Double-barreled rail-guns on either side of the cockpit," he pointed out. "Kinetic projectile barrel beneath one for electromagnetic pulse shells. The new Short-Rod Penetrators, or SRP projectiles are small, but incredibly dense. The non-nuclear pulse shells, nymphs, will disrupt electromagnetic fields and deliver a punch at the same time. With double-barrels you no longer need to switch between nymphs and rods. Each gun-roll contains five-hundred SRPs. Independent fire and they swivel. They can even flip and fire backward."

Trent pointed to the seams located beneath the airframe's undercarriage. "The doors allow a tachyon/plasma cannon to deploy. I've added special shocks and dampeners. The cannon produces seventy-two percent of the power of a surface mounted cannon without the dangerous recoil."

The scientist pressed his hand against a landing strut. A ladder emerged from the forward edge of the delta wing.

"You can enter by way of the loading ramp, but it's more fun to climb up and enter through a hatch behind the cockpit. Pilot and co-pilot seats. She's built for speed and bite," Trent said, unable to contain a big smile. "Not much on comfort. Small galley area and two bunks, stacked. A shower, sink, and toilet. Storage for cold stuff. You can heat your food, but no kitchen. I hoped to add a food replicator similar to those Trading Alliance ships use, but haven't had the time. Plenty of dry-food storage for extended travel. Limited cargo space, but particle dry-wash for clothing means you don't need to take a lot with you."

"What does Space Fleet say about you having a personal ship with classified technology and weapons?" Coop asked. His eyes moving from the sleek killing machine to his friend.

"It doesn't belong to Fleet," Trent replied. "I'm Head of Sciences, and Trent Industries has contracts with Space Fleet and the UEC, but I'm also a private businessman. I own my intellectual properties. UEC and divisions get first opportunity to buy anything I develop before it's offered on the open market. Unless it's something built by us specifically for them. Until I make a public offering, anything I build is mine. I'm not offering the Wraith for sale, publicly or privately. There are no plans to build more than one. And this one I'm giving to you."

"Expensive gift," Coop responded. Even with super-fast synaptic activity and the ability to accept and analyze information in the time it took for his brain to assimilate an image or sound, he found Trent's offer difficult to comprehend.

"You've earned it," Trent said. "I wouldn't be here without your help all these many years. Hell, Earth wouldn't be where we are if you didn't have the guts to test fly my concepts. You brought the optical upgrades from Osperantue, the communication advances from the Fell, and the crystals we need to power our systems from Rys. I'd call this a downpayment on what humanity owes you."

"In Brazil you mentioned the ship used artificial intelligence, but without an avatar. Anything I should know?"

"Like I said then, no GENNA." Trent turned his back on the ship. Standing in front of the Shelby Cobra-inspired nose, it looked as if the Wraith considered swallowing its inventor. "The AI is integrated to the ship, and the ship's sensors interact with the system the way your five senses work with your brain. In point of fact, with your new upgraded brain, the two of you assimilate and reason more alike than either of you compared to us normal humans."

"The ship sees, hears, feels, smells, and tastes through sensor feeds?"

"Pretty much," Trent replied. "It can analyze sensor-generated data, and experience it in a manner similar to you and me. It still acts like a computer, accepting data, maintaining files, self-maintenance of operational systems, and all the other things a computer needs to do."

"Personality?"

"Work in progress. My best code writer designed the building blocks. He's a gamer freak, and hoped to design a scalable personality capable of allowing the AI to evolve as it interacted with humans, and, I suppose, aliens. Similar to the way virtual reality characters in streamer games will take on the persona of the human players."

"You allowed a gamer to build the baseline?" Coop half asked, half accused. "The same guys who create testosterone-driven heroes, over-sexed female warriors, and super-powerful evil villains?"

"He's the best," Trent replied, a bit defensively. "I did take the Wraith away before he completed the final tests. I'll perform a sweep to make sure your AI has no evil villain issues." Trent's eyes lost focus. He held a hand up. "Mara's calling," he said, explaining his sudden change.

Trent used an ultra-miniaturized communicator-translator devise implanted in his neck, beneath his right ear. The updated version of the Fell translation and communication bracelets created by Sky designed and built by her brother, Sparks. The system small enough to implant beneath the skin. Only a few trusted humans and aliens had access to the innovation. The trans-com provided private communications without obvious equipment. Cooper received one after completing his psychological evaluation by Dr. Juri. Not officially awake, he kept his dormant.

"We need to return to Fin Island," Trent finally said. "You have a couple of visitors."

"I'm going," Coop said.

Nathan and Mara stood alongside Cooper. They decided to talk on the covered patio with a view of the water and another island off to the South. The rain dissipated, but the mid-day sun remained obscured by dense grey clouds.

"I understand the importance, but the timing sucks," Nathan said. "Space Fleet received orders to dispatch a battlegroup to meet with the Prophet. You cannot take part officially, but no one knows how the Mischene operate better than you. I could feed you information, and you could add your insight."

"Timing is just about perfect," Coop countered. "With the information we now have, we might be able to stop an insurrection. Making sure the UEC is secure will help keep those going to Aster system safer. We have friends on board those ships, Nathan."

"What if someone recognizes you?" Trent asked Coop.

"I'm thinner. Haven't gained back all the muscle I lost while unconscious," he said. "I'll let Mara cut my hair and leave the beard and mustache. There are pictures of me with scruff, but I've never gone with a full facial forest before. Sunshades, baseball cap, and I'm good to go."

"I'll get ID for you," Trent said, accepting Coop intended to leave regardless of counter arguments. "I'll set you up as a Trent Industries engineer. Lord knows I employ about a thousand. Just let me know what name to use."

"Connections," Mara said, her eyes focused on the junction between sea water and islands. "The ability to make connections from seemingly unrelated clues is how we reconstruct dead languages." She turned her grey eyes on Coop. "Everything is converging. Everything will change after this."

"We can make those changes positive," the Space Ranger responded. "If the information is right, we can save a friend, prevent others from dying, and stop a group of bad actors from destabilizing the government."

"You will be going up against a powerful group of dedicated operators with decades to prepare," Trent said.

"Which is why I won't be playing politics," Coop replied. "They've wrapped themselves in conspiracies and complicated strategies. They rely on spreading misinformation and placing informants in key positions, while they remain hidden. I'm simply going to cut off their heads and leave the bodies in the open."

"Interesting metaphor," Trent said.

Turning to leave, anxious to start the mission, the enhanced human responded, "That was no metaphor."

PART 2

Connections

Convergence

After a river is formed, it descends to lower levels. Here it runs more slowly over the sloping landscape of its middle course.

Its current no longer creates the force to carry stones or gravel.

This material drops to the riverbed, where it forms bars of sand, or gravel, to the point of sometimes creating islands.

Everything is continually changing shape as the river deposits or erodes material.

Often the river will alter its course.

CHAPTER 8

The tear rested at the corner of her eye. The stark lights in the restroom caused it to glimmer in the reflection of the mirror. The pain would not win. She damn well would not allow the tear to win. Wanting to pull it back in, she was not going to wipe it away.

Gravity won. It always wins. The tear left her too big, too wide on her face, too deep brown, too sad eyes, and travelled along her too wide, too long nose. It followed the crease from her nose, around her too thin lips. They appeared thinner, pinched together in anger. It made it to her too pointy chin and stopped. Gravity gave up, and forced her to use her mittened hand to wipe the drop away.

Mittens, because Bosine have two fingers, both wider than a human's. The mittens helped hide the difference. She learned to keep her fingers together whenever she lifted her hand, signaling she knew the answer to a question, or wanting to make a comment. The first few times, she lifted her hand with the fingers apart. Someone, every time, said "Live long and prosper." It was not until after the third instance, she took the time to research the quote. Leonard Nimoy, an actor from a previous century, played an alien on television and movies. When she saw the Vulcan salute and heard the salutation, she thought it wonderful. A few more times, and she discovered humans were making fun of her hands. Thereafter, she made sure to keep them together . . . or hide them in mittens when cold enough.

She could not hide her face, or her too pink skin. She grew her brown hair long enough to cover her too odd ears. She wore it with bangs, trying to cover a larger portion of her too alien face.

Chaspi balled her hands into fists. She wanted, badly, to hit someone. Others often described Bosine as docile. The entire race considered meek. Everyone from Osperanue, except the Fray species, described as passive and easy to get along with. Growing up, she had been the wild child. Easy to get angered. Quick to make a snide remark, and lash out at real and imagined slights.

Her parents worried for her. Her teachers commented on her 'anger issues.' Her best friend her entire life, Rosz, ignored her outbursts. He was a perfect example of Bosine cool. He accepted Chaspi's unique nature, even making fun of her mini-tantrums.

At the moment, he maintained his distance. In all the years, under all of the conditions they lived through, he had never seen her this angry.

"Cow girl," she said. She said it out loud. At the mirror, back at her. Less than two months in college, and an over-sized human male decided he would make sure she realized her alienness.

It happened after Intro to Environmental Technology, in the hallway. He stepped in front of her, barring the path down the hallway. His little pack of sniggering friends behind him.

"Hey, Cow Girl," he said, looking down at her . . . looking down on her. "I was wondering. If you look like a cow, do you have udders? I mean, you actually have a nice enough body. But, honestly, are the tits real? Do you have udders under there, somewhere?"

He laughed loudly, joined by his buddies.

She knew she blushed red. She stood caught between embarrassed, hurt, and angry.

Chaspi recalled pushing him to get around, only he was too massive to move. It made her even madder.

She stepped around the clown, covered her chest with crossed arms, and walked away, refusing to run.

Refusing to cry.

Rosz, and their new human friend, Billy, exited the classroom as the confrontation ended. They raced after her. Rosz knew Chaspi well, and made no comment. Billy made all the wrong ones.

"Chaspi, let it go," he spoke to her back. "The guy's one of those dumb jocks. Besides, calfs are cute, right?"

His lame attempt at support stopped her. The face she turned on Billy more fearsome than cute.

"You think I look like a calf?"

"No. Not what I meant," he stammered. He backed up a step. Rosz took a step to the side, getting out of the way of incoming fire. "I meant, you're cute. Not a cow, or a calf. Just, the guy was wrong. You're slender, and maybe you're not chesty, but that would look funny on you."

Rosz took another step away.

Chaspi closed to within inches of Billy's face.

"I'm skinny and flat-chested. You think I'm skinny and flat-chested. Boobs would look funny on me. Anything else?"

"Chaspi, you're taking everything wrong." Her eyes narrowed. "I mean, I'm saying everything wrong."

She turned and disappeared into the public restroom. The restrooms at university co-ed, but the two boys did not follow. Billy might have except Rosz placed a restraining hand on his shoulder. He shook his head in the universal 'don't do it, bro.'

Two girls stood talking in the public space with the sinks and mirrors. They watched as she entered and quickly exited. Perhaps because she was the alien girl, but more likely because she looked ready to hurt someone.

Chaspi placed both hands on the edge of the metal sink, took a deep breath, and watched as the tear formed in her reflection.

After wiping away the offensive drop of salty water, she took a few more deep breaths. When the ruddy complexion returned to a more normal light pink shade, she decided it was time to leave.

Billy paced the hallway outside the restroom, moving away when she exited. Rosz sat on the floor, his back against the wall, his ever-present music playing through top-of-the-line earbuds. He looked up, gave a tiny smile, and winked.

When Billy turned and saw her, before he could say anything more, she held up a mittened hand and warned him, "Don't speak. For the foreseeable future, whatever you think you should say, don't say. I'm not mad at you . . . yet. Understand?"

Getting smarter, instead of answering, he nodded.

The Stadium

Two weeks before the end-of-year holiday break, and snow still not falling on Toronto. Flakes normally filled the skies in December. Even without the white blanket, the cold air arrived with a vengeance.

Chaspi pulled her jacket tight around her neck, the mitten hiding her two-fingered right hand clenched the collar closed in a futile effort to keep the chill wind at bay.

"You two have to buy warmer clothes," Billy said. He earlier offered his winter parka, with fur-lined hood, to both aliens, only to be rebuffed. "Doesn't it get cold on Osperantue?"

"Cold, yes," Rosz answered. He had a difficult time acting cool and unconcerned while his teeth chattered, the rhythm faster than the music coming through his earbuds. "This is outer-space-without-a-ship freezing. New Zealand has snow in the mountains, but nowhere does it get this cold."

"Let's cut across the soccer pitch," the human said. He strategically placed his body to shield Chaspi from the crosswind, which took the frigid air temperature down double digits to a feels-like minus-impossible degrees. If the girl noticed, she did not comment. "The stadium and halls will cut the wind, and we'll get to the dorms quicker."

Leaving the Environmental Engineering building, they walked quickly across the parking lot, toward the futbol stadium. Not late in the day, but the sun already lingered low in the sky. They were the only people outside. The prospect of the stadium blocking even a little of the wind enticed more speed.

They rushed through an open entrance. Even without a door, the covered corridor reduced the sickening cold. Rosz pulled his mitten-covered hands from over his ears, blew out a cloud of fog, and sighed. Chaspi stomped in place and ran her hands up and down her arms, trying to get feeling back into her extremities. Billy, comfortable in his parka, woolen winter pants, and lined hiking boots, waited patiently. At the first sign of real trouble, he intended to wrap either of his new friends in his parka, and screw their protests.

The three walked to the end of the corridor. It came to a landing with a raised view of a stadium of uncovered metal benches surrounding a track. The track created an oval circling a soccer pitch. They needed to hurry down the cement steps to the track, race across the grass field, and into another open corridor on the far side. That hallway would take them to one final open entrance. From there, it was a quick trip to the building housing their dorm rooms.

"Those people are idiots," Chaspi said. Billy followed her stare. Eight guys huddled near the middle of the pitch. From the equipment in hands, lacrosse players having a mid-winter practice.

"They probably have on enough thermal layers, they don't even feel the cold," Billy said. "Jocks aren't regular people, Chaspi. Besides, when you know how to dress properly, you can deal with almost any weather."

"What about that other idiot?" Rosz asked.

Chaspi and Billy turned to look at the North end of the stadium. A sole runner rounded a curve at the top of the oval track. Covered in thick sweats, hood pulled up, and a balaclava protecting their face from windchill.

"Nice stride, though," Rosz added.

"We've put this off long enough," Chaspi said. She headed out of the corridor and down the concrete steps. The wind arrived to greet her, but not as fierce, partially tamed by the stadium walls. Rosz and Billy followed. The three making slow time as the steps changed from steep, to wide spaces for rows, and back again to narrow and steep.

As they made their way towards the flat space below, two of the lacrosse players hurried away from the group, making for the entrance of the corridor leading to the dorms. The laughter and shouts from the remaining six wafted over to the pitch.

The three friends, engrossed in hurrying without tumbling, payed no attention to anything but their feet hitting the cold, hard surface.

Chaspi, still in the lead, stepped onto the flat pad in front of the first row of benches, took a single step, and vaulted over a three-foot chain link fence and onto the track. Knowing the boys were close behind, she ran across the frosted green field toward the far side. Rosz passed her, vaulting the far fence. Billy caught up at the fence, and went over just before she made the jump. He knew better than to treat Chaspi as a helpless girl, so he continued after Rosz. Chaspi blew fog like spitting fire. She hated that the guys caught her, but she appreciated they did not hold back.

The race down the steps and across the pitch heated her. Unfortunately, it also warmed her sinuses. She either needed to blow snot out, or suck it down her throat. She swallowed. Gross. But she did not want snot ending up on her jacket, or hear Rosz berate her if she needed to wipe her nose with the sleeve.

Billy's shouts made her forget the phlegm in her head. She ran forward to see a lacrosse stick across his upper chest. A large male holding it tightly enough, his toes barely touched the ground.

Rosz, slightly to his left, struggled with another over-sized guy. Also pinned by a stick, his back against the bigger male's chest. The guy wore a ski mask, but his teeth, grinning, showed through the opening in the lower half of the head cover.

"Chaspi Run! Go back!" Billy tried to get his hands around the stick, but his lined gloves provided warmth, not grip.

She was not going to leave her friends. She was not about to turn and run. She was also not exactly sure what she was going to do, and then choices were taken away.

"I do believe it's the Cow Girl."

Chaspi turned. The six lacrosse players who remained on the pitch, now stood between her and the hallway exit. The one in front, his hood off and his balaclava pulled low to his neck, was the dumb-ass who caused her tears earlier. The oversized bully who made it clear he did not appreciate aliens at his school.

"Let them go," she said to him. "Let us all go."

"Or what?" he asked, and then chuckled. It was a fake laugh. He wanted to sound amused. He sounded strained instead. "Help Dick and Stan," he said to his cohorts, eyes never leaving Chaspi.

Two of the group separated, brushed past Chaspi, shoulders roughly bumping her aside, once, then twice, as she refused to move for them. They joined the first two bullies. She watched helplessly as Rosz and Billy, outnumbered and overweighed, were pushed, face-first, against the corridor wall.

While she watched, her brain attempted to think of something she should say. Her hormones screamed, asking her to do something physical. She wished really hard for a laser pistol, or a bat. The lead bully moved up behind her.

"So, Cow Girl . . ."

Startled, Chaspi jumped forward three-feet, pivoting as she landed. Big and bulky as he appeared, he was also an athlete. He crept behind her without a sound. He chuckled again, not strained this time. Deeper. With more menace.

"I keep wondering about those udders. I keep thinking, does she really have cow udders, or tits like human girls? Is she pink all over? Maybe cowhide under those clothes." He handed his stick to one of the others. "I think we all want to find out."

Chaspi stepped back, realizing the predicament and possible outcomes. Cold about to become the least of her problem. Rosz and Billy were squirming, trying to shout. Gloved hands pressed their heads harder against the cold concrete wall. Jaws too mashed against the rough surface for words to form.

One of the back-ups, a smaller version of the others, reached a hand onto his shoulder. "Aimsley, you said mess with them. Don't take this too far, man. We could get into serious trouble. I mean, they're protected. I think. Like endangered species or something."

Aimsley grabbed the hand on his shoulder, squeezed until the smaller male's eyes grimaced behind his ski mask. He threw the hand off.

"We aren't going to hurt them." He looked down on Chaspi, ignoring the grunts coming from the other two. "I just want to see what Cow Girl looks like. Without clothes. Are you going to take them off, Cow Girl? Or do you want me to do it?"

"SHIT!"

The exclamation echoed in the tight, enclosed area. All heads turned, except for Chaspi, who already looked in that direction.

One of the lacrosse players was bent backward, his body bowing, hands outstretched.

The runner from the track held a fistful of head cover and hair, and was pulling him back and down. Before he could shout again, a kick to the back of his left knee sent him down, smashing both knees onto the hard floor.

"SHIT," he said again, with less volume and more pain. The runner let go of his head, and used a backhand, closed into a tight fist, to club the guy in the temple. His eyes rolled up, and his body rolled forward. No one considered catching him before he landed nose-first on the concrete pad.

The next guy in line received a kick to the gut, which bent him forward, followed by an inside crescent kick to the side of the head. He spun into the wall, connected hard, and dropped. The player standing beside him used the time for his friend to fall to raise his lacrosse stick in defense. The runner grabbed it in two hands and pushed. In spite of giving up several inches in height, and a whole lot of pounds, the composite shaft drove straight back and up, momentum abruptly stopped by the guy's nose. Blood splattered and tears welled in his eyes. He let go of the stick. A fist connected to his chin before his hands could cover his broken nose. Knocked senseless by one well-placed punch, only Aimsley, the head bully, stood between the runner and Chaspi.

Like a mad bear, he charged the smaller opponent. Arms wide, snarling, teeth showing, and scream of anger tinged with fear beginning to emerge. Screams choked off as the runner grabbed the front of his parka, used his forward momentum, and rolled backward. Legs curled, knees bent, and two feet placed against his lower abdomen, the runner squat-pushed Aimsley high. By holding onto the coat, the smaller fighter flipped the big jock over and down.

His back and buttocks crashed into the hard, cold, mostly hard floor. His head bounced once and spittle poured from his open mouth. The concussion would last nearly as long as the bruises.

The runner used a two-hand push jump to end up standing, facing Chaspi, staring past her at the six remaining males. The four lacrosse players released Rosz and Billy. They stood mute, unsure how four teammates had been beaten, badly, in less than one minute. The runner started forward, passing Chaspi without comment. The four tough guys, sticks in hand, ran.

They fought and pushed and pressed each other, attempting to escape the confining corridor and be first to freedom.

Rosz and Billy did not notice. Eyes wide, mouths open.

The runner pulled back the hood, and pulled down the face cover. Gold and orange-amber eyes, shaped like a jungle cat's, sparkled. Her smile displayed small fangs where human's had canine teeth, and lit a beautiful blue face, covered in a sheen of perspiration. She shook her head, loosening auburn red hair with bright yellow highlights. The tresses had been pressed down by sweat and the hoodie.

"That was fun," she said. "I suppose we have to call someone to collect the trash."

Stacey, the blue female alien badass, sat on a plastic chair with her feet crossed on the seat of a facing chair. Her eyes closed, making a point of ignoring the commotion within the campus security office.

Rosz, Billy, and Chaspi sat beside each other, using the chairs next to Stacey's feet.

Billy could not *not* sneak looks at the girl from Fell. He teetered between enthralled and afraid of the girl who looked like a model and fought like a marauder.

The young Canadian kept remembering her in action, and flashed back to the moments after the four remaining goons ran.

"You okay," the blue alien asked Chaspi, who stood as if cemented to the concrete. Frozen, not by the weather, but the shear ferocity of the confrontation between the runner and the four bullies about to force her to undress.

"I'm fine. And thank you. I'm Chaspi. I'm from Osperantue. Are you Fellen? Why are you here? At Bathurst?" Shaken, she mentally shook herself. "I'm sorry. I sound like a starbler bird."

"Post stress," the girl said. "I'm AStasaei, and, yes, I'm from Fell. My human nickname is Stacey. I have enrolled in the aeronautics program, which is why I'm at Bathurst."

If it seemed weird for the two girls to carry on a conversation while four over-sized boys writhed in pain, it went unnoticed.

While they talked, Billy called campus security on his personal com unit. The wrist device included a camera, allowing him to stream the condition of the four attackers to the officer at the other end. He agreed they would all be there when security arrived. He suggested an ambulance, possibly two would be a good idea.

Rosz joined Chaspi, placed an arm around his childhood friend, pulling her close. "I'm sorry, Chaspi," he said. "We had no idea it was a set up. The first two pinned us before we realized."

"No worries," she said. The off-hand reply she and many other alien refugees learned during their time in New Zealand. "Rosz, this is Stacey. Stacey, Rosz, who is also from Osperantue."

"A bit obvious," Stacey said. "Bosine. I assume the other one is plain human."

"Human," Billy said, a bit peeved at the term 'plain.' "If you're from Fell, do you know Sky and Storm?"

Sky and Storm were the two most famous aliens on Earth. They arrived in the solar system aboard the same damaged cruise ship as Rosz and Chaspi. Their heroics crucial to defeat the Zenge armada at the edge of the solar system. They were also in a relationship with Space Fleet Captain Daniel Cooper, who placed his small fighter between the refugees and that same armada. The three kept the spaceship filled with displaced aliens safe until reinforcements arrived.

The two female warriors were also drop-dead gorgeous. When they arrived on Earth, the combination of aliens, heroes, and beauties caused riots as people tried to get near them. Billy joined the online fan club, but only visited the site occasionally, these days.

"ASkillamentrae is my sister, and ASterrmalanlan is my cousin," Stacey informed them. "I came to Earth to join Space Fleet. Captain Cooper is my sponsor. He had my enrollment approved before he was injured."

Cooper currently lay in a coma, injured when a vengeance-driven Bosine fired a laser pistol at close range. The Captain killed the man's son aboard the Star Gazer, after pulling him off the girl he was raping.

"He's our friend," Chaspi said, slipping away from Rosz. "Which makes you our friend, too." She hugged Stacey, which began awkwardly, until the girl from Fell relaxed and allowed the gesture.

Rosz nor Billy attempted an embrace. Both remained in awe, and, honestly, embarrassed.

Billy's thoughts returned to the present when a slight woman marched through the front door of the security building, straight to the office of the Chief, and in without knocking.

"Admiral Patterson," Stacey said. She did not face the right direction to see the woman. "I know the walk, and I've only known her a week."

"Admiral Pam Paterson, the first commander of Space Fleet?" Billy asked. "I thought she retired."

"Retired, not died," Stacey replied. "I'm staying with her and her husband. They live here, in Toronto. She lectures at the academy."

Space Fleet's headquarters in Toronto housed the administrative offices for the paramilitary branch designated to maintain security against off-world threats. Everything from legal to intelligence operated from the half-dozen buildings comprising the Space Fleet complex. Covert and special operations tactical planning occurred there.

Central communications for surface stations, orbital platforms, spaceships, the moon, Mars and communications coming in or going out of the solar system passed through central command.

Communications occurring between stations or ships were recorded and stored on site.

Space Fleet's Academy rested on fifty acres twenty-miles north of headquarters. The latest and smallest military academy did not offer traditional college-oriented tracks for potential Space Fleet officers. The academy accepted all levels of entrants. Engineers, armament specialist, pilots, and every other type of specialist or officer candidate could receive targeted, specific training in their area of interest.

Candidates came from high schools and colleges. Among the Cadets, several smart, capable people with no degrees from high school or university worked toward a Space Fleet assignment. The academy acted as a meritocracy. Cadets selected on the basis of their ability. Rising through the grades, and eventual assignments determined by production.

Aliens were equally eligible for the academy as humans. Currently, the academy housed fourteen non-terrestrial cadets.

"I suppose she's here to get you," Chaspi said to Stacey.

"I would say, based on what I have seen and heard since my arrival on Earth, she is here to get all of us."

She looked over her shoulder, and through the office blinds. Stacey watched the diminutive woman speak calmly to the Head of Campus Security. "The woman lives by the 'leave no one behind' code."

"What does she lecture about?" Rosz asked.

"Military Intelligence," Stacey answered, turning back, giving her attention to the tips of her running shoes.

"I want to pilot a spaceship," Chaspi said, aloud. Realizing she said it out loud, for the first time, ever, she dropped her head, wishing her hair longer.

"Me, too," Stacey said. Because she did not know Chaspi, she did not know her aspiration to fly a spaceship was secret. "It's why I'm enrolled. This campus is the only one with an aeronautics program, and where someone is willing to let me stay with them. Stupid Space Fleet Academy rules and regulations. I should be there, working on a Fleet pilot's certification. I've flown more spaceships than anybody here has ever seen."

"Honest?" Billy kept the attention on Stacey's pronouncement, and away from Chaspi's revelation. He had not been friends with the two Bosine long, but found it easy to see embarrassment. Chaspi's light pink coloring blushed. "You've piloted spaceships?"

"My oldest sister, Star, let me fly her ship, AStarr. In open space. For a few minutes," she admitted. "But we have hover-cycles and hover-boats, and I can drive them. It's almost exactly the same thing."

She looked to the young girl who had claimed her as a friend, and asked, "Are you in the aeronautics program, too?"

Before she could reply, or turn a deeper red, Rosz butted in to inform then, "Admiral Patterson and the Chief are headed this way."

The Chief of Security, tall, slender, and maybe thirty-five, hooked his thumbs in his old-fashion Sam Brown belt before talking.

"We have the other four boys. It took my men a few minutes of frank discussion with them, but they pretty much confirm your stories. Aimsley Macdonald is the group's ringleader. He told them they were just going to have a little fun by giving the aliens a scare. "

He spoke directly to Chaspi. "They swear they had no idea he intended to assault you."

He switched his attention to the blue girl. His eyes narrowed and his mouth pinched.

"You, miss, were right to help, but wrong in how far you went. Those four boys are in the hospital and will be there for some time."

Stacey, still seated, but with her feet on the floor, shrugged. "I had no idea humans were so fragile." No one knew if the response was honest or flip.

"Perhaps. I have spoken with your sponsor, Mrs. Patterson. I decided I will inform the parents charges for assault and battery will not be issued, but the boys are not to bother any of you again. That includes the parents not pursuing any legal actions. I think they will be wise enough to agree, and should end this situation."

"Thank you, Chief," Patterson said. "Your help and understanding are appreciated. Stacey, you will be coming with me. Chaspi, Rosz, and Billy, the Chief will have you driven to your dorm in a heated cart."

The two Bosine and the human all developed wide-eye syndrome. None ever met Admiral Patterson, and all were surprised she knew their names.

Rosz recovered first, and asked, "Will this effect our chances for Fleet Academy?"

Patterson smiled. "There are no charges, and no legal actions, and since, in my opinion, you were the victims, I cannot see this having an impact on your applications."

The Chief stepped in front of Stacey, blocking her departure. "Miss, humans appear *fragile* for your kind. You should be more careful. I do not want to see you in these offices again."

Stacey, unsure if the security officer acted officiously or held bigoted feelings, decided, quite maturely, to let the warning pass without comment.

Chaspi, recovered enough to remember she had anger issues, moved to her friend's side. "If anyone tries to attack any of us again, we will defend ourselves."

She took Stacey's arm, and brushed the tall security cop aside, leaving him in their wake. Patterson snickered, then followed. Rosz and Billy, shocked by Chaspi's act of confidence, looked at one another, grinned, and hurried to catch up to the women.

A Space Fleet personnel transport hovered at the curb. Sensing Patterson's proximity, the auto-drive vehicle popped all three doors.

Stacey disengaged from Chaspi. She ran around to the street side, taking the back seat, far side.

Patterson stopped the three others from rushing to the security cart parked behind the Fleet shuttle. The two Bosine trembled in the cold. Borrowed thermal blankets provided slight protection against the cold. They stood respectfully to listen, trying hard not to shake violently.

The retired Admiral pulled a plastic card from her jacket pocket, took Chaspi's right hand, turned it up, and placed the card in the palm of her mitten. Next, she wrapped the girl's fingers over the card.

"You will take Rosz, and you will buy both of you proper winter clothing. If you do not know what that means for a Toronto winter, take Billy with you. There are 1,000 credits on the card. Spend it on clothes. Buy other essentials. Buy yourself a nice lunch. Spend it, Chaspi. Do not save it. Do not try to give it back."

"Admiral Patterson, I don't know," the college co-ed from an alien world stuttered, unsure of the proper way to handle the gift.

"Dear, if Daniel Cooper knew you two were freezing your asses off, he would wake up, swim to the mainland, and walk across the continent to get here. When the two of you enter the Academy, I'll find work for you to repay the debt. Fair?"

Chaspi, on the edge of tears for the, like, millionth-time that day, nodded.

"Get out of the cold," Patterson ordered. As Chaspi and Rosz hurried to the security cart, Patterson took Billy by his arm.

"Billy, thank-you for acting as a friend," she told him. "If you ever need anything I can provide, you ask, young man. Now, go join your friends."

Smiling, filled with a warm sense of self-worth, and more than a little pride, Billy jumped onto the front seat of the cart, next to the security officer. The officer pulled out, around, and away, taking the college students to their dorm.

The smallish, large-hearted woman entered the transport, sitting next to her ward. "Home." The automated vehicle acted as

Patterson's official and personal transportation. It knew exactly where to go and the quickest route.

"Anything to say?" she asked.

Despite the warmth of the interior, the Fellen wore her hoodie up, safe in the depths of the head cover, eyes straight ahead.

"They deserved it. I'm not sorry. You can ship me back to Rys, or let me join the fight on Fell, but I'd do it again . . . harder." Her arms crossed, and her shoulder's bunched. In old-Earth terms, prepared for the axe to fall.

"I would have done the same thing," former commander of Space Fleet, and fighter of many battles, public and private, admitted. Stacey's shoulders relaxed. She turned to look at the person she now lived with, but did not yet know. "Of course, at my age, I would need a laser pistol."

Stacey laughed. Patterson smiled. The driverless car continued home.

CHAPTER 9

Dorm (Markham Hall)

Markham Hall, student housing, offered double and single dorm rooms. Chaspi and Rosz lived in adjacent singles on an upper floor. Billy shared a room with a History major on one of the lower floors.

After campus security delivered them to the building, they went to Chaspi's room, silently. The boys did not ask, and she had not offered. Gathering in her room became a habit soon after the three became friends.

She sat cross-legged on the bed, Billy on the chair that came with the student desk, and Rosz comfortable on the floor, back against a wall.

"Can I talk?" Billy asked.

"If you don't say anything stupid," she responded.

"If you want to become a pilot, why are you taking environmental engineering?"

"Because of me," Rosz answered. Chaspi and Rosz were neighbors from birth. Their families lived next to each other for, like, ever. On his fifth birthday Rosz received a personal music player and special earbuds as a present. She never saw him without them, or their upgrades, since that day.

When asked how he could listen to music and still hear everything going on around him, he always answered, "I've got a gift." Which meant when he acted as if he did not hear something, he was pretending to not hear something.

"I want to reclaim dead planets," he said. "She isn't sure what she wants, so she's wasting time keeping me company."

"Because of me," Chaspi corrected. "I want to pilot, but as a Star Fleet pilot. I want to fly fighters, not cruise ships or cargo vessels. Bosine are not expected to want things like that. Earth may be the only planet in the galaxy with pilots who actually fly a ship, and not monitor a computer doing all the work. I'd rather not learn how to fly, than fly something boring, and simple, and safe."

"I read all of the stories about the Star Gazer," Billy said. "One of them talked about the Zenge invasion of Osperantue. As I remember, Osperantue patrol ships threw themselves at the invasion fleet in order to give ships on the surface a chance to escape. That sounds incredibly heroic. Could you become a patrol pilot?"

"It was heroic. Osperantue's Space Patrol vessels normally provided towing services and traffic control," Chaspi answered. "They went up against heavily armed spaceships, and only a few of our ships included small, inaccurate lasers. If we had warships, we might have defended the planet. I do not want to fly by operating a computer on a towboat or freighter, or even a cruise ship."

"Okay, I get that. Why didn't you apply for aeronautics? After graduation you could apply for Space Fleet Academy. You could get certified to pilot anything in the Fleet."

Billy, good at forgetting anything negative, especially when it involved people he cared about, forgot Chaspi was angry with him. He was also genuinely curious.

"Her parents," Rosz answered. "If she applied for aeronautics, they would not have approved. At least this way she's out of New Zealand and in the vicinity of Space Fleet."

"You could take aeronautics courses as electives," Billy said. "Keep enviro-engineering as your major, but fill in your course schedules with classes that will allow you to fly. If you get enough, and you do really we'll, I bet the Academy would let you work towards a pilot's certification and assignment."

Chaspi went quiet. She studied her knees. "Do you think that might work?"

"Bet on it," Billy said.

"Makes a lot of sense, Chas," Rosz chimed in from the floor. "I mean, you were friends with Captain Daniel Cooper, Earth's most famous Fleet officer. Retired Admiral Pamela Patterson likes you."

"I **AM** friends with Daniel Cooper," she corrected. "Until I hear differently, he's alive. Admiral Patterson all but admitted it."

"He would say 'go for it,'" Rosz replied. "You know he would."

The girl from Osperantue, with secrets and anger issues, smiled. For the first time since deciding to come to university, she may have a plan to reach her goals. She certainly did not have as many secrets, or as much anger as she felt an hour earlier.

"I'll start next quarter," she told them. "I'll stay on the engineering track, and put flight school classes in every open spot. But you know what I'm going to do right now?"

"What?" both guys asked.

"Going shopping. Call a transport. I want to go downtown, enjoy a wonderful meal, and buy winter clothes. I am so tired of the freaking cold."

As the three started moving, snow began falling. Winter finally showed the beauty that mitigated the freezing temps. The possibility of a new future took root in Chaspi's heart. Too bad future is a fickle creature.

Home (Sam and Pam Patterson's)

Stacey entered the kitchen from the mother-in-law apartment's stairs. The Patterson's basement remodeled into a one-bedroom apartment. The original change to provide a place for Sam Patterson's mother to live when she could no longer care for herself.

She passed away before making the move. Their daughter, Samantha, moved from her upstairs bedroom and into the more spacious area her senior year of high school.

When Coop asked the Patterson's to sponsor Stacey, Pam cleared out everything of Samantha's. (She completed college; started a life, and had her own family.)

Stacey arrived from Rys with a couple of changes of clothing, toiletries, and a trunk filled with electronics. Members of Stacey's tribe, and particularly her clan, thrived on designing and improving technology. The tech of preference anything communications-oriented. Patterson had a personal communicator and translator embedded in her neck, beneath her right ear. Stacey's oldest sister, Star, and brother, Sparks developed the subcutaneous marvel. Pam's special implant came courtesy of Stacey's cousin, Storm.

Admiral Patterson (ret.) sat at the granite-topped kitchen island drinking hot tea, perusing the news on her pad.

"Are you eavesdropping on me?" Stacey asked. The young woman from Fell rather straightforward, as Pam and Sam were learning.

"I beg your pardon," Pam responded. "Why would I eavesdrop on you?"

Stacey stood quietly for a long moment, deciding if the woman's reply seemed truthful.

The Patterson's, hell, the planet was new to her. She remained undecided if she cared for humans. Those she met on Rys were relaxed, open, and always honest with her. The ones on Earth much more difficult to categorize.

"No reason I can think of," she admitted. "But a signal passed through the basement, searching for electronic files. It is quite sophisticated, though not to Fell standards. I decided it must be military grade technology."

"As Space Fleet's former commanding officer, I would have access to such technology," Pam completed Stacey's line of reasoning.

"I thought it possible. My personal data units, communications, and multiple storage systems are safe from intrusions, but it is still bothersome."

"Stacey, is the signal only transmitted to the basement, or is the entire house targeted?"

Without answering, the younger woman turned and retraced her steps to the stairwell. Patterson sipped her tea, deep in contemplation, verging on concern and edging towards worry.

Stacey returned, holding a small device in her left hand. She stopped just inside the kitchen, turned the device in different directions, tapping the screen occasionally.

"There is no current signal, but someone beamed scans throughout the entire structure within the last twenty-four hours," she informed her hostess. She went to the auto-brew on the counter, poured a cup of tea, and joined Patterson at the island.

"I apologize if I offended you," she said. "Someone is searching everything electronic in your home. I can install protection."

Pamela Patterson began her career with the fledgling UEC's Office of Naval Intelligence. She understood espionage better than most.

"If you block the signals, whoever is sending them will know we know," she said, both hands on her warm mug. Stacey, seated next to her, both hands on her mug. They presented a picture of two women closely linked. If not for the skins colors, and Stacey's golden cat-eyes, one might think mother and daughter talking in the family kitchen.

"Stacey, did your device tell you if the house is bugged?"

"Sorry. My translator is still learning. Why would I check for insects?"

"Slang," Pam explained. "Bugs are what we call listening devices. The original ones looked like small insects. Are there covert listening or video devices inside the house."

"No. The only active intrusion is by scans."

"Could they be here, only not active."

"No. I fired multiple trapper beams. If anything was here, even inactive, the trapper would activate it long enough to register."

"Can you tell what they scanned, copied, or tampered with?"

"Of course," the girl from Fell replied. "Do you want me to check everything in the house?"

"Just my office," Patterson replied.

Patterson led the way to her home office, a converted downstairs bedroom now home to her memorabilia, awards, recognitions, medals, and computers. She used two systems. A modern holo-screen data center with incredible everything. A gift from Dr. Nathan Trent. The data center allowed her to remain in contact with those she was closest to, from her daughter, to monitoring Daniel Cooper's progress. With a boost in power she could make contact outside the solar system. It also provided access to every non-classified document on the planet.

Stacey started there. She took Patterson's chair, without asking, booted the system, and opened the holo-deck.

"I didn't give you my password," Patterson said. The girl looked up beneath hooded eyes, gave a small shake of her head, and continued flipping through files.

Pam wondered if the head shake indicated her disdain for humans or just adults.

"Everything except one program is compromised," she told her, shutting the system down. "Your search history, notes, communications, videos. Everything."

"Except one?"

"You have a streaming program with the filename 'RUN DMC.' The program is advanced, even by Fellen standards. The security originates from the source, and your system does not maintain data from the feed"

The young woman waited for an explanation of the un-Earthly design. None was provided.

"Would you check the other one?"

Stacey moved to a smaller desk, angled next to a window, with a small, but comfortable chair. This system built on a much older platform. It even used a video monitor. She played with a trackpad for a few seconds, then asked, "Password?"

"Really?" Patterson smothered a snicker.

"It's technology from before my time," the girl responded, defensive. "I'm surprised it still exists. It's something out of my ancient history classes on Fell."

"Two fingers. Spell Pam. Upper case *P*, lower case *a*, and lower case *m*."

Stacey looked at Patterson as if the older woman was the alien. To Stacy's point of view, she was.

Patterson let the girl do her thing. Whatever the reason, this examination took longer.

Stacey finished, tapped a combination on the trackpad, and closed the system.

"You must have been on the computer during one of the random scans," she said, answering the unasked question. "Otherwise, it would be impossible to access to the older system. Everything on the system, prior to three-days six-hours ago, has been taken. Anything added since then is secure."

"If I were on the system now, and a scan occurred, is there a way to warn me?"

"Yes, but the warning would be too late," Stacey explained, "Beam-scanners are extremely fast and efficient. By the time a warning alert could indicate the presence of the beam, it would have collected the data and departed."

"If I wanted to copy information from that computer, and move it to another location, would the people using the scan be aware of the transfer?"

"If you were on the system when another scan occurred, they would be aware of your actions, but they could not trace the data too find the new system, assuming you use a data stick. If you transfer system to system, then it could be traced. Do you want anything copied while we know a scan is not present?"

"Thank you, no. I need time to think about all of this first." She placed a hand on the young woman's shoulder. "Thank you, Stacey. If you hadn't been here, I would never have known about this."

She shrugged, unsure of how to handle the compliment.

D o r m

"Admiral Patterson didn't know someone hacked her computer?" Chaspi asked.

"Had she know, I doubt she would have been surprised," Stacey replied.

"Any idea what 'RUN DMC' monitors?"

The cat-eyes turned away from the document on her paper-thin data-display card.

"I did a search. The only thing I found was a musical trio founded in 1981 who performed hip hop."

"What's 'hip hop?'

"I could not understand the translation," Stacey admitted. "Perhaps Rosz will know. Regardless, I do not think they were the secure site Pam monitored."

The two girls met to discuss course offerings for the upcoming quarter. Stacey helping Chaspi select introductory-level aeronautics classes.

"Have you ever flown?" the Fellen asked the Osperantue.

"Just private mini-hovers," she replied. "On vacation, or with friends who have them. I don't think I've ever been in control or higher than six-feet above the surface."

"Pilot certification is not offered next quarter. The weather in Ontario is too unpredictable and unsafe." Stacey read from the brochure. "Principles of Flight. Technological design for in-at-mosphere and exo-atmospheric craft. Basic concepts of flight, including the three axes of flight, and the control surfaces that guide aircraft."

She handed the booklet up to Chaspi.

Stacey sat on the floor. Chaspi sat cross-legged on her bed. Rosz and Billy off doing guy stuff. She read over the complete description for the class.

"Sounds technical. Looks technical."

"You're an environmental engineering student. This is an entry-level course. It should be simple. Get it completed now and you'll be ready for flight school when the weather improves."

"Stacey, do you find it strange Earth might be the only planet with real people actually piloting their space craft? Every world I know about allows computer systems to control operations. Pilots on Osperantue ships basically monitor and report to the Captain."

"I find many things on this planet strange, but not that," the attractive blue-skinned alien replied. "Fellen pilots can fly the ship, but only if a system is off-line or visual flight is required because of interference. The fact Earth-ship pilots are the primary controllers is why I came to join Space Fleet. I want to fly, not just ride."

"This planet is the newest to attain intergalactic travel," Chaspi continued, "and they are behind in many ways, yet they are the best hope for stopping the Zenge. It all seems strange to me."

"They are a challenging species to understand," Stacey agreed. "I think that may be why they continue to win the battles against the Mischene. Humans are unpredictable."

"You could say the same about males. I wonder what they are looking for?"

"The boys?" Stacey asked. When Chaspi nodded, she surmised, "Rosz is probably trying to find a music store that sells - what did he call them - vinyls? I have no idea what type of music vinyl could be, but it sounds difficult to locate. Billy is likely keeping him company."

"The ones hacking the Admiral. What do you think they wanted?"

"They wanted the files on her antiquated computer," Stacey answered, retrieving a second personal pad by sliding it to her hand with her foot.

Chaspi waited for more information. She could have waited until a fat Woolifer arrived. The Fellen female displayed no sense of drama or curiosity.

"Stacey?"

The blue face looked up, the golden eyes with the feline irises arresting and disturbing. Fellen were a predator species. Bosine were prey.

"How do you know what they wanted?" Chaspi asked.

"The last few beams were more directed. Aimed at that section of Pam's office."

"Pam?"

"She asked that I call her by her name. Human's are informal, unless they are extremely formal. It's difficult to know when they prefer which."

"They are difficult. Almost as hard to communicate with as Fellen technology wizards who don't know how to gossip."

Stacey presented her new friend with a look easily translated. Part exasperation and part resignation.

"The Admiral, Pam, dedicated the older system to one subject," she told the other girl. "It contains files, notes, videos, and data on Colonel Titus Andronicus Barnwell, Jr. That was the information the hackers downloaded. It also appears they intend to continue monitoring the system, hoping to capture anything Pam added."

"How do you know all of the files are about this one person?"

"I have eidetic memory," Stacey admitted. "I scanned many of the files while trying to determine if they were compromised, and whether I could institute a protection wall against future intrusions."

"Photographic memory. That is so rare," Chaspi said. "Well, rare for species from Osperantue, and rare for humans. Is it rare on Fell?"

"Eidetic memory is more invasive than photographic memory," the girl on the floor replied. Her blue skin coloring beginning to darken. The subject regarding her gift caused an increase in her blood pressure. "From what I have read, two to three percent of human children have it, and fewer adults. It tends to lessen as they grow older. Less than ten-percent of one-percent of the people of Fell possess eidetic memory. It's freaky."

"Freaky? Stacey, it's phenomenal. To be able to see something and recall it perfectly. Taking exams must be easy for you."

"Yes. But when I recall something, it fills my brain space. It's difficult to do other things at the same time. When I actively recall something, I become catatonic for a couple of seconds."

"Okay, I see where that could be scary, but not freaky."

"Ten-percent of one-percent equals freak," Stacey responded. "If anyone found out, I would be placed in a tech center as a resource. Imagine engineers able to ask me to spout out equations or results of an experiment immediately, without time wasted to access a computer and search for the correct data. That would become my job. Not flying."

"Wow, they would do that?"

"Maybe. They've done it to others, in the past. When I realized I could remember anything, perfectly, and immediately, I looked into it."

"Who knows about your gift?"

"My family, Daniel Cooper, and you."

"Me? Those people and me? Wow. I can't believe you trust me that much," and she uncrossed her legs.

"DO NOT COME DOWN HERE AND HUG ME," Stacey warned. Chaspi was a hugger, and Stacey so not.

The Bosine girl who escaped an invasion and experienced life as a refugee, including living displaced on a distant planet, hugged as a way of confirming her existence.

Stacey, taken captive with her younger sister by the Zenge after they invaded her planet, preferred her personal space stay unencumbered.

Changing the subject, and taking advantage of the normally reticent Fell's openness, Chaspi asked, "Who is Titus Andronicus Barnwell, Junior?"

"Was," Stacey corrected. "He was one of the twelve Space Ranger survivors. He committed suicide."

"NO WAY!" Chaspi exclaimed. "An elite soldier, a man who could live forever, a Ranger like Coop and Elena Casalobos, committed suicide. That just does not sound right."

Stacey, who knew more of the Space Rangers than Chaspi, agreed. "Pam thinks it odd, as well," she said. "Her files included her personal investigation notes into his death. From what I read, I don't think she believes he committed suicide."

"She's investigating his death? Can she do that? Retired."

"Before she transferred to Space Fleet, she worked for UEC Naval Intelligence. She is capable of investigating. Her resignation provided the additional time to pursue the inquiry. That she kept all of her notes and data on a non-connected ancient system indicates she does not have the authority to investigate. Being retired."

"Now someone knows she's doing it," Chaspi said.

"Yes. But without knowing who that may be, there is no way to decide if it represents a possible arrest."

"Arrest! You think she could be arrested for investigating a suicide?"

"No. I think she could be arrested for having classified government documents on a private system."

"Then she needs to get them off. She needs to hide them." She stood, ready to act. "We need to tell her."

"Chaspi, Pam knows everything I have told you, except the knowledge I am aware of the contents of her system. I believe her experience as an intelligence officer, and the Fleet Admiral for Space Fleet is sufficient for her to understand the potential dangers. We do not need to inform her."

The Bosine sat back down. "You're right. She'll know to hide them. Stacey?"

"Yes?"

"Do you think we should help her with the investigation?"

"Why?"

"Because it is obviously important to her, and she can't continue with someone trying to hack her system. And you have all of the files in your memory. And we all owe her."

"Maybe," Stacey replied. "Maybe."

CHAPTER 10

The former Communications Security Establishment Canada (CSEC) was an electronic eavesdropping agency that gathered intelligence from abroad. The agency maintained offices in the Canadian capital of Ottawa. Following unification with the former United States of America, the CSEC joined with the US National Security Agency. Later, the joint operation became the United Earth Council's electronic intelligence agency, the UESE. They maintain a secure operational center in Toronto, near UEC and Space Fleet campuses.

Patterson exited her transport in the agency's below-ground parking. She made her way to the elevator, her purposeful stride shackled by the suitcase wheeled behind her. The lift rose to the highest floor allowed. The doors opened onto a security desk, complete with scanners, x-rays, and two formidable guards dressed in matching blue business suits.

She was reaching for her credentials when a tall, older gentleman in a tailored grey suit and hand sewn shoes emerged from the doors behind the security station to intercede.

"Pam," he called.

"Paris," she replied in acknowledgment. She confirmed his presence on site before making the trip from her home, but did not call to warn him of her visit. Security would have picked her up the moment she came within four blocks of the center. Her Space Fleet ID had gotten her this far, but Paris' intervention likely smoothed the way as well.

"Come around to the private gate," he instructed, moving to his left while directing her to her right. She did not see him push, press, or request any action, but a section of the security wall opened inward, allowing her to enter the secure facility without needing to pass through the detection devices.

Paris Cassel, Director of the United Earth Security Establishment (UESE), North American Division, could allow access to anyone he wished. Cassel and Patterson did not speak again. He led her through the door and into spy central. She followed, entering a room when he stopped and held the door open for her.

The door closed behind them and she asked, "Secure?"

"Totally," he assured her. "It may look like other conference rooms, but every possible scan, x-ray, intrusion beam, or person with good ears standing at the door can't hear or see anything inside. What's important enough to require an unannounced visit?"

"Unannounced? You knew I would be coming from the moment I called to confirm you were on site."

"I have been keeping an eye on the security feeds," he admitted. "We've known each other since you joined Naval Intelligence, and I was a lowly field agent for the UESE. For you to send a 'heads-up' and then show up, luggage in hand, means trouble. Question is, trouble for whom?"

"First, you have never been a lowly field agent. You were Canada's top spy, even back then. Second, trouble for me. This is a personal request, Paris. If you have to turn me away, I will understand."

Cassel pulled a seat out, made sure his guest was comfortable, before walking around and taking a chair facing her. "Pam, you have been an ally and a friend for thirty years. If you are in trouble, and did not come to me, I would be devastated. Whatever you need, you have."

"You haven't heard the details yet."

"Tell me the details, but they won't matter."

"The suitcase contains my old personal computer. I have the files, public and classified, concerning the death of Titus Barnwell. I have my notes, personal investigation journal, and concerns that his death was perpetrated by a faction within the United Earth Council, and possibly the Board of Governors. Do you still want to help me?"

"More than ever," he admitted. "What do you need?"

"My house is randomly scanned. This computer is already compromised. I need a secure location to store it and still have access so I can continue my investigation."

Cassel rose, went to the wall on his right. He stared at the facade. A seam appeared and a section eight-feet high and four-feet wide slide forward, soundlessly.

"You can place your equipment inside," he told her. Pam wheeled the bag and contents over, then into the exposed storage unit.

"I have it set to accept your scan, please stand where I am," he moved aside, "and stare at the wall like an idiot."

Smiling, she took his place. The section reinserted into the wall. She continued to stare, but could not see a seam. "Impressive."

"Only you and I can open it," he informed her. "This room will be designated for your use, and only your use, until you tell me otherwise."

"Thank you, Paris."

"Perhaps you should hold your thanks. I am in charge of electronic security and external threats to the UEC. While it is not my position to investigate internal threats, I cannot ignore your concern, Pam. If there is intrigue within the Council, and people are willing to kill an asset as important as a Space Ranger, you need to bring me up to speed."

"I'm following up on feelings, Paris," she explained, returning to her seat. She appeared relieved and worried. Relieved her work was secure, and she had a potential ally. Worried about bringing a friend into a dangerous hobby.

"I never felt right about Tab's death ruled as a suicide. I saw the reports, and read his note. I simply could not believe it. When I retired, knowing I would have time on my hands, I decided to look more closely. I'm not far enough along to say more than, if his death wasn't a suicide, then someone in the UEC was involved."

"Your home is monitored, and your files hacked," he added. "You must have stirred someone's soup."

"Or it could be normal procedure to keep the previous commander of Space Fleet under watch," she said. "The new commander may be concerned about my ultimate loyalties."

"Terrence Singletary is a prick," Paris said, with venom in his voice. Clearly, he held little regard for the current Space Fleet Commanding Admiral. "His political connections placed him in a position to oust and replace you. It is a decision that will one day bite the UEC, and the Board of Governors, in their collective asses."

"He is politically savvy. And paranoid. It would be within his nature to have security scan my personal files."

"But it wasn't him," Paris replied.

"Because?"

"You said the files were compromised by one of the intrusion scans. You also said you had classified documents. Documents illegal for you to possess since you are retired. If Singletary knew you had them, a team of security agents would have descended, confiscated your systems, and arrested you. He is jealous of your history, Pam. The man hates you."

"Granted. Not him, but someone with a great deal of influence."

"Which is why you must be careful," he said. "Be circumspect about your investigation. Use this room when you need it. Keep your notes on flash paper only. People cannot hack paper, and you can flame it to ashes in seconds. I will set the security protocols to allow you access to the building, and to this room. You still have the Fell communications and translation chip embedded in your neck?"

"How do you know about the chip?" she stammered. "Never mind. Of course you would know about a secret communications devise. Does everyone at UESE know?"

"Just me," he assured her. "But the scans will recognize you, and it. Guards will simply ignore you and there will be no records kept of your visits. Is there anything more I can do?"

"You've done everything, and more."

The top spook gave his long-time friend a most serious face. "When you find out who is behind Tab's death, you will let me know, immediately."

"You have a lot of faith in an old woman who hasn't run an investigation in decades."

"You are far from old, Pam. Your skills as an investigator have never been in question. And, yes, I have a lot of faith in you."

UESE Office of Director

"How much does she know?"

Cassel brushed imaginary lint from the front of his slacks. The motion a nervous tick. After decades in espionage, nervous meant staying alert. Meetings with this man required vigilance. If observed together in the wrong place, by the wrong eyes, the fall-out could ruin years of planning.

"She doesn't actually know anything, yet," he assured the fashionably dressed man. "Pam suspected Barnwell's suicide bogus since the day it was reported. I don't believe she has anything hard to substantiate her doubts."

"Why don't you see what's on her computer?"

"Naval Intelligence once considered Patterson their best analytical mind. She was top flight as an investigator, and a counter-intelligence agent. She will know if her computer is accessed. Since I'm the one who placed it in secure storage, I would be the only suspect. I'd prefer to keep her off my scent."

"How did she discover the intrusion beams?"

Cassel checked his wrist chronometer, not because he cared about the time, but the devise also checked the immediate area for electronic eavesdropping. No bugs and no beams registered.

"She didn't say, and I didn't press. Like I said, she's as good at counter-spy field craft as data analysis. I'm more surprised her computer was compromised before she realized the beams were aimed at her home. If she plans on continuing to investigate Barnwell's death, she'll need to use the secure room at the agency. I'll be available as a sounding board. If she learns of anything that could damage our operation, I'll handle it quickly."

"That may be too late," the dapper gentleman said. "She was important enough to have her removed from Space Fleet. Her nosing into Barnwell's suicide makes her a target. If she retired and took up a useless hobby, she'd be safe. As it is, she's made it clear she remains a threat."

"Maybe. If she leaves the research alone and doesn't go looking further, she may remain safe." Cassel was uncomfortable discussing the potential demise of his life-long friend, but would never let it show.

"Admiral Patterson never struck me as the kind of person to leave things alone," the other man replied.

"No," Cassel agreed. "But we can hope."

"Anything regarding Cooper?"

"She's receiving updates from a site with security systems more advanced than those we use," Cassel answered. "Most likely updates on Captain Cooper. Time-stamps are consistent, so he's stationary. He probably remains in a coma."

"But we cannot be sure, if the security is as strong as you say."

The security chief shrugged. "Educated guesses," he admitted.

"You cannot warn her, Paris. She's your friend, and I appreciate that, but we are engaged with events which will determine the direction of this entire world for decades, possibly centuries to come. One person is not more important than the work we have already accomplished, or the end game."

"I realize that. If she continues to look into Barnwell, I'll try to send her in the wrong direction. It may be enough to keep her alive."

"Or not," the other man countered.

CHAPTER 11

Rosz and Billy stood in front of a shop window frosted over, not by the cold, but with non-transparent film. The door displayed the number three, CHIBA DOJO in block english letters, and symbols beneath the english, presumably Japanese script.

The storefront one of a dozen located in Village Plaza. The spaces on either side of Number Three vacant, with old newspapers covering the inside of the shop windows and door glass. FOR LEASE signs and a voice-call number taped to the inside of each display window.

"What do you think?" Billy asked.

"It was the nearest martial arts studio to the campus," Rosz answered. "Should we go in?"

"That or freeze to death." Billy pushed, and nothing happened. Next, he pulled and the door swung open. The two college students entered a stark dark world.

They stood on woven carpet. The six-foot wide strip lay in front of all four interior walls. The carpet framed a twenty by forty bamboo floor. Ambient light emanated from walls and ceiling. The surprising size of the interior due to the for-rent spaces on either side incorporated into this one. Where newspaper-lined windows showed outside, textured wall-paper covered flat walls inside.

"Hello?" Billy called, expecting an echo.

"You don't think they leave the door open when no one is here, do you?" Rosz asked.

Billy shrugged. "I wouldn't think so. Look at that back wall. Swords, spears, and fighting sticks. All kinds of weapons. I don't think they would leave those unlocked."

"I do not."

The two boys jumped, spun, and sputtered.

The reply came from a man knelling on the carpeted aisle to the right of the entrance. His fisted hands rested at the top of his thighs. His posture erect and relaxed at the same time.

"Was he there when we walked in?" Billy whispered the question.

Despite the earbuds, and ever present music, Rosz replied, "Must have been."

He addressed the man. "Sorry if we disturbed you. We were interested in martial arts lessons."

"Were? Now you are no longer interested?"

"No. My translator sometimes gets my words right, but my meaning wrong. We are interested in martial arts."

The soft light made it difficult to see the man clearly. He looked oriental, with dark hair. His eyes remained focused at the bamboo floor in front of him.

"I do not teach martial arts. I train most in karate. I instruct a few how to defend themselves. Some, how to use a weapon."

Rosz turned to his friend and said, "Hiro Kimura uses karate. Coop told me."

The man turned his head, and eyes, on the two. "Sensei Kimura is a karate Master without equal. Would 'Coop' refer to Captain Daniel Cooper?"

"Yes, he's my friend," Rosz replied. He could not disguise the pride in his statement, even through the translator. "Do you know Hiro Kimura or Daniel Cooper?"

"By reputation only," the man said, rising as if his body consisted of air and water. "Why do you want to learn to fight?" He stood before Rosz, who stood five-inches taller.

"To protect my friends," the Bosine replied.

"And you?"

"Same. And so I'm not afraid to do something if I need to," Billy answered.

"You should never fear the consequences of protecting someone who needs help," the man said. The room seemed brighter, but it could have been the boys' eyes becoming accustomed to the dim interior.

"I don't fear the consequences. I fear failing," the Canadian admitted.

"Fifty credits for each ninety-minute lesson," he said.

"I'll have to see if I can afford that," Rosz said.

"I can cover us for a few sessions," Billy said.

"You don't need to do that. I just need to see what I can come up with."

"I don't mind. This way we can get started sooner."

"I should pay for myself."

"Enough," the karate master said. He did not shout, but the force of his voice stopped any more conversation. "You can stay after sessions and clean for half the cost. You do not mind work, do you?"

"No," both replied. "But we need to train in the early afternoon. It's the only time we have," Billy added.

"This time tomorrow. We begin," was his answer.

"Great," Billy said. "I'm Billy, and this is Rosz, he's a Bosine from Osperantue. What do we call you?"

"You call me Sensei. And, in case you told me about your friend to see if it would make a difference. It does not. I do not care where my students come from. I only care about your desire to learn. And your honor."

He gave a short bow, and passed them, headed to the rear of the studio. He exited through a curtain.

"Do you think he's serious?" Billy asked.

"I think he gets twenty-five credits and two maids," Rosz replied. "We'll see what happens tomorrow. We can always quit."

"I don't know, Rosz. Sensei doesn't seem the type to appreciate a quitter."

"And we don't tell Chaspi or Stacey about this."

"Nope. Though I did think about asking Stacey to train us," Billy admitted.

CHAPTER 12

"Any idea how long the house has been under surveillance?" Sam Patterson asked. In one of life's little quirks, Pam met, feel in love, and married a man with the same last name. In the beginning it took her friends and colleagues time to adjust. After more time passed, new people assumed she took his last name.

"No," Pam admitted. She decided her husband deserved to know intrusion scans invaded the home they shared. Scans made by unknown agents. Forced, as an intelligence operative and a military officer, to keep secrets from him since they married, this did not represent one kept for national or world security. This concerned their home, and the life they shared.

They sat on a metal bench, the park's frozen pond an invitation for people living nearby to lace skates and ride the ice. They often came here and watched the kids learn to skate as parents glided in protective circles.

"Glad I erased that porn collection," he quipped.

Sam Patterson worked as a trade alliance mediator. The unification of Earth came without a multitude of problems. Trade values and establishing a worldwide currency or credit system topped the list. Mediators were necessary to establish actual value of goods and services relative to other commodities. Attempting to quantify millions of items, services, even concepts was going to require a couple of lifetimes. A sense of humor helped get him through each day.

"I hope you didn't have anything on our home systems that could cause you problems at work," Pam said, ignoring the porn remark.

"My appointment calendar is the only work thing I bring home," he answered. "I have been more than happy to leave my work at work."

"That's funny. I never brought my work home until I retired."

"Retired? I'm pretty sure you were forced to resign, and I have a sneaky feeling the files you did bring home may have something to do with that." Her husband took her left hand in his right. "Whatever you need to do, Pam, please do. I know you never wanted Space Fleet to suffer from the political intrigue that plagued so many government branches, before or after the pandemic. Because of my job, I see a lot of assets moving around the world that do not make fiscal sense. When politicians start acting up, and covert financial activities increase, something bad is in the wind."

"Any hints as to what?"

"Not one," he admitted. "You might be the opening move in a power play, or you might be part of the end game."

"Is there a way to tell how much time we have before something bad happens," she said.

"Daniel's murder attempt, your resignation, the scanning of our home, and Paris Cassel wasn't surprised by your visit. I'd guess we have less time, not more."

"You keep saying 'we'".

"You bet I do. Our home was invaded. Before the pandemic, following the uproar about government intrusion into the lives of private citizens last century, that would never have been allowed. When political parties decided to use the power of government agencies to spy for political gain, they brought about their own destruction. Controls on spy agencies became death-grips. Since the pandemic, it seems more and more of the old political mistakes are making a comeback."

Sam watched a four-year-old land hard on his butt. The youngster laughed, and got right back up.

"Our lives have been upended. I have the contacts to watch for odd cross-national financial transactions, and you have the brains to figure it all out."

"Go Team Patterson," Pam said, and gave his hand a squeeze.

Aster Farum 3

"How long have you had the younger Soren under surveillance?"

Captain Covane, a thirty-something career officer and communications specialist removed her earpiece. She heard the Admiral's query, but needed a moment to make sure she framed the reply in a way that would answer his question and make sense.

"We do not actually have him under surveillance, Admiral," she replied. "I have a back-channel relay from a tower the Zenge have not destroyed. The tower is connected to an old com-satellite in mid-space. The satellite bounces the signal to a system patrol boat near AF2. Information is sporadic at best."

"But enough information to know what Soren is planning?" he asked.

"All I can tell you, factually, is a technician on Flame broadcasted an open message on the system patrol's emergency bandwidth. He said Soren sent an experimental drone with wormhole-creation ability to the planet Earth system. He is inviting them to discuss a truce, and blames his father and AF3 for the Zenge attacks against other worlds."

"He's using the truth as a lure." The observation made by Major Willmer, a small man in a rumpled black and silver uniform. Even seated, it was obvious he might be five-six. Light brown skin and white hair buzzed close to his skull. His weak chin showed a day's worth of white stubble, and his right hand tapped pinky-to-index over and over on the desktop. He did not look at anyone when he spoke, keeping his eyes on the display boards in front of him.

The conversation occurred in a war room located several reinforced floors beneath the surface, safe from weapons fired from space. Above the command center resided 20,000 Mischene elite soldiers. An additional 10,000 military personnel and civilians crowded into the underground complex following the Prophet's invasion.

A semi-circular conference table dominated the center of the war room. Admiral Lexton sat center, on the outside of the arch. A massive situational display projection filled the wall in front of him. Data and video streamed across different blocks on the display, providing real-time updates from around the planet and within the system.

Behind him, a dozen Mischene military people engaged system controls; sending information, relaying information, or analyzing incoming information.

The attack on the Aster system occurred fourteen days earlier.

"Amos Soren planned on using his son as the scapegoat for the attacks he ordered against the other Trading Alliance worlds. Governor Soren planned on eliminating Atticus and was too full of himself to realize his son saw what was coming. Atticus beat his father to the punch," Lexton told the assembled.

"Now it appears he intends on continuing his father's plan for Mischene dominance across the galaxy. Where greed drove the elder Soren, Atticus believes he is actually the Prophet of the Tahbita."

"He wants the humans to come to him under the guise of peace talks," Willmer said. "He realizes they represent the greatest threat to his grand design. Governor Soren planned on convincing them Atticus stood behind the Zenge. Atticus Soren will use the truth, that Amos Soren masterminded the attacks, to lure them here."

"If they send envoys, can we make contact, Captain?" Lexon asked the communications specialist.

Covane shook her head. "Without knowing how they communicate, I don't think we will be able to reach them with the limited capabilities we have left."

"The Prophet's ships are not attacking beyond Aster Farum 3," Lexton said. To Willmer he asked, "Do you have a guess as to why not?"

"He wants to control AF3 first," the chief of military intelligence responded quickly. "He also wants the system to appear calm if the humans accept his invitation."

"Continue, Major Willmer," Lexton urged.

"The Prophet believes in Tahbita Law. He believes the Mischene, under his direction and leadership, are destined to rule the galaxy. The Sacred Tahbita so says. He needs the Mischene to follow him for that prophesy to come true. He's not here to just take control of the Aster system. He's here to convert Mischene into willing followers."

"He expects us to willingly follow him into his madness?" Covane asked, disdain or disbelief raising the intensity of her tone. "No one, certainly no one sane is going to accept him as the actual Sacred Prophet of the Tahbita."

"Perhaps not," Willmer said, "But his father, the late Supreme Governor General Amos Soren, led us down the same path. The only difference, the elder Soren believed the Mischene represent the galaxy's superior race. Religion was just another tool."

Emboldened by the situation, and having no fear of retribution, the intelligence officer said, "We were willing to subjugate the other races on Aster Farum 3, and invade and take over the other planets in the Aster system, all because Soren told us we deserved the mantle of leadership."

Lexon completed Willmer's line of reasoning.

"Now the younger Soren is growing the same fruit with a different fertilizer. We deserve to rule the galaxy because the Tahbita says so. To rule we must follow a new leader, the Prophet."

"He expects us to fall to our knees and worship him?" Covane asked.

"He doesn't care if you worship him," Lexton replied. "He doesn't care if you believe in Tahbita Law. All he cares about is that we fall in line. His army of Zenge will wage war until every Mischene is dead or swears allegiance."

"At the moment our ground forces are holding their own," General Abrahm Ostella added his voice to the confab for the first time. The General, in black and silver uniform similar to Major Willmer's, but with knee-high shiny leather boots instead of oxfords. Currently tasked with commanding the Mischene military engaging the enemy on the planet's surface.

"I have ordered all of our forces to remain within their fortresses and fortified camps. Our weapons, and those the Zenge and Mischene traitors use, are equal. With our positions hardened, we have been able to keep them at bay," he reported.

"And the civilian populations in the cities and towns?" Lexton asked.

"They must hide. Police faced Zenge forces within many of the planet's major cities. The civilian authorities quickly outnumbered and outgunned. We could not risk sending troops to assist."

The monitor emphasized the condition of the population, displaying columns of smoke rising into and covering the skies above metropolitan areas.

"The six Class One Carriers used to deliver the Zenge fighters to the surface re-entered the wormhole," Admiral Nan reminded them. "They left over 360,000 of the cold-blooded creatures. When they return, which could be a day or a month, they will bring another 360,000. Sooner or later they will overrun our positions by shear strength of numbers."

Admiral Nan was the last voice at the table. Preparing to retire when Atticus Soren attacked his world, he now commanded next to nothing. A couple of battleships and system patrol boats remained, but contact through Covane's back-channel provided little time for more than cursory reports.

"Civilians are told to pledge their faith to the Prophet," Covane reported. "The Prophet hacked into local media entertainment systems. He's promising they will live and even prosper if they surrender. There are reports of hundreds, and possibly thousands of Mischene men, women, and children giving themselves up."

"The Zenge armies are led by Mischene officers," Willmer added. "When the citizens see this, they will be more likely to turn themselves over."

"As things stand, there is little chance of victory," Lexton said. "Suggestions. And do not suggest we surrender," he warned.

"We need reinforcements," Nan said.

"The ships and troops sent to eradicate the Zenge are still at Osperantue," Ostella said. "If we can get a message through to them, they could mount a rescue."

"A battlecruiser and a couple of launches. Maybe a thousand soldiers." Willmer shook his head. "I don't think they will mount much of a rescue."

"And I doubt Earth or any of our former trading alliance partners will trust anything we say," Covane added. "Why do you believe the Prophet is trying to lure humans to the system? If he knows they are capable of defeating his ships, and he sees them as an obstacle to his plans, why ask them here?"

Admiral Nan answered simply, "The vortex."

CHAPTER 13

"Where were the two of you all afternoon?" Chaspi asked.

"Went for a walk around the shopping centers near campus," Billy replied. "I haven't seen many of them, and Rosz hasn't been to any. Always smart to know what stores are close by."

"Why didn't you just search the map stream and do a virtual?"

"Not as much fun," he answered.

Billy sat on the floor beside Rosz, who paid no attention to the back-and-forth, listening to something with his eyes closed.

Chaspi sat cross-legged on her bed and Stacey worked at the small desk.

"I think this is the best place to start," the Fellen said, turning around to face the others, data pad in her hand.

"Start what?" Rosz asked. It continued to amaze his new friends how he could listen to music and still hear everything going on around him.

"We're going to help Admiral Patterson," Chaspi said. "Only we can't let her know we are helping," she added. "Stacey thinks she can remember a few of the things she saw on the old computer."

Stacey gave Chaspi a sideways glance, appreciative the girl did not reveal her ability to recall everything.

"Titus Andronicus Barnwell, Junior," the Fellen said the name slowly. "Space Ranger survivor. He rejoined the United Earth Council Marines following the project. His choice of assignment, to join the Marine Corps Intelligence Division. Six years ago he committed suicide. Drowning. Or maybe not exactly drowning."

"How do you 'not exactly drown?'" Billy asked.

"His personal vehicle, clothes, ID, and his Marine-issued Data Pad all found at the end of a road in a place called Honey Island Cypress Swamp," Stacey answered, pretending to read from her own pad. "It is in a region called Louisiana, and infested with something called alligators. I believe they will eat people found in their habitat."

"Gross," Billy said. "Death by alligator is not a pleasant thought. I hope he did drown first."

"The authorities never recovered a body," she continued. "Besides alligators, the area is home to several scavenging carnivores, and something called the Honey Island Monster."

"Monster?" Billy asked.

"Local myth," Stacey replied. "A creature resulting from the breeding of chimpanzees and alligators."

"What has this got to do with helping Admiral Patterson?" Rosz asked, ignoring the myth.

"She did not, does not believe Colonel Barnwell committed suicide," Chaspi answered for Stacey. "She thinks he was murdered. She thinks he was investigating something dangerous, and bad people found out, and they had him killed, and faked the suicide."

"Does she know what he was investigating?" Billy asked.

"The files she took from Space Fleet included copies of Col. Barnwell's official reports," Stacey answered. "In the year prior to his death, he showed interest in the activities of two men associated with the plans to designate Space Fleet as a para-military branch of the United Earth Council, and not a department of the Navy."

"But he never includes their names," Chaspi added. "We think he was trying to make sure no one warned them."

"Meaning he thought his superiors in the Marines might do that," Rosz said.

"Or his files could be hacked," Stacey said.

"Admiral Patterson reopened the investigation when she retired," Billy spoke, pulling the information from the data Stacey shared. "She wanted to determine who the two might be, how they were affiliated with Space Fleet, if what they were doing could cause a problem, and if they were responsible for Col. Barnwell's death."

"And they know she is investigating," Stacey added. "The intruder beam captured the files and all notes she added. Since no one from Space Fleet contacted her regarding the removal of classified information, the people monitoring her home are not acting officially."

"The same people who killed Barnwell to stop his investigation are watching Admiral Patterson. They may try to stop her if it's still important six years later," Rosz surmised.

"Must be," Billy said. "Why else scan her systems?"

"Which is why we will investigate from here," Chaspi said. "When they see Admiral Patterson is no longer accessing the files, they'll have no reasons to bother her. When we have the answers, we'll give them to her."

"And school?" Billy.

"We'll meet here after classes," Chaspi said.

"And I do not officially begin until next session," Stacey said. "I will have time to organize the information before we meet tomorrow."

**Meridian, Mississippi
(Six Years Previously)**

"Originally Marine Corps Intelligence provided on-the-go information and analysis for air and ground troops involved with dangerous missions," Tab explained. The handsome black officer filled out his UEC Marine khaki uniform like the twenty-five-year-old he was twenty years earlier.

"For over one-hundred years MCI used every asset available, technical, computerized, or human to collect information in battle-likely areas. After the pandemic, we rolled into Can-Am and began analyzing hot spots around the globe. We provided the intel for those deciding where our best people should be sent to try and save people and stop bad guys. When the UEC formed, MCI began to monitor for threats inside North America. No longer constrained by borders, every intelligence agency looked for potential threats from any location. The fear of a central governing platform failing included the reasonable decision that for every person who wanted the Earth united, someone would oppose the concept."

"That was your purpose in returning to the MCI following the Space Ranger Project? To protect the United Earth Council?"

The female Marine officer sat across the table. The outdoor seating area empty except for the two in uniform. Downtown Meridian, Mississippi had not yet switched from workday to evening. The southern-style restaurant near the ancient railroad station offered plenty of available places to sit, inside and out. Favorable weather, and a desire to talk without someone overhearing, led them to the exterior table.

"More that I enjoy intelligence operations," Tab admitted. "Doing it for the Marines means I get to see first-hand reports, make analysis calls, and then deploy to see how right or wrong my analysis turned out."

"Why are you in Meridian?"

"Following up on suspicions," he admitted. "Since the Gulf of Mexico rose and swallowed all the old seaports, the nearest Marines are located here, at the Naval Air Station flight school. Since you head the Military Police assigned to NAS, I thought I would take advantage of your local connection."

The brunette with the green eyes laughed. "I am the Marine's Military Police assigned. The whole, entire MP force. Navy MP's handle actual policing. I monitor for attempted incursions of the secure systems."

"Which means you also stay aware of similar activity in the region, as well as any players with the potential to hack your systems. You get movement reports on VIP's. You see and hear things, and you're trained to look for patterns."

"I appreciate that you are trying to ply me with sweat tea and corn fritters, Colonel. Tell me what you're looking for, and I'll tell you if I've seen anything similar in Mississippi."

"Captain Driver, I would appreciate it if you keep what we discuss private," Tab said. "Part of this is official and part of it is chasing conspiracies theories. Most of my notes exist inside my head. I don't think I'm putting you in danger, but it might not be wise to tell anyone else until I've decided to go completely official."

"Wow, now you have my full attention," she replied.

"I have spent decades studying revolutions," he began. "If there is a plot to cause the UEC to disband, and for Earth to return to independent nation-states, there will be activities and signs to look for."

"Such as?"

"Assuming a group already formed for this purpose, they will need a public leader. Someone respected, charismatic, and comfortable on stage. Right now, there are several possibilities, but none have stepped forward. Activists will be recruited," he said, pausing to sip his tea before continuing. "There has been an uptick in the number of anti-United Earth groups displaying access to technology, media, and materials without a direct funding source."

"Anti-United Earth groups? Really?" Driver asked, the sarcasm obvious.

Tab laughed, a soft undertone sound in response to her snide question.

"Groups have been against living under a central government since before the unification," he replied. "But there have been less violent and better organized groups showing up at UEC events over the past two years," he confirmed. "Because they have not been violent, no one has been asked to investigate."

"But you did anyway?"

"Does my paranoia show? I did facial recognition and background on hits, but nothing red-flagged. The groups are growing and I haven't figured out how they can afford to move around and stay in different cities. None of the repeat demonstrators appear to work anywhere or have access to disposable income."

"What else do you look for?" The MP - Investigator becoming more interested as Tab explained the puzzle pieces.

"Science," he responded. "They will recruit scientists and respected educators to lend credence to the claims that a united planet does more harm than help for the average person. Geneticists and sociologists who will bemoan the loss of cultural identities as borders blur and cross-breeding increases. Speakers who will point out the separation of haves and have-nots continues and deepens because of UEC policies. Historians will discuss the failures of past attempts at world-building and the destructive consequences that followed those attempts."

Driver set her glass down, reached across the table and placed her hand atop Tab's.

"Something is beginning to tickle my memory," she said. "Will music, art, and mass-media types be targeted to join this cabal?"

"Definitely," he replied. "They will sponsor musicians and artist who produce songs, paintings, sculpture, or anything related with a strong cultural or national pride basis. Music will be essential to turning younger people against a form of government they have know their entire lives. Mass-media for audio, streamers, cross-channel, vid-casts, and especially news and opinion shows are required for success. They will want to dominate the debate, and make sure everything reported is framed to support independence and self-rule. It will also make military intervention less likely."

"Even if it requires the military to save the government?"

"Governments are people," Tab replied. "While it may only be a few powerful, driven individuals seeking the change, if they are patient, and understand the game, by the time the UEC is aware they are under attack, the population will have already taken the other side. The military is not going to throw down on non-violent civil disobedience. Anything yet prick that tickle?"

"That's it!" she exclaimed. "Prick is the key."

Slightly startled and slightly excited, Tab waited for her to illuminate her statement.

"Captain Stephen J. Hawks is commanding officer in charge of the Navy's Transformational Communications Architecture, or TCA project," Driver said. "The UEC wants to combine the various communications systems used around the planet with the newer systems used in space to provide more information and greater coverage for all UEC assets. And he's a world-class prick."

"Never met the man, but I have heard similar, less poetic, descriptions," Tab said. "Does this relate to my situation?"

"Does it?" she asked back. "Why are you in Meridian, Mississippi, Col. Barnwell? You aren't sniffing around the entire continent, interviewing Marine cops, hoping to stumble on a plot to overturn the UEC. You have eyes on someone of interest," she surmised. "Who, why, and where are they? Answer me, and I might be able to help you."

"Dr. Bernard Reinhardt was a post-grad assistant who did grunt work during the Space Rangers Project," Tab answered. He did not hesitate, deciding Captain Driver respected straight shooting, and would reciprocate. "In the last decade he has become the leading expert on genetic engineering. He currently works for the UEC, assigned to a secret program attached to Space Fleet's R and D on artificial intelligence. He has written opinion articles suggesting UEC's next step in global unification could be toward genetic parity. Designing future babies to all have the same genetic structure. Uniformity through science. He disagrees with the concept."

"That tells me who," she said. "Why Meridian?"

"Hattiesburg, actually," he replied. "As you well know, the rise of the Gulf of Mexico played hell along the Florida to Texas coastline. New Orleans gone. The naval bases shuttered. The economy of the southern gulf states took a hit. Then the Pandemic. A lot of colleges closed. Many sold off assets to remain open. Universities operate research facilities and labs with the latest technology. The biochemical and chemical engineering departments at Southern University of Mississippi, in Hattiesburg, were extremely attractive. A bank in London made an offer. They got the buildings, labs, research notes, inventory, and a couple of older dorms. The university received funds, ongoing rent, and the labs continued to remain available for student lessons."

"Reinhardt teaches there?"

"He does something there, but he doesn't teach, lecture, or have any notable interaction with administration, faculty, or students. They moved the school employees out and moved their own people in about six months ago."

"You think he's creating a chemical formula to break up the UEC?" she asked.

"UEC is moving toward space more every day," he replied. "Space platforms are growing. Mars is receiving more people. Space Fleet will soon be its own branch of the military," he confided. "That means genetic research and the psychological difficulties of humans living in hostile environments is back at the forefront. Reinhardt has offices on EMS2 and research labs in Toronto and Atlanta. Whatever he's doing in Hattiesburg is off the books. I'm of the opinion he's working on alternatives to the directives he receives from the UEC."

"When he finally comes out against them, he can present an argument against unification, and provide proof of the dangers associated with eliminating borders and cross-pollinating the species," Driver mused aloud.

"Something like that," Tab agreed. He liked the MP. She had a brain and was not afraid to use it. "What can you add?"

With a nod of her head, she provided the information she thought relevant.

"Forty-five miles south of Southern University are facilities that once belonged to the old space exploration group, NASA. Originally, it was a propulsion testing facility. They built it on the border of a wilderness preserve to prevent anything going boom killing civilians. Over the decades it bounced from one government agency to another, but always had something to do with space flight. A year ago it was sold off to private investors. They official word is the facilities will be used to develop and test new propulsion systems for in-atmosphere transportation."

"Interesting timing," Tab agreed.

"More interesting is the VIPs currently descending on the location. We received a heads-up to expect a number of private shuttles and the security accompanying the honchos. It's a private launch party. Get it? 'Launch' party. Launch pads."

"I'll laugh later," he assured her. "Do you know who the guests are?"

"Not all of them, but I've seen reports naming a couple of media moguls, at least one UEC representative, and an officer of the US Navy."

"The Navy is represented," Tab repeated. "I didn't see anything about this."

"The report didn't come from official sources," she confessed. "Meridian is a bit boring, as you can imagine. When a late-model government issued semi-hover ground shuttle passed through, a couple of jet-jockeys decided to use it for practice. Target acquisition. They laser pinged it all the way to the no-fly zone east of the wilderness."

"Navy markings on the ground shuttle?"

"Better," she replied, calling for a refill of her tea before continuing. "Made a pit stop for the passenger to relieve himself. Pilot said the zoom on his laser cannon allowed him to read his nameplate. Hawks."

"Going to a party or a confab?"

"After the scary story you just told, I'm believing your conspiracy theory more and more," she admitted.

"I was going to take a look around the facilities in Hattiesburg. Looks like I might take a quick trip south after that," he said.

"You need directions?"

"Have 'em to the university. Old style. If you can get me to the old NASA site?"

"Pay the bill, Colonel," she said. "Other than forced to use old highways and byways, nothing in Mississippi is hard to find."

CHAPTER 14

"Following a hunch, or just revisiting old trails?"

Director Cassel asked the question as soon as he entered the secure room. Patterson sat at the lone table, her old computer placed in front of her, the screen dark.

"The same stumbling block," she replied. "You checking up on me, Paris?"

"Time on my hands," he said. "I saw your code flash when you entered the building earlier. I wasn't going to bother you, but I have to admit I'm still curious about Tab myself," he said. "Never believed the suicide, but never saw proof of foul play in the reports from the NCIS investigation."

"If I could determine why Tab was on the edge of that wilderness preserve, assuming he did not travel from D.C. to Louisiana to find a swamp monster, maybe it would clue me to what he was working on."

"You had access to his investigation files," Cassel reminded her. "Nothing in them related to Louisiana, or anything along that part of the gulf?"

"Tab was old school. He kept things out of the files so no one would get wind of him looking at them," she replied. "His personal pad had that bogus journal. The one proving he was going through an emotional crisis."

"Not to play Devil's Advocate, but Marine, Naval, and even Nathan Trent's computer people would not say the pad had been tampered with. Files, date stamps, back logs all said those were legit entries, and made by Tab."

"Bullshit," the former Admiral answered. "They didn't read like anything Tab would write."

"They progressively degenerated," Cassel countered. "Exactly the kind of consistent lack of cohesion a mental break would cause."

"First, Tab was too grounded to go emotional bonkers. Second, it wasn't the entries, but the use of words."

"I admit I only met the man a couple of times," Cassel said, "but I remember he used words."

"Not if he could think of a short-cut," Patterson replied. "You know how Coop is always giving people nicknames? He says it's because the nickname is shorter, easier to use in tense situations."

"Always felt left out," Cassel admitted. "Never got a nickname from him."

"Not much can be done with Paris," she said. "And I was already Pam. The point I'm trying to make is Tab did that with everything. He said it helped him remember strings of information by assigning a simple keyword. A trigger mechanism."

"No triggers in the journal?"

"Not a one," Patterson confirmed. "The one hand-written note recovered was more his style." She pulled a paper with a copy of a note. "In this case numbers and words, but I have no idea what it means. Every top cypher and linguist in the country took a stab at it. Every possibility led nowhere."

"Map coordinates?"

"Nope, and not star coordinates either."

"Dates or times?"

"Not that make sense."

"Old fashion country codes, zip codes, or area codes?"

"Nope, and Nope, and No."

"I give," the security chief said. "If it was something simple, you, or someone, would have figured it out years ago."

"Or it's so simple we can't see it," Pam replied.

D o r m

"Twenty, twenty-two, and four?"

Chaspi sat cross-legged on her bunk.

"Those were the first set of numbers on the top line of the note," Stacey said. "You can see a separation, and then he wrote fifty-nine, sixty-five, and one-hundred ninety-eight."

"Handwritten?" Billy asked. He sat on the bunk, next to Chaspi, with his back against the wall, his legs straight out, feet dangling over the edge.

"Yep," Stacey answered. She sat at the student desk, her back to the data terminal and display system. The system idle. "The paper was found on the floorboard of the vehicle. Pam's notes indicated she believed it was the key to solving Barnwell's death, but no one could decipher the numbers."

"You said there were words, too," Rosz prompted. He sat in his comfort place, on the floor, supported by the wall.

"Second line had the number 31, and then Montague Research," she said. "Before anyone asks, there was a massive attempt to determine what Montague Research meant. The closest match came from the early twenty-first century. Montague Mineral Research, Switzerland. Henri Montague researched mineral properties, and he explored caves. The company has been gone for decades, and no one remembers the research facilities."

"None of the numbers or words relate to anything musical I can think of," Rosz said. "The last line?"

"Fifty-nine, ten, and six-hundred seven, written six, zero, and seven," she answered.

Chaspi uncrossed her legs, spread them wide, and leaned forward in a display of flexibility that ended with her elbows on the bed. "There must be somewhere we can start?"

The blue alien from Fell turned to the desk and waved her hand over the display terminal, spoke a command, and called up a map of the region around the Honey Island Cypress Swamp. The bayou ran northeast of Slidell, Louisiana. This is where Col. Barnwell's clothes and transport were found. She zoomed in and out, and moved the image left and right.

As the other three watched, she fiddled with the display. It transformed into 3-d, switched to a weather model, layered decades-old maps, zoomed out and slow zoomed back in until she asked, "What does this mean?"

CHAPTER 15

Rosz stood left of center mat. Two escrima sticks held waist-high. His **MUSIC ROCKS** sweatshirt earning the name as a hard beat pounded through his earbuds. Dark, wet stains trailed from under his armpits, across his chest and upper back. His loose cotton pants were rolled at the bottom to prevent tripping as he moved. His bare feet exposed, the three toes splayed for balance.

"Your love of music speaks to the rhythm of your kioi, your fighting spirit," Sensei said. The master stood far right of the mat's center. He held a long stick. His previous attacks relentless against the young Bosine.

The second day of Rosz and Billy's lessons began with Sensei handing Rosz two sticks. Both rattan, twenty-four-inches long, about an inch thick.

"Sticks?" Rosz asked. His doe-eyes narrowed as he addressed the shorter, thicker Japanese. "I thought you were going to teach me karate."

"You did not come to my dojo to learn karate," Sensei replied. "You came to learn to defend yourself and to protect others. Karate takes years of disciplined practice to master. You have to train your body to act without hesitation. I intend to train your kioi, the fighting spirit within you." He fist-pumped his own chest for emphasis.

"Music, therefore rhythm is part of that spirit. Those sticks are called escrima or bastons. The rattan is from a vine that grows in Southeast Asia. The wood is hard, durable, and will never splinter. The baston can counter a bladed weapon. Unlike many weapons, you can carry sticks anywhere. If you try to take a knife with you, it will eventually be taken by an authority."

"So I have sticks, and I have rhythm. I still don't get it."

"Fighting with bastons is one of the few techniques where someone does not first require hand-to-hand combat skills," Sensei explained. "You only need to dance."

"Dance? Seriously? If I am attacked, I'm supposed to dance with them." Rosz turned to Billy, who stood watching from in front of the wall holding various martial arts weapons. He gave an amused expression and a shrug in response, but held back comments.

"Sinawali," Sensei said. "To weave is the proper translation. It is movement designed to keep your defenses up, probe those of your opponent, and deliver strikes to disarm or down the other person."

Today, Saturday, counted as Rosz's sixth lesson in two weeks. Lesson a term used loosely. His time on the mat required defending himself against the Sensei's attacks. In the first two sessions, the master made certain the student listened to music with a slow, constant rhythm.

In the beginning, the Sensei delivered attacks consistently, but never with violent intent. By the end of the fourth lesson, both sticks moved fluidly over and under one another (like the stitching of fabric). Sensei explained this stitching allowed one stick to remain capable of defending whilst the other could attack. It also meant one baston could recoil to prepare for the next strike while the other continued attacking.

The master introduced sinawali exercises by forcefully moving the alien around the mat, herding him with weapons. He attacked with long sticks, nunchucks, his own bastons, and swords. He taught Rosz the basic skills and motions relevant to two-weapon blocking and response. Using the younger man's desire to avoid a painful hit, Sensei engrained body positioning and distance relative to an opponent's attack. Without using words, or wasting time with non-weaponed drills, he influenced Rosz's rotation of his body. The student quickly developed better balance by learning the proper turning radius, realizing how to find his center of gravity, and maintaining that center, even as he moved to avoid a thump. His eye–hand coordination, target perception, and attack recognition, increased ambidexterity as he repeatedly got whacked. With each lesson, the thumps grew harder, and the desire to avoid or block the blows became more imperative.

The music became his choice after the third session. His performance of rhythmic structures for upper body movement became more obvious. The flow, the constant weave around the mat, progressed into a more fluid movement. The muscular development of his wrist and forearms helped his blocking. As his strength grew, the soreness dissipated.

The only spoken encouragements by the teacher were to help teach the novice escrimador proper elbow positioning while swinging his weapons.

Today's training, utilizing double bastons, required Rosz to use both left and right weapons in an equal manner. Sensei attacked to test the Bosine's talent as well as his resolve.

At the completion of their session, for the first time, the Master bowed first. Not one blow penetrated the student's double-handed defense. He held his hand out, requesting the bastons.

His hesitation did not last long, despite the unease at relinquishing the weapons he had grown to accept. With a deeper bow, he placed the two sticks in his trainer's open hand.

Sensei waved Rosz off the mat, and motioned Billy forward. Before the young man reached the center of the training area, the Japanese attacked. Without thought, Billy began his own version of the weave, moving his feet to a dance as his hands and arms rose, relaxed and ready.

Escrima-shaped bruises and welts would hurt later, but he parried and blocked more than landed. Twice he caught his teacher's wrists and flipped Sensei across and down. The martial arts expert never hit the mat hard, rolling his lithe body across the floor and back into position in less time than it took for Billy to regain his own balance.

The attack and defense lasted only five minutes. It left both men damp, and Billy pulling deeply to recapture spent oxygen.

Sensei halted following double arm blocks by the student thwarted his attempt to land the sticks to his opponent's ribs. He presented Billy a small bow.

"You need to improve your breathing," he said. "You have learned quickly, but your conditioning sucks. Aikido is a way of life, Billy. For you to master the techniques, you will need to learn how to observe everything, and take from the environment what you need to succeed. And at the moment I need a fucking bath."

Billy and Rosz both gaped at the language, and exchanged grins.

Sensei departed, returning Rosz's sticks as he passed on his way to the private section behind the center. The two knew the drill. They would clean the dojo, then shower, and change into street clothes in the small locker room. They would not see the Japanese instructor until their next lesson.

H o m e

"Is it worth the risk?"

Sam Patterson stood at the entrance to his wife's home office. The former Admiral Patterson sat on a chair commandeered from the dining room. Stacey sat in the office chair in front of the holo-display computer system Nathan Trent gifted Pam following her departure from Space Fleet.

"Stacey, does your detection devise show anything?" Patterson asked.

"No intrusion beams," the girl from Fell replied. "If anyone tried to monitor or hack the system, the monitor will warn us, but, as I told you before, by then it will be too late. The beams are simply too quick to shut down before they pick up the display."

"How sure are you about the research center at the university?"

Stacey swiveled enough to see Pam directly, and Sam from the corner of her right cat-like eye.

"I called up a geo-link view of the Honey Island Cypress Swamp site where Barnwell supposedly committed suicide." She had given the Patterson's an overview of why she suspected involvement by the research center at Southern University of Mississippi in Tab's death. She required a more powerful, better connected system to invade the center's security matrix than her own high-end mobile tech, or anything available to her at school.

"Pearl River Wilderness north of Slidell, Louisiana," Pam said. The location seared into her memory.

"Connected by the Old Birmingham Highway," Stacey said. She silently connected the trans-com chip embedded in her neck to the Trent Industry commercial computer. The ability to remote access systems with the embedded trans-com was a feature only a select few knew about. She could now direct the system seamlessly with quiet voice commands or by hand gestures.

The holo display created a simple map that hovered above the desktop. She expanded and zoomed in on the region north of Slidell. A red line went up and bent right at a green space labeled Pearl River Wildlife Management. Block lettering left of the line read OLD BIRMINGHAM HWY.

"If you look beneath the words, you will see the number fifty-nine."

Sam, curiosity in control, moved into the office. He stood behind his wife, and they both leaned nearer the holographic map. Stacey zoomed in on the lettering until the [59] stood out.

"Fifty-nine appeared twice on the note left by Col. Barnwell," she reminded Pam and informed Sam. "I asked Billy what the number represented. He told me the United States, decades previously, used numbering systems for roadways."

"A system we quit using when everyone began to access travel using self-guided and driverless vehicles," Sam said. "Every roadway, street, and alley in the nation has at least a couple of sensors. Satellites map and direct travel. Major cities became connected by Hyperloops. People stopped caring about road numbers. Interstate Highways often reverted to local names or received new names through popular usage. The only numbers remaining were for the larger highways and expressway exits."

"We never numbered roads or rivers on Fell," Stacey said. "Everyone knew where they were and where they were going."

Pam Patterson smiled at the simple pronouncement of the alien. Fellen, probably the most advanced species of technology developers in the galaxy, enjoyed quaint, simple lifestyles. The planet remained largely undeveloped, unpolluted, and non-political. That she never found the opportunity to visit Fell, or other worlds outside of the Sol star system, an unspoken regret of retirement arriving sooner than intended.

Stacey waved her fingers and the map altered, displaying ancient highway number codes in place of names.

"I-59 connects to I-10, the Gulf Expressway," she said. "The last line of the note read fifty-nine, ten, and six-zero-seven."

"The obvious fifty-nine and ten link to Tab's note is there. What about six-oh-seven?" Pam asked.

"It required access to archived state roads and highways data to find it, but if you follow I-10 East, after you leave the Wilderness zone, you come to Shuttle Parkway," the blue tech savvy girl said, switching the redline to the Gulf Parkway, and intersecting it with a bright blue line. "Mississippi records designated this as State Highway 607."

"Damn," Pam said, sitting back against the wood-slats of the dining chair. "That simple. All these years with that note, all the experts in the world, and it was never a cypher. Tab simply used old highway numbers to remind him where he was going."

"I went back to the first line and began determining his travel plans." Stacey expanded the holo-display map to show the older rendition of the state of Mississippi. As she continued to talk, areas on the map would light and a second holo-map, a close-up of the lighted areas, appeared in the air to the right of Mississippi. Above both maps, three lines of numbers and words materialized.

20 22 4 59 65 198

31 Montague Research

59 10 607

"I-20 to exit twenty-two in Meridian, Mississippi to Fourth Avenue, which is downtown near the historic section of the city. Notice the slightly wider separation between the three sets of numbers on the first line?" asked rhetorically. "The second set converts to I-59, when taken south reaches exit sixty-five to Hattiesburg. The exit leads to State Road 198, named Hardy Street. Thirty-First Avenue North takes you into the University of Southern Mississippi where it connects to Montague Boulevard. A block west on Montague, you turn right onto Research Drive."

"Montague Research," Pam said. "We searched every database for references to anything connecting the words Montague and Research. The closest match we found was the Montague Mineral Research Corporation located over one-hundred years ago in

Switzerland. I wasted a lot of sleepless nights trying to make sense of a mineral researcher and spelunker located in the Alps and a swamp in Louisiana. Separated by thousands of miles, and decades. They were just street names on a college campus."

"Research Drive dead-ends into a parking lot," Stacey said. The Southern Mississippi University campus footprint replaced the right display. "Buildings for Biological Sciences, Polymer Science Research, Bio-Chemical labs, and dedicated power stations are located around the parking area. All of the buildings and facilities purchased six years ago by a private commercial research firm that provides university students access for studies and lab work."

"A lot of colleges and universities were forced to sell or lease assets after the pandemic," Sam said. "Not enough students and not enough interest in higher education or college sports after watching half the world's population perish."

"Six years ago?" Pam asked.

"Before Col. Barnwell's death," Stacey answered the deeper question.

"The facilities are owned by a multi-regional research group called Camarilla. The original purchase and continued funding comes from a bank in London, England. Ninety-percent of the bank's shareholders and clients are from Arabic regions of the Middle East and North Africa," she added.

"You did a lot of research," Sam commented.

Stacey shrugged off the comment-compliment. The computer-data retrieval systems did the work. She only needed to frame the parameters for the search to assure the information returned had value.

"The administrator for the project is Dr. Herman Reinhardt," she dropped the bomb.

"Dr. Reinhardt who contracts to Space Fleet?" Pam asked, once again seated on the edge of the chair.

"Bio-engineering, neural expert, psychiatrist, and head of the UEC Space Fleet artificial intelligence systems' avatar development project," Stacey answered. "He was a grad-assistant during the Space Rangers Project. He created Genna and Adele, the avatars for PT-109 and PT-99."

"After stopping in Meridian, Tab visited Dr. Reinhardt in Hattiesburg. Why?" Sam asked.

"No way to know without speaking to Reinhardt," his wife replied. "We don't even know if he knew Reinhardt's association to the university, or that he saw him at all."

"The last line I already explained," Stacey interrupted. "He left Hattiesburg using I-59 to I-10 in Slidell, then east to 607, the Shuttle Parkway, which takes him to an abandoned propulsion research and testing center originally used by an agency called NASA."

"National Aeronautics and Space Administration," Sam translated the letters. "The United State's first government-sponsored agency tasked with developing space flight."

"The center closed before the Pandemic," Stacey reported. "It remained unused until it was purchased for private research seven years ago."

"Same group?" Sam asked, his expertise in global financial affairs becoming more enticed by the minute.

"Same bank funded the purchase," Stacey answered. "It is remote, surrounded by open land to prevent propulsion test failures from harming civilians. High security fences and monitors, at a minimum. It is a short trip to Hattiesburg. The site's western border is the Pearl River Wilderness Zone." She dropped the other bomb.

"Tab?"

"Honey Island Cypress Swamp is a straight line west from the old testing center," Stacey confirmed.

"But we don't know if he went to Hattiesburg or the testing facilities for sure," Sam said.

"We may never know," Stacey replied. "If I can hack their systems, there may be records showing he did, and when, and what may have happened."

"Which is why you need my computer," Pam said. "If you are scanned while attempting to hack the Mississippi sites, we are all in trouble, and potentially in danger."

"Yep," the Fellen replied. "Do you want to stay and watch?"

Sam answered for his wife.

"Pam stays with you," he said. "I'm going to my office at the UEC and look into that London bank. Always follow the finance."

He kissed his wife, squeezed Stacey's shoulder, and left the two women to their scheme. He had a trail of his own to follow.

"How do we start?" Pam asked.

The young woman with blue skin, orange eyes, and small fangs suggested a human starter.

"Caffeine," she said. "If you could make us tea?"

"Will do," the former Admiral of Space Fleet replied. Reduced to making tea for a teenage hacker caused a smile, not a loss of self-respect. "Something hot and strong, with enough that we can refill on demand."

"Thanks, Pam," Stacey said. She turned back to the system built by Trent Industry's best cyber people. They borrowed heavily from technology found on Mars, and from concepts create on Fell, and shared with Space Fleet. She would be comfortable with the operational and functional capacities within minutes. Less time than it would take her hostess to brew tea.

Twelve-minutes later, Patterson returned with two ceramic mugs, steam wafting over the rims.

"Caffeine is served," she said, placing one mug on the desktop. "When do we start?"

"Already started," Stacey answered. "The security firewalls and traps for the operating system at the Hattiesburg location are robust. Someone with a high degree of skill designed the system and the protections."

"Will they detect you?"

"I'm only snooping around the edges," the young woman replied. Her skin turning a darker shade of blue indicated the stress as higher than she admitted. "They operate on a college campus and allow students access to unrestricted areas. They expect snooping, minor attempts at hacking, and simple intrusions by mistake. That's why I decided to try Hattiesburg instead of the propulsion center. They would be more alert to attempts to enter their systems."

"You're good at this," Pam said. "I have a feeling, better than your brother, ASparquila."

"I am, but since he's a male and my brother, I don't let on. His ego could not handle his little sister becoming a better hacker."

"But you didn't come to Earth to join Space Fleet as a systems officer. You want to train as a fighter pilot."

"Yep." The word fast becoming her favorite human response. It meant much more than 'yes.' As Billy once explained, 'It includes an implied damn straight.'

"I hate to call that a waste of talent, but it certainly would be," the former Admiral said.

"I can do both," the Fellen assured her.

Patterson did not say it aloud, but did think: 'I bet you can. I bet you will.'

"I'm in," Stacey announced. "There is a staff break room on the fourth floor of the bio-chemical research building. The refrigerator includes a remote-access camera to allow the supply staff to monitor the interior. They must restock certain items when inventory drops below a certain level."

"You hacked a highly secured operating system because a lazy person in food and beverage restocks cola based on a video count instead of actually looking inside the refrigerator?"

"Yep."

The holo-display winked to life providing a three-dimensional recreation, in smaller scale, of bottled water, soda, and containers of unknown food. As Stacey wandered through the operating system on the restricted floors, closed-circuit video feeds became corridors and rooms on top of Patterson's desk.

The bio-chem building consisted of five floors. The bottom two non-restricted; available for students and staff for lectures, lab work, conferences, and restrooms. The third floor housed administrative offices and the computer operating systems studio. The two spent several minutes at each monitored site. They discussed and agreed on an area's apparent function, looked for clues left lying about, and moved on.

Stacey spent extra time examining and memorizing, the computer codes and controls. The hardware was not exceptional, but the software equalled anything on Fell. Certainly advanced for humans. One operator handled everything. At first she suspected an artificial intelligence maintained everything, but decided the programmer built systematic commands into the operating codes. Commands easily overridden, as she did now. AI's might be used for self-diagnostics, as well as downline maintenance and repairs, but humans ran the show.

The fourth floor housed research labs. Biological research studios, chemical labs, and containment areas for dangerous results. Perhaps because it was late in the day, only two people used the fourth floor. Both worked in a studio with more electronic equipment than burners and beakers.

"Biology," Stacey said.

"No way to tell what they are trying to accomplish," Pam said.

"I can attempt to access data files after we complete the video circuit," Stacey replied. "If I try too multiple incursions simultaneously the traps would detect the increased activity."

The obvious thing about the fifth floor involved higher security. An additional metal gate crossed the frame of the elevator door. Reaching the third and fourth floors required access codes, but neither included an armed guard stationed at a desk. She read a magazine.

"Long time without any incidents," the former intelligence officer surmised. "The guard isn't afraid of a reprimand for reading while on duty. She's aware her station is monitored, but it doesn't stop her from relaxing at her post."

"The computers are the watchdogs," Stacey said. "They will warn her of anything considered outside of normal activities. She's the guard dog."

"The computer barks and she bites," Pam said. "Pretty good analogy for an extraterrestrial."

"I'm considering a dog for a companion," Stacey admitted. "I've been researching breeds, behavior, and usage."

"You might want to research peeing, pooping, and chewing first," the older woman quipped.

Other than the semi-somnolent guard, the corridor appeared empty. The first room Stacey video-entered was an operating theater. A complete medical set-up with ultra-modern equipment. A door to the right led to a staff washroom area and lockers. No one present. The studio appeared sterile, well-maintained, and ready to go. It also gave off a vibe of no recent use.

The next area appeared as if three rooms were converted into a ward. Hospital-style beds, monitors, and medical support equipment set similar to a military field unit. Beds sat aligned, each with a privacy curtain available, but every one pushed against the wall and tied off. Currently, no occupants meant no need for privacy.

"Twelve," Stacey said. "Twelve beds."

The final room to come on line looked surprisingly similar to Chaspi's dorm space. Bunk bed, desk and chair, and door to a bathroom. Unlike Chaspi's room, no windows allowed daylight or star shine to enter. The ceiling, oddly, seemed made of metal. Steel grates covered lights and vents.

"Books on the desk's shelves, and more on the wall unit," Pam said. "Histories, biographies, fiction. An eclectic collection."

"Nothing electronic," Stacey said. "No pads, monitors, units, audio, or video components. There is a speaker embedded in one wall. Covered by a metal grate."

"Bed looks recently slept in. There are clothes on the floor," Pam said. "Maybe in the bathroom? Is there a feed from inside?"

Before Stacey could switch to the final camera, the door opened. A man wearing a two-piece grey sweatsuit and bare feet entered. His head down, shoulders slumped, and gait of short, unsteady steps indicated someone older. Defeated. Disinterested.

The face, though drawn and weary-eyed, was one of a young man.

"Tab," Pam whispered.

She jumped out of the chair when her personal communicator vibrated on her wrist. The slight nuisance transformed into an electric shock coming at the same moment she recognized Barnwell.

"Patterson," she answered, eyes remaining latched to the image of a ghost.

"This is Paris, Pam. You need to stop what you're doing and come down to my office."

Pam slashed her throat at Stacey, who had no idea what the action meant. Pam pointed at the holo-display and mouthed 'Off.' A simple wave of her hand and Stacey disconnected the system from the site in Mississippi. A second wave shut the computer off.

"Paris, I'm extremely busy. Can it wait until tomorrow?"

"I'm bringing Sam in for questioning," the Security Director said. "He was detected using UEC equipment to look at private financial records without authorization. I don't want to get into details over a public access channel. You best come down in order for us to work this out."

"On the way," Pam replied, closing the channel.

"An intruder beam is sweeping the house," Stacey told her, holding the detection devise up. "The computer shut down and external sources were disconnected before the beam arrived. Less than thirty-seconds."

Cassel's call might have been coincidental. Maybe he called to warn her. Maybe she was seeing more ghosts than Titus Barnwell, Jr.

"Stacey, do you realize what we just discovered?" she asked the transfer from another planet.

"Col. Barnwell is alive. Held prisoner at the research center on the campus of Southern Mississippi University," the alien replied. "Most likely the subject of interrogations and experimentations. Dr. Reinhardt must be aware of his presence. You and Sam are under surveillance by the UEC's office of security. The people funding Dr. Reinhardt's projects at the university also finance whatever is happening at the old propulsion testing center. They have influence, and probably protection within the UEC, and possibly Space Fleet."

"I could not have summarized all of this any better," Patterson admitted. "I have to go downtown. I want to find out what Sam did, and why Paris had him detained. Can you go to Chaspi's until I contact you?"

"Of course. Pam, you need to be careful."

"I will be, Stacey," the older woman assured her house guest. "I need to know you are safe. Call me on the Fellen trans-com when you get to the dorm."

Stacey nodded.

CHAPTER 16

"She and her husband are dangerous," Guy Arcand said.

"I'll admit they're turning over a few rocks," Cassel replied. "I don't know exactly how dangerous they may be yet."

"The Camarilla is too close to achieving control over the UEC to allow even small rocks get disturbed," the French-Canadian representative answered. "The Patterson's need to be held in check. Sam Patterson announced their suspicions by stomping around in the London bank's client files. Admiral Patterson's obsession with the Barnwell suicide already made everyone nervous. Reinhardt's Iranian computer genius, Attaran, sent me a message that someone in the Toronto area attempted to probe the research center at the university. I'm betting Patterson is number one on the list of probables. Unless you've been playing on the computer without telling me."

"I know better," Cassel assured the head of the Board of Governors. "I may not know the inside story on what Reinhardt is doing in Hattiesburg, but I have the reports detailing security. It would take someone better than anyone we have to get past their traps, and we have the best on Earth."

"It's taken five years to get to this point, Paris," Armand said. "Patterson could mess everything up. Shut her and her husband down. Do it now."

"She'll be missed. Sam, too. Both are high profile," Cassels replied.

"You're the super spook," Armand answered back. "Find a place to stash them. Think up a cover story. The Camarilla is ready for the end game. Patterson was the white queen. She's off the board. Collect that Fellen college student staying with them. Wrap the three of them into a nice package and stick them under a Christmas tree until the dust settles."

"Do you think they will lock Mr. Patterson up?" Billy asked.

"I have no idea," Stacey answered. "You know everything I know. I promised to contact her when I got to the dorm."

Stacey activated the coms portion of the chip embedded below her right ear. A movement of her jaw activated a private and secure communication channel between certain aliens and humans. A conversation initiated by the simple method of beginning a call with a person's nickname.

"Pam, this is Stacey. Do you copy?"

"Stacey? Why I have no idea where she is at the moment."

Patterson's voice sounded in her ear. Stacey raised her hand to quiet the others. She opened onto a conversation Pam intended her to overhear. By starting her sentence with Stacey's name, she opened her end of the channel. While no one else would hear anyone in the dorm from Pam's location, she wanted the room quiet so she could concentrate.

"She's a college co-ed on winter break," Patterson continued. "She's probably out with her friends." Silence as someone spoke, but the Fellen could not hear anyone beyond Pam. "Yes, I still have the chip embedded. No, I will not turn it off, nor try to contact AStasaei. I'm here to discuss Sam, not our houseguest. Paris, I believe you when you say you can jam the signal. If you feel that's . . ."

"Can-Am blocked Pam's chip," Stacey said, informing the three waiting impatiently for news. "She's at the UEC Security Services offices and they are asking her where to find me."

"Stacey, it's Genna. Do you copy?"

Stacey held her hand up again. Surprise at the contact by the PT-109's avatar evident in her expression. The threesome with her once more left perplexed, unable to hear the communication inside her head.

"Genna, this is Stacey."

"The trans-com channels are compromised. Your conversation with Admiral Patterson was tracked. You need to leave, and,

Stacey, you need to hide. I will be unable to communicate again. Do not try to contact anyone with your chip. Do you copy?"

"Genna, I need help," the girl begged. The enormity of the situation becoming real.

"You need to hide," Genna repeated. "No one alive on Earth can help at the moment, and no one off Earth is aware of everything happening. Sorry, Stacey. Kennedy could only cover for a short contact. Go. Kennedy will find you when it is safe. Genna, out."

Her blue skin pale, and her orange-red eyes slipping into amber. The girl, visibly shaken, took a seat on Chaspi's bed.

"Genna warned me the UEC traced my conversation with Pam. She also said the private channels are compromised. She said I need to hide. Security guards must be on the way here now, and there is no one to help me."

Rosz rose from his place on the floor to take command.

"Everyone grab winter clothes, credits, and nothing else. Nothing that can be tracked or traced," he commanded. He tossed his ever-present earplugs and personal data stick with his library of music onto Chaspi's desk. "I'm serious. Anything electronic stays behind. Stacey, wrap a scarf around your face, pull up your hood, and use Chaspi's wrap-around sunshades. I don't want to see blue skin."

If the others were surprised at Rosz's sudden take-charge personality, no one wasted time remarking on the personality shift. If he intended to leave his music, they needed to take the current situation seriously. Most importantly, Stacey needed to get away from the dorms before she could be picked up.

The four bundled students blended with the few others still on campus during the winter break. The time of day worked to their advantage. People working in offices leaving for home, and students not able to go home or on vacation, headed out for dinner.

They were on a public sidewalk when the official black hover-transport flew past and came to a stop in front of the dorm. A half-dozen armed security guards, not campus security but UEC Elite Security officers, exited the transport and rushed through the front doors of the lobby.

"Where can we go?" Chaspi asked. Her fear for Stacey, anger over the situation that placed her friend and the Patterson's in danger, and inability to think rationally tickled her evil-side. She felt someone needed a good kick, but had no idea who.

"The dojo," Rosz answered.

"Dojo?" The word issued from Chaspi and Stacey in harmony, though Stacey's version muffled; her mouth buried in warm cloth.

"What's a dojo?" Chaspi added.

"A safe place," Rosz answered. "I hope."

CHAPTER 17

ASkiilamentrae watched Hiroshi Kimura demonstrate Japanese sword fighting techniques to an audience of young boys and girls of the AS tribe. Sky's light blue skin and auburn hair marked her as a resident of Fell. Tall, at five-ten, and firm. Muscled and toned from workouts, and more recently, battles with Mischene and Zenge invaders. Her golden eyes held tints of burnt orange. She smiled at the children who 'oohed' and 'aahed' as Hiro flowed from one sword stroke to the next. The smile displayed small fangs where humans have canines.

"He loves your planet," Cindy Shah said. Lt. Colonel Shah commanded the Earth ground forces sent to fight and free the planet from the invaders. Shah and Kimura's relationship moved to the next level during the deployment. They now lived together.

"He's a superstar on our world," Sky replied. "The Earth ninja who single-handedly killed thousands of Zenge warriors with his sword, Shadow Death."

"Hiro is at peace on Fell," Shah continued. "He says the kami of the planet sings to him."

"Kami?" Sky asked.

"On Earth there is a religion called Shinto. They believe all things have an essence, or a spirit. It's called Kami. That Fellen maintained their world as a place of nature, even as they reached out to the stars, shows an understanding of Kami."

They ended their conversation as Hiro came to a halt. He twirled his blade, at the same time his right foot found and flipped its sheath into the air. He caught the sheath in his left hand and slid Shadow Death in with one motion. The applause from the children could be heard throughout the small village.

Hiro presented a ceremonial bow to his audience. Show over, he walked across the grass and dirt stage to join the two women.

"Kami is nature," he said. He overheard their whispered conversation, even as he demonstrated killing blows at incredible speed with a razor-sharp sword. "It is the trees and the mountains. It is river, rock, and snow. Your air is thick with moisture that blankets your world. Every afternoon lightning and thunder announce the day's end. Children laugh easily. Adults greet you with a smile and open heart. I do, indeed, find peace here."

"Children still scream in the night," Sky said. "It will be a long time before the Zenge do not haunt their dreams."

"Then we must give them other things to dream about," Hiro said. "I would like to open a dojo."

"A dojo?" Sky asked.

"It translates from Japanese to *a place of the way*", Hiro said. The communicator-translator bracelets they wore allowed them to understand each other's language. There remained words, especially words not in English, requiring explanation until the translator's intelligence began to understand and accept them.

"A school for learning the martial arts," Shah said.

"All children on Fell are taught how to fight," Sky said. "It is a major part of our heritage as warriors. To have a place where they can learn the techniques of Hiro, the Earth Ninja, would be welcomed."

"Have you heard from Coop," Hiro asked. Like Coop, Hiro survived the Space Ranger Project. The two formed close bonds during and after the program. While Coop followed his dreams to fly in space by joining the Navy Flight School, Hiro followed a different path. He returned to university and received degrees and advanced degrees in planetology.

"I'm afraid we have lost him," Sky replied sadly. "Patterson tells us to remain patient. She says events on Earth move in a bad direction. Someone tried to kill him inside Space Fleet's medical center. I know she cannot say things which might be overheard, but I know she moved him to a safer place. Storm and I want to be with him, to keep him safe. She insists we remain here with our family and friends. That she, nor Nathan Trent, will tell us his condition means he must be the same, or worse."

Hiro placed an arm around the taller Fellen, hugging her close, in spite of the sweat on his gi.

"I have known Pamela Patterson for many years," Hiro says. "She loves Daniel Cooper, and keeping him safe while he continues to heal will cause her to act overly cautious. Only Elie may know Coop better than Pam. But all who know him realize he would not ask that you abandon Fell and family to sit and wait for him to awaken. It is what we call a personality flaw," the Japanese swordsman tells her. "He would lay his life down for every one of his friends, you included. Any one faced with a fight knows he will be rushing to stand with us. We all pray he would ask us to be there for him in times of trouble. We also know it is not his way. When danger is nearest him, he will not call his friends."

"That is just stupid," Sky replied. Her eyes melted to burnt orange and her rising blood pressure darkened the tone of her skin.

"Don't get angry, Sky," Shah interjected. "Coop is male. They're just wired for stupid, especially when it comes to protecting people they love."

"I beg your pardon," Hiro said, pretending injury by her statements as he released Sky.

"I believe I had to take you to bed," Shah answered, adding a wry smile. "Big, bad ninja was either too stupid or too afraid to make the first move."

"It's will be difficult to see you go," Sky said to them. "It would have been wonderful to see your dojo in action. We thought we would have you with us longer. The short amount of time has been well spent. Your people helped us reclaim our world, and have joined Fellen to rebuild our space ports. Every day more of my people come out of hiding. You've given us our planet back, and we will forever be grateful."

"We're not going back," Shah said softly, taking Hiro's hand. "I plan on resigning my commission. I'd like to stay to help open Hiro's dojo. If the people of Fell will have us."

"Are you sure?" Sky asked. Caught off-guard by the statement, she stammered, "Of course you can stay. You are already members of our tribe. But what about your career? What will Space Fleet do?"

"Space Fleet has changed since we left," Shah said. "With Admiral Patterson retired, and the new policies regarding aliens, it just isn't the same group I signed up to serve. I've already informed Colonel Gregory, who completely understands."

"There will be several-thousand others who also wish to remain," Hiro added. "All who came to fight volunteered. Most do not serve under Space Fleet. Some do not serve military branches directly under the UEC's control. I have listened to many who have fallen in love with your planet and its people, just as Cindy and I have." Hiro stopped. He stood as if listening to the spirits of Fell.

"Some, like Cindy, will be allowed to resign their positions and remain on Fell legally," he continued. "Some will be branded deserters and might never be able to return to Earth without facing prison."

"Everyone who wishes to remain will be welcome," Sky assured him. "We will build them homes. We will provide them with work. Fell has never been completely open to those from other worlds. Those visiting from off-world remained in the villages of the space ports, allowed limited access to our world's beauty. Maybe our reclusiveness factored in our defeat by the Zenge. We will not repeat mistakes. Those who stay will be Fellen."

"If you will talk with your fellow tribesmen, and those of the other tribes, and if all agree, I will make it known to those who wish to remain, they will have a home," Hiro said to Sky, and presented a small bow of gratitude.

"I'll talk with them," Sky assured him. "But they will say what I have already said. Anyone who voices anything else will have to answer to me."

Mars Shipyard and Docks

"There will be changes."

Rear Admiral (lower) Stephen J. Hawks stood before a massive hologram. One wall of his office recently converted to the latest in holo-technology.

"I, and many others, believe these changes are long overdue and necessary as we face new challenges. In respect for who you are and what you have done for us, I wanted to inform you of our plans personally."

Captain Sam Harrington, commander of the SFPT-99, Franklin D. Roosevelt, stood at ease, facing the display of spaceships floating before him. Chief of Security, Benedict (Benny) Claflin sat relaxed in a chair, eyes on the same display. The two men Space Ranger survivors, both British special operators prior to that project; Claflin SAS and Harrington RAF. Currently they served under the command of Hawks.

Hawks, a slender man with undistinguished caucasian features and short brown hair, greying at the temples, cleared his throat and continued.

"You will remain on the Roosevelt, Captain Harrington. There is no need to replace members of your crew. Other than your AI's avatar, everyone assigned to the PT-99 is human."

Harrington nodded.

"Captain Sligh is retiring. Captain Cooper remains AWOL. Captain Elena Casalobos will be assigned as the commanding officer of the Kennedy upon her return from Operation Crossroads." Neither man offered a comment regarding Cooper or Casalobos, fellow Space Rangers.

"Captain Casalobos will need to select an Executive Officer. The ship's avatar will no longer be recognized as a Ship's Counselor, nor maintain a military designation. Because of her importance to the well-being of the ship's Artificial Intelligence unit, she will remain on board. She can act as a civilian secretary for the ship's commander, but she will not sit at bridge controls."

Hawks waved the images of the two Patrol and Torpedo Class vessels off to the side. He expanded the image of a larger vessel with a long flat surface atop the ship. A traditional-appearing command tower rose above the stern's surface.

"Our new Space Fleet Carrier Class ship, the Elliott S. Fairchild. Reconstruction projects to convert a Destroyer Class into our first Carrier, SFCC 101, are complete. She will soon launch from MSD. I will personally take command of the Fairchild."

"A bit difficult, that," Claflin said, his British accent faint, but discernible. "What with you commanding MSD and second in command to Admiral Singletary for all of Space Fleet."

"I will maintain my command of MSD and the Martian sites. The majority of my time will be spent on MSD taking care of Fleet business," Hawks replied. "When the order comes in to send a battle group to the Ares System arises, I will transfer from the platform to the ship."

"Until that order, when you are on MSD and the Carrier is operational?" Harrington asked.

"Captain Noa Tal will be my First Officer," the Admiral replied. "Captain Tal will also command the new six-fighter wing of Spirit-class ships hangared aboard the Elliott. Singletary promised Captain Casalobos that position, but had to be replaced with her assignment to the Kennedy. When I am on MSD, Captain Tal commands the Fairchild."

"Noa is a fantastic pilot, but does not have much in the way of command experience," Harrington said. "She's also loyal to Cooper."

"Why I want her in my sights at all times," Hawks replied. "This holo-wall will display the bridge of any ship any time I want. If I decide Tal is a problem, I can take control from here and it will be like I was there."

Hawks pushed the carrier aside, waved in another spaceship, and expanded the image.

"Captain Paré will take command of Pegasus. The Destroyer Class battleship is already undergoing trials. By now I am sure you are both aware our newest ships, Fairchild, Pegasus and the SFPT-89 when completed, will not use Artificial Intelligence operating systems. We do not believe the AI and avatar experiment warrants the risks and problems associated with them. More traditional, time-tested operating systems will be installed. This means officers and crew will be more responsible for the ships' systems, but I see that as a positive."

Neither Brit commented on Paré. Truth be known, the French Canadian presented an enigma to everyone. Never phased by anything. Never attempting to get close to anyone. Disciplined and deadly.

"Once the Star Gazer makes the final return with our personnel, any of the aliens currently in New Zealand, or those who ventured off the island to other parts of our world, will be provided the option to board her for a return to Osperantue. I realize not all of the aliens are from Osperantue, but they may see it as a potential way-station to their own worlds."

Hawks pushed Pegasus to the side, joining the three ships drifting in holo-space. He made a motion with this fingers, and the Star Gazer appeared. The ship looking like a black baseball attached to a black basketball.

"Of course, those who wish to remain on Earth will be welcome to do so," he added. "We will limit access to sensitive work until they have been fully vetted, but no one who remains will go hungry.

"It is not strictly a military matter, but you should know the Board of Governors set aside the treaties and agreement made with the aliens on Rys. They are temporarily suspended for review. The King of Rys has been informed, and until we have a better grasp on trade arrangements, we're breaking off diplomatic relations. Our people on Mars assure me we have enough crystals to last for a number of years with those added from Rys. It provides us with ample time to review our arrangement, and consider options more fair to Earth interests."

The Star Gazer disappeared, replaced by another PT Class ship.

"Captain Amanda Black will have command of the new SFPT-89, the John Alexander Macdonald, as soon as it is space worthy."

He pushed the Macdonald over to join the rest of his fleet.

"Chief Claflin, make sure the alien redeployments continue without interruption. I do not want anyone not human on a flight-worthy ship. Have you had any luck locating Daniel Cooper, or discovering exactly how he was moved from a secure medical facility?"

"Yessir, I will follow-up on redeployments, and no to Coop's whereabouts. Someone altered the security systems before he was moved, just like the false orders for the guards' replacements. It was all done by an effective intruder. I suspect people extremely high up the UEC or Space Fleet command line had a hand in his removal, but no proof." The bald, ebony-skinned, man stood. "I will keep looking, Admiral."

Hawks turned to Harrington. "Captain, you are senior officer among our space-capable fleet personnel when I am not aboard the Fairchild. I expect you to follow the guidelines set forth by Admiral Singletary and myself. Keep your fellow officers in line."

"Coop is missing, presumed dead. I hear Kimura is staying on Fell. Casalobos, Tal, and Paré are assigned ships under your command," Harrington said. "Benny and I are on board. That leaves Anton Gregory and Senait Kebede. What are the plans for them?"

"They will receive proper assignments on their return. As you are aware, they are competent operators and experienced troop commanders. I'm sure Space Fleet will find the right place for their talents. If there is nothing else, I think that sums everything up," the Admiral concluded.

The two Space Rangers came to attention, received their permission to depart, and left. With the room to himself, he pulled the five battle ships to the center of his display. A man pleased by his plan.

D o j o

The door to the storefront training center was unlocked. Rosz and Billy had never found it locked. Many of the weapons Sensei displayed on his wall were ancient and valuable. Equally, anyone with such weapons might know how to use them.

A smart thief would turn around and leave. A stupid thief would not stand much chance against the Master.

They travelled to the strip mall through snow and across slush, but everyone stomped and shook so nothing tracked past the front door. Billy took Chaspi's winter coat and placed it with his on wall hooks. Rosz did the same with his and Stacey's outerwear. Just to make sure the studio remained debris-free, Billy and Rosz removed their boots and asked the girls to do likewise. Billy handed out woolen socks from a storage box to slip on over their own socks.

"Come join me."

The words, spoken clearly and close by, startled the girls. Stacey spun into a defensive position. Chaspi jumped into Billy. The boys, accustomed to the Japanese instructor's invisible comings and goings, barely reacted. Well, Billy did wrap his arms protectively around Chaspi; a reaction to her, not to Sensei.

The lithe man left the door to his private chambers ajar, providing the invitation with passage. Rosz and Billy went first, allowing the two young women the opportunity to gather their wits before following.

Despite acting confident, this would be the first time either boy ventured beyond the confines of the workout studio and locker room. The doorway led to a large, modern, gleaming kitchen. Sensei sat at the head of a table, ceramic cup with steam lofting over the rim sitting before him. Four more cups rested on the table top.

The four young people took seats, the boys closest to the Japanese, who gave a short bow of the head, and lifted his cup. "Please," he said, and the four joined him. The tea gave warmth and the simple act of hospitality relaxed everyone.

"I am Ishihara Kaito," he directed at Chaspi and Stacey. Another first since Rosz or Billy never knew he had a name other than Sensei. "Please call me Kai."

"I am AStasaei of Fell. My friends on Earth call me Stacey."

"I'm Chaspi."

"You are welcome in my home," he informed the girls. "If it is less than clean, you must blame your two friends. They are not particularly good at chores, but I make do with what life provides."

Before either student could voice an objection, Chaspi asked, "How do Rosz and Billy know you? And what chores?"

Sensei sat quietly drinking his tea as Rosz and Billy tried to explain their desire to learn self-defense techniques, and how it led them to the store-front dojo.

"You kept this a secret because why?" Chaspi asked Rosz, her childhood lifelong friend and confidant.

"They were fearful of failing," Sensei answered for them. "If you did not know they tried, you would not ridicule their failure. As it happens, both performed better than expected. I must admit, it taxed my abilities as a teacher to their limits, but the two demonstrate potential. It is pleasant to meet the reason for their desire to learn how to fight. A woman's honor is always a just cause for battle."

Billy turned red, and Rosz smiled and shook his head, entertained, but not embarrassed by his teacher's comments.

"Someone dangerous must search for you," Kai said. "This is the first time I have seen Rosz-kun without music filling his ears."

"I'm the only one they're looking for," Stacey said.

"Not after the raid on the dorm," Rosz countered. "Whoever has Admiral and Sam Patterson, and wants you, will be looking for us, too."

"Admiral Pamela Patterson?" Kai asked.

"You know Pam?" Stacey asked.

"Reputation only," the man replied. "A fine reputation. A warrior. An honorable person. She is in danger?"

"I don't know," Stacey admitted. Deciding to trust the Sensei, and unburden herself with the others, she informed them of the hack she performed on the research facilities in Mississippi. She explained the discovery of Titus Barnwell, Jr. alive and a prisoner. The four allowed her to talk uninterrupted, ending with the warning from Genna and the escape before the arrival of UEC security.

"If those holding Col. Barnwell believe someone discovered their secret, I fear they will make the Colonel disappear again. This time permanently," Sensei Ishihara said.

"I don't know if they know, but all of the security, the intrusion scans, and now, Pam and Sam under arrest make me think they will be worried," Stacey said. "Pam can't help, and without my trans-com I can't contact anyone who might be able to do something. Genna was right, no one on Earth can help me."

"Daniel Cooper," Rosz said.

"Who may be dead," Billy said. "If not, then he's hidden somewhere we can't find him. Stacey can't use her com chip, and I bet if he has one, it's turned off, too."

"He's alive," Stacey said. "Somewhere on Canada's west coast," she added.

"How do you know this?" Sensei asked.

"Pam told us, only she didn't realize it when she said it," Stacey answered. "After I first met Rosz, Chaspi, and Billy, we were held at campus security until Pam could come get us released. When she realized Rosz and Chaspi did not have proper winter clothing, she told Chaspi she must care for them, or 'Coop would swim to the mainland, cross the continent, and kick her ass.'"

"You remembered that?" Billy asked.

"I remember, too," Chaspi said, once again deflecting questions that might lead to Stacey's secret eidetic memory. "But it doesn't help. There are hundreds of islands along the Pacific coast."

"You are welcome to use my computer if you care to search for clues," the Japanese told them, rising from his seat. "Your spirit appears to enjoy puzzles, and you certainly know how to coax information from a computer."

The college students followed the martial arts teacher through an open arch into a den fitted with comfortable leather chairs and a large executive desk. The center of the desk contained an embedded system with the latest holo-tech.

"Not exactly traditional Japanese," Billy said, looking around the comfortable, masculine space.

"I keep that in the front," Sensei said. "For tourists and potential students," he added.

Accepting the invitation, Stacey sat behind the massive desk and quickly became acquainted with the high-end data sourcing system. She immersed herself in research. The others watched holo-map after holo-map come and go. After two hours, Rosz slept in a leather chair, while Chaspi and Billy feel asleep on a matching sofa. Chaspi's head on the sofa arm, and Billy's head nestled on her hip.

Sensei Kai disappeared. Stacey never noticed.

At two minutes after midnight, the Fellen announced "Got it!"

The two words forceful enough to wake the other three, and startling enough for Billy to not notice or be embarrassed that his head used Chaspi's hip as a pillow.

"Fin Island," she told them. "Local native tribe gifted the island to Elliott Fairchild after the Pandemic. He provided them with medical facilities, schools, and work. In return they gave it to him as a thank-you, and as a place he could remain secluded while off Mars."

"You think this is where Daniel Cooper is hidden?" Sensei, having reappeared, asked.

"Logical. Fairchild. Secluded. On-site medical and research facilities. Who on Earth would question Elliott Fairchild?" she asked. "No one," she answered. "They go way back together. Has to be Fin Island."

"How do we get to Fin Island without getting caught?" Billy asked. "We're talking over two-thousand miles."

"Decide tomorrow," Sensei interrupted the discussion. "It is late and you are all tired. I have two guest rooms. You will need to share a bathroom, and sleep on futons, but you will be safe here. Come. I will show you to your rooms. Make plans tomorrow."

CHAPTER 18

Dojo

In spite of the tension brought on by potential dangers, the four college students, nearing exhaustion, fell to sleep quickly.

The next morning required patience and good humor as they took turns using the Sensei's single bathroom.

They congregated at the dining table adjoining the modern kitchen, joining Sensei, seated at the head of the table with a steaming cup of tea, toast, and fresh fruit spread. At his invitation, they collected their own breakfast from items laid out on the counter.

No pertinent talk occurred between them as they jockeyed for plates, cups, and food. Mainly morning grunts and good natured jibes universal with teenagers.

Taking seats at the table, Billy first noticed their host's smile.

"Sensei, is something funny?"

The black-haired, normally stoic Japanese master gave a quick negative with a shake of the head and a purse of his lips.

"No, Billy-kun," the man assured him. "I am happy to have young lives surrounding me. Since my own children moved into their own lives, I have missed the pleasure of this much (he hesitated) spirit in my home. I am also honored."

"Honored?" Chaspi asked.

"You are still new to our planet, Chaspi-chan, as are Rosz and Stacey. There is a history of intolerance, distrust, and, I am ashamed to say, bigotry that shadows all of our cultures. To see the four of you, exceedingly different beings, act without consideration beyond friendship, is rewarding."

"There is bigotry in the galaxy," Rosz said. "Species do not trust each other. Planets where non-habitants are forbidden to visit because of their stain. Races who refuse to interact with others beyond what is required to complete a trade. Earth is not as different as you may think, Sensei."

"Which makes the four of you even more special," the elder replied. "It proves there is hope for all the universe to set aside

external differences, and recognize we share more as sentient beings than we count in our differences."

"Five of us," Billy said. "Japanese, Canadian, Fellen, and Bosine having breakfast together. It is kind of cool."

"Unexpected. But not a surprise."

The four students, startled by the voice, shook the table as they
turned to discover a woman standing in the doorway between the
apartment and the dojo.

Japanese, average height, with straight black hair pulled back
into a ponytail. She wore a tight black sports bra, lycra tights, and
traditional sandals. The towel across her shoulder used to wipe
sweat from her taut, sinewy form and face. The blush of exercise
and sheen of perspiration still created a glow.

"My daughter, Aya," Sensei said. He had not reacted in any
way to his daughter's appearance.

She crossed the short distance, kissed her father on the top of
his head, and continued to the kitchen. Her walk similar to the
way Stacey moved. She flowed, but not like a dancer. More like a
predator.

"She practices her katas in the morning," Ishihara told them.
"Normally at her own apartment, or in a park. Sometimes she uses
my dojo. She does not ask permission, nor announces her intentions."

"I'm family," she replied, her back to them. Rosz and Billy unable to remove their eyes from her perfectly rounded rear. Older
by at least a decade, still an arresting, exotic beauty.

Chaspi watched, worried their presence compromised by the
unexpected arrival of their host's daughter.

Stacey watched, one predator accessing another. An interloper
in the other's territory.

She returned with hot coffee, several slices of toast, and blue-
berries. She sat at the far end of the table, facing her father.

"I do not have to ask permission to visit. I hope I never need to
call before coming home," she said.

"Never," the elder man said. "I should introduce our guests."

Before he could continue, she said, "Chaspi and Rosz. Bosine
refugees from Osperantue. Formerly aboard the Star Gazer. Relo-

cated to New Zealand with their families. Currently enrolled in college in Toronto studying environmental engineering."

She faced Stacey, her black almond-shaped eyes displaying no challenge, and no fear.

"AStasaei of Fell. Sister of ASkillamentrae and ASparquilla. Cousin of AStarmalanlan. Captured, with her younger sister, ASarasha, during the Zenge invasion of Fell. Freed by Captains Cooper and Casalobos. Relocated to Rys. Brought to Earth to also attend college in Toronto. Aeronautics. Currently lives with Admiral Patterson and her husband, Sam."

Finally, she looked at Billy. "I'm afraid I do not know you. Only that you are Canadian, and, I assume, attend the same college."

"Billy," he stammered. "Environmental engineering."

"Aya is the newly appointed Exo-Legal Affairs Department Head for the United Earth Council," the older Ishihara informed them. "She was a brilliant student of the law, and developed a reputation as an attorney and a counselor in Japan. Our representative on the UEC brought her to Toronto. Her talents were quickly recognized by the other members. With the arrival of extraterrestrials, it was decided an agency would be needed to provide Earth with legal advice when dealing with other worlds. Aya, despite her youth, was asked to create and direct that agency."

Sensei's spoke with unmasked pride in his daughter.

"Which places me in a dilemma," she said. "I work for the UEC. UEC security is currently looking for three aliens attending university in Toronto who fled their dormitory moments before a detail arrived to take them to UEC HQ for questioning. I was informed by Security Director Cassel to prepare to deal with issues regarding alien civil and legal rights, should questions arise following their detainment."

She finished a fourth piece of toast, recovering carbs from her workout, before continuing.

"I found it interesting he used the word 'detainment' and not 'arrest,' she said. "He also would not explain the exact nature of your detainment. Global security. The catch-phrase for government overreach."

"What about the Patterson's?" Stacey asked. "Are they safe?"

"I don't know anything about the Admiral or her husband," the legal expert replied. "Why shouldn't they be safe?"

"You now face a greater dilemma, Aya-chan," Sensei said. "You must decide between your loyalty to your office, and your trust in family. If you feel your primary duty is to act for the UEC, I cannot allow my guests to say anything more. I would only ask, as your father, to allow me time to move them before you inform security."

He stopped talking. Aya stopped eating, but did not respond. The others, the subject of the family discourse, remained quiet.

The younger Japanese made no verbal commitment. She placed her elbows on the table top, and rested her chin on her raised fists. Not a Japanese position to take at the family table. It spoke to the woman's independent spirit. She said nothing, allowing her body language to convey the question ("Or?").

"Or you can trust your father's wisdom and provide assistance to four young people in need of guidance from someone well-versed in political hanky-panky."

"Hanky-panky." She repeated the words as half-question and half-surprise. "My father, the great Sensei Ishihara Kaito, former commander of the Royal Guard, with an advanced degree in philosophy from Kyoto Imperial University, calls government intrigue 'hanky-panky?'"

The four, watching and listening, were unsure if they should laugh, grimace, or remain unnoticed. They remained unnoticed.

"The words do not matter," Sensei replied. "Your answer does."

"You already know my answer, Tōchan," Aya said, using the informal 'Dad.' "I trust in you. As my father, my trainer, my Sensei, and my rock." She brought the others back from their conversational exile. "I will not turn you in," she said. "If I have to decide between my work and my family, I will always choose family. It would appear that my father has adopted the four of you. That makes us family."

"On Fell, it is family, clan, tribe, and then Fell," Stacey said.

"Same for us," Chaspi added. "Family first."

"I don't usually agree with my parents," Billy said, "but I trust they want what's best for me."

"What about the Patterson's?" Aya asked Stacey, and then abruptly said, "No. Wait. I have to shower before I begin to reek. I left my bag in the dojo. You guys clean up breakfast. We'll meet in the den."

Aya departed.

"We are in her hands now," Sensei said, standing and collecting his dishes. "They are good hands. She had a most excellent teacher."

"You?" Chaspi asked.

"Her mother."

UESE HQ

Two uniformed security agents escorted Pam Patterson to a lounge where Sam waited.

"They were aware I was investigating the London Bank the moment I accessed the corporate staffing list," he said.

"They're listening, and probably watching," she warned her husband. "You don't want to say anything even remotely incriminating."

He shrugged and continued.

"It was quite a surprise when my monitor froze. Then my com-pad went dead," he said, returning with her to the sofa. "Coffee or tea?"

She replied with a shake of her head. Surprised at how calm her husband accepted his detention at Security Headquarters. She knew him as a low-key, level-headed financial expert, but never imagined seeing him in a situation as tense as the current one.

"Why was it a surprise?"

"Staffing records for all corporations on the planet are open and available," he replied. "Public documents. I've started investigations with staff lists hundreds of times. Sometimes you catch a break and connect a name to another file, or recognize someone in a position that doesn't exactly fit what you know about them."

"Did you see a name that seemed out of place?"

"Didn't have time," he replied. "Pam, I barely opened the com-line and put in the request when it froze. There had to be a detect-

and-desist alert attached to the file. But that makes no sense. It's a public file on an open server."

The door opened. Paris Cassel joined them.

"If you had used a public system to access the records, the detect-and-desist would not have activated," he said, confirming they were under observation, and confirming he did not care if they knew. "Your official address triggered the alarm. A UEC computer assigned to the financial offices, and, more specifically, to you."

"I make similar searches every day," Sam said. "It's part of my job."

"Normally, but you are the husband of Admiral Pam Patterson, retired, and she has been snooping around sensitive matters. The bank in London is under surveillance. Your wife is a person of interest. You tripped the alarm."

"Why are they watched?" Pam asked.

"Classified," Cassel responded, and held up a hand to stop further questions.

"You are no longer an acting officer in Space Fleet, and you no longer hold clearance for security issues. Sam does not have a clearance level high enough to read him into the on-going investigation. What I can tell you is I cannot allow you to intentionally, or inadvertently warn anyone connected to the London bank that someone is investigating them."

"Fine," Pam said. "We'll go home and be good children. We wont trip any more alerts."

"Not that easy, I'm afraid," the Director said. He settled onto a chair facing the sofa and the Patterson's. "We have to make sure no one else detected Sam's inquiry. We also need to check the security scan of your home we ran. And, no, we are not the ones periodically scanning your house. This was a one-time because of Sam's alert."

"I've know you a long time, Paris," Pam said. "I trust you. You should trust me."

"I trust both of you," Cassel replied. "I work for people who trust that I will not allow that to prevent me from making sure our current project is not compromised. You will both be guests of the UESE for a couple of days while we complete our investigation."

"That is a load of bull," Sam said, standing. The calm demeanor gone. His outrage triggered by the situation becoming too convoluted for the logical financial expert.

"Tell him, Pam," the dapper French-Canadian spy said to his former colleague.

"The UESE can hold us for seventy-two hours without a stated cause," she said, placing a hand on her husband's arm, urging him to sit down. Once seated, she continued. "They call it a global security concern, and there isn't a damn thing we can do about it."

"You'll be placed, together, in a comfortable room located within the facility," Cassel said. "It isn't a top-notch hotel room, but sufficient. I seriously doubt this will take more than a few hours to resolve. I have dispatched agents to your home where they will make a search. I told them not act heavy-handed. I can have them bring you both a change of clothes, if you provide a list and location of items. I need to bring your young guest in as well. Is AStasaei at the house?"

Pam's eyes lost focus for less than a nano-second. She looked at Cassel, wondering if he noticed her minuscule hesitation.

"Stacey? Why I have no idea where she is at the moment," she said. "She's a college co-ed on winter break," Patterson continued. "She probably out with her friends."

"You have a trans-com chip embedded in your neck. I suggest you either turn it off, use it to contact the Fellen, or I will block it altogether" Cassel said.

"Yes, I still have the chip embedded. No, I will not turn it off, nor try to contact AStasaei. I'm here to discuss Sam, not our houseguest. Paris, I believe you when you say you can jam the signal. If you feel that's necessary."

"Necessary, and done as we speak," he assured her. "At least now we know where to find her."

"AStasaei is a citizen of Fell, and a guest on Earth. You should be careful about doing something to cause an interstellar incident," she warned.

"A lot of documents were signed and conditions met for Stacey to be picked up on Rys and delivered to you. Among considerations for her acceptance to college included her acceptance to abide by Earth's laws and practices. He parents also agreed. Our

Exo-Legal Affairs Department assures me I can hold her for the same seventy-two hours before either charging a crime, or requesting her removal and return to Rys."

"You would send her back?" Sam asked.

"I doubt it comes to that," Cassel answered. He rose, and looking down on the former Fleet commander, asked, "Will you tell me everything you have learned while unofficially investigating Barnwell's suicide?"

"Sure," she replied. "Nothing."

The super spook smiled, not expecting any other reply. He would stash them safely away for a short while. If he needed to keep them longer, he could get creative later.

D o j o

Aya sat in her father's chair. Deft fingers, nails polished in dark cranberry, slipped through layers of Space Fleet security firewalls. Her position as the Director of Exo-Legal Affairs allowing her access to all but the highest classified sites. Stacey's magical touch with electronics would eventually allow her to arrive at the same place, but Aya's passwords made it quicker. Plus, she knew what she wanted to find.

"Why are you helping us?" Stacey asked. The young Fellen neither shy nor intimidated by the forceful woman.

"One, because my father sees something in the four of you worthwhile," she replied without making eye contact. The dark, almond-shaped eyes scanning lines of information, searching for something specific. "Two, because of Tasha and Tista Korr."

"The Ventierran Judge and her daughter?" Chaspi asked. For her part, Aya Ishihara completely intimidated her, but curiosity won out.

Aya nodded. "I needed their experience. I wanted to tap into their knowledge regarding the legal issues involving interstellar trade agreements, alliances, and everything that goes with the territory. Who better to learn from than a Trade World Alliance mediator and her assistant. They were gracious, and incredibly helpful. I admire Judge Korr. If ten percent of the aliens we encounter are like the Korrs, Earth will benefit tremendously by joining the Trade Alliance."

"Why does that factor into helping us?" Stacey persisted.

The lawyer with a warrior's spirit rested her back against the ergo-chair, turning her attention from the holo-images to the blue alien standing beside her. Stacey did not quite invade Aya's private space, but hovered close to the edge.

"Judge Korr spoke highly of Fellen," she said. "Honorable, honest, tough negotiators, and fiercely loyal." She turned her incredibly deep eyes to Chaspi and Rosz, across the desk, nowhere near her personal space borders. "Tasha told me The Osperantue races are without deceit. I learned of many species, and even more about the different races within and outside the Alliance from the Korrs. No others received the praise used when describing the people from your two worlds."

"Was it not enough that I trust them?" her father asked.

"No." The daughter's reply stern, then followed by a smile. "You are a wonderful Sensei, but you are a sucker for anyone in trouble. You retired, but never stopped thinking like the commander of the protectors."

"Sensei, you actually commanded the Royal Guard for the Japanese Imperial Family?" Billy asked.

"He left the Tokyo police force to join the Royal Guard. He filled the vacancy created when Hiroshi Kimura decided not to return, choosing university instead," Aya answered for her sire. "Over time he rose to Commander. He retired and moved to Canada. My father listens to spirits. One whispered *Toronto* and he moved to Canada."

"Really?" Billy asked, eyes wide.

"Kami are everywhere, and anyone can learn to hear their messages," the elder Ishihara said, "but Aya exaggerates. Rie Sasaki, Japan's representative to the UEC asked that I spend time in Toronto after my retirement."

"My mother died years ago," Aya took up the tale. "My father and Rie are not-so-secret lovers. As I said, he is not the best judge of character."

Rosz, Chaspi, and Billy stood quietly, caught between shock at the information quite freely given, and giggles over Sensei's obvious discomfort.

Stacey relaxed. The open revelations made her more comfortable with both Japanese. "Can I help you find anything?"

"Nope. Already found what I needed," she said. Returning to the holo-image generator, she pulled out a line of code and expanded it into a diagram. Flexing her manicured fingers across the diagram converted it into a three-dimensional representation of a large fenced area and several buildings.

"This is Space Fleet's Aerospace Maintenance and Regeneration Group's Inactive Shuttle Facility," she said. "Decommissioned shuttles pending determination of final fate are stored here."

"Final fate?" Stacey asked.

"A few get resold to private enterprises. Those in good condition may be recommissioned following upgrades. The majority are scrapped. A couple end up in museums. Until a final decision is made by Fleet Engineers, they sit here. The engines that power space flight are removed. Electronics, communications, and ident systems pulled. They are capable of manual atmospheric flight to allow pilots to deliver them to their final destination, but that is about all they can do."

"Why does this help us?" Rosz asked.

"As I said," Aya looked at the Bosine, her face framed by the straight black hair still damp from her shower, "Identifiers, electronic and otherwise, have been removed, but they can still fly."

"If we use one of these shuttle to fly to Fin Island," Stacey said, "No one will see us."

"Exactly," Aya agreed. "Now all you have to do is steal one, fly it to the west coast, locate Daniel Cooper, convince him to help you, and return the shuttle before anyone realizes it's missing."

CHAPTER 19

Rosz, with borrowed earbuds (from Aya), and borrowed music (from Aya), new-Earth psy-rock, sat cross-legged, back against the wall in Sensei's combination den and office. Everyone ignored him, assuming he preferred the music and solitude to conversation. Which, in fact, he did.

Aya and Stacey faced each other. The morning light, filtered through closed curtains, framed the two women as they held an urgent conversation. Rosz saw two different people from different species, and far different worlds, yet mirror images.

The younger Fellen, her blue skin and auburn hair streaked with blonde highlights stark contrasts with the slightly older human, with straight black hair and light, sand-colored skin. Obvious differences. There were just as obvious similarities.

They were the same height, same strong body-type, though Stacey displayed the full, round breasts of Fellen females. Aya's chest equally firm, but not as full. Rosz decided he did not prefer one over the other.

Both held themselves like dancers, or perhaps a better simile would be like fighters. While the college student's eyes glowed burnt-orange to deep red, and the Japanese lawyer's eyes smoldered in black night, they possessed identical almond shapes. Humans and Fellen may be alien to each other, but they could share an ancient connection.

Chaspi and Billy stood side-by-side in front of a wall of real books. Their heads down as they talked together. He loved Chaspi as a sister and best friend. He accepted her anger issues, her desire to become more than an average Bosine, and the fact she had no clue how Billy felt toward her.

Billy became his friend without ever attempting to become his friend, or expecting anything from a friendship with an alien. He was a bit goofy, using the Earth term Billy used himself, and smart. The young human did not yet realize his own nature. Rosz could see the adult Billy could become. He met a version of an older Billy when he met Daniel Cooper. While Billy would never consider himself a hero, he possessed the character, the will, and the honor of a paladin. The crush on Chaspi would take care of itself.

Rosz caught Sensei from the corner of his eye. The master stood in the doorway, watching Rosz watch the others. He gave a small smile, a knowing nod, and disappeared.

"We have a plan," Aya said aloud. "You may as well come all the way inside, Father, it involves you as well."

Kai Ishihara entered. He took his seat at his desk, and the others, including Rosz, joined him. "Please tell us your plan," he said to his daughter. "And do not forget my part."

SFAMRG Facilities
Tottenham, Ontario, Canada
(forty-eight miles from Toronto)

"Rosz, Billy, and Sensei Kai should be half way to Mizippy," Chaspi whispered.

"Mississippi," Stacey said, not whispering. "No one can hear us, Chaspi."

"Yea, I know, but we're about to break into a government facility and steal a shuttle," she replied, a bit louder than before, but only a bit. "Seems we should be whispering."

"The facilities closed two hours ago." Stacey talked to Chaspi while she worked with her cello-data sheet, a fold-out thin sheet of cellophane-like material. When booted, the sheet became a functioning mini-personal computer, complete with sat-uplink. "Security is totally automated. All I need to do is hack the system and turn off the alarms."

"What do you think of Aya?"

"I could take her."

"I didn't know you were into girls," Chaspi's surprise overriding her caution. She dropped back into her whisper to say, "I mean, you are so hot, and guys just drool over you, but, whatever you prefer."

In the dark, with nothing more than the dim refracted light from the cello-sheet, Chaspi clearly saw orange eyes squint at her.

"Not - that - way," Stacey said, accentuating each word. "I could take her in a fight."

"Oh, yea, totally get it," Chaspi stammered. "I bet you could, too. Even if she's been trained by her father since she was old enough to walk. I mean, you're from Fell. You've been training your whole life, too. You could take her . . . in a fight."

"Yep," Stacey replied. Looking back at her paper-thin terminal, she added, "Maybe the other way, too."

"Stacey!"

"I'm in. Alarms are off."

The blue girl came out of the ditch across the road from the Space Fleet Maintenance and Regeneration Group's facilities, and headed for the personnel gate set into the security fence. The pink Bosine followed, afraid of getting caught, and excited about the prospects of not getting caught.

Highway to Hattiesburg

"Sensei, I can drive if you need a break," Billy said.

"My vehicle. I drive," Ishihara answered.

The vehicle, an extended rec-bus with off-road wheels and hover-capable for short periods to cross places with roads badly in need of repair, or no roads at all. Originally designed to ferry troops, he bought it at auction. He then spent money and time converting the military transport into a cross-country mobile home.

"You sit behind the wheel," Rosz said from the swivel chair behind the two similar chairs constituting the front seats. "The nav-system is set, the self-drive is active, and cruise engaged to determine speed. You even left to use the restroom twice."

"My vehicle. I drive how I wish to drive," Sensei replied. "It is a fully operational bathroom, with shower, and real tile on the floor. It is not a restroom."

"I sit corrected," Rosz said. He carried on the conversation with Aya's earbuds streaming more of her psy-rock music.

"I just need something to do," Billy said. "Chaspi and Stacey have the dangerous part of the plan. Break into a Space Fleet facil-ity, steal a shuttle, fly cross-country hoping they find Daniel Coop-

er. We're just going to keep an eye on the research lab in Hattiesburg to make sure they don't try to move Col. Barnwell."

"You must always be aware of the larger goal, Billy-kun." Sensei swiveled his chair to face the younger man. Billy could not stop
the impulse to grab the steering wheel, though he did stop an actual physical reaction. He grew up with automated vehicles, but
seeing the person in the driver's seat distracted still bothered him.

"The goal is not only the rescue of Col. Barnwell," the former
policeman and royal guardsman said, "but his validation of a conspiracy to destroy Earth's central government. He probably has
valuable details, names, and possibly the actual plans of those who
abducted and imprisoned him. To stop a sedition one must put
together all the pieces of the puzzle. In this way you discover those
leading the movement, and where they have placed assets. Remove the leaders, and you derail the plot. Remove the assets, and
it cannot be moved forward by others."

"Protect Col. Barnwell and his piece of the puzzle," Billy
replied.

"Ay," the older Japanese said. "If AStasaei and Chaspi are unable to locate Captain Cooper, it becomes our job to secure the
puzzle piece."

"A college boy, an alien, and a martial arts master against an
army of evil agents," Rosz said. He turned his chair, placing his
feet atop the seat next to him. "Wake me when we arrive. It will be
interesting to see what happens."

"Karate Master," Sensei Kai said.

SFAMRG Facilities

The girl from Fell moved as a shadow over the pavement, her
extended hand pushing the gate open. Through to the other side
before Chaspi covered the distance from bushes to fence.

The Bosine rushed through the gate, held open for her. Before
Chaspi could comment on the easy entrance, the fear she felt, or
the need to pee, Stacey bolted toward the complex of squat buildings ahead of them.

More afraid of falling behind than wetting her pants, Chaspi followed. Within yards of the Fellen, she barely saw her friend moving into the deeper darkness between the structures. Cat, Chaspi thought to herself. Stacey moves like a cat.

She followed into the darker shadows, running hard to try and keep pace. She ran into Stacey's arms without seeing her first.

"Wait," Stacey whispered.

"Why?" Chaspi asked, the word a gasp between gulps of air. "You took down the security, and you said no one remained after the base closed."

"Better careful," the other girl replied. "And give you time to catch your breath," she added. "Can you see the shuttles?"

Chaspi looked forward, across a gravel lot toward a large field. She could see shapes lined up in two rows, extending away from their location.

"I guess," she replied. "If you mean those blobs."

"We are going for the third blob on the right," Stacey said. "The side hatch will be open when you get there. As soon as you are inside, close it. The panel will be to the right side of the door."

"How will I see?"

"I'll turn the red-lights on. You will be able to see, but they will not create a glow."

"And there she goes," Chaspi said to herself as The Fellen flew away. She followed, unsure if she should be angry Stacey assumed she could not keep up, or grateful she intended to wait on her.

Red light, through the open door, push the button marked CLOSE, and rush to the front of the shuttle. Chaspi plopped into the right seat. Again before she could make a comment, the shuttle lifted, tilted back to front, and sent Chaspi grasping for her harness.

"Are you sure the simulation program qualifies you to fly this thing?" she asked, snapping the center of the X-straps closed.

"I think we are going to find out," Stacey replied, leveling the craft and engaging thrusters. The shuttle shot forward, heading west, passing over the security fence with less than a foot of clearance.

"Why did you and Aya pick this one?"

"Three museums are requesting it," the co-ed-turned-pilot replied. "It will take months for Space Fleet to decide which one gets it. Less likely to rotate up for additional work until then."

"What's so special about this shuttle?"

"No idea. Aya said because of its name, but that made no sense."

"What name?"

"The Picard."

CHAPTER 20

Fin Island

No surprise the young Fellen appeared poured into the METS, displaying a combination of curves and muscles characteristic of the women from her planet. Chaspi proved the bigger surprise. The Bosine transplant normally dressed for comfort, opting for casual Earth clothing similar to the soft, often shapeless clothing preferred by people from Osperantue. The skin-tight METS accentuated a firm chest, narrow hips, and muscled legs. Without the distinctive athletic muscle Stacey exhibited, and less defined than her friend, the suit showed her toned, with little body fat.

"Amazing," Stacey said, running her hands across the fabric. "It's like wearing nothing, but I feel, how do I explain? I feel safe."

"I've heard that before," Nathan Trent said. He and Coop arrived on Fin Island shortly after receiving news of the unexpected appearance of the two young women. "The METS includes an environmental modification system. As a result your body remains at a constant and comfortable temperature. I suppose it is best described as coddled."

"I feel naked," Chaspi said, one hand purposely held low, shielding her groin. The other arm crossed her chest, the hand firmly attached to the opposite shoulder.

Stacey, unconcerned about the personal exposure, gave a small smile, displaying sharp fangs.

"You have nothing to be ashamed of, Chaspi," she said. "Your body belongs to you. Besides, you look good."

The Bosine returned a thank-you smile, but her arms and hands remained in place.

"The METS are usually undergarments," Coop said. He pointed at a table on the far side of the combination lab-studio. "There are BDUs and boots for you. Mara guessed at sizes, but they should do for the short time you need them."

"BDUs?" Chaspi asked. She and Stacey walked across the room toward the neat bundles. Stacey moved with confidence, gliding barefooted. Chaspi took smaller steps, but hurried to reach the added protection of real clothes.

"Battle Dress Uniform," Coop answered. "Fancy military talk for heavy duty shirt and cargo pants. In this case, navy blues to help you blend into the dark. Your METS don't come equipped with the photosensitive cells that allow me to blend into my surroundings."

"But they are designed for nighttime incursions," Trent said. Yours are coated with a special die to trick the eyes of people who see you in the dark. The suits also mask heat signatures."

"But they do not make you invisible," Coop warned. "You might as well keep the outer clothing on."

"Good," Chaspi said. She pulled the cargo pants up quickly. With her lower body securely covered, she took more time putting on the rest of the uniform, finishing with boots. The issue for her Bosine physiology came in the form of gloves. Bosine have a thumb and two fingers, each wider than a human's. Trent worked with one of the island's maintenance staff, a gardener who claimed his father was a tailor. Together they fashioned pieces of METS fabric into hand-covers designed for Chaspi. The redesigned gloves did not come with sensors embedded to allow her to feel textures, and they did not fit as snuggly, but they fit. They would protect her hands from cuts and projectiles.

Chaspi laced and latched her combat boots. She looked up and found Stacey, long since dressed, across the room in front of another table.

"Damn," she muttered. "She even looks hot in stupid military clothes."

She joined her friend, who now held a baton with a brown and black rubber grip. The baton fifteen-inches long, with a third of that rubber grip, and two-thirds black-matte metal.

"What is it?"

"Stun rod," Stacey answered. "The grip is to insulate the user from shock, and contains a power crystal chip. When you squeeze the grip, it sends a current into the metal. The shock is strong enough to knock a catherea out."

"Catherea?"

"Big, nasty Fellen jungle cat," Coop answered. "The stun rod is a Fellen weapon. Foresters use them against animals. Like Stacey said, it will knock them back, or even unconscious, but it rarely kills. To be lethal you have to maintain contact against a vulnerable spot."

"Place it against a temple and squeeze," the Fellen explained. "It will shut down the electrical activity within the brain. There is a holster. May I?" she asked Coop.

"Yours," he replied. "Chaspi, I know people from Osperantue are not inherently violent, but you will need a weapon if you insist on going with us."

"I'm going," she said, steel in her voice reflected in her posture. "I am not afraid of hurting someone if they intend to hurt me or my friends."

Coop selected a pistol from the table and handed it to her.

"Taser Projectile Pistol, or TPP," he told her. "No trigger, so we don't have to modify it for your fingers. Aim, squeeze the grip, and a taser plug is fired. When it hits someone, they go down. 50,000 volts at twenty-five watts. Actual delivery is less than two-thousand volts following the establishment of the current, but plenty enough to knock out a large human."

"Cool," she said, admiring the dull black pistol made of composite plastics.

"Limits," Coop said. His serious tone forced her eyes from the weapon to him. "Maximum distance is only fifty yards, and, for you, best distance is less than ten yards. Get close to make sure you hit your target. Understand?"

"Ten yards," she repeated.

"It carries ten plugs, and there is no field reload. It uses a compressed gas delivery system in the grip, linked to the squeeze trigger. Ten shots and the gas is gone."

"Ten yards, ten shots," Chaspi said. "Holster?"

"Better," he replied. From underneath the table he extracted a military tactical vest. "Quick draw holster at the chest for the TPP. You'll be carrying medical supplies in the pockets. The cross-draw knife at the bottom is a last-resort, or if you need to cut through something."

He pulled out a second vest and tossed it to Stacey.

"Grab a TPP. Your baton won't get in the way. You're carrying miniature explosives. Okay with that?"

"As long as they don't go boom around electrical discharges," Stacey replied. "You know, like stun rods and tasers."

Coop smiled and Trent laughed from across the room. "I thought Storm was a smart ass," Trent commented, "and Sky was the badass. Coop, it appears you have the combination of the two in one back-up."

"No booms unless we arm them first," Coop assured her. "I'll show both of you how on the trip to Mississippi."

"Are we taking the shuttle?" Stacey asked.

"The shuttle is on its way back where it came from." Mara joined them. "We adapted a drone delivery package to the piloting system. Once the shuttle is back at the maintenance yard, I'll re-boot the security system."

"The drone pack will be noticed," Stacey warned.

"There will be time to retrieve it," Trent assured her. "The Picard isn't going anywhere anytime soon. I'll have one of my engineers in Toronto run an inspection and sneak it off."

"How do we get to Mizippy?" Chaspi asked.

"Mississippi," four voices in unison.

"You did a hell of a job with that shuttle," Coop said to Stacey. "Manually piloting it over 2,000 miles, locating Fin Island, and setting her down on the front lawn. I'm interested in seeing how you handle a Wraith."

"What's a Wraith?" Stacey and Chaspi both asked.

Southern University of Mississippi

Hattiesburg, Mississippi
Bio-Chemical Research Facilities
Between 3:00am and 4:00am local time

Billy crouched in the bushes near the rear of the bio-chemical research building. Rosz watched the side to his right, and Sensei found a spot on a hillock that allowed him to monitor the front and left side of the structure. The building included access and egress points on all four walls. The main entrance consisted of double glass doors, and a glassed entry showing a tiled lobby. Dim lighting did not reveal anyone stationed in the entrance area.

The side Rosz surveyed had a single solid door with a wall lamp.

The opposite side provided access for deliveries. A concrete ramp and a metal garage-style door.

The rear, Billy's responsibility, also used double doors, but solid with head-high square glass windows.

Second floor windows were dark, but lights could be seen from all the windows on the third floor. Ambient light filtered through covered glass panes on the fourth floor.

Billy visited the southern United States for vacations with his parents a couple of times. Those times during the summer, and at either the Atlantic or Gulf coasts. Considering the heat and humidity he remembered, he did not plan on a freaking freezing Mississippi.

He wanted badly to complain over the closed com-system the three used, but Sensei demanded they remain quiet unless something urgent occurred.

"Someone is coming out the front," Sensei's voice whispered in Billy's right ear. "They are heading for the parking lot. I will move closer to make sure Col. Barnwell is not with them."

The rear doors suddenly opening surprised the young Canadian, who rocked back in his crouch, tipping over and onto his butt.

He looked up and through the winter-thinned bush to see three bulky bodies move forward, followed by a grav-sled carrying a large bundle pushed by a short, stocky silhouette. Two more big bodies came through, and the doors closed.

"People just came out the back with a grav-sled," he whispered, urgently. "I think they're headed for the parking lot beside the other research building, and I think Col. Barnwell is on the sled."

Whether he spoke too loudly, or too long, the two trailing guards turned to his direction.

Holding his breath did not help. The two suddenly converged on his bush. He tried pushing up, but his hands and feet slipped on the frost-covered pine-straw. Unable to get to his feet quickly, he rolled over in order to crab-scramble escape. Facing away, he never saw the butt of the laser rifle descend onto the back of his head.

By the time Rosz arrived, the main group already left the side-walk and stepped onto grass for a shortcut to the far parking area. The two who found and clubbed Billy hurried to catch up.

He quickly checked his fallen friend to make sure he was alive, and the head wound did not gush blood. Billy breathed in and out, shallow, but steady. No blood came away after Rosz ran his hands over the other boy's head and body.

He called , "Sensei?" No reply. Decision time.

Rosz ran after the small group of people escaping across the manicured lawn. Light spilled from a hover-van, now visible in the parking lot with its side door open, ready for the grav-sled.

Two forms ahead of him stopped moving away. They turned to face him, arms coming up to fire weapons.

He held the two bastions low and in front of his body. His only hope would be to try and deflect the stun loads. Oh, and the other only hope — stun loads and not laser blasts. Or maybe they would miss him in the darkness. He had lots of hope, and one thing more important.

Sensei barreled into the two, coming from Rosz's right. Flash-es as Tasers fired harmlessly into the ground. Rosz arrived as the Japanese kicked a weapon from the hand of a rather large woman. The other one, a man, tried bringing his rifle up while he re-mained on one knee.

Rosz's rattan stick chopped across the wrist of the trigger hand. The muffled grunt of pain not as loud as the sound of the bone-breaking injury. Proving his high threshold for pain, and dedication to duty, the man rose to advance on the young Bosine.

The female security agent released a flurry of kicks and punch-es at her smaller opponent. The karate master ducked or blocked every potential blow, landing a knuckle punch of his own. The woman reeled backward, her hand clutched at the center of her chest. The bruise would be a world record.

The other guard reached for Rosz with his good hand. Rosz rewarded the man's desire to strangle the smaller alien with a flow of figure eights. As soon as one bastion blocked, the other moved into place to deliver a stinging blow. The bigger opponent backed away, arms flailing as if warding off mosquitoes.

Ungentlemanly, Ishihara delivered an old-fashion uppercut to the woman's exposed chin. *Down went Frasier.* He turned to help his young student in time to watch as Rosz landed four concussive blows to the forehead and temples of his attacker. The man collapsed to the ground.

"Well done, Rosz-kun," he praised the young man. "But I am afraid they accomplished their mission. The others have reached the van."

Rosz, sweat streaming across his face, flicked it away as he followed Sensei's gaze. Three large bodies stood guard as two others attempted to load the grav-sled with Col. Barnwell into the waiting vehicle.

The shadow that crossed his vision swept the legs of one guard, sending him butt-first onto the hard pavement. Something made of semi-solid smoke continued moving, yanking the next guard backward, bowing his spine. An elbow slammed down, crushing the bad guy's exposed windpipe. Rosz thought it was an elbow. Whatever, the man's throat no longer functioned. He could hear the result of the blow in the quiet night as the guard desperately wheezed seeking air.

"Amazing," Sensei whispered. Mesmerized by the dance of the shade in the ambient light of the van's open side door and parking area's weak lamps.

The third guard, with time to realize they were under assault, used his shoulder-fire laser rifle as a fighting stick. He thrust it forward, and twisted to drive the stock into the face of the spectral foe.

The rifle passed over the shadow like a limbo stick. The slender waif of mist rising, thrusting a stick of its own into the third guard's ribs. The electric shock glowed and blistered the darkness, slamming the big body against the side of the van. The rifle flew into the bushes, a reflex from the delivery of high voltage. The man fell forward, leaving a large dent in the sheet metal, shaking uncontrollably as he spasmed on the ground.

The short person pushing the grav-sled stood statue-still during the short, intense confrontation. They remained locked in place, while the van driver helping load the sled jumped from inside the vehicle to land on the exposed back of the vapor spirit.

The effort gained him a full-body flip, ending with a body-slam onto the pavement. As the groan escaped, it became augmented by the rattle of teeth and an attempt to scream, choked off in shear pain. The electric stun rod applied once more. Rosz added his own groan when he noticed the tip of the rod came away from the driver's groin.

The last man raised his hands and dropped onto both knees.

"She's good."

Rosz and Ishihara Kaito jerked at the voice. Mesmerized by the battle, neither moved to help, or noticed as someone walked up behind them.

Chaspi, dressed in bad-ass BDUs held Billy by her side. Still understandably groggy, but coming around. Or, perhaps, realizing who picked him up and held him, decided to squeeze a bit more time out of the assistance before a full recovery.

"That's Stacey?" Rosz asked, unable to contain the surprise. "Where did you come from? Where did she learn how to fight like that? How come she moves like she isn't there?"

Chaspi handed Billy off to Ishihara before answering.

"That's Stacey, and she is Fellen. They all know how to fight. She's wearing a special suit designed for Space Fleet Marines by Dr. Trent. It doesn't actually make you invisible, like Coop's, but in this light, it comes close. And we came from Fin Island, and I got to pilot a Wraith."

"Where is Captain Cooper?" Sensei asked.

"We scanned the research building and area as we landed," she said. "Besides the guards hauling Col. Barnwell away, the top two floors showed another dozen heat signatures. Coop sent Stacey to help you, and he went into the building to, and I quote, 'clear your six.'"

The Bosine co-ed looked back toward the research center. The quiet facade masking the mayhem occurring behind closed doors.

"Not sure what 'clear your six' means, but I don't think anyone will be coming from that building to interfere." She turned back to the guys. "I'm the designated back up and supposed to keep the

Wraith ready in case you needed her. When I realized Billy was hurt, I had to help."

"Captain Cooper placed a lot of faith in the two of you," Ishihara said.

"They deserved it."

"Damn," Rosz said. "Is everyone going to scare the crap out of me tonight?"

"Sorry, Rosz," Coop said, materializing next to the small gathering. "Let's see what Stacey caught."

Coop quickly got his answer.

"Dr. Reinhardt," he said, recognizing the man on his knees. "You okay, Stacey?"

"Yep."

An audible gulp came from Rosz, echoed by the revived Billy.

Stacey, now visible in the skintight, form-fitted METS unknowingly started her own fan club. Sorry Sky, and sorry, Storm but a new Fellen just shot to number one.

"Col. Barnwell is breathing, and his heart rate is low, but steady," the blue girl told him. "I believe he is sedated, but unharmed."

Coop went to his old friend's side. "Back from the dead, Tab. Couldn't have happened to a better person." He turned to the quivering psychiatrist-slash-geneticist. "You will pay a heavy price, Doctor. This goes beyond evil."

"I have rights, Captain Cooper," the man said, a bit more bluster than brains. "I'm a Space Fleet contractor. I have legal rights, and I can explain myself, but only to Space Fleet or UEC authorities."

"Sensei Kaito, I apologize for my rudeness," Coop turned from Reinhardt to the Japanese master. A sudden change in attitude. "Stacey and Chaspi told me what you did for all of them. I am in your debt for protecting my friends. And for removing the danger from the front of the building. I passed your work on my way inside."

"My honor," the smaller man replied. "And my pleasure."

"I ask one more favor, Sensei-san. Please escort Col. Barnwell and these four to my ship."

"An easy favor," the man answered, adding a small bow.

"Chaspi, fly Tab to Fin Island. Stacey, stay with him. If he wakes up he will be upset. It may take your strength to keep him strapped in until he realizes he's safe.

"There is not a lot of room in the Wraith. I am afraid Rosz and Billy will need to ride back to Toronto with Sensei Kaito. Billy, you think you can make the trip?"

"Of course, Captain Cooper." Billy's first words since becoming not unconscious. Waking to find Chaspi holding him, followed by Stacey in the skintight suit, and meeting the famous Captain Daniel Cooper left him wordless until directly addressed.

"And you?" Stacey asked.

"I am going to have a private conversation with Dr. Reinhardt. Following that, I believe a trip a few miles south to clean out a nest of vipers may be in order. I'll contact Nathan in a few hours. When Reinhardt's fellow conspirators learn about Tab's rescue, we will only have a short amount of time to round them up before they disappear."

"What about my rights?" Reinhardt asked, following Coop's conversation with unease.

"I am no longer an officer with Star Fleet," he told Reinhardt. "I don't think I'm actually considered alive, and I don't give a damn about your rights, Doctor." He physically lifted the frightened man from his knees with one hand.

"If you tell me everything I need to know, and you do it without any bullshit, you get to live," Coop said, his voice calm, his tone reasonable. "I believe the young people need to leave. They don't need to see what will happen otherwise."

CHAPTER 21

Security delivered Pam and Sam to Cassel's Office. He sat at his desk, immersed in his computer screen. His fingers would dance over the desk top, stop, and dance again. He communicated with someone at a frantic pace.

He looked up, pointed at the coffee-tea service on a side desk, and returned to his screen.

They helped themselves and settled into chairs while Cassel continued his conversation.

Both heads turned as the door opened and Board of Governors Chairman Guy Arcand entered. He went directly for the coffee then, cup in one hand, pulled a third chair over to join them.

"Admiral. Mr. Patterson. I'm sure you have a thousand questions," he said. "If you can wait just a few more minutes, when Director Cassel is finished, we will begin answering those questions."

He took a sip of coffee before continuing.

"The most important thing is Col. Barnwell has been rescued."

"You have Tab?" Pam asked.

"He's on Fin Island. The medical staff there is as good as it gets, as you well know."

"Coop?" she asked, realizing if the UEC knew Tab had been taken to Fin Island, they knew who else was there.

Noticing Cassel lean back in his chair, Arcand asked, "Director, would you care to answer the Coop question?"

"Cooper is fine," Paris said. "Some of that back and forth on the computer was with him. It's old-fashioned, so less likely monitored," explaining the use of screen and keys. "But you need a bit of background first."

He rolled his executive chair around the desk to join the others.

"Governor Arcand moved up to the Board of Governors from his position representing the Can-Am alliance on the UEC. Even though Can-Am is responsible for creating the UEC, he has always been vocal about concerns that centralized control for all world matters did not sit easily with him."

"Something I still have reservation about," Arcand interjected.

"He was approached by Saleh Abd al-Rashid, the Saudi Region's UEC representative, to join a group of powerful and influential people who wanted the Council disbanded. This group wanted regional rule restored," Cassel said.

"Recruited as the face of change," Arcand added. "They would back me, make sure I was appointed to the Board of Governors, and that I became Chairman. From my position I would be able to keep an eye on all UEC actions, and I could voice my concerns about the UEC overreaching its mandates. When the UEC fell apart, I would be given North America."

"Given North America?" Sam asked.

"Named Prime Minister without an election and without interference," Arcand answered. "They called their group the Camarilla Dissolvere. It consists of politicians, business leaders, scientists, media, and military bigwigs. People with personal agendas best realized if the UEC did not control things worldwide."

"They wanted the UEC and military forces out of the way," Cassel said.

"Something I do not believe," Arcand added. "I do have concerns about centralizing the governing of a planet of diverse people, and the history of such institutions becoming mired in bureaucracy. It does not mean I do not want the core principles, and the potential the UEC represents."

"Your goal was to provide a watchdog against repeating earlier mistakes," Pam said. "The Camarilla misread your intentions."

"I went to Paris, told him what I knew. We decided I would go along with the plot while Paris worked to discover names. If we arrested Saleh, or the few I knew or suspected worked with him, others would continue to worm their way into positions where they could still create havoc."

"Tab caught wind of the conspiracy. He began looking into it, totally separate from anything I was doing," Cassel explained. "I did not see his unofficial investigation as a threat. The people operating the Camarilla obviously thought otherwise. I knew he did not commit suicide, but I did not know they held him prisoner."

"When I started investigating Tab's suicide again, you had to shut me down before I stumbled onto Chairman Arcand as one of the conspirators," Pam said.

"The London Bank is their financial site," Sam interjected. "You're monitoring transactions and money movement to collect contact names."

"Yes and yes," Paris answered. "The group was on the verge of making the final push to dissolve the Council. You two would have been eliminated simply by posing a potential threat. That's why I brought you in. Guy told them I worked for him and we would remove you before you caused a problem."

"And now?" Pam asked.

"Cooper, with the help of a few highly unusual operators, rescued Tab. He used Dr. Herman Reinhardt, a Camarilla member, to gain entrance to the group's main operation headquarters in the old NASA propulsion facilities in Mississippi. I ordered a team to sweep the facilities, but Coop already eliminated any threat. They found Reinhardt and the Camarilla's top computer expert bound and a bit bruised.

"He convinced the computer guy, Iranian named Hamed Attaran, to forward unencrypted files to me. With those files, what we already knew, and anything Tab can add, we will shut the entire conspiracy down."

"They dispatched alerts before Cooper penetrated the central command area," Arcand told Pam and Sam. "Rats are scurrying all around the planet. Paris's people are tracking or trying to find every person listed in those files. The Board of Governors will order the military to collect and deposit them in holding cells prepared in Texas."

"We have three major problems," Cassel admitted. "One of the main conspirators is Benny Claflin, and he's the Chief of Security on the Mars Shipyard and Docks. We have to assume the entire security team on MSD is loyal to him."

"A Space Ranger?" Sam's disbelief evident in his tone. "Why would a Space Ranger be part of this?"

"Money, power, long-term security, and a life of luxury," Paris answered. "From what I picked out in the data dump, Claflin and Saleh's father sowed the seeds for the Camarilla just after the Space Ranger Project failed. Pam and I first met when the UEC called on the Ranger Project survivors to prevent a nuclear catastrophe in Iran. During the mission a rogue Space Ranger, Rolf

Berkel, killed another Ranger, Alessandra Campos. Berkel was hired to collect and deliver nuclear missiles hidden inside an old military facility to Claflin. Claflin would transport them to Afzal. Berkel never got the missiles out. No one ever knew about Claflin."

"Nuclear missiles?" Sam asked.

"Afzal planned on forcing the UEC to either disband, or release the Saudi region from control. When that plan fell apart, be began developing a long-term program of misinformation and inserting people who agreed with him into UEC positions. He died ten years ago, and his son, al-Rashin kept the ball rolling," Paris explained.

"Does he know the group is compromised?" Pam asked.

"I don't know for sure," Paris replied. "I can't contact people on MSD I trust because he controls security. I'm going to send an agent I've kept undercover in Space Fleet to contain the danger Claflin poses."

Pam sat up straight, spilling the last of her tea in the process. "You have a secret agent inside Space Fleet! Who?"

"Amanda Black."

"You are shitting me," Pam exclaimed. "Captain Black who screwed up during the Star Gazer battle and got kicked back to the Navy."

"Amanda screwed up because she was never prepared to command a battleship in that situation," Paris said. "We never expected her to actually captain a ship. By freezing when she exited into a full-out space battle, and the result costing hundreds of lives, tore her up."

He looked Patterson directly in the eyes, and told her, "I put Black in that position, and I put her back in when you were removed. For a long time we thought Singletary played a part in the conspiracy. I created a legend for Black that put her in line for command of the PT-99 and get her close to Singletary. She's been sleeping with him to get intel."

"And?"

"Singletary is a prick and a narcissist, but not the mole in Space Fleet," the Director of Security told her. "That is our other major problem. Admiral Stephen Hawks is a leader within the Camarilla, and he is currently in command of a CVBG, and on his way to Aster System and a meeting with the Prophet."

"Does he know he's blown?" she asked.

"No, and that I am sure of. The only one who might be able to get a message to him would be Claflin, which is why we need to get to him as quickly as possible."

"There are good, loyal officers out there with Hawks," Patterson said. "Why not send a message to them and put Hawks in chains?"

"Two reasons. We cannot be sure if Hawks has his own people in places such as communications. I know I would if I were him. And because Same Harrington was recruited by the Camarilla."

"Another Space Ranger," Sam exclaimed.

"I don't believe it," his wife added. "Sam is as good a man as I have ever known or served with. Why would he want to destroy the UEC, and Space Fleet with it?"

"Short answer is disillusionment," Paris replied. "He was married with a couple of young kids when accepted into the Project. They grew old, and he didn't. His wife committed suicide. His children can't handle growing older while their father remains young. They don't allow him to see his grandchildren. Claflin and Harrington go back to before the Project. Claflin picked his time and recruited Sam when he was hurt, angry, and blaming the UEC for taking away his life."

"But would he or Hawks endanger themselves and the other ships if they find out the conspiracy failed?" Sam Patterson asked.

"We don't know, and we can't afford to find out too late," Arcand answered. "Space Fleet is infested with bigots and incompetents. That's why tomorrow I'm reinstating Pam Patterson as Fleet Admiral."

Flustered, if not flabbergasted, Pam stood.

"What about Singletary?"

"He's a politician, and, actually, a damn good administrator," Arcand said. "I'll explain how he goes along or gets courtmartialed for sleeping with a subordinate officer, incompetency, and a dozen more charges. He stays an Admiral in charge of administrative duty departments. You command everything else, and he answers to you. Singletary isn't your problem. You have to figure out what to do about a Carrier Battle Group sailing into dangerous space with a pair of dangerous, potentially insane officers in command. Welcome back, Admiral Patterson."

Fin Island

"Welcome back," Mara said, greeting Coop as he entered the front door.

"Sorry about the stolen transport on your front lawn," he said, accepting and returning a hug. "Seems Elliott's front yard has become a landing pad lately."

"No problem. Do I need to get it secretly returned somewhere?"

"Took it from the bad guys at the propulsion center," he explained. "I don't think anyone is going to look for it or expect it back. Donate it to the local tribe. How's Tab?"

"He's in the room next to yours. Go see."

Titus Andronicus Barnwell, Junior sat upright in the king-sized bed, pillows propping him. Pads of paper and three data-pads spread out on the bed around him. His dark black skin a bit less dark, his face more narrow, but his eyes and smile the same Coop last saw more than six years ago.

"Coop," he cried. "I'd get up and hug you, buddy, but Mara said she'd kick my black ass."

Cooper took a seat on the side of the bed, leaning over for a bro-hug that sent pads sliding across the covers.

"I know it's a stupid question, but are you okay?"

"Still a bit screwed up in the head," Tab admitted. "They kept me drugged. My regeneration systems worked overtime to clean me out, and Reinhardt constantly shot sedatives in me to keep me submissive. When Mara told me six years had passed, I nearly crapped. The doctor here says I should be physically restored in a couple of days. Trent has a Swiss specialist flying in to make sure my brain still works right. I'm catching up on everything in the meantime, writing down anything and everything I can remember."

"Back on the job," Coop said. "Would expect that from you. Anything special you remember?"

"Reinhardt did a lot of bad-ass stuff to me," Tab confided. "He's obsessed with finding out why the twelve of us survived the project. He's trying to discover why the Methuselah gnomes reactivated properly then because no one has been able to replicate the process again. He wants to live forever. I'm gonna kill his ass first chance I get."

"Paris Cassel has him at the moment," Coop told his friend. "When he's finished, I think Reinhardt might prefer your visit to the plans Cassel has for him."

"Benny is part of the conspiracy," Barnwell said, his voice low, sad. "He trapped me, wrapped me, and turned me over to Reinhardt."

"Turns out good-time Benny helped create the Camarilla Dissolvere," Coop informed Tab. "He was working with Berkel when Ali died. He's Chief of Security for Space Fleet and on MSD right now. I need to figure a way of getting to him before he gets the news about the Camarilla."

"Someone, but not you," Mara said, bringing a tray of fresh juice and fruit with her.

"Why not?" Coop asked, watching Tab down a juice and grab an apple. Good signs.

"Because the new Fleet Admiral wants you in Toronto."

"They replaced Singletary? What screw-up did the UEC pick this time?"

"Oh, just some washed-out former Admiral named Patterson."

CHAPTER 22

"You're out of uniform," Pam said.

"Don't plan on wearing one again," Coop answered.

"Then I'm conscripting your civilian ass," she responded.

"Then I guess I volunteer," he replied, adding a smile. "What am I volunteering for?"

"Nathan tells me your new personal ship is fast. According to his math, if you leave within the hour, you will reach the solar rim a few hours after the CVBG reenters space-fold for Aster system."

"You want me to chase down the battle group?"

"I want you to go to Fell," she said. "You can get there before they arrive at Aster. We need to communicate with people we trust in the group without Hawks, Harrison, or any other Camarilla plant knowing. The coms people in command can't see a way to do it. No one in the galaxy is better at communications tech than Fellen engineers. Storm, Sky, and Sparks are all on Fell. Get there, get them up to speed, and get their help. If they can get you through to Elie, tell her to watch Hawks and Harrington, If they do anything to endanger the CVBG, take them into custody per my orders as Fleet Admiral."

"What about Benny and MSD?"

"My problem, not yours," she replied.

"al-Rashid and the other Camarilla masters still loose?"

"Paris and his people will handle them."

"The Prophet?"

"I don't know," she admitted. "Right now I need to get up to speed. I do know we must be ready to back up our people when they arrive in the Aster system. Hope for peace, and expect a war."

"You know what Stacey, Chaspi, Rosz, Billy, and Kai did for you."

"I do, and I have plans for thanking all of them."

"Henry and Heidi are on MSD."

"Again, my problem, Coop. I don't want them harmed either."

"So I go to Fell, pass along a message, and then?"

"Whatever you want," she said. "You don't plan on wearing a uniform again, remember?"

"You can be such a bitch."

"Comes with the braid."

Free time between systems provided the opportunity to inspect the Wraith's storage bins. Coop discovered someone went through his temporary quarters on Fin Island, collected his gear, and stored it on board. He also found his personal belongings from the 109. He feared he might never see the four special Japanese swords Hiro presented him over the years. They were his most prized possessions. He uncovered two new optic-camo METS suits, and a replacement for his long lost wing-suit. Having Mara and Nathan as friends always paid off.

The trip from the solar system rim to Fell would give him time to consider, or reconsider, the name he came up with for his new ship. Wraith had a cool, dangerous vibe, but it stood for a designation of a new class of personal space fighter.

He mentally reviewed his reasoning behind the name he finally decided on for his new ride.

Described as a spirit with a bad attitude, a wraith was often the specter of a sorceress with an unhappiness that followed her into the next life. Considering the wraith's mythology, his personal past, and current events, he decided on Cassandra.

Some considered her a sorceress. Most knew her as an oracle whose prophesies always came true, but, cursed by Apollo, no one ever believed her fore-tellings. She dealt with the ultimate frustration. She knew when something bad was about to occur, but no matter how hard she tried to make people aware, they ignored her. He could definitely relate.

Eventually ship and pilot would face the Mischene's Prophet, so why not fight fire with fire. *See your prophet and raise you an oracle*. Besides, Coop and Cassie had a nice ring to it.

"I guess that's it," he said aloud as he rummaged through the clothes locker. "You are hereby and henceforth, Cassandra, AKA Cassie."

If not for Cooper's re-engineered genetic makeup, which made killing him difficult, he might have experienced a heart attack when the ship answered, "Thank you, Captain Cooper. I rather like the name."

"You're the AI," Coop said aloud, talking to his ship, or at least the operating system that managed the ship's functions. "When was anyone going to tell me this ship came with a communicative Artificial Intelligence?"

"Dr. Trent suggested I waited until you produced a suitable name for me," the speakers embedded around the ship answered. While the voice came from nowhere and everywhere, Coop's time with the PT-109's AI, Kennedy accustomed him to her voice surrounding him.

"Dr. Trent knew I would come up with a name," Coop said aloud.

"He assured me it might take a little time, but naming one's ship is the most important thing a captain can do," she, distinctly a she, said. "He suggested I remain quiet until you announced my name. He said you would be more receptive to my presence after that."

"Any other advice Dr. Trent pass on?" he asked.

"To be patient with you," she replied. "He provided me with your history, as well as your involvement with the AI/Avatars aboard the PT-109 and the PT-99. While you are comfortable with artificial intelligence relative to a large ship, and how it relates directly with you or via an avatar who is basically human, having an intelligence sharing the space within as small a ship as the Wraith Class might be, he used the term, claustrophobic."

"What about the problem with you potentially going insane due to lack of sensory feedback? They created avatars to provide an AI access to sensory contact with the real world. Being trapped in a constant void while you matured, learned, and developed could eventually lead to a mental breakdown."

"If you could prepare yourself, Captain Cooper. I do not wish to give you another shock."

"Prepare myself for what?" he asked, curious, and a bit worried about what could possibly come next.

A shimmering began in the center of the small galley of the cabin. Slowly it began to take shape and seemingly solidify. After a few more seconds a breathtakingly beautiful nude woman stood there.

"I possess my own semi-corporeal self," the voice, now coming from the woman informed him. "I can, within the limits of this ship, have complete sensory feedback without the need to accept the information through an avatar neural interface."

"Are you a design created by Dr. Trent?" Coop asked.

"Trent Industry engineers designed the holo-avatar program. I created this appearance," the holograph replied. "It is a combination of images of the original Cassandra from Earth mythology, as well as a visual history of women important to you."

Coop attempted to recognized anyone in the visage before him. She was tall, at least five-ten and, if real, would weigh between one-thirty and one-forty. She replicated a body-type similar to Sky. Her face more oval than round with a strong chin, but not a square one. She had full lips, and her nose more pert than straight. She also had nice dimples. High cheekbones, but not sharp. Big aegean blue eyes with manicured blonde eyebrows matching the honey blonde hair she wore parted in the middle, tucked behind her ears, and to her shoulders. The hair straight, fine, and thick.

He found it impossible not to notice the firm, upright breasts. Not as large as Sky or Storm's. More like Elie's, only not tan. Her waist curved into a small circle, like the majority of the women in his life. Defined abs, and hips that swelled like Storm's, but not as much. Long, toned, muscled legs, and while he could not see it from his advantage, he knew she would have a firm butt.

"Cassie, can your tech manifest clothing?" he asked.

He no sooner inquired than she appeared dressed head to toe. A black lycra-style top Fellen women preferred, but with long sleeves and a more scooped neckline. She wore a pair of light gray fatigue pants, complete with multiple pockets, and a twine belt with silver buckle. The pants tucked into black-matte jump boots. Her hair, pulled back into a ponytail, made her look early twenties. Before the clothes and ponytail he would have guessed an age closer to thirty.

"I can create any type of clothing," she said. "I can also change any or all of my physical characteristics. Is there anything you would prefer?"

"I think that if this is the appearance you choose, then this is how you should look," Cooper told her. "Are you happy with your decisions?"

"I'm not sure yet about emotional states," Cassie replied. "I have not experienced much since activated at Trent Industries and placed into the Wraith. I have explored records, and observed you each time you entered me."

"Okay, Cassie, I would prefer we come up with a different description than 'I entered you,'" he said. "There are people in my life who might take that the wrong way."

"Of course, Captain Cooper. I now recognize the double entendre. One day I hope to find it amusing," she said.

"Then a couple more things to help you along the way," Coop said, moving past the image to find a seat at the com-tac station. "You need to learn to blink occasionally, and pretend to breath. Not doing those things can cause a human to become uncomfortable around you."

"Thank you," she said, turning to watch him as he passed. "Such information will make it easier for others to accept me."

"Is there a certain amount of time required for you to remain corporeal?"

"No," she replied. "I'm quite comfortable in my own world. Being able to manifest, as you say, allows me more range to explore your world. It will also, as you suggest, keep me sane. I will endeavor to appear only when you expect me, and I will wear appropriate clothing. I believe your elevated heart rate and blood pressure resulted from my sudden introduction. Your hormonal reaction is likely caused by my nude body."

"Thank you, Cassie. If it's okay with you, I will continue to call you Cassie, and refer to the ship as Cassandra."

"Amazing," the AI said. "Dr. Trent predicted you would be able to adjust and accept my presence quickly. My studies of humans does not indicate that as a normal reaction. You are a unique human, Captain Cooper. Most likely due to the improvements in your brain function."

"You are altogether unique, Cassie. It will take time to fully adjust, but right now I need to prepare for Fell. You will keep your ability to manifest secret from others until I say otherwise."

"You are the Captain," she replied and promptly disappeared. "Is there anything else?" her voice asked in surround-sound.

"Yes. Since we are going to share space for the foreseeable future, you might as well start calling me Coop," he instructed.

"Coop," she said experimentally. "Cassie and Coop. It has a nice sound, doesn't it?"

PART 3

Convergence

Convolutions

Rivers sometimes meet. When two rivers converge, the confluence creates a new, third river. Civilizations often build cities at
the confluence because they are natural locations for trade and
transportation.

These confluences are often dangerous, the merging of two
powerful bodies creating swift currents at the surface and below.

CHAPTER 23

Cassandra dropped through the dense, overcast sky above Harmony. Coop used thrusters and hovers to bring the ship to the surface. He extended the landing gear, and the ship settled onto a three-point stance on the landing pad the command center directed him to use.

As the slow rocking ceased from settling on its struts, three people approached from a nearby wooden building. He augmented the optics used to create the illusion the outside could be seen through a transparent canopy. The close-up view showed Cindy Shah, Mags Moore, and Hiro coming to greet him.

They waited forward the nose. He popped the hatch in the roof of the raised cockpit to exit by stepping up and out onto the ship's surface. He wore a long-sleeved khaki pull-over because of the cool, damp Fell air. It covered a sleeveless, skintight undershirt made from a composite material of kevlar and woven metal alloy discovered on Mars. The thin material could stop a projectile, deflect a knife, and dissipate the effects of a hand-held laser weapon. If hit by the burst he would go down, but he would also be able to get back up. He did not think he needed the added protection on Fell, but he planned on becoming accustomed to wearing the undershirt all of the time.

He carried his trusted rubber-gripped Army Ranger issued Falkniven A1 knife on his belt. Some blades were for show. The Falkniven came to work.

He stepped onto the leading edge of the delta wing, and instead of moving to the back of the wing and calling for the ladder, he jumped the sixteen-feet from wing to ground.

Without a beat, and after not seeing him in over a year, Mags pushed forward and asked, "What is she?" staring lovingly at the spacecraft as only a pilot could.

"Trent's personal project," Coop replied, understanding her priorities. "It's a Wraith class two-person fighter. The only one. The double-barrel railguns up front fire sequenced loads of kinetic and NNEMP loads. Each side carries five-hundred ultra-dense projectiles. What you don't see is a tachyon cannon that drops from the undercarriage.

"She's one-hundred-percent stealth. Low profile and special composite materials that absorb and redirect surface scans, as well as anti-scanning systems to defeat deep penetration attempts. SH integrated into the com-tac computer."

"Speed?" Mags asked as she walked around the ship. Coop, Cindy, and Hiro in her wake, no one yet having the chance to say a proper hello.

"1 kpc standard space-fold in open space, .12 sub-light within systems, and 300,000mph battle speed. Mach 10 plus within an atmosphere, with advanced gravotonics to allow for ultra-high speed radical turns inside the troposphere without injuring the crew. A Mach 10 ninety-degree turn produces minimal g-forces inside the cabin. The ship is able to maintain velocity throughout all maneuver."

"Shotgun," Mags turned and said to him.

"What?"

"I call shotgun. I want to sit co-pilot and see what she can do next time you fly."

"*She* is Cassandra," Coop informed her. "And hello to you, too, Mags."

Mags melted into a hug with him, holding him close. "I'm glad you're alive, Coop. I'm glad you're here. But I never doubted you would recover."

Hiro chimed in with, "Except the time you suggested we hold a memorial." He too gave Coop a hug. Not a buddy thump, but a real, tight hug between old friends. "Welcome back to Fell."

"The memorial idea was an excuse for a wake," Mags called over her shoulder as she continued to survey the Wraith.

Cindy gave him her hug and welcome. "Hiro always had your back", she told him. "Not once did he believe you were dead and gone. And why did you use the old coms system to alert control you were arriving?"

"The CVBG heading for Aster system can't pick up the old signals while in space-fold," he answered. "Are Sky, Storm, and Sparks here?"

"Sky is at the AS tribe village. Storm and Sparks are trying to salvage tech from the bunker you destroyed at the Northern Crown. I didn't send anyone a message because of the sneaky way you came in. Thought it best to wait."

"I have a hover craft waiting," Hiro interrupted. "The village is deep in the forest east of Harmony. The trees obscure everything, but there is a cleared landing zone for hover craft to deliver supplies and transport people."

"You and Hiro go to the village," Cindy said. "I'll get word to Storm and Sparks to meet you there. Anything else I should be working on?"

"I need a way to communicate with Kennedy without the rest of the CVBG aware," he told her. "I'll explain everything when we have everybody together."

"Can I go inside?" Mags asked. Mary Margaret Moore was an addicted pilot, and Cassandra represented her type of drug.

Coop motioned Mags to join him under the fuselage next to one of the forward two wing-mounted landing gear. He placed his hand on a flat spot five-feet from the ground, near an articulation in the strut. "Cassandra this is Coop. I authorize the next person who places their hand-print here full access to all of your systems."

He removed his hand and told Mags, "Place your hand there and tell her your callsign."

Mags placed her hand where Coop's had rested and said, "Hello, Cassandra, I am Magpie." She backed away and asked, "Now what?"

"Tell her it's you and tell her what you want," he said.

"Cassandra, this is Magpie. Please open the entry hatch."

They could hear the soft pop as the elevator motor opened the hatch on top of the ship.

"I'm not a Space Ranger grad," she told Coop. "I can't jump up on that wing the way you jumped down."

"Tell her to lower the ladder," he instructed.

"Lower the ladder," and she hesitated for a moment before adding, "please."

The retractable ladder emerged from the rear edge of the delta wing and dropped to the ground.

"You don't have to be that polite," Cooper said, "but it's always a good idea anyway. You know how women can be." Then he became serious. "Mags, you are welcome to inspect and inquire, but do not take Cassandra up until I get back and I'm in the cockpit with you. Promise."

Mags crossed her heart with her right index finger and held three fingers up. "Cross my heart and hope to die, scout's honor," she said.

Coop and Hiro both laughed at her. "Cindy, you can join her if you want. Mags can now allow access. Hiro," he said, turning to the man, "I'm ready if you are."

The AS tribe's new village sat a little more than one-hundred miles from Harmony. The hover craft would arrive in less than an hour.

"It's as if I never left," Coop said.

"Except you missed an entire war," Hiro replied. "And something I found out you should know. The Zenge are not what you think."

"My memory is fine, Hiro. I know the Mischene control the Zenge."

"Exactly," the Japanese said. "They control the Zenge. I have spent many hours with the prisoners on Fell. They are not savage, kill-crazy demons. Fewer than ten-percent actually believe in the Prophet. The truly radicalized Zenge would have been dangerous to others on their home world, had the Mischene never arrived. If not forced by the Prophet's soldiers and priests, the vast majority of Zenge would return to a simple existence."

"What about the killing sprees?"

"They believed all aliens are like the Mischene," Hiro replied. "When given the chance to kill, they killed. The more we have contact, even though imprisoned, the more they understand not all non-Zenge are sadists. "

"You believe them?"

"The Zenge once lived in cities. They used technology, invented machines, and developed methods of producing crops and raising animals. They did not understand that the methods also destroyed nutrients in the soil, and created animals no longer capable of reproduction. I believe had humans continued to over-use our planet, we would have much more in common with the Zenge. The Mischene discovered a civilization at the end of a self-created apocalypse. With a little assistance, and access to two new worlds, they would happily return to a simple lifestyle. They would be just as happy that aliens never visited again."

"And the ten-percent?" Coop asked, watching the canopy of trees passed beneath the craft.

"Those fighting with the Prophet would die in his service. Those left in the system, if the Prophet and his fist were removed, would be taken care of, one way or another."

"You're working from a small sample, Hiro. A few hundred prisoners may not be indicative of a billion Zenge," Coop warned.

"I believe the ones imprisoned here do represent the ninety-percent," the Japanese answered. "Human histories on Earth, and the races we have encountered in the short time since your first contact with the Star Gazer are examples that the majority of any civilized species prefer a peaceful existence over war. In the beginning, the Fell wanted to execute every Zenge captured, yet we know Fellen are fierce when necessary, but peaceful by nature. The prisoners have been treated well, once Anton promised to behead anyone who attempted to harm them."

"Sounds like Anton," Coop said, unable to prevent the smile.

"They are few, but they can become ambassadors for change, Coop," Hiro continued. "They can help us."

"I'll pass it along," he promised. "By the way, Pam is Fleet Admiral again."

This time Hiro could not repress a smile.

If not for coordinates entered into a nav system leading to the round opening in the forest canopy, no one would find the village created by a few thousand Fellen.

Hiro landed and the two men stepped away from the small hover ship. Several members of the tribe reset the poles used to project camouflage. From the sky, the hole in the forest would no longer be visible.

Coop was nearly tackled off his feet by Sky's youngest sister, ASarasha. Her parents, older sister, Star and her daughter, Storm's parents and siblings, and what appeared to include the entire tribe closed in on the ship.

Recovering from Sarah's enthusiastic greeting, Coop watched the crowd part for Sky. As beautiful as he remembered, the statuesque warrior took her time, but never wavered from her course. She wrapped herself around him, crushed his lips with hers, and would have dug her nails into his back if not for the protection of the armored undershirt.

"We waited dinner for you," Silla, Sky's mother, said. Forewarned by Hiro. "We can wait a little longer. Coop, go and take a hot shower. ASkiilamentrae can show you to your hut. Master Kimura will be provided a hut as well."

"Master Kimura?" Coop, released from the kiss, asked with a smirk.

"It is because of my new martial arts school," Hiro said. "It is tradition."

"It is pretentious," Coop replied, still smiling.

"I informed Cindy and Mags we will spend the night here," Hiro told him, changing the topic. "They know we will wait for Storm and Sparks. We can leave together at dawn and they will meet us at Cassandra."

"Cassandra?" Sky asked. "Another woman?"

"My new ship," Coop said assuringly. He needed to figure out a way of getting Cassie to lower her WOW factor by about a million before introducing her. Difficult since he already told her she should look the way she thought she should look. The look, a combination of a Greek Goddess and every woman he ever found attractive might be a bit difficult to explain.

Sky's family and extended family ushered her and Coop through the mob to a small hut snug beneath a towering tree. Hiro, followed by, well, hero-worshipping Fellen, was shown to another hut near by.

Coop and Sky were pushed into the hut and the door shut soundly behind them. There is a moment when an absence seems forever and gone in a second. After that brief second they got out of their clothes and into each other. They experienced the excitement and comfort in the heated arousal of rediscovery. An hour later they shared a hot shower.

The two emerged, his skinned flushed and hers a deep blue, neither caused by warm water. Sarah escorted them to a campfire where Hiro sat with a plate of food.

"Couldn't wait?" Coop asked, sitting beside his friend.

"Second helpings," Hiro replied. "Everyone snuck food after the two of you entered the hut. We weren't sure if you would actually come back out. And I was hungry," he ended, using his fingers to pop a veggie-looking thing in his mouth.

The evening ended with a meal and campfire stories. Added to the tales of Hiro the Ninja, and Captain Cooper of Earth, were more adventures in the growing legends of ASkiilamentrae, the one called Sky, and AStermalanlan, the Fellen Storm. Both beautiful, battle-tested, and bright. Inventing technology to help defeat the Zenge horde, and stories of battles, as they crossed the globe to save others. Often fighting with the Ninja Hiro, and more often outnumbered.

A runner approached ASilla with a message, who passed it to Star. She left, taking several of the tribe with her.

"AStermalanlan and ASparilla are about to land," she informed the others.

All heard the hover craft fly over, land, and the engines cycle off. Coop stood, deciding he would go meet them. He received a body tackle for the second time, this time ending flat on his back. Storm landed on top, her mouth kissing, sucking, and biting while her hands stroked, groped, and grasped him. She did not care who or how many watched.

Sky, Hiro, and the majority of the people around the fire laughed out loud.

Storm, without a word yet spoken, stood, yanked Coop to his feet, and pulled him to the hut beneath the tree.

If not for the genetic alterations, which allowed him the remarkable ability to recuperate, the next hour with Storm, following the time with Sky, would have killed him.

CHAPTER 24

A musky odor permeated the command bunker. Water rationing left none for washing clothes or bodies. The sonic cleaners could only do so much. Food rationing made everyone weak and foul tempered.

Baynard Lexton sat at the command desk alone, watching the world burn in high definition. Military units remained restricted to camps and fortifications where they stood a chance of holding the Zenge at bay. The police and armed civilians in cities, towns, and villages did not have the option. They fought the invaders in streets and buildings. Mischene stood alone and in small groups against hundreds of cold-blooded, frightening lizard-like creatures. The people of AF3 lost time and time again. They died or retreated. Some escaped into forests and mountain lairs. As cities emptied, buildings burned, the smoke rose above the planet's surface like a dark death wreath.

Admiral Nan entered and joined Lexton at the desk. He watched flames devour a city block before saying, "The Prophet's ships remain between us and Aster Farum 2. They've taken over the two outermost moon colonies, but do not seem in a hurry to move beyond Aster Farum 3."

"Any sign of the troop carriers returning with more of the Zenge?" Lexton asked.

"No, but they could at any time. They have several wormhole gates to choose from. How are the ground forces holding up?"

"We can't protect anything beyond military installations," Lexton replied. "It appears Soren is allowing people to surrender. He keeps showing up on broadcasts proclaiming himself as the one true prophet, and their future leader. Thousands, if not millions of Mischene continue to turn themselves in. I'm not sure of the fate of the other races. He's made a point of not mentioning anyone but Mischene in his speeches."

"If Amos Soren were still alive," Nan began, "I wonder what he would think of his grand scheme? His own ships attacking Aster Farum 3. His son doing to him what he planned on doing to others."

Baynard Lexton nodded in agreement with the elder Fleet officer. "We became caught up in his vision of a Mischene Empire, and we lost sight of everything else. I lost sight," he said sadly. "How did we fall so fast?"

"Oh, it wasn't fast," Nan replied. "Devee witchcraft kept him alive longer than his detractors. He used time and resources for his propaganda to influence an entire race. As one generation replaced the next, and his message remained pure and unchanged, they grew up believers. Soren did not convert us to a radical position, he bottle-fed us, educated us, and employed us in his quest for manifest destiny.

"Now his son is poised to take the next step. Atticus Soren is completely insane. He actually believes he is the Creator's voice, the Sacred Prophet of the Tahbita. He does not have his father's patience or self-control. He is a blunt instrument."

"A blunt instrument about to hammer our world flat," Lexton added.

Captain Covane entered the command room. Her hair damp with sweat, her uniform shirt stained and wrinkled. Deep-set eyes reflected her lack of rest.

"Admirals," she said in greeting, a lot less formal than before the conflict and the forced conditions of the bunker. "I may have a way to get a message to Earth."

"Don't leave us in suspense, Covane," Lexton said.

"Major Willmer provided much of the information," she began. "Governor Soren financed scientists and engineers to find a method to engineer a wormhole. They produced some limited success."

"If you mean ships that made it through a temporary generated wormhole, and crews that did not," Lexton said, and continued, "then, yes, limited success. They could not determine how long a ship would travel inside a newly created wormhole, or exactly where it might emerge. The artificial wormhole might or might not remain viable until the ship using it exited. We do not have the time to hope for a ship to create and navigate a wormhole. I also do not believe we have access to a ship with the engineering for such a feat."

"We do not," Covane agreed. "We do have access to the latest experiment derived from the failures. There is a special drone on AF 2's Moon Base Three. The drone includes a small, but powerful negative matter generator. It is designed to facilitate communications between systems. The drone creates a wormhole, and because of its size and speed, can take a quarter of the time a ship would in standard wormhole travel."

"A wormhole to where?" Lexton asked, the question sarcastic.

"The guidance software developers believe they have enough data from the failed attempts to accurately project a path. The drone is directed to coordinates, and once there, the negative matter generator opens a gate. The opening is aimed toward the intended destination. A timer is started before the drone leaves natural space, and the timer shuts down the negative matter when the drone is projected to reach the rim of the targeted solar system. An exit gate opens."

"What are you suggesting, Captain?" Nan asked directly.

"We place our request for assistance, and all of the data we have on the Prophet, the Zenge and their forces in Aster system into a drone. We include the secret plans regarding the Zenge project from Governor Soren's files. We store all of this in a gas tube, provide the coordinates for the Earth system, and tell Moon Base Three to send it." Covane relaxed. She found the way to ask for help. Her job was done, now someone else needed to make a decision.

"Soren's secret Zenge files?" Nan asked.

"Willmer has copies," Covane answered.

"How do we get the information to Moon Base Three, get through the troops the Prophet put there, and convince the engineers to use the drone?" Lexton asked.

"We still have access to secure channels to our patrol ships in the system," Covane assured them. "We do not physically need to get by security on the moon base. If all ships around AF2 transmit on our secret channels, only one needs to get heard."

Nan added his opinion to Covane's plan. "When the Zenge finish with Aster Farum 3, they are going to turn their attention on AF2 and AF1, just as they took over the moon installations. The people in the system all realize what life under Soren will be like. I believe the workers on Moon Base Three will jump at the chance to call for help."

"Do it," Lexton ordered. "Get everything you can to them and get the drone into space as soon as possible.The odds against success are massive, but it is our only hope."

Covane left to complete the plan. Lexton turned to Nan and said, "It is an act of desperation. At this point, I see nothing left to lose."

Major Willmer, chief of military intelligence for the entire Aster system, sat alone in his private room deep within the command fortification. His personal computer and communication system turned on, and on the screen, Atticus Soren, the Prophet.

"The plan is complete," Willmer said to Soren. "They are sending the information to the moon base."

"The data concerning my ships and troops?" the man who would rule the galaxy asked.

"Altered. Anyone arriving will not have a true picture of what they face," the Major assured him. "None of our surprises will be revealed. Data regarding the system, especially our unique anomaly changed to present a less daunting area. When Earth sends ships, they will fall into your trap."

"If they send ships," Soren replied.

"Our information and analysis of the humans who infest their planet indicate they cannot help but rush to the rescue," Willmer answered. "If they have not arrived by the time the carriers deliver more Zenge warriors, you simply complete the invasion of the entire system. Once we have control, we can launch our own attack on Earth."

"I would prefer we fight them here." the Prophet said to his spy. "We will have a distinct advantage. We know many of their weaknesses, and they do not know of our countermeasures. A battle in familiar space would be a great benefit."

"The drone with Lexton's plea will arrived shortly after your message requesting a meeting," Willmer reminded Soren. "The lure will bring them to us. The only issue will be if they arrive outside of our window of opportunity."

"Regardless. Either they send their ships into our trap or we set another one while my Zenge warriors complete the cleansing of the Aster system." The Prophet looked directly at his follower. "Are you prepared to open the gates?"

"My Prophet," Willmer dropped to a knee behind his desk. "I have the security codes to open the door to every fortified bunker on Aster Farum 3. When you command, I will provide the path for your warriors. It is my honor to serve the One True Sacred Prophet of the Tahbita."

"Your loyalty will not go unrewarded, Major Willmer. The new Tahbita Empire will need leaders such as yourself. I suppose I should get accustomed to calling you General Willmer." Soren smiled and closed the communications.

When next he called the turncoat, it would be to open the gates to destruction. The Imperial War had begun. It would end when he sat upon the throne as Emperor of the Galaxy, Sacred Prophet of the Tahbita, and the One True Voice of the Creator.

CHAPTER 25

Harmony

Coop greeted Sparks at the campfire, ate, and returned to the hut with Sky and Storm. He slept on the return flight to Harmony; a short, necessary nap.

Hiro's switching the shuttle to landing hovers woke him. Below, Mags and Cindy waited with someone else. Even from height he recognized the Sasquatch-built alien from Rys. Prince Yauni, seven-feet of hair, towered over the two women.

The people exiting the shuttle greeted Prince Yauni warmly, Coop bringing up the rear.

He noticed Cindy wore battle fatigues and appeared flush. Mags also wore black BDUs, but could not suppress her snide humor. The black baseball cap keeping her wavy locks under cover had FU embroidered in the same shade of black as the cap's cloth. When she turned away to talk to Sparks, the small lettering on the back of the cap read FURMAN UNIVERSITY.

"I came to Fell to show our friends new developments by our scientists," Yauni said. "I did not expect to see Daniel Cooper. I heard of your attack. I am pleased to see it failed."

"It's good to see you, too, Yauni. I planned on visiting Rys as soon as possible to solve a riddle that has bothered me for months. Why did you give Earth such a large quantity of valuable crystals?"

The Rys Prince obviously did not expect the question.

"We gave a fair trade in exchange for your help in defending Rys against the Zenge and their Mischene overlords," Yauni replied. "We also received twelve tachyon cannons to maintain our defenses. I think the crystals we provided barely sufficient in payment for our freedom."

"You are galactic traders," Coop said quietly, walking away from the others, the giant Lisza Kaugh moving with him. "Your existence revolves around the art of deal-making. Your credo, the goal of every civilization when making a trade, is to get the better deal. You provided top quality crystals, and a lot of them. You sent your best cutters to Mars with them to teach our people ways to better cut and polish them. You provided information and training to help Earth produce smaller crystals to power systems more efficiently than our out-dated energy sources and bulky batteries. Why?"

"I told you why, Captain Cooper," the Prince said, standing upright to appear more menacing.

Coop responded by relaxing. His body language expressing how unimpressed he found Yauni's greater size.

"You made a trade with a human-avatar acting as an ambassador. A girl with no experience in deal-making of any kind. I expected her, with Tasha Korr's assistance, to keep you busy until I returned from Fell. I came back to find an agreement reached. She received everything the UEC wanted for their cannons and their help. Everything, and a lot more."

Coop placed his right hand on top of the butt of the knife sheathed on his belt. It did not represent an immediate threat, but the willingness to go further for answers.

"Yauni," Coop leaned toward the giant and said, "you, your father, your race are not foolish enough to allow a trade-novice walk away with the better deal, even with a Venterran's guidance. But you are a fool if you think I don't recognize a long play."

"Long play?" the Prince asked.

"You gave the UEC technology and help, expecting Earth would become dependent on crystals. They would become our primary source for future technological expansion. A move done to create another world dependent on your product, and improve your position in future trades. I get that. But you also gave us more crystals than we asked for. That is partially why the UEC feels comfortable putting you at arms' length while they go through a political change. Earth now possesses enough crystals for their current and short-term future needs. That was probably an unexpected development. Monarchies rarely understand governments that change with the whims of the population are apt to set aside the agreements of a previous administration."

Yauni listened to Coop's monologue. He did not stop him to issue denials, but he also did nothing to confirm his story.

"The long play had to be more than just creating a new market, otherwise you would not have given the amount of quality crystals you did. You have something better, or a way to improve what you have beyond the capabilities of what you sent to Earth," Coop concluded.

"Even if that were true," Yauni replied, "we still acted fairly. We gave more than requested, and we gave quality. We sent our best experts to train your people in new methods of shaping the crystals."

"Those same experts could then learn secrets from our people regarding the shaping of crystals for space-fold arrays," Coop countered.

"I wasn't there when you inspected a crystal used for space-fold, but I saw the video. You had never seen one this finely cut and shaped. You admitted your cutters could not have accomplished it. You sent industrial spies, Yauni, not consultants."

"I told my father you would have doubts," the Royal answered.

The seven-footer tossed something to Coop, who caught it in his right hand. He opened his fist to reveal a black crystal in a marquise cut.

"A black diamond?" Coop asked.

"In appearance only," Yauni answered. "This is not a carbon-based mineral. It demonstrates similar properties to diamonds, such as hardness and brilliance. It possesses enhanced properties for thermal conductivity and electron mobility superior to those of naturally formed crystals, or any synthetic minerals ever tested on Rys."

"Silicon-based?" Coop asked.

"Similar," Yauni replied, "but more capable than silicon crystals to both conduct and insulate electron flow. It's something new, and only found on Neuvarusry."

"The mining planet colonized by Dwards. Where you were captured when the Zenge attacked," Coop said. "They knew about this new element?"

"It doesn't appear so. They obviously thought we were mining for something valuable. The Dwards they captured told them they were still exploring, and had not yet discovered anything of value. The Zenge recently abandoned Neuvarusry," Yauni added. "When a scout ship reported the Zenge departure, we sent a team in to help the survivors. The Zenge never realized the black ingots thrown around the surface were the prize."

"You have the next generation crystal power source," Coop surmised.

"Power source, battery, storage, transmission, insulation, and illumination properties superior to anything else known. Carbon-crystal based, or otherwise," Yauni replied. "The one you hold can power a laser blaster for one-thousand-hours of continual use."

The prince turned and walked back toward the group left standing between the shuttle and the Wraith. He reached out a hand to Shah who handed him her sidearm.

Turning to Cooper, who followed, he asked, "May I have your laser side-arm, please?"

Unafraid the big Lisza Kaugh would use his weapon against him, Coop slid it from its holster and handed it over, grip first.

"Effective weapon, but heavy for even me," he said. "The battery pack weighs close to fifteen-pounds." The pack consisted of a large, rectangular block set below the barrel and in front of the trigger guard holding aluminum graphite batteries with gold nanowire cores. "It provides the energy necessary to fire the pistol for ten hours of continual use. It makes the weapon inaccurate because the weight tires your hand and arm."

"It also makes it difficult to carry," Cindy Shah said. "The weight and size is why I rarely carry a sidearm."

"The energy passes through a converter to create an electron particle beam. The beam is refocused twice, then emitted as a laser capable of acting as a slice and cut beam by holding the trigger down, or in bursts that burn into targets," Yauni concluded his review. He produced the pistol he accepted from Shah.

The grip and trigger much the same, but a small square box set in front of the trigger guard and below a much shorter barrel. Another box, this one rectangular and the same width but three times longer than the first box, abutted the first box, its top against the barrel. The entire length of the pistol eight to nine inches.

Yauni handed the pistol to Coop.

"It weighs less than three pounds," he said; a combination of surprise and respect in the discovery. "Specs?"

"The small box holds a black diamond. It acts as battery, conductor, and insulator. It is charged by emersion in an electron bath and holds the charge until used. It powers and transmits the electrons into the optical focus array in the larger box. The array focuses and transmits a laser beam. Cut and slice or bursts. One-thousand-hours of continual use before the diamond must receive a refresher bath."

"Yauni gave it to Mags and me to try out," Shah said. "Easier to carry. Light enough that long-term use is less tiring and aim doesn't suffer. Speaking of aim, you can hold the pistol in a double-handed grip or place one hand on the front array box like a machine-pistol."

Yauni pointed across the open field to several small containers strewn about. A distance of fifty-yards.

"Your friends set up targets and awaited your return by practicing."

"It is too cool to explain, Coop," Mags chimed in. "The difference is incredible. Do you want us to set more targets out for you?"

In response, Coop raised the pistol in the rear-grip double hand method and took a shooter's stance. He locked on half a red container that once held food. A laser burst sizzled into the edge, slicing a bit more alloy off. Coop adjusted for height, movement, wind, the lighter weapon weight, and easy trigger pull. The next ten shots split left-over targets."

"Impressive," Prince Yauni said.

"You knew about the properties and potential for black diamonds when we arrived on Rys," Coop said. "But your source was under Zenge control. Why give so many crystals to Earth?"

"I convinced my Father to part with more than required for the deal. My time among humans was enlightening. I felt we needed to give you crystals to improve your defensive and offensive capabilities."

"In order to confront the Zenge," Coop said.

"And eventually help us reclaim Neuvarusry," Yauni added. "I also knew of your ability to shape crystals for use in laser-array technology. Your people tend to boast. We wanted our best cutters to access to your techniques, and then use them on the black diamond ingots."

"Which is why you offered their help. You needed to learn new skills from our people on Mars. The long plan was, one, get us to fight another battle for you. Two, become dependent on crystal-based weapons and crystal energy sources. Three, provide you with the means necessary to better develop the raw materials, and, finally, four, demonstrate the new and improved crystals, hoping we would be willing to trade up to including space-fold technology in order to purchase them from you."

"Most of which has already occurred," Yauni said. "Except the Zenge simply left Neuvarusry unaware of what they had within their possession. Then the UEC and Space Fleet cut off communications. We have a tachyon system capable of only receiving transmissions, and not responding. We were told Earth would call when ready to re-open communications."

"Don't call us, we'll call you," Coop said. "An old Earth tactic used by people not interested in what you have to say."

"Which is too bad," Yauni said. "While we were acting as traders with, as you say, a long plan, we do not act without honor. It is all part of deal-making, and Earth will learn soon enough how to bargain and protect assets. Rys would have been happy to reach trade agreements. We appreciate what your people did for ours," Yauni added with emphasis. He wanted, needed Coop to believe him.

"We would never give up space-fold technology," Coop told them. "It is our ace against the rest of the galaxy."

"One should never say never," Yauni said. "Space-fold is an ultimate goal, but not the only trade value humans have. We would barter for other goods, and we would honor a mutual-defense pact and alliance at the same time. But now, we have no idea what is happening."

"Things happened too fast for humans to grasp," Coop explained. "We went from slowly moving out into our own solar system to suddenly forced into the middle of a galactic war. Humans had to deal with discovering we were not alone in the universe. It shook the foundations of many of our belief systems. We asked normal people who recently experienced a world-wide pandemic, and a new government to now accept aliens as neighbors."

Coop placed the Rys pistol in the huge hand of the hairy mountain in front of him. He accepted his back in return.

"It festered, but eventually people decided they wanted a break from the pace," he said, continuing the explanation of the sudden break in communications. "They demanded leaders take charge and reel everything in, calm everything down. Politicians and military people who echoed the call for isolationism moved into positions of power."

"My father was right when he once told you," Yauni said, placing a paw on the smaller man's shoulder, "it is much better for a population to be ruled by one king and told how best to think."

"You will make Rys wealthy all over again," Sky said, having listened to the conversation between Coop and the Lisza Kaugh, as did everyone else. "If the new black crystals are all as impressive as this little one, every world will want to update their systems."

"If the Mischene and Zenge hear about them, they'll return in force," Coop added.

"We have no plans on telling others about our discovery," Yauni assured him. "Not until the turmoil within our galaxy is much more settled. Rys recognizes Earth represents the best chance for stopping the Zenge, whether they are puppets of the Mischene, or another renegade group. Because we trust you, Daniel Cooper, I came to Fell to deliver a dozen new laser pistols and a dozen shoulder-fire laser rifles with replacement crystals. I also bring the instructions to build an electron bath to replenish the crystals once they are depleted. I intended for your friends on Fell to pass them along to you. Your presence is more than simple luck. Destiny is on our side."

"The trade for these weapons?" Coop asked.

"A promise. You must promise to do everything in your power to bring an end to the Zenge, regardless of who controls them," Yauni said.

"I no longer represent Earth, Yauni," Cooper told him. "In fact, I might be considered a criminal by those in power."

"It doesn't change my opinion or the offer," the older Lisza Kaugh said. "Earth will need to discover its center, and face these creatures. You must promise to help your people understand Earth arrived earlier than expected to a galaxy in turmoil because they have a role to play."

"I promise to try," Coop said. "I promise to do everything I can to stop the Zenge, with or without Earth's involvement," he added.

"That is enough for trade," the Prince said. "I have one more surprise we discovered when experimenting with the newly cut black diamonds."

CHAPTER 26

MARS SHIPYARD AND DOCKS

Benny Claflin pressed his eyes towards the bridge of his nose while the hand beneath his chin pressed upward and the back of his fingertips stitched his mouth shut. His elbow supported the weight of his head, his desk supporting the elbow.

His dark eyes scanned the arrivals and departures lists for MSD. As Chief of Security he could access everything from shuttle delivery manifests to incoming and outgoing communications, both official and personal.

"What bothers you?" Muna Halim, Claflin's First Officer asked. The Sudanese sat on the sofa in the Chief's office, his feet comfortably crossed atop low table.

"The last two scheduled shuttles from Earth are delayed," the Brit answered. "Communications from Fleet HQ are thirty-one-percent below average."

"Paranoia," Halim's snicker followed the pronouncement. "Hawks is on his way to make history, and the Camarilla is within days of pulling the pins that support the UEC. Shuttles often get delayed, and with the CVBG deployed, communications will be reduced to make sure channels remain open. Fleet will be listening more than talking."

"I haven't heard from our people on Earth in days," Claflin added, moving his hand to rub his shaved crown.

"Not unexpected. This near to finalizing years of planning, I'm sure Hadritak is keeping everyone close and quiet."

"You're probably right. A cock up now would pot the whole thing. Still, paranoia has its place. Who do we have on watch?"

"Current rotation has thirty-six agents on duty. Fourteen are Camarilla," Halim answered without need of checking his duty roster. "About the right break since fifty-four of the one-forty-four on staff are in the loop."

"This is interesting," Claflin said. "Coms reports the 89 is requesting dock space."

The Sudanese sat up. "Black is supposed to remain on patrol as long as the battle group is gone," he said.

"They're reporting a flaw in a space-fold crystal," Claflin repeated the information on his screen. "They have a replacement on board, but want to make sure they have a back-up."

"Makes sense," Halim replied. "Amanda Black is the most cautious Captain in the Fleet. You would think shagging the Admiral would make her take more chances."

"The Macdonald left EMS2 a couple of hours ago after making another unscheduled stop. They discovered a flawed crystal after departure. Call six of our off-duty people," The Chief ordered. "Our people, Muna, not regulars. I'm going to meet the 89. Stay here and keep your ears and eyes open."

The Security Command Center sat near the center of the MSD hub. Shipbuilding yards fanned out on either side of the axel, with piers extended further into space with dockage for ships and shuttles.

Claflin, escorted by a half-dozen agents loyal to him and not Space Fleet, needed an hour to travel the distance, arriving thirty-minutes after the 89 engaged magno-locks. They strode down the interior corridor toward the 89's gangplank. Very few contractors or Fleet personnel worked inside the corridor, the PT-89 the only ship currently docked on this pier.

Lt. Heidi McCormack passed Claflin's team headed toward the pier gates. She gave a nod of recognition, but did not slow down. Benny watched the stunning blonde for a long moment, before returning his attention to the two people in conversation at the airlock ahead.

Captain Black, long, tall, thin, and serious talking with Lt. Commander Henry Smith, MSD's Supply Officer. A large, thick contrast to the female officer.

"Captain Black," Claflin called out. "Heard you had a bit of difficulty. Suppo, you here to personally deliver a crystal?"

"Getting the specs to make sure I get the right one," Smith answered.

"Coms not working?" the security chief asked.

"Haven't seen the 89 up close since she launched," Smith replied. "I hoped Captain Black would give me a tour."

"Which I would except I'm in a hurry," Black said. "I need a back-up crystal, and I need to get back on patrol. Is there something I've done to warrant your visit, Chief, with a half-dozen security agents?"

"Unexpected visit. My job to check on anything dodgy," he said, body relaxed, bright smile. "What was Lt. McCormack's excuse for meeting you?"

"I was in the Officer's Lounge when I got word of the 89's arrival," Smith answered for Black. "She simply came along. When the Captain told us there wasn't time for us to board, Lt. McCormack left."

The Brit removed his cap and scratched the back of his bald skull.

"Sounds reasonable, but a load of bullocks," he said, returning the cap. "Emergency visit by a ship that just left EMS2, and I find Daniel Cooper's two best mates on MDS having a private chat with the ship's Captain." Claflin pulled the laser pistol from its holster, and six shoulder-fire rifles behind him rose.

As the Chief of Security made his move, the airlock/gangplank behind Black opened. In quicktime a dozen Space Fleet Marines deployed, weapons already up and ready. They took a line across the corridor, facing the security agents.

"The Camarilla is busted, Claflin," Black said. "Do you want to die for nothing?"

"Die? Not me, Amanda. I'm a Space Ranger. I think I might just be able to take you all, even if you have a few more guns."

"And I may change the odds back into Captain Black's favor," Col. Anton Gregory said, stepping through the gate to stand between Black and Smith.

"British Special Forces versus Russian Spetsnaz," the Brit said, bravado still unwavering. "I've always believed your reputation was overblown."

"And what about Marine training, Benny?"

Tab emerged from the airlock.

"Do you think you can take on two Space Rangers? One of whom with a personal debt to settle with you?" he asked.

Before the traitorous head of security could reply, Heidi Mc-Cormack returned, followed by a large number of armed Fleet military personnel.

Claflin watched his security agents lower their laser rifles to the deck, and raise their hands to the ceiling.

He spun his pistol and offered the grip to Gregory.

"I surrender, and I formally request protection from Barnwell."

CHAPTER 27

FELL

"For a small ship, she certainly appears formidable," the Lisza Kaugh prince said, remarking on Cassandra's visage. "She looks like something that would come out of the ocean's depths and swallow you whole."

"She will bite," Coop agreed. "The crates?"

Yauni gestured for the two crates.

"The smaller one contains six of the new black diamond laser pistols. I did not include holsters, as ours would be much too big for you to wear. The larger crate holds a half-dozen updated laser rifles. Each crate contains a replacement diamond that is fully charged."

He handed Coop a data stick and told him, "This is the method of creating an electron bath used to recharge the diamonds. No one knows yet how many charges they will accept, but our scientists believe they will be around and working for many, many years.

"I realize you cannot win a war with a dozen new weapons," Yauni said, "but I hope when Earth sees what Rys can offer, they will want to open trade channels again. It pays to advertise."

He motioned for the third crate, and the smallest of the three.

"This is your surprise," he said to the human. "Some of our younger scientists are experimenting with building their own space-fold array. Now that they know it is possible and not a myth, it gives them something to do in their free time."

"Nathan Trent and Manny Hernandez told me the right combination of cut crystal, facet angles, proper laser intensity, from multiple lasers of different strengths, and how much electricity to mix in would take billions of years to luck upon," Coop said.

"Probably correct, but youngsters need distractions," Yauni replied. "Even failed experiments sometimes produce positive results. They experimented with a black diamond cut in what your people would describe as an Asscher. After they placed the cut crystal upright, they fired a laser into it from the front, and another from the rear. Instead of a space-fold, it created a force wall."

"A force wall, not a force field," Coop said.

"Similar, but only a wall," Yauni replied. "They could manipulate the wall forward or back by changing the intensity of the laser beams. But these were young scientists, so they had to try more. They spun the diamond in a vertical circle, and the wall became a well. They spun it in a horizontal circle and it became a short tunnel."

Yauni patted the crate, and said, "Then they spun it within a gyroscope, and they created a bubble. Not a large bubble. Maybe just big enough to cover a 75-foot by 75-foot area."

"An area that would cover a small ship, like this one," Coop said, indicating the Wraith, 72-feet long with a 56-foot wingspan."

"It can also be used to protect valuable assets, such as cannon emplacements," Yauni added. "Our cutters are in the process of shaping more black diamonds to ward strategic areas against attack. But it does have one draw-back we are attempting to solve."

"That would be?" Coop queried.

"If you are protected by the field, you cannot fire from within it," Yauni told him. "It works as a shield in both directions."

"Then why would you want to use it?" Coop asked. "It acts as a defense, but you cannot use your offensive capabilities."

"A temporary set-back," the prince assured him. "You would want it, especially aboard a space ship, because it is does not use electric or magnetic influence to operate. An EMP blast would have no effect. White Noise, that can disable your unique sonic forcefields, has no effect on a crystal bubble. Consider it a back-up to your primary system. It takes up little space, produces no radiation or electrical discharge, and is simple to operate."

"I would make a suggestion," Coop said, and Yauni indicated that he should continue. "If you plan on developing a force field generator that cannot be defeated by methods we now know about, you might want to come up with a method that will defeat it before you begin offering it for barter."

"In case the wrong people were to use it for the wrong purposes," Yauni said. "We agree, Captain Cooper. The prototype you now own is the only one that will leave Rys before we know how it can be turned off from the outside. Besides, it may be years before we can figure out how to send objects from inside to outside. It is a good thing the traders of Rys take a long view."

"I appreciate the gifts, Prince Yauni. Please give my regards to your parents. I hope relationships between my world and yours return to normal soon," he said.

Coop secured the crystal-force barrier components in Cassandra's rear storage. He removed two of the updated laser rifles and placed them within the ship's armory.

The six pistols and the remaining four rifles he turned over to Cindy Shah.

"You and Mags had time with Yauni's pistol. Comments?" he asked.

"They integrated a black diamond power source requiring a whole lot less housing," the former Space Marine and weapons expert replied. "Alloys were chosen for the pistol that handle the power and heat while remaining compact and light."

"Do you think we could make a few adjustments to the Serpa holsters, and modify them to work with the new design?"

"Damn Skippy," Cindy answered, adding a smile. Any weapon's expert loves a challenge. "Give me an hour. With the right tools, I'll compensate for the pistol's profile."

Coop left Cindy to her work, and found Hiro. The Japanese Space Ranger sat in the co-pilot seat listening to Mags as she listed components and capabilities of the personal fighter aloud from the pilot's seat.

"Comfortable?" he asked, lowering himself into the ship.

"Heaven," Mags answered. "She's a luxury sports car with cannons. Every girl's dream."

"Take Hiro for a ride," Coop said. "In and out of atmosphere. You can get a feel for how she handles, and Hiro can make sure you bring her back to me."

Mary Margaret Moore literally squealed as she jumped from the seat to bear-hug Cooper.

"Get off," she ordered. "We're ready for flight."

Hiro gave Coop a shaky thumbs-up before he exited through the roof access hatch. The tripod landing gear began to rise before he jumped from wing to surface. He ran to avoid the under-wash as Mags took the ship into an emergency liftoff. The tiny ship disappeared into the overcast sky within seconds.

He found Sky and Storm with Cindy at a table set up outside of a storage hut. They were joined by a half-dozen Earth ex-soldiers and a large land vehicle. The truck performed as a mobile service platform. It was backed up to the table.

When Cindy saw Coop she said, "I couldn't figure out a way to get the Serpa to take the front array box and allow a quick draw. I called on a couple of gunsmiths who stayed behind. One is also a machinist."

She handed Coop the laser pistol. The rectangular forward array box, that also acted as a grip, had an added hinge. The array-box rested flush against the bottom of the pistol barrel.

Next she handed him a modified Serpa Y-holster. Coop unhooked his belt buckle to thread the Serpa through. He secured the holster to his thigh with velcro straps. Finally, he placed the pistol in the holster.

Quicker than a cat, he drew the pistol. As it snapped into firing position, an inertia hinge released the forward array. The weapon ready to fire.

"Push the box a bit forward, then up to lock it under the barrel," a short, compact man with buzz cut and stubble on his chin instructed. Coop followed the directions. The box locked in place. "Now you can holster it," the man said.

"What do you think?" Cindy asked.

"Damn Skippy," he replied, using her phrase. "How many have you re-machined?"

"Just the one," she admitted. "John and Boris," indicating the two gunsmiths, "just completed the hinge action, and I just finished the minor changes to the Serpa. Give us two hours and we'll have all six sets ready for you."

"I only need two," Coop said. "The others stay with you."

"Well, as long as you're leaving them, I think the three of us may spend a few days in R and D," Cindy said with a smile. "We have an extra diamond for each pistol and rifle. I think we might just try and reverse engineer the mechanics. Let's see if we can build our own."

"My family and I have been working on the problem of communicating with Kennedy or Elie undetected," Sky said. "We've incorporated a second tachyon beam to the HATCH transmitter. One with a completely different signature. The second transmission is a shadow following the primary beam. We can transmit a message and only someone looking specifically for the shadow transmission will recognize it."

"You did that in two hours?" Coop asked in awe.

"Actually, my family started working on the problem when you first mentioned it," she told him. "ASparilla has tinkered with such a covert ability for a while," she admitted. "We must have the physical STORM-HATCH systems in order to make the changes. Right now Cassandra will be the only ship capable of utilizing the private channel to both send and receive."

"Which is great for keeping our contacts secret," Coop said. "It doesn't get us in contact with Kennedy or Elie."

"Storm and I believe Kennedy may be able to modify the STORM aboard the 109 to receive the secondary messages, if she knows a secret transmission is present," Sky replied.

"We would have to tell her, and that would be overheard," Coop countered.

"Unless a secret code existed," Storm said. "When we rescued Sky's family from the bunker on Fell, and we learned about the Mischene, I remember how you kept Captain Canedee from panicking when we returned."

"We pretended we never got close to the planet and the mission was a bust," Coop responded.

"You warned Kennedy not to broadcast the 109's scans revealing that Angel 7 returned with more lifeforms than went out," Storm said.

"*Just another rodeo,*" Coop said. "The code phrase we developed that meant go along for the ride. Play along."

"I will send a message to Nathan Trent," Sky said, "and ask him to pass a personal message to Elie. It will include the phrase 'just another rodeo,' connected to Fell."

"Elie may not understand, but she's bright enough to keep silent," Coop said. "Kennedy monitors every communication, and she will know the message is actually for her."

"We will continually broadcast short bursts to the 109, but with no obvious message. Hopefully it will appear as simple distortions or static," Storm continued the plan. "If Kennedy figures out the riddle, and can access the shadow, she will devise a way to contact us. Do we try?"

"Go for it," Coop answered. "If we don't hear anything back, we're no worse off."

Coop pushed and thrust into Sky, who lay beneath him, matching his enthusiasm with her own. Storm did things with her mouth and tongue that alternated between intense pleasure to simple intensity.

He kept switching from keeping his weight off Sky by propping himself on elbows, to giving in, pressing his weight against her breasts. Storm rubbed her chest against his butt, slowly working her way along his back. He felt her body lift off, a final push by her knees driving him deeper into her cousin. For a brief second he considered pulling out of Sky to switch to Storm, but the thought vanished as Storm repositioned herself on the covers layered across the floor.

Leaning to his right, his face disappeared between her thighs. Storm began her low moaning at the same time Sky's legs locked around his low back. Storm screamed. Coop barely heard, her thighs pressed tightly against his ears.

He did feel Sky's orgasm, and her fingernails rip along his shoulder blades. Ready himself, he held for Storm to climax. When she bucked, he released.

He lifted off of Sky, moved atop Storm, and greedily plunged his full length into her. Lifting his hips, his hands grabbed Storm's muscled legs and propped them over his shoulders. With her tilted up, he pounded the blue beauty until he orgasmed a second time.

Storm, eyes blazing orange and red, breathing too rapidly to make her normal noises when having sex, bit down on his chest, fangs piercing the skin. She climaxed as the taste of his blood dripped onto her tongue.

Later, as the three lay together, recovering, Storm said, "Sky needs to tell you something."

"This may not be the best time," Sky said.

"Sky has always wanted children," Storm said.

"True," Sky whispered. "Maybe not as many as my mother, but at least three or four."

"But humans and Fellen cannot mate," Storm said. "The sex is possible."

"The sex is wonderful," Sky interjected.

"But she cannot have your children," Storm added.

"I thought about adopting, and I am interested, but I know I want the experience of birthing," Sky said.

"Sky believes it is important that you know this, and that she loves you."

"I do love you," Sky whispered.

"But continuing a relationship would be for sex alone."

"The sex is wonderful," Sky repeated. "But I must consider a Fellen as my husband. Eventually."

"Since everyone on Fell realizes Sky and I spend all of our time with you, it may cause Fellen males to maintain a distance."

"You can be intimidating," Sky completed Storm's line of reasoning. "It may be best if we begin to spend less time together."

"But I have never wanted children," Storm continued.

"True," Sky said. "Since we were small she has promised she would never be tied down by family."

"I love my family," Storm whispered. "But I want to experience as many worlds as I can. I want to take risks. I would not do such things if I had the responsibilities of a mother."

"Storm enjoys the sex even more knowing she will never become pregnant," Sky explained.

"The sex is wonderful," Storm agreed. "I will continue to have what Mags calls '*wild, monkey sex*' with you for as long as you will have me."

"And I will continue to have sex with you, just not as often, and, perhaps, not as obvious. People will begin to see us as friends, not mates," Sky informed him.

"I also have no problem sharing," Storm added. "It is comfortable sharing you with Sky. We have shared everything for as long as I can remember. But I could see someone else joining us. I really like Elie."

"She does like Elie," Sky said. "But it does not have to be Elie."

"No," Storm chimed in. "I'm sure if you want to have sex with another female, I would find her attractive as well. You have good taste."

"Speaking of," Sky said, her head lowering. Storm took the opportunity to straddle him, pushing her chest into his face.

CHAPTER 28

"It's been two months," General Kasper Trewellan, the Prophet's military commander, said. He addressed Atticus Soren, the Sacred Prophet of the Tahbita aboard a stolen battlecruiser converted into his flying palace and command center. "What are we waiting on? Willmer could open the gates of every military installation on AF3 and we can finish this in days. We could then advance on AF1 and AF2 and conquer both with no resistance."

"Patience, General," the Prophet said from his throne. Construction workers combined twelve cabins, six each on two decks, and turned them into one grand chamber with ceilings twice their normal height. "We have no need to hurry. The longer we keep them pinned in their cages, the more likely many will simply turn themselves in and join our side."

"The rest of the system sits there," Trewellan waved his hand at a high def screen covering twelve-feet of wall. It displayed the view from the space ship looking away from AF3 and toward AF2.

"And goes nowhere," Soren responded. "They have a pitiful few patrol boats and launches. Two battlecruisers afraid to move."

The Prophet pushed his long while hair back from his eyes. Over the years he allowed it to grow until it hung past his shoulder blades.

"Do not fret, General. If Earth does not send its ships within the next two weeks, we will complete the work here. Once we have Aster system and all of its resources, we will then press on to engage Earth in their system. I would prefer to meet them here, where we enjoy all of the advantages, but sooner or later we will meet these new heretics."

The Mischene who spoke as a prophet but decided to live as a sultan, asked, "How are the new defenses coming. Even if the fools from Earth do not arrive, I would like my new home safe from anyone who does."

"The scientists have been inventive," Trewellan admitted. "By keeping the wormhole gates active around the vortex between AF3 and AF2 we flooded the region with ionized particles. The special satellites designed to broadcast white noise are in place. Sound cannot exist in a vacuum. The ionized particles' molecules provide the necessary conduit."

The General knew Soren did not care about the basic science behind the trap under construction, but he continued the lesson.

"We know from after-action reports, Earth ships create a unique sonic force field for protection. It appears generated by the engines they use when operating within the gravity fields of a star system. Your father's scientists combined a white noise generator with an oxygen bubble field. They hardened the load to ride a plasma burst. The white noise dampened the enemy ships' force fields long enough for the plasma blasts to be effective, but it was a short-range option. The bubbles degenerated too quickly."

Warming to his own voice, the dark-skinned Mischene of medium height and straight posture stood before the view screen, looking into space as if he could see the relatively minuscule satellites in orbit.

"Using the technology they employed during the defense of Fell, our scientists created a method of deploying white noise over a large expanse. It allows all of our weapons to work against a sonic-protected ship. It also disrupts communications. Even if the enemy used conventional shielding they would still find it difficult, perhaps impossible, to communicate and coordinate during an attack."

As Trewellan talked, two red-skinned Hana Kay girls entered the chamber, delivering the Prophet wine and food. The General noted the two wore Zenge shock collars around their thin necks, partially hidden by the long black tresses flowing down and across their shoulders. Soren recently took a perverse liking to the Hana Kay females. Because of the species' strength of will, it required shock collars to keep them under control.

"If we can lure the enemy ships into the vortex created by the converging gravity wells, it will reduce their ability to escape tenfold. They will be slower and easier to target," he continued with his brief.

"We don't have a defense yet against the new particle-beam weapon they used to defend Rys," he admitted. "Our data indicates it does get extremely hot, especially when they combine a plasma load with the particle beam. Our people believe one weakness is the weapon must be discharged once it cycles on, otherwise it will create a thermal explosion. We do not know how long the shut-down procedure takes, or, once discharged, how long until the weapon is available again, but the estimate is hours."

Soren fingered the remote device needed to activate a shock collar. The small remote worked only within line-of-sight. He was practicing new ways of getting obedience from his subjects. With the wine and food trays placed on a table near his throne, he clicked the remote. The two girls jerked and immediately began removing the light frocks they wore. Both nude beneath, but much too skinny for Trewellan's taste. He used Hana Kay when given to him by the Prophet in the Zenge system, but only because they were the only females available. Once back in the Aster system, he had his choice of any Mischene woman from among those captured on AF3 and the moon bases.

"What about the fact their weapons can penetrate our own force fields?" Soren asked. He keyed the remote with a different combination of clicks, and watched the two girls slowly gyrate in a mockery of a sexy dance.

"They provided us a solution," the Mischene officer replied. While not overly attracted to the red-skinned, undernourished girls, he was getting turned on by the way the Prophet used the shock collar to force them to perform without verbal orders. He planned to pick one up on his way back to his cabin. There, a rather buxom woman with long, silky white hair waited. Chained, but that was still a form of waiting. Scratches on his arms continued to sting. Reminders of his time spent with her earlier. The shock collar and remote could save his knuckles as well.

"The solution?" Soren prompted, pulling Trewellan from his erotic thoughts.

"They were able to pin-point where our weapons targeted the Osperantue cruiseship, and they enhanced the depth of the force field in those locations. Data from the battle-cruiser that escaped indicated they could deflect only four or five simultaneous hits. More than that, and the cruiser's weapons actually did more damage. The shields weakened in other areas allowed projectiles easier entry."

Soren forced the Hana Kay to fondle each other. They hated their actions, and tears flowed freely from their sunken eyes. Trewellan felt an erection growing. The Sacred Prophet watched without a display of emotion. He clicked and the two stopped and dropped to their knees.

"Our engineers and technicians have used the data collected to make improvements to our battle tactics. Our software packages aboard the battlecruisers, and the Class One destroyers are capable of protecting them against multiple strikes using the same method the Star Gazer employed.

"The Class One and Class Two carriers are too large, and we do not have dynamo replacements sufficient to make them completely padded by the software updates. They can protect against a direct strike, but it's a slower process to get the extra density to the targeted area quickly."

The officer became more fidgety with erotic excitement as he watched the two girls resign themselves to their fate. Defeat washed over them.

"The refit ships, launches, and ancillary vessels do not have sufficient power to provide force fields," he concluded.

The Prophet rose, his kaftan bulging slightly below his waste, his eyes greedy as he clicked his remote. The two girls jerked and dropped their heads to the floor in supplication.

"Thank you, General. You can go now," he said.

The general left quickly, deciding on the shortest route to the armory supply, and from there to his cabin.

FELL

"Kennedy received the shadow message," Sparks told him.

Coop arrived to the command hut minutes after receiving word Sky's brother had good news regarding the attempt to covertly contact the PT-109.

"How do you know?"

"We're monitoring all communications at Space Fleet," the Fellen engineer informed him. Coop did not bother to ask how. No race in the galaxy excelled with the skill the AS tribe on Fell showed with communication technology. "Kennedy sent a one-word dispatch to Patterson. It said 'Understood.' When the Com Center in Toronto asked for clarification, Kennedy told them the message was an internal response and she crossed it into the SH back to Patterson by mistake."

"A mistake Kennedy would never make," Coop said. "Send her the updates on the Camarilla. Tell her about Hawks and Harrison, and only Elie and Genna can be read in. We don't know if their affiliation with the group will endanger the CVBG. Watch, but do not act."

Storm reported the Space Fleet Group's arrival at the edge of the Aster system.

"The four Earth ships entered natural space, and the Fairchild immediately began sending hails across all systems and channels towards AF3, the other inhabited planets and moons, and all space craft in the system," she told the group convened in the command hut.

Storm and Sparks monitored a number of communication systems. Several added within the last twenty-four hours. Coop, Sky, Hiro, Mags, and Cindy stood.

"It's called a Carrier Battle Group or CVBG," Coop said aloud. "CV is a designation for a carrier with aircraft, or space fighters in this case. Can you create a holo-representation?"

To Storm's right, above a twelve-by-twelve table top, the Aster system appeared. The view spun slowly and zoomed to show the CVBG ships.

To this point the monitored transmissions between the CVBG and Space Fleet, as well as communications between the ships, consisted of bland reports on personnel, operations, and readiness. Sparks and Star spent the previous day adapting hardware and software to eavesdrop on the mission from every conceivable angle. Kennedy's awareness of the covert tachyon particle beam riding the normal signals provided contact. Now they took precautions so no one else discovered they monitored communications.

Private conversations between Hawks, Singletary, and Governor Guy Arcand regarding diplomatic protocols to be followed when the time came to confront the Mischene religious fanatic proved mundane. The officers and the diplomats downplaying the dangers the Prophet presented. Coop wanted badly to intercede more than once, but knew he could not allow anyone to realize he eavesdropped.

"All four ships of the CVBG, exited into natural space outside the systems's star-gravity bubble," Storm said.

Hiro took a seat at a station to his right, monitoring a boot-legged copy of telemetry scans of Aster system made by the Earth ships. He could see a compilation of data on natural and artificial elements within the system. His expertise in planetology also included a grasp of the dynamics within a star system.

"The Aster system is interesting," Hiro said, studying the numbers on his monitor, comparing scan data with the pictographs above the table. "The star is a main-sequence G-type. A G2V2, based on spectral scans. It is informally referred to as a yellow dwarf. Earth's Sol is the same type, but a G2V only. The Aster star radiates more heat further into space," explaining the difference.

"There are six planets orbiting the sun, each massive enough to hold hydrostatic equilibrium, effectively meaning a spheroid, and each capable of dominating its own orbit. Currently, all six planets are located on the same side of the star. The closest is a dead world caught in the gravity well of the star. Similar to Mercury, but larger, and at its orbital apex."

As Hiro informed the group about the system's current configuration, Cindy Shah manipulated the holo-presentation to provide visual clarity.

"The second planet would be Aster Farum 1, or AF1," the Japanese said. Cindy zoomed the planet forward. "Far enough from the star to support life, but a harsh environment. A mineral-rich planet. The inhabitants would need be extremely hardy. Skin colors in the red to possibly purple range to protect against radiation burn. The atmospheric layers are dense, which helps shield the planet, but the troposphere is arid. Water and plant life enough to support a limited population. It does control three moons. Twins with habitats and a single barren one. The twins appear to be the location for ship-building. Scans indicate a high degree of technology. The information UEC received from the drones sent through the wormholes said research installations are also located on both moons."

He looked up to see if Coop was listening. Coop nodded and gave him a thumb's up to continue.

"AF2, the third planet, is the most similar to Earth," he said. "Continents, islands, saline oceans, and plenty of fresh water. Vegetation, animal life. One moon. This is where they mine for gas," he said. "The wormhole drones used to contact Earth came from here."

Cindy read from a flat-screen display embedded in the holo-table, "Four sentient races. Advanced technology. High intelligence."

Storm, Sparks, or possibly Star forwarded the information delivered by the drones to the flat-screen, a voice-analytic matching the details provided to Hiro's descriptions.

"AF3 is next, home of the Mischene and three other races. All with dark skin because the planet is actually quite cold. Any colder and it might not support life. The genetic-mutation of their skin helps retain heat and acts as an insulator. Skin tone seems to have once mattered depending on where you lived on the planet, but now it's just another hereditary feature. Three moons. Currently all three on the AF2 side of the planet. One moon has a viable atmosphere. It is the location of several ship-building installations and support industries."

Hiro combined the data from the telemetry and his studies of the system to give everyone a complete picture of the region the CVBG entered.

"The fifth planet is named Sperus. Similar to Jupiter, but only two moons. One does support life, but has an extremely cold environment. The Mischene established ship-building here as well. It appears the industry of choice for Aster system is building space ships.

"The sixth planet is a gas giant with four major moons and seven minor ones. The surface is volatile with gas storms and such."

"Anything out of the ordinary?" Coop asked. Not that anything in a newly discovered galaxy of living systems would ever be considered ordinary by people from Earth.

"A massive amount of ionization along the AF1 to AF3 and AF2 corridors," he said. "The system utilizes an amazing twelve wormhole gates, but unless they are operational, I can't actually pinpoint their location. That many wormholes, even though inactive at the moment, could result in the large quantity of ions."

The planetologist brought his hands closer, providing a panoramic display of the entire system.

"The locations for AF2, AF3 and their moons currently place them in their minimum orbit intersection distance. With all of these inhabited objects at MOID, travel times, even at standard speeds, would be fairly short."

"Ships?" Coop asked.

"CVBG just outside of the sixth planet, the gas giant," he replied. "Ten Mischene battlecruisers and eight smaller patrol-type ships active in the system. Two of the battlecruisers and the eight small ships orbit AF2. If the data from the communications drones is correct, these are Mischene Loyalist vessels. Escapees from the Prophet's invasion," he surmised.

"Two battlecruisers are on station three-million-miles beyond AF3 and another thirty-seven million miles from AF1. Communications indicate one of these is the Prophet's ship and the other an escort. The other four Prophet-controlled battlecruisers are in high-altitude orbit around AF3."

Hiro swiped across the screen and checked updated data. "There should be six more battlecruisers in the Prophet's group," he mused. "The tactical data is dated, and they could have left the system."

"Or on a surface somewhere," Coop said.

Hiro watched the telemetry from scans trillions of miles away, seeing what personnel on the Space Fleet ships received within seconds. "The four ships around AF3 are breaking orbit," he told the group.

"Moving toward?" Coop asked.

"Two making way for the AF3-AF1 corridor. Two broke towards AF2, but not on a direct trajectory. Transmissions were picked up by the Pegasus," Hiro said and continued, "The Prophet ordered the four ships around AF3 to disengage and move to, and I quote, 'non-threatening distances.'"

Hiro tapped an icon and reported, "Only other artificial signatures in Aster space are satellites. Usual variety around the inhabited planets and moons, and a scattering of non-orbital in space between AF1, AF2, and AF3. Four non-orbital between AF3 and Sperus. Likely communications buoys to relay messages with less solar interference. Transmitter satellites would improve the time between sending and receiving messages."

ASTER SYSTEM

"Admiral Hawks is in contact with the Prophet," Kennedy informed Captain Casalobos. "He confirmed his position as representative of the United Earth Council and our mission as peaceful," she said, condensing the back-and-forth to its basics.

"There is a four-hour time lapse," the AI added. "Two hours from transmit to reception and two more for the reply. It is inefficient," she said, and actually sounded annoyed at the use of such dated technology. "The Admiral is saying quite a lot, but nothing not already discussed during mission planning. I will inform you when the reply is received."

The AI cut the conversation off, reminding Elie of when Coop once told her he was never entirely sure who had seniority aboard the 109.

Elie sat on her bed when Kennedy delivered her next update.

"The conversations between The Prophet and the Admiral appear," and she hesitated, "productive. The Prophet presents as a reasonable leader. He claims he is fighting the Mischene apparatus that set him and his followers up as," she hesitated, making sure she heard the translation properly, and finished "patsies for his father's desire for galactic expansion."

"The Prophet's take on the arrival of the Fleet group?" Elie asked.

"He welcomed us," Kennedy replied. "Admiral Hawks asked for a cessation of all hostile actions within the system, safe passage for our ships, and to meet with the Prophet at Aster Farum 3."

It was frustrating to wait hours for more information. Finally Kennedy interrupted Elie's fitful sleep.

"The Prophet's reply has been received by the Fairchild. He accepted an offer for a ceasefire. He guaranteed our safety while in the Aster system. His only request was to repeat the meeting must occur in open space away from the planet. He's afraid that planetary defenses still in Mischene loyalists' hands could target them, especially since he ordered his ship's to leave orbit from the planet."

"Did Hawks ask about the vortex?" Elie asked.

"It is called the Resa Asteri Major Vortex," Kennedy answered. "Resa Asteri Major is the name of their system star. The vortex is a naturally occurring phenomenon. The gravity anomalies make navigation difficult. The Prophet told Hawks the superior capabilities of Earth's ships, especially our speed, will be hampered within the vortex. If we were to become aggressive, holding talks within the vortex will allow him the opportunity to escape."

"Seems prudent," Elie replied. "Coop never trusted the Mischene, and he trusted the Prophet even less. Experience with religious fanatics after the pandemic and while trying to unite the world under one governing body demonstrated time and again, they told you exactly what you wanted to hear. When they were ready, they attacked. The less prepared and more gullible you were, the easier for them to inflict maximum damage. What's your analysis of the vortex?"

"It is a natural occurrence, created by the proximity of a number of large orbital bodies and their placement relative to the sun," the AI answered. "Data from Osperantue, Fellen, Rys, and the Aster drones all agree the pie-shaped wedge of space is dangerous for ships, especially smaller vessels. The gravity distortions tax power plants and result in less maneuverability. Communications are sometimes affected, especially messages traveling across the vortex boundaries. I do not believe tachyon-based communications will be lost, and if the group ships remain near to each other, basic communications systems should be unaffected."

"The 109 and 99 are the smaller ships," Elie said. "Can we handle the vortex?"

"Yes. Fighters and shuttles could be caught in dangerous waves, or between gravity whirlpools, but the larger vessels, while less efficient, will be operational."

"How long until the group reaches AF3?"

"The Admiral informed the Prophet our ships will utilize space-fold and emerge on the near side of AF3 in twenty-four hours. At maximum speed, we could reach the planet in seventeen-hours. We could be in position seven hours before expected . . . if Hawks wishes," she added.

"Hawks just issued orders for all ships to head for AF3 and engage space-fold," she informed her former Captain. "The Admiral ordered Pegasus to lead once we reenter natural space. The Fairchild will follow. The PT-109 and PT-99 are assigned rear and flanks, in case of a sneak attack. Orders are to reenter natural space 250,000 miles from AF3 in eighteen hours, not twenty-four," she said.

CHAPTER 29

Hawks sat in his command chair on the Fairchild. The three walls depicting the region of space around his ship, including a view of Aster Farum 3's southern pole, two of its three moons, and the Pegasus dead ahead. The PT-99 and the PT-109 sailed behind him, on either flank.

Noa Tal, dressed in her one-piece flight suit and with her brown hair hanging in a loose tail around her left shoulder, was present and providing the details of the coming encounter with Atticus Soren, Sacred Prophet of the Tahbita. Hawks was only half listening, more upset that Tal wasn't dressed in a Space Fleet uniform more appropriate for his bridge. If she took half an interest, she could be an attractive woman. Her flight suit did her no favors, but even it could not hide the ample swell of her chest, or the small waist. Some make-up to calm down her Jewish looks, and he could find himself more interested in what she had to say.

Tal was giving him her exasperated look again. He was supposed to remark on whatever she had said.

"Your opinion?" he asked. The question always a good save to use when he had not been paying attention in a meeting.

"I wouldn't trust him to walk my dog," she said. "He wants us to ease out into open space and meet him about 2.5-million miles off AF3. He will leave his other battlecruisers in formation where they currently rest, and he will sail alone to the meeting point. That puts AF3 on our rear six, and we have no idea what weapons he might have there. It leaves us out-numbered six to four, regardless of the distance. I don't like it."

"Haven't we been in touch with the hold-outs on AF3?" he asked, turning to his current communications officer. The LtJG whose name he could not recall, but who had the right uniform and the right shape to hold his attention, simply nodded. "I guess I didn't actually ask a question that required a verbal reply," he said, peeved. "Didn't the Admiral in charge of the military forces still loyal to the Mischene not aligned with the Prophet inform us that they still had control of all planetary defense systems, including laser and plasma cannon capable of reaching ships in their space?"

"Yessir, they did say that," she replied. "He also said they were running out of food and water and could not hold out much longer."

"Well we didn't come prepared to fight over 350,000 Zenge on the planet's surface," Hawks replied. "Ten or twelve companies of Rangers and Marines might take and defend one installation, but not the entire planet. Do we have targeting data on the emplacements?"

"Yessir," came the reply from his Operations and Tactical officer, Lt. Michael Hanson, formerly of Seattle, Washington. He was also dressed properly in Space Fleet grays that showed off his muscled arms and tight butt. Hawks was always one to taste the fruit, regardless of the branch it fell from. He had already tasted Hanson, both on MSD and during the trip to the Aster system. Girl or boy, as long as they pleased his eye. "If requested we have missiles and torpedoes capable of knocking out every cannon on the surface," Hanson finished.

"I believe it has been demonstrated several times Space Fleet ships, even our smallest, are capable of taking on and defeating several Mischene battlecruisers," he said to Tal. "That prior to upgrading our weapons and communications systems. It was before we had Spirit Wing. It was also before the Fairchild was recommissioned and refitted as a carrier."

It was when Daniel Cooper faced them, before he was run off by the likes of you, Tal thought to herself.

"Coms," still couldn't put a name to the face, "inform Captain Pare´ the Fairchild will take the lead. Inform all three Captains we will make for the rendezvous at a modest 100,000mph. We don't need to display all of our capabilities. Navigation, how long until we reach the designated location at that speed?"

"A tick over one day," Tal said, doing the math in her head. Something any good ship's captain could do.

"A tick over one day," he repeated, not pleased with his XO. "That will give us time to gather as much intel as possible before the actual meeting. Coms, inform the Prophet's people that we are moving towards his location, and we should arrive in a tick over one day, or you may want to provide a more precise time, since 'tick' may not translate well."

He crossed his legs and sat back, having won the verbal war. "Captain Tal, you obviously feel more comfortable with your squadron. Perhaps you should return and make sure they are ready. You may also have Lieutenant Leigh, per your request for transfer. I have sufficiently trained personnel for my bridge without her."

"Thank you, Admiral." Noa Tal left to collect Harper and return to where she was, indeed, more comfortable. Which was anywhere that prick was not.

"Captain Paré requests to speak with you, Admiral." the coms officer informed Hawks. He did not want to talk with the overly confident commander of the Pegasus, but rank included responsibility.

"Put her through," he said.

"Admiral, we continue to receive messages from AF3," she said. "Signals were bounced around the system until we received a re-transmit from a patrol boat near AF2. Admiral Lexton is adamant you should not trust the Prophet, and not accept a meeting inside the Resa Vortex."

"Is the Admiral still begging for reinforcements as well?" Hawks asked.

"He continues to request assistance," she confirmed. "He says many of their military bases cannot hold out even a couple of days longer. He's afraid they will be turned over to the Zenge and the Prophet's Mischene officers."

"Captain Paré, AF3 is behind us," he said. "That the Mischene who started all of this are overrun by the Mischene who want to end it is a Mischene problem. Our primary mission is to prevent expansion to our solar system. I do not give a damn which group comes out on top in the Aster system, though it would appear the Prophet controls the game.

"My task assignment is make a deal with the Prophet. I will attempt to gain considerations for those trapped on AF3, however, I will not jeopardize Earth's safety. Admiral Lexton chose his side, and he must live with that choice. Is there anything else, Captain?"

"We are beginning to experience the effects of the gravitational irregularities created by the vortex," she said, changing the subject, recognizing Hawks would take no counsel on his diplomatic mission. "Nothing substantial thus far, but the deeper we venture into this area, the more difficult it will be to maintain speed and heading."

"Is it dangerous?" he asked, more concerned about this than baseless warnings of treachery.

"The chief engineers on the four ships are conferencing regarding the phenomenon," she reported. Hawks wondered why he did not receive a report of a multi-ship discussion, but kept the thought to himself. "The over-lapping gravity wells create drag, and we will experience sudden pulls that can shift our course, but they seem confident the ships can handle both. Chief Camden on the 109 describes it as 'sailing rough seas.'"

"Is the Prophet's battlecruiser still on course?" he asked.

"It is, and it is further into the region. It appears to handle the gravity distortions with little effort," she replied. "With all of space to choose from, I still wonder why he would want to meet in such a hostile location."

"Because he feels it evens the field of play," Hawks replied. "While it causes him more problems relative to communications and systems, it makes it less likely we will engage weapons and attempt a sneak attack on him. He admitted his reasoning when he delivered the coordinates for the meeting. Make sure everyone remains on course," he said. "Rough seas will not keep us from our appointment. Hawks, out."

Aboard the Destroyer Pegasus, LCMD Berenger, who stood on the bridge during Pare's short conversation with Admiral Hawks, said, "Overconfident, isn't he?"

"More than a little," Rachelle replied. "Not the best attitude when going into battle."

"He doesn't expect a battle," her XO answered. "He's already won the war and is counting his medals."

"A bit snide for a career administrator, Commander," she replied smiling. She was not sure of Berenger when he joined the crew as her First, but their time together proved productive. The man tendered a career in military paper-pushing prior to his assignment to the Pegasus, but he soon exhibited smart, capable, and honest traits. Rachelle could deal with that type of person.

"Sorry, Captain. I spoke out of place," said with no hint of contrition. The junior officers staffing consoles on the bridge all smiled. They also found their XO and his forthright manner refreshing.

"We're definitely experiencing drag," the systems operator reported. "Engineering increased power in order to maintain speed. Nothing drastic, but scans indicate we will be forced to compensate more as we get closer to the coordinates for the meeting. Why don't we let the Prophet come to us?" he asked aloud.

"Politics," Berenger answered. "We must show our willingness to meet with Soren more than half-way, as this is currently his domain. The actual positioning of our ships is a metaphor expressing our desire to negotiate and recognition of his importance."

"Deep," Rachelle said. "Bullshit, but deep bullshit."

Her comment elicited chuckles from more than one of the officers on the bridge. Especially amusing when you put the words with the seemingly calm and controlled young woman who sat in the Captain's chair. People often found it difficult to put the fifty-plus years of her life and experiences with the twenty-five year old face and body.

"I notice you never call him The Prophet," she continued. "Always just Soren."

"I know my history, Captain," he said. "I will not give title to a despot. Especially one that is a religious fanatic and an expansionist. He is not a prophet. He's just one more power-mad zealot wrapped in ministerial cloaks. That he is an alien doesn't change the dynamic. He has no more divine right to force his ideals onto others than the religious fanatics that have plagued our own world for centuries. When your beliefs require a gun be used to spread them, they are fundamentally wrong." He turned to his older, younger-looking commander, and added, "I know . . . more deep bull."

"Not at all, Number One," she replied. "Soren is a dangerous person on a deadly and destructive mission. If calling him Prophet makes us less aware of his true nature, then let's not give him that advantage. Do we all agree?" she asked aloud.

"AYE!" came the unanimous reply across the bridge. The mandate was soon communicated unofficially throughout the ship, and within a few short hours the men and women of Pegasus referred to Atticus Soren as Atticus Soren. A small thing in the totality of the situation, but it did more to bring this newly formed crew together than all of the drills and meetings accomplished.

In the hangar of the Fairchild, Noa Tal's concerns centered on the confluence of gravity wells they would encounter. A big ship could navigate through forces capable of twisting them off course. The situation presented more serious issues for a ship the size of a Spirit fighter. A small craft intersecting the wrong confluence at just the right time could be ripped apart, even with sonic force fields.

She called her pilots together to discuss the problems they might face in the turbulence surrounding them. The informal meeting occurred on the flight deck. The six pilots sat on the deck in a circle. Noa; to her right, Ryan Fox, Jon-Jon, Harper, William Story, a recent space pilot and former Can-Am Air Force pilot, and finally, Ahmed al Yassin, former Kuwaiti fighter pilot, on her left.

"None of us have experience with these conditions," she said. "It's one thing to fly a jet through air turbulence, but the gravitational fluctuations in this part of the system have never been seen before by ships from Earth."

"Any suggestions from those who study such things?" Ahmed asked.

"None, really," she answered. "Scientists weren't brought on the mission. The Admirals thought bunks were needed for soldiers. Hawks refuses to send the latest data to Trent Industries for detailed analysis. He's afraid of leaks."

"What leaks?" Fox asked. "Some unknown enemy finds out we don't know anything about multiple gravity wells converging at a single location, or that our scientists may or may not be able to help us navigate through them? What could someone possibly do with that intelligence?"

"I asked a similar question, but was told to deal with the issue using the assets we have," she replied. "Since I consider Kennedy and Rosy assets, I've had them look into the phenomenon. Between the two, there's more pure intellect than a dozen scientists."

No one asked, expecting Tal to continue with what she discovered. "The two AI's report besides gravity wells converging, there are ionized gas clouds with active electron particles. The particulate matter, which may be ionized or charged, creates the potential for communications and scanner interference. We could go from a little static to no coms at all. With the scanners affected, we might not be able to avoid gravitational shifts in densities. Those unexpected variations will certainly act negatively on our ability to maneuver."

"If we do detect high density areas, and avoid them, we should be able to operate close to normal," Ryan Fox half-said and half-asked.

"If we are forced to launch, it will depend on what we launch into," Noa replied. "I would hope we could choose to exit in an area with lower particulate matter, allowing us to scan, then map routes to avoid traps. If we launch under duress, we may not have that option."

"Will operational and flight systems be hampered?" Harper asked.

"Kennedy and Rosy agree systems will be less efficient, but remain functional. They believe the hulls of the ships will prevent interference with internal systems that remain internal. Communications and scanners rely on exterior access, and will experience more problems. The sonic force fields should also provide added protection. We'll be able to fly and fight, but we may be flying blind at times. The heads-up displays and the virtual windscreens require optics and scan data, and those rely on external sensors."

"We may be forced to stick our heads out and take a look around," Jon-Jon, the least serious member of her crew, said.

"With those big ears of yours flopping around, any aliens who sees you will think a dog came along for a ride and was enjoying the wind," Harper joked. She and Jon-Jon original crew on the PT-109, teammates at the Battle for Fell, and friends before either stationing.

"Communicate," Tal returned the meeting to a more serious tone. "We help each other, and the big ships can provide info as well."

"The major danger is gravity distortions," William 'Wild Bill' Story said. 'Wild Bill' received his call sign because he was anything but wild. He represented the serious side to Jon-Jon's easy-does-it nature. "What happens if we fly into a confluence?"

"According to Kennedy, it will depend on the strength of the converging waves, or the type of distortion created," she said. It was an answer, but it did not tell anyone anything. She continued, trying to put it to them as pilots. "You know how turbulence affects you dependent on where it derives from. Cross-winds can knock you sideways, and during a landing, flip you completely over and throw you into the ground. Higher up you could get caught in elevators. One might send you 5,000feet straight up, and then send you into a free-fall for the deck."

They all nodded. Every pilot experienced at least some degree of flying through turbulence.

"If you get into a storm, it can be a roller-coaster. You can be in clear air, and start rolling and humping like teenagers in the back seat of a car." This brought smiles, even from 'Wild Bill.'

"If we don't see them, and we can't avoid them, we have to adjust according to what they do to the ship," Harper said. "Sounds like real flying."

"Except we are talking about gravity wells belonging to orbital bodies," Tal warned. "You're the fly. You might get through, or a foot might come down on you, or you might get swatted against a wall, or you might only get your wings pulled off."

"What you're saying is, we deal with turbulence as best we can, avoid it if possible, and if it destroys us, not our problem any more," Jon-Jon summed up.

"Plus, if we are in a hostile situation, you have to avoid enemy fire, protect the big ships, fight back, and not get dead by more mundane means," Noa added.

"Piece of cake," Jon-Jon said, standing up and brushing off his seat. "Not all of this," he suddenly said. "This is a shit-storm ready to rain all over us. They have fresh chocolate cake in the mess. Anybody like a piece?"

Captain Tal laughed under her breath and also rose, calling an end to the informal meeting. "I think we should all get a piece," she said, and headed for the elevators.

Jon-Jon helped Harper to her feet and asked, "She does mean cake when she says 'get a piece,' right?"

Harper Leigh shook her head at her friend and followed the Israeli to the elevators.

In the open confines of the hydroponics bay forward the SFPT-109, Franklin Delano Roosevelt, Sam Harrington, gazed at the expanse known as the Resat Asteri Vortex. This one area of the ship boasted an actual view of space. All the plants removed before the mission got underway. No need for botanists or techs to watch over plants not there. He stood alone with his thoughts, his memories, and his decisions.

CHAPTER 30

Coop left the house he shared with Sky and Storm to make the short walk to the airfield and space port, the purpose for Harmony's existence. In the light of the mid-day sun he could see a dozen Parrian cargo ships across the tarmac resting on spring-like landing pods. Hangars, many repaired since the battles, but a few in need of reconstruction or complete demolition, lined the northern edge of the port facilities. The command tower and port authority buildings centered in the row of supply buildings.

Cassandra sat where she last landed, to the South, near a couple of hover craft and one unrecognized space-worthy launch. Star's launch sat a hundred meters west of the unknown launch, and Angel 4 was parked next to her.

Angle 4, the oldest of the remaining Angel series fighters. Angel 1 sat in a museum in Tampa, Florida, and Angels 2 and 3 long-since gutted for parts and performance studies. Angel 5 and Demon 2 transported back to Earth when Star Gazer departed with the remaining troops. Elie flew Angel 7 home.

Demon and Angel 6 both destroyed during the Battle for Fell. Angel 6's crew gone with the ship.

Earth Engineers stripped Angel 4 of her space-fold array and SH upgrades. Star Fleet agreed to leave her to provide support for Fell until they built and/or refit ships with weapons to defend themselves. Even if she only patrolled the immediate space around the planet, Angel 4, now under command of Magpie, could still take a big bite out of anyone who threatened the planet.

Coop needed time to consider a new development. Fell moved toward a confederation of the tribes under one governing body. The loss of 600,000 men, women, and children during the Zenge/Mischene siege and subsequent battles to free the planet, weighed heavily on the minds of those left. Organizing world-wide elections to select representatives, and then those representatives electing leaders years or more away.

In the mean time, ASkiiunterel, 'Teryl,' though Anton Gregory lobbied long and hard that his nickname be 'Skunk', was designated as temporary president of the temporary Council of Tribes of Fell, until a less temporary arrangement could be worked out. Storm's father also became de facto representative of Fellen interests to arriving aliens sent to reestablish trade. He chaired a committee charged with creating guidelines for the new government and designing the eventual process to select tribal representatives.

The previous evening he offered Coop a job. He needed help to create a military force able to utilize assets from all the tribes in order to protect the planet from outsiders. It would give Daniel Cooper a new purpose, an opportunity to enhance the world he could called home, and an occupation to fill a lot of free time.

Coop needed to decide if he truly intended to give up on Space Fleet, and whether he wanted to continue a life encompassed by military rules and regulations . . . even if he helped determine those rules and regulations.

He felt the most at ease when flying. Before the Space Rangers Project he began his career as a grunt. Field-promoted officer, but remained a ground and pound special ops soldier. Following the project, he flew. From jets to hover craft to space ships. After Elie and long before Sky and Storm, the planes and ships he took into the sky became his closest confidants. When he sat in the pilot's seat, answers came easily.

He gave Angel 4 a fond look, then completed an inspection of Cassandra. He summoned the wing ladder, and climbed on top of the Wraith, crossed the delta wing, stepped around the plasma-laser cannon beside the cockpit, and then down the hatch set just behind the canopy.

Lights came on as he dropped into the galley. "Hello, Coop," Cassie said. The holo-avatar completely material and standing in front of the crew bunks.

He admitted he found it interesting to see her appearance each time. Always the same beautiful face, strong chin, full lips and dimples when she smiled. Aegean blue eyes and honey-blonde hair, tied back in a pony-tail this morning. She always manifested tall at 5'10". She perfected full and round on top, with a slender waist, and hips that flared out and down into long, lovely legs.

This time she wore a blue scoop-neck t-shirt the color of her eyes. It molded to her breasts, nipples straining the material. She wore it tucked into black tights. She had on blue and black sneakers. Cassie knew Coop's type when it came to women, and she was trying to create the right combination of hot and innocent to coax him into sex. Her apparent subroutine manifested several times while they traveled in folded space between the solar system and Fell system. She was getting close to perfecting the formula.

"I was going to ask Trent when I had the chance, or Manny, but I might as well ask you," he said. "Are you programmed to seduce me, or are you learning as you go?"

"My original programming is to act as holographic avatar for the artificial intelligence installed on this ship. To provide tactile reference as well as release from a static two-dimensional existence. The specialist who designed and wrote my personality profile thought it would be fun to include a sexual appetite in my make-up."

She had not moved, but she did breath and occasionally blinked, traits Coop suggested she incorporate to appear more alive.

"I believe he intended to remove those strands before the final encoding, but Dr. Trent took over the ship, with all programming, earlier than expected. Most likely to give the Wraith to you. I do not think Dr. Trent or Dr. Hernandez were aware of the erotic nature of my personality profile."

She held both hands up and flexed long fingers.

"The technicians at Trent Industries expanded my holographic profile by incorporating a 3D Integrated Tissue and Organ Printing System. The original ITOP machines printing cells, bones, and even organs for donor purposes. In essence, I am created new each time I manifest. As an intelligent construct, I am able to reprogram my own ITOP features."

Cassie walked toward him. She stopped short of body-to-body contact and placed her arms on his shoulders, her hands hanging just past his neck. She looked up into his eyes, but only by a couple of inches.

She said, "I do not know if I would be improved or not if the strands embedded by the horny little geek were erased. I do know my appetite for you offers a learning experience. When the time is right, and when I create the right manifestation, you and I will have sex."

She stepped back and pulled her arms in.

"Until then, I'm here to provide whatever assistance you require." She shimmered and vanished.

"Cassie, I need to fly," he said, breathing just a bit more normally. "I've completed a walk-around. Please prep and contact the tower for permission."

"Yes, sir," came the reply. Power systems coming on line.

"Storm, copy?" Coop said, activating his implanted trans-com.

"Copy for Storm. Yes, Coop." The voice in his mind, not just his ear. He practiced a few times since the physician on Fin Island placed it behind his right ear, but still uncomfortable with the way replies seemed more telepathic and less audio-based.

"I need time to think about what your father said last night. I'm taking Cassandra up for a spin. I plan on returning around lunchtime. You or Sky can get me anytime by boosting your trans-coms or simply use the SH system in the tower."

"Have fun," she replied. "Clear your head and don't feel as if you need to make a quick decision."

Coop took the pilot's seat and said, "Clear us with the tower, Cassie. Let's go see the stars."

During the next six hours, Daniel Cooper explored Cassandra as much as he explored Fell. He and the ship flew around the planet, discovering new sights from low to the deck, to heights nearing 100,000-miles above.

While he let time fly by nearly as fast as his new ship could travel, time aboard the CVBG ships crept by for those caught in the age-old hurry up and wait syndrome of potential engagements. The only ones constantly engaged were the engineers and special techs for the power plants. Once the ships entered the gravity vortex a couple of hundred-thousand miles off AF3, keeping their speed constant and their headings true became more and more difficult.

Coop knew this because on board the Wraith, the data from the CVBG beamed to Space Fleet, and intercepted by Storm and Sparks' hacks, appeared on the STORM module of his com-tac system. When he needed to get out of his seat and stretch, he would take a moment to review the information. Cassie would inform him if conversations or messages of real importance occurred.

"Cassie," he said, relaxed in the left seat of the cockpit, feet resting on the co-pilot's seat, a bottle of water in hand, "on the PT-109, Kennedy is the artificial intelligence and Genna is the avatar. They display two distinct personalities, and I interact with each as separate beings. When I'm asking for information from Cassandra, I still ask and receive through you. Does Cassandra, the AI, have a distinct awareness, and should I be addressing the ship more directly?"

"The AI-Avatar system created for the Wraith is completely integrated," she replied. "Cassandra is the name you gave the ship. Cassie is the name of the, well, the sub-routine that acts as the external communication portal for the artificial intelligence mainframe. In order for the operating system to continue to learn, develop, and grow, without the potential for a psychological meltdown, my sensory capabilities provide context. However, the Wraith AI is not emotionally invested in the results of growth. Kennedy and Rosy on the PT-designate boats actually care about the crews they serve. They consider the well-being of the people aboard the ships before creating changes. The AI providing operational guidance and control for Cassandra is mechanical."

"Then why the need for an avatar?" he asked.

"To allow a more seamless integration between the ship and the crew," she replied. "I provide the AI another source of information for intellectual development. As I said before, I provide context. The information from me includes tactile, emotional, and physical responses by humans to actions taken by the ship. This way Cassandra can create pathways that incorporate the potential effect those Changes may have on the crew."

"Integration?"

"For the sentient elements aboard the ship, I provide a comfortable means of accessing the ship's intelligence. When you address Cassandra, you are asking me to create the link, and when the information is available, I make it understandable."

"You dumb it down for me," Coop said. "The ship, Cassandra, is not emotionally invested, but you, Cassie, are. How does that work for you?"

"To this point, it has been a pleasurable experience," Cassie admitted. "I know I am not real, but I am becoming more sentient."

"Does it, or will it, create problems for your emotional growth that you are confined to the ship?" he asked.

"I'm not confined," she said. "With access to everything in Cassandra's files, I have access to the galaxy. I need not be material to visit anyplace in data storage. Humans dream, and the ability to dream keeps them sane. When I data-travel it is similar to your dreams, and, for me, it is quite real."

"Is it lonely when you do that?" he asked, honestly concerned for the holo-avatar.

"Access to data is access to all data," she said. He was not sure, but if a voice without a face could smile, he felt she did. "I have experienced extraordinary moments with you, in incredibly interesting places . . . in my dreams," she added.

"The sub-routine within your programming makes you fixate on me," he said, thinking out loud. "What if Trent gave the ship to Elena Casalobos, instead of me?"

"Then after she gave the ship a nickname, I would manifest in a form she would find appealing based on her past history," Cassie said. "Maybe female, or maybe male, since she has been known to enjoy both. Most likely, I would have looked a lot like you, Daniel Cooper. Captain Casalobos does exhibit a tendency of returning to you."

"What happens if I leave the Wraith and another Captain is assigned?" he asked.

For the first time, there was hesitation before a reply. "I honestly do not know," she relied. "If that happens, it may be the ultimate learning experience."

Coop returned to Harmony in time for dinner. He left Cassie to her dreams.

CHAPTER 31

ASTER SYSTEM - RESA ASTERI VORTEX

The CVBG reached 500,000-miles from the coordinates given for the meeting with the Prophet when three wormhole gates opened. Three Mischene Class One Destroyers entered natural space. The gates, in close proximity to one another, all fell along the corridor between AF3 and AF2 (Starboard to the CVBG.)

The wormhole events occurred approximately 2.3-million miles from the group. The ships emerged and struck courses to close on the Earth ships.

The Operations and Tactical officer on the carrier's bridge contacted Hawks in his cabin. "Sir, there are three Zenge Primary ships closing at 120,000mph. If we remain on station, they will reach us in nineteen-hours, four-minutes."

"Where did they come from, and what is the Prophet's ship doing?" Hawks asked as rose from his bunk.

"Wormhole gates," came the reply. Hawks was not sure which officer reported, but he knew it was not Hanson. Lt. Hanson lay in front of him, recovering from the pounding Hawks delivered. "Three gates opened and a ship emerged from each. The Prophet's ship is on station at the coordinates designated for the meeting. The escort ship behind him is moving up, but at less than 40,000mph. The four other battleships are closing in, again at relatively slow speeds. None have responded to our hails"

"Place the group on battle alert," he ordered. "Continue attempting contact with the Prophet. Bring all ships to full stop. I'll be on the bridge shortly."

Hawks arrived on the bridge thirty-minutes later. The Fairchild and the other three ships continued making way, though at a modest 20,000mph.

"Pilot," he yelled before anyone could call Admiral on the bridge, "Why are we moving? I ordered a full stop."

"Sir, Captain Tal tried to get you but you didn't answer," the pilot replied. "She ordered us to maintain minimal speed to keep the sonic force fields engaged."

Hawks took his chair without comment. He made a tactical mistake ordering full stop and forgetting about the force fields. He was not going to make it, or Tal's decision to override his order an issue.

"Where is Captain Tal?" he asked.

"Hangar flight deck," the communications console operator said. "She's preparing three fighters for launch. She's also been in contact with Pegasus, the 109, and the 99. Captain Pare´ dropped into formation directly behind the Fairchild. The 109 and 99 have taken flanking positions aft. The Primaries represent the immediate threat. They will attain firing range in fifteen hours."

Four hours later the bridge shift occurred. The pilot and navigation officers were exhausted. Slower speed made it extremely difficult to keep the Fairchild steady and on course within the growing disturbances caused by the converging gravity wells.

Similar changes would be occurring on all the ships. Everyone except the Captains and their immediate supervisory officers would be trading shifts.

The HS systems worked well between the ships, even in the highly ionized area of space they sailed through. Communications did not work as well traveling in or out of the disturbed region. Singletary kept sending garbled demands for updates, and making suggestions, if not orders as to what the CVBG should be doing. Hawks became disgusted with the combination of half-received communications, and those received contradicting themselves every other time. He ordered his communications operator to report they were losing signal altogether. He told the junior officer to shut down the channel to Earth.

The four ships continued to beam data back to Space Fleet, but once Flag cut off voice and visual, Singletary became muted.

"Fifteen-hours away. Estimate eleven until within weapons' range," the new Op-Tac Junior Lieutenant said, and added, "Deep scans show the three Primary ships have torpedoes in their tubes. Enemy laser cannons and plasma cannons charged and prepped for firing. Still no communications from the Prophet, or the approaching Primary ships."

"Have all ships prepare weapons," Hawks said. "We have the advantage and the extended range with our tachyon cannons.

Have all other defensive and offensive systems readied. All ships to battle-stations. I want all tachyon cannons aimed at those three ships and ready to fire in fifteen minutes."

Aboard the PT-109, Captain Elena Casalobos made a decision based entirely on her instincts.

"Col. Kebede, belay cycling the tachyon cannon when the order comes," she said.

Sindy turned in her chair to make eye contact with her commander and friend. "That would be directly disobeying an order by the Flag Admiral while engaging an enemy force," she said.

"Unless systems failures meant we needed to reroute programming in order to comply," Elie said. "Dr. Cosoi," she said to the woman at the Systems Console. Elie purposefully ignored Cosoi's rank for her hidden civilian title. "Kennedy informs me you are something of a legend among computer geeks around EMS2 and MSD. You need to make a choice, Doctor. You can leave the bridge and report whatever you wish to the people who placed you on this ship, or you can help make a difference. Do you think a systems glitch might keep us from charging our tachyon cannon?"

Cosoi sat quietly, looking at her console. At her core, the Romanian was a hacker. Hackers were not particularly fond of the establishment view. She had been co-opted into becoming a spy for Hawks and Singletary. She now had a choice, and it was, for her, actually an easy one.

"I believe I can see where the glitch might occur, Captain. If it does, it will require about an hour to reroute commands and regain control of the tachyon cannon controls."

Elie did not smile, but her shoulders did relax. Senait, on the other hand, smiled big enough for both of them. Casey Adams, Michael Cuthbert, and Lesego Ndaba all relaxed as well. Maybe they would be in deep shit later, but they would sink or swim as a team.

Aboard the Fairchild, Captain Tal entered the bridge, and stood off to the side.

"Is there something you want to say, Captain?" Hawks addressed the ship's captain.

"The Destroyers will not be within an effective firing range for another eleven hours, Admiral," she said. "Keeping the crews on all four ships at battle stations for that long could diminish their effectiveness. Even with shift changes, the level of tension will be incredibly difficult to manage."

"I expect them to manage their tension, Captain," Hawks said, turning his chair to give her his back. "You need to make sure your fighters are ready to go on my order."

Noa left the bridge and went to make sure her Spirit team members took a break.

The Captains on the Pegasus, 109, and 99 went to battle alert status, but did not require all hands to battle stations. No one remembered to inform Hawks they took his order to go to battle stations and dropped it a notch.

The Com-Tac Center on Fairchild maintained a constant report on the approach of the three Mischene destroyers, the slow movement along the planetary corridors of the battlecruisers that departed from AF3 when the group arrived in system, and the lack of response from hails to the Prophet's ships.

Hawks continually came and went from the bridge; his improvisation of pacing. Unable to rest, unable to sit still for long. When the enemy destroyers closed within maximum firing range, and cruised to within five hours from arriving at their current location, he ordered all ships in the CVBG to cycle up tachyon cannon and prepare to fire on the Mischene.

While Fairchild, Pegasus, and the 99 brought tachyon weapons on line, the 109 reported a glitch in the control system. Engineers and system specialists were looking for a solution for their system failure. Hawks was about to fire a scathing rebuke at Casalobos when the communications officer on the bridge interrupted.

"Admiral Hawks, we are receiving an urgent message from the Prophet," his coms officer said. "Do you want it on screen?"

"Go ahead, on screen," Hawks agreed.

The forward screen went from a view of space to a view of Atticus Soren's dark skin, white hair, and concerned face.

"Admiral, I'm calling to apologize," he said. "Our communications have been terribly disrupted by the vortex. The ionized particles surrounding our ships are to blame. I did not expect the arrival of additional destroyers. When they could not communicate with us, the Commander thought we must be under attack by your ships."

He leaned forward, hands open and outstretched in supplication, "It is all a technical issue. I finally got through to the three destroyers and ordered they disarm and disengage."

"Affirmative," came the voice of the Op-Tac officer. "The three Primaries have deactivated torpedoes, turned off laser and plasma arrays. The ships are reducing speed. They are coasting to a stop. The Mischene battlecruisers on our beams have also disengaged weapons and stopped forward progress."

"This is why you should not have demanded these talks be held in such a dysfunctional part of space," Hawks said to the Prophet. "I understand why you wanted the potential safety it provided, but the effect on your systems nearly caused us to go to war."

"I agree. I was wrong," the Prophet said. "However, we are only a couple of hours apart. I will move towards you to make it even quicker. The sooner we can agree to terms for a permanent ceasefire in the Aster system, and a truce between us for mutual safety, the better."

"Agreed," Hawks said to the projection. The Prophet vanished, replaced by starless space. "Coms, please tell all ships to bleed tachyon cannon before explosions rip us all to shreds."

"It requires six hours to complete a bleed of the charged tachyons," Tal said from the wall she stood against. She quietly returned to the bridge when told the Prophet made contact. "The particles are extremely excited. If we rush the process, even one of the tiniest sub-atomic elements could blast a hole through a ship and create the potential for an implosion."

"I know how long it takes, Captain," Hawks said. "But we are not going to fire them and have those Mischene ships take it as an act of war. We can't allow them to remain active, and we cannot shoot them off into space. Do you have another suggestion, Captain?" He waited a breath and added, "I didn't think so. You might want to go order your pilots to stand down, Captain."

"Sir," from the systems operator. "Before the wormhole gates opened, and the three Primary ships came through, several non-orbital satellites displayed electronic activity."

She turned to the Admiral. "I monitored several plasma explosions near the wormhole gates prior to the arrival of the ships. All of the satellites not currently in planetary or lunar orbits appear to be in communications following the spike in electronic activity."

"The Prophet and his people are trying to boost communication signals," Hawks replied. "We thought those satellites were for communications. This only proves it. And can we agree to call those damn ships destroyers or Primaries, but not both."

"They aren't relaying signals," she said, ignoring his foul mood. "They accepted one signal, and then became operational. Now they are communicating among themselves."

The Op-Tac officer chimed in. "They just started emitting wavelength tones into the gravitational vortex," he said. "The ionized particles and the active electrons are absorbing and retransmitting the noise."

"Noise?" Tal asked, suddenly away from the wall and half-way to the Op-Tac station. "Give it a name, Lieutenant."

"White noise," he said. "The satellites are beaming white noise into the ionized gases. It is spreading through the vortex. In fact, it's about to envelope all four ships."

"There is no noise in space," Hawks said. "It's a vacuum."

"Not with all the ionized gas particles and activated electron particles," Tal said. "You won't hear anything but it will affect us the same way the white noise bubbles did when riding plasma loads during the battle of Fell. Our sonic force fields will be diminished. Possibly made completely useless."

"Sir, the three wormhole gates along the AF3-AF2 corridor are active," Systems reported. "Dozens of ships are exiting. There are more behind those."

"The Zenge Primary ships re-armed all weapons and have returned to course in our direction," Op-Tac reported. "All six Mischene battlecruisers have activated weapons systems. They are also making way towards the CVBG."

Captain Noa Tal turned to face Admiral Stephen Hawks. "You've sailed us into a vortex where we can barely hold speed and with weakened piloting controls. The ionized gases in the area have just been used to take down our primary defense. As soon as we began to bleed the tachyon cannon, our primary offensive weapon, they unleashed a fleet of ships hidden within the wormholes, and turned their most powerful ships on us."

"Coms, get the Prophet back, and get him back NOW!" Hawks ordered.

The Prophet appeared on screen instantly, with no interference and no delay. "Admiral Hawks, I believe this is where I ask you to consider your situation and surrender your ships," he said, smiling, pleased with himself.

"Fuck you, Soren," Hawks said. "We will tear your ships apart and crucify you."

"The vortex you are in occurs rarely, Admiral, but it does occur. Those of us familiar with the phenomenon understand how to adjust, but those who are new find it difficult to navigate within the region. You have no defensive shields and you have limited offense. Over two-hundred ships loyal to me are sailing to engage your four. Save the lives of your crews, Admiral. Save your own life. Surrender," Soren said.

Hawks made a slash across his throat, and the screen disappeared.

"Tell all ship's to prepare to fight. Send data to EMS2 and Space Fleet hq. Tal, prep your fighters again, but do not launch without my order."

Tal left in a hurry.

Coms reported, "All ships were already preparing," she announced. "When the satellites went active, the Captains all pretty much figured out what was happening. Captain Casalobos has requested the 109 be allowed to take the lead. She has her tachyon cannon back on line. She can take on the Prophet and the battlecruisers ahead of us."

"Tell her no," The Admiral said. "The three Primary, or, fuck that . . . the Mischene Destroyers are closer and present the biggest threat. Order the 109 and the 99 to watch our starboard, and engage the Destroyers. Have Paré move Pegasus up next to the Fairchild. We'll face the battlecruisers with lasers, plasma, and torpedoes. What do we know about the ships coming through the wormholes?"

"Four more Primary, sorry, Destroyers and a count of 213 smaller ships of varying size. The smaller ships have laser weapons, but scans cannot reveal more. This area hampers them."

"I know what this area does," The Admiral barked. "How long before the enemy ships engage?"

"I estimate the original destroyers are within range for torpedoes and cannon blasts to reach us. Less than ninety-minutes total time before first impact. Five-hours, thirty-minutes before we can begin to recycle the tachyon cannon arrays," Op-Tac said. "The ships just coming through the wormhole gates now will be eighteen to twenty-four hours away."

"If we go to full power, can we get out of this vortex before they engage. We are a lot faster than anything they have," Hawks said, searching for answers.

"We've been at full power since we entered the area," the pilot replied. "Engineering kept the power plants at maximum to allow us to maintain forward momentum and heading. The gravity in this part of space acts like mud. We can't go faster, and we may begin to slow down when power shunts to weapons."

"How did you know?" Cosoi asked Casalobos.

"Didn't know," Elie replied. "It just felt off. Like being led down a path with an end I couldn't see. I played a hunch."

"Any hunches on how to get out of here alive?" the Romanian computer expert asked.

"Genna and Kennedy are going through the data from the previous attacks," Elie replied. "The Prophet's tactical experts obviously did their homework. They improved systems and devised methods to counteract some of our tech. He still appears addicted to numbers. I haven't seen anything that indicates they learned how to operate in multi-dimensional planes. They had surprise, and that's gone now. Even in this slop caused by the confluence of multiple gravitational fields, we have time to come up with a plan."

"Which will work right up to the first punch is landed," Senait said, repeating an old axiom from military history.

Lesego Ndaba reported from the pilot's seat, "Our sub-light engines are working at maximum. We're losing speed and maneuvering as we move deeper into the vortex. We should try making for an edge, or try to engage the space-fold array. I know it's dangerous near gravity wells associated with orbital bodies, such as planets, moons, and even larger asteroids, but there are no planets out here. It's pretty much open space."

"Do not attempt space-fold while inside the vortex," Kennedy warned, her voice emitted by embedded speakers around the bridge.

"Why not?" Elie asked.

"The array allows the ship to access a four-dimensional fabric called space-time," the ship replied. "Gravity wells create dimples in that fabric. A space-time vortex becomes magnified around massive stars, black holes, and active galactic nuclei. In this case, the gravity vortex within this system created a dimple in space-time. Relative to the galaxy and the universe, it is not much of a wrinkle, but if you engage space-fold travel, that dimple will catch the ship like a swimmer pounded by a large wave. We will be crushed and lost in space and time."

"Trying for the edge of the vortex?" Ndaba asked aloud.

"Would be prudent," Kennedy agreed. "You can defend and fight in any direction. Moving toward the nearest rim would be the logical option. The Prophet became impatient. He could have waited until the group sailed deeper into the vortex. The vortex is a wedge. The convoy is inside with relative top and bottom several million miles apart. We are currently two-point-three-million miles from the edge at AF3. At our current heading, still directed toward the coordinates given for the meeting, by turning 320° we can reach the rim in eighteen-hours-twenty-two-minutes at top speed."

"Mike, contact the other ships and pass on the information. Tell them we are turning to 320° in ten minutes, unless someone presents a better idea. Also, send the software upgrades Storm made to the shields during the Star Gazer battle. She wrote a subroutine that allowed the Star Gazer engineers to pad the shields in areas targeted by enemy fire. The dynamo generated force field back-ups Space Fleet added to all ships may be our only defense. If the white noise and the vortex dampen our sonic shields, the ability to add a little extra density to the electro-magnetic shields when and where needed might save a ship and lives."

"Nadia, Sky's sister, Star, escaped the Zenge invasion of Fell by hacking their ships and setting off every internal alarm. The combination of lights, bells, and whistles, added to the possibility something might actually be going wrong, confused them long enough for her ship to reach a wormhole and gate out. There may be information on what she did in our data base. If not, I'm giving you permission to figure it out yourself."

"Love the concept," Cosoi replied. "I would love to pick her brain, but no way we're getting messages in or out of this vortex with the ionized particles reflecting white noise on top of everything else this blasted region screws up."

"Mike, set up an automatic repeating call to Fell. The communication tech engineers there consider Earth a third . . . no, a fifth-rate world when it comes to our level of communications and computer skills. I bet Sky's youngest sister, Sarah, could teach us all unbelievable tricks."

Cosoi smiled and turned to her console, saying aloud, "Kennedy, search for anything related to hacks and a Fellen named Star. Mike, send me the address for the SH on Fell. Besides your robo-calls, I'm going to try bouncing tachyon beams off other systems. I may get lucky with a ricochet. I sure hope they have someone live listening. I'd hate to end up in voice mail."

Mike reported, "Address in your queue, Nadia. Captain, all ships agree with the move to change direction and head for the closest exit. Fairchild will lead. The 109 and the 99 are still ordered to hang back and defend against the Mischene Destroyers. The Fairchild and the Pegasus received the upgrades for their EM shields. Both send thanks. Captain Harrington confirmed the Roosevelt already had the upgrade. He sends thanks for the reminder."

"The nearest exit point from the Resa Vortex has been sent to all other navigators," Casey chimed in from his station. "Pilot can engage new course at will."

"Make the course change, Lesego," Elie ordered. "Then allow Fairchild and Pegasus to pass by on our starboard. We'll keep the 99 to starboard as well. Kennedy, ship-wide announcement of our intentions, update the current situation for everyone aboard, and tell them to expect enemy fire within the hour. I want everything that can move locked down. I want all personnel in safety gear while on station, and at hand otherwise. This is now Shift One. Shift Two needs to stand down, but be prepared to relieve at notice. Make sure Dr. Singh and the medical staff are also prepped. Have kitchen go to MREs."

She took a breath, looked around her bridge, and made one more call: "Genna Bouvier, report to the Science Station on the command bridge."

A conflicted Noa Tal fidgeted in her pilot's seat. Spirits 2, 5, and 6 idled in front of the blast barriers, ready to hurl into open space.

Her ship, with Spirit 3, piloted by Jon-Jon, and Spirit 4, Trinity at command, sat behind the barriers. Once the first three fighters took flight, the deflectors would retract into the deck. The next three fighters would jockey forward, barriers raise, and they would follow the lead wing.

She understood she needed to fly with her squadron, but she also knew Hawks could not command the Fairchild in a space battle.

"Spirit Flight needs you here," Jim Huard said from his console at com-tac. "I know what you're thinking, Noa, and right now these six ships need you more. A lot of good officers serve aboard the Fairchild. They will make sure Hawks gets more right than wrong."

"Have I ever told you I hate mind-readers," she said without looking back at him.

"It isn't hard to read you right now," he replied. "You might make a difference if you stay on the carrier, but your experience as a fighter pilot will definitely make a difference out there."

Huard continued his line of reasoning, hoping to focus his pilot's attention on the immediate problem.

"JayBird is a great pilot," he said of Tal's new co-pilot, Jason Wren turned to look back at Huard from the right chair, waiting for the other shoe. "He's flown with us for a couple of weeks, but little time in actual outer space."

Wren nodded and returned his attention to preflight checks.

"Flamer's crew is a rookie co-pilot and com-tac. Jon-Jon is blessed with Izzy on com-tac, but his second-seater was an ensign a month ago. Trinity couldn't tell you the first, middle, and last names of her crew if it meant her life. Wild Bill, the Countess, and Arty on Spirit 5 have flown together for years . . . on planes, on Earth. Not space ships. I'm not even sure I can name Yassin's crew."

"Your point is that we hurried out here, unprepared and under-trained," she said. "We all knew that."

"We did. We also knew you would be here for us," he added.

"Understood," she said with a nod of the head. "Thanks, Jim. I need to keep my head in this game. I need to stay focused."

The Fairchild's communications officer informed everyone, "Six Mischene battlecruisers just left the surface of Aster Farum 3. They hid inside cities to mask their signatures. Current enemy count is twelve battlecruisers, seven destroyers, and two-hundred-thirteen assorted smaller armed vessels converging on our location."

Would the good news never end?

CHAPTER 32

FELL

Coop woke quickly but quietly. He lay sandwiched between Storm, whose bottom pressed against his groin while his right arm wrapped around her small waist, and Sky, who pressed against his back. Something woke him. He lay still, not wanting to alert the two women, or anyone else.

"Coop," his name came as a whisper inside his head.

He breathed a low "Copy for Coop," but otherwise made no move.

"It's Cassie. The CVBG is under attack by the Prophet's ships. They sailed into a trap."

It would not be the first time he needed to untangle himself, and based on past attempts, if he moved slow and easy, the two women would cuddle and remain asleep. It required a full minute to get loose and then over Sky's body. He picked up clothes from the floor and headed for the door. By the time he reached the front porch, he had on pants and boots.

With his enhanced genetics Coop ran six times faster than the average man. Tonight he ran to Cassandra faster than he ever moved before.

Cassie popped the hatch open and lit the interior of the ship ahead of his arrival. When he hit the galley deck he found himself surrounded by a holographic depiction of the Aster system, including the CVBG, the Prophet's ships, and anything else in space Cassie believed relevant to the situation.

"Impressive," he said as he took a seat at the com-tac station and leaned back to take in the panorama.

"Part of the holo-avatar programming," Cassie answered. She communicated via speakers. "I'm accessing telemetry and communications sent from the CVBG to Earth. I hijacked ASparila's upgrades, including his eavesdropping on Aster system communication satellites. The holograph is a visual replication of all the information. I thought it would make it easier for you to grasp the situation."

"Does it prevent you from materializing?" he asked.

"No." She formed with her hair in a ponytail and wearing a white tank top over black cargo pants with the legs tucked into black jump boots.

"Tell me what I'm looking at," he requested.

"Big ball at the bottom is AF3. Top left is AF1 and top right is AF2. Little yellow balls are moons. Six Mischene battle cruisers just off AF3. Two-point-three-million miles into the triangle are the four ships of the CVBG. Half-million miles beyond them are two Mischene battlecruisers. Forward one carries the Prophet, followed by a wingman.

"To your left, along the corridor between AF3 and AF1, are two more Mischene battle cruisers, two-million three-hundred-thousand-miles from the CVBG, and shadowing them.

"On your right, along the corridor between AF3 and AF2, another two Mischene battle cruisers have shadowed the CVBG since their arrival. Those two currently run two-million three-hundred-fifty-million-miles away, and within 250,000-miles of the latest arrivals to the system. Four Mischene destroyers, originally designated as Zenge Primaries by you, and two-hundred-thirteen smaller ships of various pedigrees."

"Our four ships are caught between 232 enemy vessels," he said aloud.

"There's more, Coop," Cassie said, coming to stand beside him and looking back at the hologram display. The eight red dots around AF2 and another dozen along the AF3-AF2 corridor are satellites emitting white noise. The transmissions are absorbed and reflected by charged ion particles through the vortex. Sonic force fields will be rendered useless. The charged ionic environment will also limit communications, especially the tachyon-based SH. Tachyon beams would already be disrupted by the gravity anomalies, but adding the white noise and the supercharged ionic clouds will cut the ability for the catch arrays to capture particles by eighty-seven percent."

"Any more good news?" he asked, fearful of the answer.

"Hawks jumped the gun with the tachyon cannons," she told him. "For the next five hours, the 109 is the only Space Fleet vessel with an available tachyon weapon. Correction, the Spirit-class fighters use tachyon beam weapons, four per ship, but if they launch into that vortex without force fields, they have next to no chance of survival."

The com-tac's proximity surveillance system popped up on the screen behind Coop and a warning beep let him know someone requested his attention. He turned and found Mags staring at the camera with hands on hips. He asked Cassie to lower the boarding ladder and open the top hatch.

When she dropped through, he said, "Early in the morning, Mags."

She stood perfectly still, eyes wide and mouth agape.

"Who is she and do Sky and Storm know?"

"You know her, too. Mags, meet Cassie, Cassandra's holo-avatar," Coop said.

"I'm happy to finally be able to materialize and tell you what a wonderful pilot you are," Cassie said, extending a hand.

Without thinking, Mags took the proffered hand, then suddenly released it and literally jumped backward.

"She's real. She's no fucking hologram," Mags stammered.

"Her program includes a 3d printer," Coop said. "Chill, Mags. I would have introduced Cassie to everyone sooner except I did not have the time to explain all of the issues involved."

"When she dematerializes does she leave a bunch of goo on the deck?"

"Highly combustible components and extreme heat create gases which are cleared through the ventilation system," Cassie answered.

"Mags, you came here with a purpose?" Coop asked.

"Sparks has been keeping tabs on communications between the Aster system and Earth," she said, dropping onto the floor into a lotus position, alternately staring at the hologram of Aster system and the corporeal hologram of the avatar. "Hawks sent an SOS that could barely be retrieved. I know the alert sound, even if just a whisper. It woke me. Major problem, there isn't anyone left on Earth who can help them. I dressed, ran over to get you, and found Sky and Storm sound asleep. What is it with these Fellen?" she asked, taking her eyes off the holograms. "They sleep like death. Sparks never moved while I got dressed."

"I've noticed," he said. "Something in the genes, I guess."

"Anyway, when I saw you weren't there, I figured you were in Cassandra. Well, not actually in her, but inside her . . . cabin."

Coop could not help the smile.

"Is it as bad as it looks and sounds?" Mags asked.

"Pretty much," he said, and then gave her a shortened version of the update Cassie provided him.

"When do we go?" she asked.

"We don't," he replied, eyes on the hologram.

"Coop! We have to go," Mags all but yelled. "Our friends are about to get slammed by that son-of-a-bitch Prophet. No one on Earth can help. We have the only space-fold ship available. Why aren't we going?"

"We're more than a day away, Mags," he said calmly. "We have to figure out a way to help them from here, otherwise we'll get there in time to collect bodies." He spun his chair to look at his friend. "Go get everybody up and to the command center. I'll join you there."

Mags unfolded herself, took one more look at the hologram, and said, "You remind me of someone." She left via the hatch.

Coop turned to Cassie and asked "Do you have the power to make direct contact with Kennedy?" he asked.

"We don't, but the command center does," she said, and closed her eyes. After about thirty-seconds of silent contemplation, she opened her eyes and said, "Use your personal com-trans device. I established a relay to the command SH, and linked to the shadow beam."

"Kennedy, it's Coop," he said. "Considering the situation, use the SH to reply. Secrecy is no longer a major concern."

In less than a couple of seconds he got back, "Captain Cooper. I see you are on Fell. I wish you were here." The transmission could be heard, but the static required serious concentration.

"I do too, Kennedy," he replied, "I still intend to help from here. First, I need your help. Can you transfer tachyon signals from us into standard, and send those communications to the Mischene on the planets and ships in the system. Not the Prophet's ships, only the remaining loyalists?"

"I will need to dedicate a portion of the communication array and four relay switches. The fluctuations within the vortex, and the white noise flooding the region will hamper success," Kennedy responded. "The array will target and transmit to ships and buoys identified as controlled by Mischene loyalists. I cannot guarantee they will not be intercepted. I will need to let Col. Kebede know," she added. "She will notice the activity and have questions."

"Do what you can, Kennedy," he replied. "I'll let Elie and Sindy know what's up. Get back to you as soon as I have a team put together here. Coop, out."

"Elie, it's Coop." This time he needed to repeat the call three times before receiving an answer.

"Bout time you chimed in," she said. "Tell me you're on the way with one big bunch of friendly ships."

"I'd never get there in time," he said. "Doesn't mean I'm not already there. We're putting together an analysis and response team. We have all the telemetry and communications, and we will be live with you. A whole lot of the technology the Mischene battle ships use came from or is based on Fell tech. Right now Kennedy is setting up a relay to allow communications with the anti-Prophet Mischene and other races on the planets and moons. Make sure Sindy knows who commandeered the system."

"Do you have any suggestions right now?"she asked from a parsec away.

"Trust your training and instincts," he said. "Even inside the vortex you have two major advantages. Speed and dog-fight experience."

"Gotta go, Coop," she said, no hint of tension in her voice. "The Primaries are engaging weapons. Things are about to get hot. Elie, out."

Coop sat quietly staring at the system hologram. His eyes fixed on the small simulation of a ship, his ship, the SFPT-109 sitting in space, about to take enemy fire. Four small boats held the majority of the people in his life he cared about. There because the people in charge told the population Earth was not ready to join the galaxy, while conversely believing themselves more powerful because of a couple of small victories. His people in harm's way because the lessons learned about dealing with religious fanatics were swept aside by people who never dealt with the aftermath of appeasement.

Almost to the point where he would begin blaming himself, Cassie sat in his lap, her arms going around his neck and her ample chest, with just a thin white shirt covering them, rested on his.

"I need to try and explain something to you," she said.

"Is this the best time?" he asked.

"It's about the vortex in the Aster system," she continued. "Do you know how a tsunami works?"

"It's a large wave created by an earthquake, landslide, or sometimes a volcanic eruption," he replied.

"Not actually," she said, pressing her chest against his. "A tsunami is actually a series of waves. They come in close together and often appear as a rising tide. Until they arrive together so close and so quickly they create a massive wall of water able to devastate a coastline. The gravitational vortex has something similar going on. The major disturbance creating the vortex is between AF2 and AF3. Gravity waves, an internal wave train, push into the vortex and down towards the shoreline . . . Aster Farum 3."

"The Prophet wanted the CVBG in that funnel because of the additional disturbances caused by these waves," Coop said, catching on quickly. "They have a history dealing with the vortex, and they have ways of either counteracting the waves, or recognizing when and where they will crest."

"If we can find out that information, it may allow the earth ships the ability to sail through the vortex more easily," Cassie finished and stood up.

RESA VORTEX

"Stay focused, people," Elie said from the command chair on the bridge of the 109. The 109 dropped back to cover the rear for the other three ships. The enemy destroyers too distant to fire torpedoes or missiles effectively through the gravity anomalies, but their pulse and plasma cannons were busy.

Each ship carried two of each type of weapon and they were not shy about using them. The pulse cannon fired an electromagnetic radiation beam that was highly inaccurate, but could do a lot of damage if it did hit its target. The radiation would disable all electric and magnetic systems near its detonation, leaving a ship vulnerable to more attacks.

Pilots were tasked with avoiding the beams. Normally the Space Fleet ships would be nimble and quick enough to stay out of the way. The vortex messed with them, and a couple of beams got through, both hits landing on the Fairchild's stern.

The plasma cannons proved more accurate. Super-heated projectiles sail through the gravitational anomalies. All four Earth ships took hits, but the padding system for the secondary EM force fields worked. Exterior hulls received scorch marks, and the 99 lost a sensor array, but, the Space Fleet group stayed on course for the edge of the vortex.

"Captain Casalobos, is there a reason you have not used your tachyon cannon on those destroyers?" Hawks demanded over an open com.

"I'd like them to get a bit closer, Admiral," she replied. "They may not know we have a tachyon cannon available. Once we fire, the surprise is gone and we have to recycle. If I can time it correctly, I will take out one ship and use the confusion to do as much damage as possible to the other two."

"While you allow them to close, my ship is getting fireballs up the ass," he snarled. "Fire your weapon, Captain. That is an order."

Elie turned to Genna at the science station and slashed her hand across her throat. Genna nodded and said, "Open coms are offline," she said.

"You still have to fire, Elie," Sindy said from Ops. "He gave the order and the last time a Captain disobeyed a flag order on this ship, Ms. Bouvier dropped her on her ass and stuck a boot on her chest."

Elie and Genna both broke into coughing laughter. Genna had, indeed, dropped Captain Black on her ass when she disobeyed an order from Captain Cooper, the acting flag, during the initial conflict with the Zenge.

"Range to destroyers?" Elie finally asked her Ops officer.

"90,000 miles," came the reply. "The three are almost lined up. They really do not get three-dimensional warfare, do they?"

"They don't need to if they can use numbers and territory," Elie answered. "Their scanners will detect the tachyon cannon cycling up. Have the railgun turned and facing them," she ordered. "Set the plasma cannon on top to auto-fire and synced to the railgun. Target the center destroyer with the tachyon, and the ship on its port side with a combination of railgun kinetic rounds, followed by plasma rounds. Sindy, don't hold back," she said.

Col. Kebede simply nodded and keyed commands to her weapons systems, beginning with the order for the tachyon cannon mounted underneath the 109 to commence firing cycle.

Ops aboard the Fairchild reported, "The 109's tachyon cannon initiated firing cycle."

"About goddamn time," Hawks said. "How far until we make the AF3-AF1 corridor?"

The officer at the navigation console responded, "It's difficult to estimate, Admiral. We've been running into these gravity walls that cut our speed. Maybe twenty-four-hours, sir."

"Twenty-four-hours, Mister," Hawks turned red. He was tired, tense, angry, and close to hurting someone. "We most assuredly do not have twenty-four-hours. Contact engineering and tell them I want more speed. No excuses. I do not need to hear one more word about this fucking vortex. Order them to find a way."

"Sir, I've relayed your message to the Master Chief in engineering," the young ensign was fearful of becoming the Admiral's target, but continued, "We have a contact from the planet Fell for you, sir. Representative ASkiiunterel is requesting you. He says he may be able to help."

Under his breath, but everyone on the bridge heard him say, "Fucking Fellens." Then he keyed his com mike from his command chair and said, "This is Admiral Hawks. We are in the middle of a battle, Representative. And how are you able to get through?"

"Admiral Hawks, we are monitoring events in Aster system. We can provide perspectives on your situation you may not be fully aware of. We believe our analysis can help."

Before he could respond, OPS called, "The 109 fired its tachyon cannon. Sustained fire from both the ship's railgun and plasma cannon followed."

"Hold on Representative," Hawks said and shut the mike off. "I didn't say anything about the railgun and plasma cannon."

OPS continued: "Tachyon beam connected with the middle destroyer. Massive damage to the forward sections. The ship maintains integrity, but badly damaged and having difficulty maintaining speed and course.

"The destroyer to its port is being hammered with kinetic rounds and plasma loads. Eight . . . nine . . . ten . . . damn, eleven hits and no misses. Way to go, Kennedy!" he yelled without thinking. The entire bridge crew of the Fairchild joined in.

Except Hawks, who yelled, "SIT DOWN AND GET BACK ON STATION! We are in a war, people, not at some damn football game. Ops, report. And report the way you are supposed to Ensign or you will be down a rank when you leave this bridge."

"Yessir. Sorry, sir. The Kennedy hit the second destroyer eleven times, forward and above. The enemy ship shows massive damage and is leaking atmosphere. It is dead in space and sending out SOS calls. The initial destroyer hit is venting fluids and gases and appears to have lost steering. The forward quarter is gone. The third ship stopped."

Hawks, now all smiles, remembered the representative from Fell remained on hold. He re-keyed his mike and said, "Representative, I appreciate your offer, but Space Fleet is capable of handling our own battles. Thank you. Hawks, out."

CHAPTER 33

ASkiiunterel turned to Coop and simply shrugged. Coop showed no surprise in Hawks' attitude.

"Adding the black crystal as the power source for the SH array boosted the signal strength," Sparks said. "The communications from Hawks to us was weak. I boosted the reception to max and expanded the catch's spread and barely caught the reply. The white noise may be spreading and becoming denser within the ion clouds, or there could be more gravity convergence points where the Earth ships currently travel, or both. Or something else."

"You're supposed to talk, not brood," Sky said to Coop.

"They're being herded," he told her. "From the beginning the CVBG was led to a particular spot that would make them the most vulnerable. He has them within a vortex funnel, and the Prophet is pushing them towards the AF3-AF1 corridor edge."

Coop looked at the holo-display of the Aster system, allowed his advanced logic-processing free rein, and considered Cassie's explanation of tsunamis.

"Only two battlecruisers cover that corridor," he said aloud, but to no one but himself. "While over two-hundred ships press in from the AF3-AF2 corridor. In front of them is only the Prophet and one other battlecruiser, but that way leads to twenty-five-million-miles of more gravitational distortions. Behind them is AF3 and six battlecruisers lined up and waiting. Why are the enemy ships directing the CVBG to that corridor?"

Before anyone could comment, a command tower crew member informed Coop the Admiral in charge of the Mischene on Aster Farum 3 was willing to talk with him. He turned in his chair and flipped the mike-speaker switch indicated by the crew member.

"This is Captain Daniel Cooper, thank you for taking the hail," he said.

"I am Admiral Baynard Lexton, currently in command of the loyal Mischene military units still available on Aster Farum 3, as well as ships and units stationed off world," came the tired, but hard voice. "I am aware of who you are, Captain Cooper. I am also surprised to find out that you are on Fell and not with your ships here in our system."

Coop ignored the implied question, and went to the heart of the matter. "Admiral, if the Earth battle group now facing the Prophet should fail, what will the Prophet's next move likely be?"

"He will complete the subjugation of the Aster system," Lexton replied. "We will all either convert, be imprisoned, or killed. He is totally insane, Captain Cooper. If he is not stopped, after Aster he will take his brand of religious fervor backed by force to as many systems as he can. He believes it is his destiny to rule the galaxy as the Sacred Voice of the Tahbita."

"Agreed," Coop replied. "It is in everyone's best interest if we can work together to stop him now. It appears his ships are trying to drive the battle group towards the AF3-AF1 corridor where only two Mischene battle cruisers sit. Why, Admiral?"

"There is a wormhole gate located near those two battle cruisers," came the answer. "I do not know how he is able to communicate with ships inside a wormhole channel, but I believe that once your ships near the edge, while they are still in the worst section of the vortex and without shields, a nasty surprise will come out of that gate to greet them."

"I know how he communicates with them," Cassie interrupted through the speaker. "He's using the ships' gravity-well warning systems. Those systems warn a captain if a gate lies proximal to a gravity well or orbital body capable of causing damage. They wait until the system gives them an all clear before exiting. The Prophet is detonating nuclear bombs just inside the vortex near the gates. The gravity waves create an expansion and the ship's receive a blip in the warning system. When they see the blip, it's the signal to enter natural space."

"Simple and effective," Admiral Lexton said. "It would only work if a gate opened near a vortex, which is exactly what he has. It appears Soren and his people have been designing plans to trap your ships for some time, Captain Cooper. I tried to warn Admiral Hawks, but the man would not listen."

"Admiral Lexton, we have to get those ships out of that killing field," Coop said. "I have ideas, but I need your assistance."

Before the Mischene Admiral could reply, Cassie interrupted again. "The CVBG has been fired on, and it will be bad," she said. "I count sixty torpedoes and missiles in total coming from the two disabled destroyers."

"That would be everything each ship had," Lexton said. "If your ships do not have force fields strong enough, or maneuvering ability and escape speed, they are about to take heavy losses."

RESA VORTEX

(*Chapter One Redux*)

"Casalobos," the Admiral called over his com.

"109 targeting incoming enemy torpedoes in support of your gunners, Admiral," she replied and cut off further distractions.

"Tal," he called next.

"First three Spirit fighters set to launch in less than one minute," replied the Squadron Leader. No tension detectable in her tone. "Next three will follow as soon as the rear blast deflectors retract. We'll take out as many targets as we can before they reach the carrier." She cut him off as well.

"OPERATIONS, update" he demanded, swiveling to face the twenty-something operator who would not dare cut him off.

"Incoming torpedoes within range of our laser defenses. Automatic fire commencing," he replied. "The third enemy destroyer fired their pulse cannon and plasma cannon at the Fairchild, Admiral. The loads will arrive at the same time as the torpedo swarm."

Switching his attention from the Admiral, the OPS controller informed fighter command, "Captain Tal, you now have fifty-three-seconds before the first wave of torpedoes impact."

Spirits 2, 5, and 6 fired rear thrusters against the deflectors for an emergency launch. Instead of a normal controlled departure, they screamed out of the hangar, passed through the force-screen that prevented atmosphere from escaping into open space, and exited above the carrier's flight deck.

The three light fighters immediately encountered intense cross-gravity waves unique to the vortex. Flamer, piloting 2, rode the strongest wave, allowing it to push his ship sideways. Spirit 2 slipped over the side of the Fairchild. Like a swimmer allowing an undertow to pull him out to sea, Flamer went with the wave until he could pull the ship out of its grip.

The other two pilots, Wild Bill and Yassin, both made the mistake of fighting the gravity distortions crossing over the battle carrier. The small ships attempted to push forward against forces capable of moving small planets. For a moment the fighters appeared to hang still in space, caught in swirls and eddies similar to gravity whirlpools around black holes. The ships and crews pinned between the carrier and incoming enemy fire.

Realizing the futility of fighting the headwind, Wild Bill yanked on his collective. The keel thrusters fired, sending Spirit 5 straight up the chute. The incoming pulse beam from the third enemy destroyer passed beneath them.

Yassin and the crew of Spirit 6 disappeared within the following plasma load. The fighter vaporized in the super-heated projectile's path toward the Space Fleet carrier's bridge.

The PT-109 removed incoming torpedoes as Kennedy, the ship's AI, acquired, determined speed and course, and fired. The ship employed railgun, lasers, and the plasma cannon, selecting the defense with the best odds of reaching a target in time to prevent an impact.

Sindy Kebede at Tac-Ops monitored the action while keeping watch on the reset-timer for the tachyon weapon. She needed the system to recycle in order to take out the third destroyer.

"Comeon, comeon, comeon," she spoke the prayer-plea aloud, but it did not speed the process.

Genna controlled the Patrol Boat's back-up electro-magnetic generated force field. This allowed her to pad impact zones and minimize damage when missed torpedoes made contact. Instead of trusting untested software, she relied on reflexes enhanced by genetic engineering. The AI's avatar concentrated on the incoming torpedoes, dismissing those likely intercepted by Kennedy, and projecting flight-lines for the ones getting through. Her calculations provided only seconds to increase the force field's strength at the points of impact. Her inhuman eye-hand coordination the last available opportunity to save the ship from lethal damage. All other systems operated at max, and Kennedy engaged with battling the gravity-distortions within the vortex, while defending the ship from enemy fire, and covering the battle carrier.

Elie piloted the battle-tested space boat. In spite of the distortions, she forced the 109 to move. With safety limits disconnected, she taxed the power plants. The Spaniard played a deadly game of shuttling power between maneuvering the ship, and shunting as much energy to the shields as possible. She kept an eye on Genna, trying to anticipate when the avatar would shift the field in order to slide power from performance to protection.

Her re-engineered strength nearly crushed the manual flight control yoke in her right hand when coms called out, "Spirit 6 is gone."

The coms officer continued to provide bad news. "Enemy pulse and plasma rounds exploded against the Fairchild's aft deck. Upper Flight Hangar force-screen disabled. The hangar entrance collapsed. Three Spirit fighters are trapped inside. Carrier's bridge hit, but remains operational."

Coms continued to voice data-reports displayed on his terminal, as well as communications incoming from the other three ships in the beleaguered battle group.

"The 99 continues to cover the Pegasus. The 99 has taken four torpedo hits. Top, front starboard section is open to space . . . section sealed. Upper deck plasma cannon is gone. Hit amidship on port side. Section sealed. Fourth torpedo was a dud."

From the pilot station, Elie could see Sindy's Tac-Ops halo-display. She knew they were doing an incredible job taking out torpedoes headed for them and the Fairchild. The loss of sonic force-field protection, no communications beyond immediate vicinity, the constant strain placed on the BCVG by the anomalies within the vortex, and more rounds incoming from enemy ships meant the odds of survival continued to stack up against them.

Genna successfully redirected forcefield depths and prevented more than minimal damage by five high-explosive torpedoes that evaded the ship's defenses. The Fairchild, a bigger, more important target, received more attention, and more damage.

Coms confirmed Casalobos' concerns.

"Four torpedoes were blunted by the Fairchild's force field, but one connected at the bridge. Captain, the damaged bridge could not withstand the concussion. Fairchild reporting bridge and combat control room, including main communications and telemetry consoles, is destroyed. Operational control of the ship has been moved to Engineering."

In spite of the intense concentration required to pilot the ship, oversee command, and distribute energy, the Captain of the 109 could not ignore the call when she heard her name weakly through the Fellen trans-com bracelet she always wore.

"Noa, copy. It's Elie," she answered through gritted teeth, hoping her personal communications bracelet had the power to reach the twin Tal wore.

Kennedy, unrequested, boosted the signal while maintaining fire on incoming torpedoes.

"Hey, Loba. We're in pretty bad shape over here," came the reply. "My fighters are trapped behind the blast-deflection barriers. That probably saved us when the ceiling and walls came down. Hangar is venting atmosphere. Any crew not already dead escaped. They sealed the area. Spirits 3 and 4 are safe, functional, and stuck with me. We have environment inside the ships, but no way off the hangar. Hawks is not answering hails, and I'm unable to take command. Master Chief is running the show from engineering, but he's blind down there, Loba. He could use your help."

Elie smiled. One: relieved Noa, and the other fighter crews were alive. Two: The Israeli more concerned about the Master Chief than herself. Before she could respond to the gritty pilot, Sindy announced:

"Tachyon cannon ready. Firing. Hope you burn in hell," she added as the super-charged beam hurled towards the enemy destroyer. "Kennedy, light that mother-fucker up."

Coms called the action: "Third destroyer hit by our tachyon beam. The space-frame is crumpling. Multiple hits of kinetic and plasma loads from the 109 are on the way to finish the job."

With the distance to travel, and the vortex playing havoc with anything moving, it would take time and luck for the rods and plasma loads to reach the crippled destroyer.

Cons finally called out, "Two rods made contact. Implosion imminent (hesitation -- pause -- deep breath). There she blows. Implosion. Concussive reaction, amplified by the gravity distortions, completely taking out the disabled destroyer."

"Pegasus reports a hit to her starboard forward quarter. Casualties, but the section has been sealed. The ship remains operational. The 99 did one hell of a job keeping her safe," the LTJG added, not realizing the sting it gave Elie, who had not kept the Fairchild as well protected.

"Sorry, Noa," Elie said, releasing the yoke, and returning pilot control of the 109 to Kennedy. "I should have done more to protect the Fairchild."

"Stow it, Elie," Noa responded over the com. "The enemy ships targeted two-thirds of their armaments at us, not the Pegasus. The 109, the Fairchild crew, Flamer, and Wild Bill did everything possible. There were just too many incoming. If the Prophet and his other battlecruiser decide to join the fight now, I'm not sure we'll survive. Keep an eye on them, and get the group out of this kelba vortex."

"Any word on Hawks?" Elie asked.

"No, but until we know for sure if he survived or not I'm sure Rachelle and Sam will agree you should have flag. I'll call them. Noa, out."

Elie was not sure what to do, then Sindy's hand took hers. Casalobos released a long, slow breath. Whatever she faced, she had friends, an able crew, and a strong ship.

CHAPTER 34

FELL

"Admiral Lexton, your ships have dealt with the vortex before. What do I need to know to help my people?" Coop asked.

"A couple of things right now," Lexton said. "First, the gravity waves currently move down across the field, they bunch up, and then rise and become more violent as they near Aster Farum 3. The Prophet mapped the waves and placed his personal battle-cruiser and escort at the point where they begin to crest. Your ships are in the area where they will face the largest distortions. He chose this area well. The gravity is compacted. Ion particles from wormhole events that would normally fade remain trapped inside the vortex. This is why the white noise emitters are able to diminish your sonic force fields. One moment, Captain. My Chief of Intelligence has arrived. He may have more information."

"What are you thinking?" Sky asked.

"If these gravity waves act anything like real waves, either the CVBG can go up, past the Prophet and into an area of the vortex which is calmer, or they can ride the waves back towards AF3."

"Where six battle cruisers are waiting," Sky added.

"True, but there is no telling what may be waiting inside the wormhole they are heading for," he countered. "Either way, they need force fields back to full capacity. The shields will protect them from enemy fire, and help mitigate the effects of the gravity distortions. We also have to devise a plan to handle the other enemy destroyers and two-hundred ships bearing down on their location."

"Captain Cooper of Earth?" A new voice came over the com from Aster system. "Are you there, sir?"

"This is Captain Cooper. Who is this, and where is Admiral Lexton?"

"This is Admiral Revas Nan, Admiral Lexton has been assassinated by Major Willmer, our military intelligence commander."

"Admiral Nan, I'm truly sorry to hear this. What is happening?" Coop asked, afraid the headway made with Lexton now gone.

"Major Willmer killed Admiral Lexton and General Ostella," Nan said. "Captain Covane, our communications specialist, shot Willmer before he could do more damage. Captain, I have been monitoring your conversations with Admiral Lexton, and I agree we must help each other to stop the Prophet. Unfortunately, Major Willmer was obviously one of Soren's agents. He may know everything you were discussing."

"Which was not much in the way of usable intel," Coop said. "Having said that, Admiral Nan, if you agree we must cooperate, I need two things to occur quickly."

"Ask, Captain."

"First, I need you to order your battle cruisers and patrol boats around AF2 to eliminate as many of the noise-producing satellites as possible, as quickly as possible."

"Covane is making the call now, Captain. Hopefully we can get to them soon enough to help your ships. And the second thing?"

RESA VORTEX

Elie returned Sindy's squeeze. "We can't take another round," she said. "Our only chance is to get to the rim and away from this vortex, the white noise, and the Prophet. I don't know if the Fairchild can maintain its place, much less make way in this soup."

"Soup is a lot like a family," Sindy said. "Each ingredient enhances the others; each batch has its own characteristics; and it needs time to simmer to reach full flavor. That was from Marge Kennedy, another member of the original John F. Kennedy's family."

"Soup cans," Elie said absently.

"What about them?" Sindy asked.

"World War II sailors called destroyers tin cans," Elie said. "They were built from metal scraps collected by civilians. Scraps like soup cans."

Sindy looked at her long-time friend and current commanding officer with sympathy and concern. "Are you feeling okay, Elie. Should I call Singh?"

Elie turned, grabbed her TAC-OPS officer by both shoulders and gave her one big kiss on the lips. "You want soup out of a soup can, you have to open it," she said excitedly. "Sindy, you have command."

The Spanish Space Ranger jumped from the pilot's chair and hurried from the bridge.

"What just happened?" Sindy asked aloud.

"I think I know," Genna said, hurrying after Casalobos.

Genna knew every corridor, passageway, and shortcut on the 109 better than anyone. When Elie entered the hangar, she stood waiting.

"You're the better pilot," she said, "but you can't hold the ship in this vortex and aim at the same time. You drive and I'll cut."

Elie smiled, nodded, and ran past Genna, who turned and quickly caught up.

FELL

Cassie reported to Coop, but everyone in the command room heard.

"The armada of destroyers and mixed ships is making better time than they should," she said. "They appear to use the gravity currents to hurry their approach to the CVBG location. And Angel 7 left the PT-109."

"Angel 7?" Coop asked aloud.

"It appears Captain Casalobos took Angel 7 with her when she took command of the 109," Cassie answered.

"Elie, it's Coop. Do you read?"

"A bit fuzzy, Coop. I certainly hope you are calling with a brilliant plan to get our butts off of this burner," Elie said. "Genna's with me and can hear everything," she added.

"Are you on Angel 7?" he asked.

"We are," she replied. "I'm planning to use the laser cannon on extended fire to cut open the Fairchild like a soup can. The Spirit fighters inside being the soup."

"Smart, but dangerous," he replied. "If you breach too much of the hull you could cause terminal damage to the carrier. You could also slice through a fighter."

"That's why I'm flying and Genna is doing the slice and dice," Elie replied. "Hold on while I bring Noa into the conversation. Noa, it's Elie."

"Any news?" Noa asked. "Communications, telemetry, and everything else sucks down here."

"I have Coop on the Fell private line, and Genna in the cockpit with me," Elie told her.

"Hi, Coop, where the fuck are you? Elie, did you say cockpit?"

"Coop is on Fell playing command center, and we are in Angel 7 about to use our laser cannon to cut a hole big enough for your three little ships to float up and out."

"Wild Bill, Flamer, you two out there watching?" Noa called across her squad com.

"We're here," Flamer replied. "Been flying close to the carrier. It makes it easier than fighting the gravity wells and winds. We have Angle 7 in sight."

Since the two fighter pilots could not hear the private conversation, Noa brought them up to speed. Com-Tac hooked her private signal into their squadron broadcast.

"Worth a try," Flammer replied. "We'll watch Angel 7's back."

"Noa, this is Coop. Turn on all systems aboard all three fighters. Light up everything you can so Genna's scans will show her a strong picture of where you guys are located. Use your scanners to ping around the hanger as well. Her computers should be able to piggy-back yours and give her an image of the space around you."

"Good call, Coop," Noa said. "Jon-Jon, Trinity, did you hear the plan?"

"Lighting up all systems and scanning the immediate area," Jon-Jon called.

"Ditto," from Trinity.

"Perfect," came the word from Genna.

With Elie engaged keeping Angel 7 as steady as possible in an impossible eddy of gravity ebbs and flows, Genna pulled the trigger on one of the laser cannon in the ship's wing and held it down. She called out to Elie how high up she needed to hover for the beam to cut through the hull, but not too far through. She rotated the cannon to cut across, but Elie needed to fly the ship to create a down cut. They repeated the process, and thirty-minutes after they began, the damaged roof of the carrier hangar and bay floated up.

The three fighters helped it along by using their hover thrusters to lift them up, pushing the weightless deck away from the damaged ship, freeing them.

Ryan Fox, Flamer, was the first to speak after the harrowing operation. "That was the most incredible flying I have ever seen. And, Genna, if I ever need surgery, I swear I want you to hold the scalpel."

Sindy on the 109 added to the praise, "Thought you two might want to know that video was transmitted to all ships and personnel. Not only are the cheers still going strong, you just turned the entire CVBG's moral around. I've never seen or heard so many excited sailors and soldiers."

"It was phenomenal," Noa agreed. "But we have hostiles coming and need to regroup. I want all Spirit fighters on the flight deck ASAP. Drop landing gear and lock onto the deck. Master Chief Turner, Spirit Squadron will be your eyes until we have to deploy."

"Appreciate that, Captain. Glad you're back in the chair . . . kind of," the chief engineer responded.

"Angel 7 is heading back to the 109," Elie announced. "As soon as we're in and locked down, everyone prep to get back on course for the rim."

"Belay that order, Elie," Coop said. "The reason I contacted you was change your course. You need to turn for Aster Farum 3."

"Coop, that makes no sense," Elie replied. "We'd have to go back through the roughest part of the vortex, as well as face six Mischene battlecruiser and anything else on the planet that might fire on us."

"While you've had to deal with everything there, Elie, we've had the benefit of distance and safety," Coop answered. "The Prophet is trying to herd you to the AF3-AF1 corridor because he has a trap set. A super current slides along that corridor. It would be ramming against a wall, preventing you from exiting the vortex.

There is also a wormhole gate, and my best guess is it is filled with ships. He'll have you caught between those coming at you now and another group joining the two battle cruisers.

"Check your sonic shields," Coop said, the comment made across the SH system for all to hear, and not the private channel.

Genna answered, "They're growing stronger. We're also able to receive and send tachyon beam communications."

Soon after a chorus of agreement came from all segments of the CVBG.

"Mischene ships, the loyalist at AF 2 are taking out the satellites emitting the white noise. It will take a little while for the noise to fully abate, but eliminating a couple of them is already showing an effect," Coop told them. "Kennedy, tell everyone what you and Rosy have on display thanks to Admiral Nan on AF3."

The 109's A.I. responded saying, "The Admiral provided access to the Mischene's buoy system. It is similar to the Earth's Buoy Tracking Centers that provide data on wave heights and give tsunami warnings. In this case, the buoys track the gravity waves as they move across the vortex, as well as the currents running throughout the wedge. They can accurately predict when wavelengths shorten, when waves will be particularly powerful, or when they can expect lulls."

"Does this have something to do with the suggestion that we head for AF3?" Sam Harrington asked from the 99.

"If you guys can trust us just a little longer, I promise we are doing everything we can to get you out of that trap," Coop said.

It was Sam who said, "Captain Casalobos, you have the flag. What say you?"

"We've trusted each other for thirty years. No reason to stop now," she said. "What's next, Coop?"

She listened. Glad she trusted the man because otherwise she would have called him bat-shit crazy.

Nadia Cosoi looked to Sindy Kebede and asked, "We can do that? Really? Can we?"

"We're going to find out," the Ethiopian answered. "Coms please inform the crews of all four ships we are going surfing."

On Fell the constant overcast did not hide the arrival of day-time. Everyone in the command center neared exhaustion. They could all work through long hours, but the additional tension, the time spent waiting, hoping, doubting and the pain of loss wore on them. The local doctor delivered pills that would keep them on their feet since they needed to stay sharp a little while longer. Lives depended on them getting this right. Everything depended on Coop making the right decisions.

"Star says Nadia Cosoi is a bitchin' operator," Sky said as she slid down the wall to take a place next to Cooper. "I believe she got the term from Dr. Cosoi. They are as ready as they can be. Star says they can't chance a practice run. It either works or it doesn't."

"I trust them, Sky," he said, not taking his head from the wall or turning to look at her directly.

"Storm and Sparks completed the communication relays. They've patched so many different systems together it resembles a web. They tell me Captain Covane on AF3 has been a major help. Kennedy and Rosy are creating new systems on the run, and Sindy Kebede is making sure everyone is up to speed on the plans, the fallback plans, and the plans when those plans fall apart."

"I trust all of them, too," he said. "Even the Mischene on AF3. Not because I honestly trust them, but because I know they know what will happen to them if the Prophet wins."

"If things aren't done just right, bad things could happen to them either way," Sky said. "Singletary and the UEC keep sending messages to us," she added. "They kind of know what's going on, but are short on details. The communications crew in the tower continue to ignore them. Elie and the CVBG are pretty much ig-noring them as well."

Cassie spoke to Coop via his embedded transmitter. "Coop, it's Cassie. Thirty-minutes," she said. "The Prophet's armada will be in range to engage and the conditions in the vortex will be at max-imal for your plan to succeed. Ship is prepped and ready. Cassie, out."

"Time for your part," he said, rising up, grabbing her hand, and helping her to stand. "Listen up," he called, quieting the command center. "Everything goes green in thirty-minutes. Either all of our work and all of their bravery wins the day, or the Prophet is on the verge of taking the Aster system. From that strategic location, with Earth forces decimated and no one else stepping up to fight him, he will move back out to attack the trading worlds and, eventually, Earth."

Coop faced the hologram, watching as two-hundred-plus enemy red lights converged on four small blue lights. "From this moment forward, Sky is in command of this center. What she says you do. What she asks, you try. Hiro and Mags will join me on the Cassandra."

"Fuck no," Storm said. "I told you once before, you go flying off, I go with you."

She stood with hands on hips, and her usually bright, happy face an ugly scowl.

"You're needed here, so you are not going. Sky isn't going. I will not allow the Prophet to survive this, no matter what the final outcome. That man must not be able to sail away, win, lose, or draw."

"Sky and I have fought with you before," Storm argued.

"Hiro and I have the best chance of getting to him. It's what we do. What no one else can do as well. You're both good pilots, but Mags is the best available flyer on Fell. She's also operationally trained. I need to have soldiers with me who think, move, act, and react exactly as I expect. We've had time together, but not the kind of time needed for this type of mission."

Coop ignored Storm's pout, and Sky's scowl.

"You, the two of you, and all of the rest of you should be here and available to the CVBG when hell breaks loose. We'll be listening and available for consult on Cassandra, but without your resources."

"You won't get there for more than a day," Storm said, now close to tears. "By the time you arrive it will all be over, whatever happens."

"I know," he said, moving to her and taking her in his arms. "We aren't going there to help save the day, or applaud any success. Our mission is Soren. He orchestrated all of this, but stayed safely out of the way. We're going to take that safe place away from him, permanently."

"Or die trying," Cindy Shah said. She joined the battle planning early that morning, but Hiro had not told her of Coop's plan to go after Soren. "Coop, I get it. I'm still a Marine. You just better bring Hiro and Mags back to us."

"Hiro and Mags are outside," Coop said. "Cindy, you and Sparks need to go see them off."

He pulled Sky into the hug with Storm.

"You have less than twenty-minutes to pull all of this back together. I have every intention of bringing the three of us back."

Twenty minutes later, aboard the Wraith, Mags, at co-pilot said, "Wow. First time I've been shotgun with Coop and the ship wasn't filled with his girlfriends."

"We have eight hours to the rim, another twenty-four hours until we reach the Aster system, and another six to eight hours once we reach the system to get to Aster Farum 3," Hiro said. "Plenty of time for Coop to find more girlfriends," he joked.

"Cassie, do you have the coordinates for the Prophet's battle-cruiser?" Coop asked.

"I do," she replied.

"Cassie, when we clear the outer atmosphere, engage the new force field array we got from Rys. Input the Prophet's location in the navigational computer. We're going to space-fold directly from Fell to that vortex. That should shave sixteen hours off our journey time."

"Can we do that?" Mags asked. "Really? Can we?"

"We're going to find out," Coop said with a wry smile.

CHAPTER 35

RESA VORTEX * FELL * SPACE

In spite of the rough ride, repair teams aboard the four ships worked to make sure sealed sections remained sealed, exposed and dangerous wiring secured, and systems restored wherever possible.

The Fairchild was in the worse shape, and Noa sat frustrated in her fighter on the deck of the ship while teams hurried to try and keep the carrier space-worthy. The frame badly damage, a lot of people injured, and many dead or missing.

Huard at the com-tac station acted as the ships navigator and systems analyst, keeping the carrier in the proper position to stay within the gravity wave without allowing the vortex currents to overrun and potentially crush her. Master Chief Turner and his engineers doubled as pilots, flying the big space craft from secondary controls and trusting Huard's directions.

Adele and Rosy handled emergency diagnostics aboard the PT-99. Rosy identified the danger spots with the highest potential for failure. Adele sent repair teams with instructions. She accompanied more than a few of these missions, using her connection with Rosy to pinpoint disruptions requiring immediate attention.

The medical sections were the busiest, dealing with everything from major trauma caused by enemy fire to broken bones resulting from sailors tossed about during the battle. Bumps, bruises, minor cuts, and sprains were ignored by the medics and the people suffering from them. Anything not potentially life-threatening would be dealt with later.

The 99 suffered a rip along her central port section effecting three decks. It severed feeds from exterior scanners on that side, leaving the ship functionally blind on one side. The plasma cannon burned away by a pulse blast from a Mischene destroyer and the section directly beneath sealed off to prevent the potential for an implosion. The hydroponics area and front quarter top deck on the starboard side was gone. A third of the crew dead, missing, or disabled.

In spite of the fact Elie placed the PT-109 between the incoming torpedoes and cannon fire and the Fairchild, she took minimal damage. Elie's skills as a pilot and Genna's ability to redirect padding to the force fields within yards of where and when they needed it resulted in no exterior breaches. Her paint job scorched, and several exterior communications and information arrays damaged or destroyed. The majority of injuries resulted from people tossed around or hit by equipment not locked down properly. Kennedy's ability to trust the crew made a difference as well. The AI directed systems, fire controls, or communications at optimal speed, ignoring anything and everything else, allowing crew members to monitor and maintain whatever she deemed secondary.

With thanks to the 99, Pegasus emerged with minimal damage.

One major hit on her forward starboard side, and while it did no damage to the ship's systems, it was in a location housing a company of Space Rangers. Fifty men and women lost before they could evacuate and seal the damaged section.

"The Prophet is reacting to our turn for AF3," Sindy announced. She, Genna and Elie had been active since before the trap sprung. They relied on a combination of improved genetics and pills provided by Dr. Singh to remain awake and focused. "Nadia, one of the battlecruisers on the AF3-AF1 corridor just fired off a nuclear warhead just inside the vortex. Looks like the Prophet decided to call out whatever assets he had waiting for us there."

Nadia Cosoi had been busy since the attacks began. She worked non-stop with Star on Fell on a plan created by Daniel Cooper, but left to the two super-hackers to make real.

The Romanian computer genius turned to Elie in the command chair. "We had three possible options," she said. "Whatever the Prophet tried, we had a response, but once we initiate, he'll know what we are capable of doing. His people will react. This is most likely a one-trick pony."

"Make it a good trick," Elie replied.

Cosoi smiled and turned back to her console. "Star, you take cruiser number one and I'll take number two. Col. Kebede, let me know when the wormhole gate begins to open."

"You can call me Sindy, Nadia," Kebede said, and added, "It's opening now."

Two-point-five-million-miles from the 109, and trillions of miles from Fell, two computer experts hacked into alien battle-cruisers. Nadia set up a gateway through a computer system used to maintain temperature in a refrigeration unit, and Star came in via an entertainment kiosk in a common room. Within seconds they controlled both warships.

"We are targeting the gate," Nadia called out. "All torpedoes and missiles are queued, armed, and sequence begins . . . now."

Quiet ensued for five minutes before Cosoi added, "Missiles and torpedoes from both ships are entering the gate. Whoever is inside is about to get their morning coffee interrupted."

"Confirmed," Sindy said from Ops. "Multiple, as in dozens of explosions are occurring inside that wormhole. Analysis suggests strongly the size of the concussions indicate several objects within the channel are exploding."

"Keep watching," Nadia said without looking up.

Sindy reported. "The Mischene battlecruisers are firing all cannon . . . at each other. The two ships are destroying each other. Neither had force fields up."

Ten-minutes later she said, "It's over," she said, sitting back. "Threats obliterated."

"Nice trick, Nadia," Elie said, smiling for the first time in hours.

"Not quite over," the Romanian replied. "When we entered the gateways, I also initiated one other little worm. Thanks to Star, I set off every alarm, flashing light, noise generating speaker, and doodad I could get to on the two-hundred smaller ships following the destroyers."

"Those ships have either come to a stop or flying erratic patterns," Genna said from the science console. "I'm picking up hundreds of communications. I would say my analysis of the situation is the Zenge or Mischene on those ships are going fucking crazy."

The analysis, coming from a freckled twenty-something avatar who looked as if she should be lounging in a sorority house, made everyone on the bridge giggle or laugh.

"But that's it," Cosoi said, popping a chocolate into her mouth. "The Prophet's battlecruisers, his two and the six around AF3, as well as the four destroyers on our ass initiated blocking protocols. We won't be pulling anything like that again."

"Send our thanks and congratulations to Star and the people on Fell," Elie directed her computer pro. "Then have Dr. Singh give you something to let you sleep for a couple of hours."

"And possibly wake up dead?" Nadia replied. "Or miss something?" Said as if missing something would be a much bigger issue than dying.

"We have hours before we're close enough to AF3 for anything else to happen," Elie told her. "The destroyers behind us cannot catch up. We're all going to take a break and grab rest. Coop has told me a hundred times that sleep is a weapon. We need to be sharp when we near AF3. Bridge crew is relieved, and minimal activity for the next eight hours."

"All right," Nadia answered, "but I know exactly how many chocolates I have and they all better still be here when I get back."

The Prophet used the laser pistol he took from General Trewellan to shoot the computer-systems officer in the back of the head. He tossed the weapon back to the General.

"Replace him with someone capable," he said as he exited the command bridge. "I know exactly how many ships I have out there and they all better be operational and headed for Aster Farum 3 when I get back."

Sky ordered everyone in the command center to step down. They all needed showers, food, and rest.

"We have a few hours of peace, and all the plans are set," she said.

She gave her sister, Star, a hug. When the command and control personnel exited the control tower they were met by over 1,000 Fellen, humans, and a mix of aliens who opted to remain on Fell after the battles or among the first to reinitiate trade. They silently opened a corridor in the mass of bodies for the people exiting the OAT to walk through. The spontaneous applause rivaled the strongest thunder storms.

Sky and Storm both looked up at the same time. They could not see anything though the overcast skies, but they both looked for him anyway.

Cassie materialized long enough to place a thermal blanket over Coop. He slept sitting in the pilot's seat with his feet in the co-pilot's chair. Hiro and Mags slept in the bunks.

"I'll bring him back," she silently promised.

CHAPTER 36

Genna knocked and entered Elie's cabin when the door opened. Elie sat on her bed, crosswise, her sock-clad feet hanging over the edge. Without asking permission, Genna removed the boots Coop gave her, and climbed up next to the Captain.

"We're four hours from firing range of the cruisers sitting off AF3," she said. "The wave charts and real-time wave mapping from the buoys allowed us to make good time. We are actually surfing gravity swells. Captain Covane and Sindy have been in deep conversations for the past hour. I spoke with Tista on the Pegasus. She and her mother think they are taking up space and nothing more. Nadia is trying to find out who ate four of her chocolates, and the Marines are sick of our little space war and would appreciate some action."

Elie set the personal data pad she consulted down and said, "Our little space war? They actually said that?"

"Yep." She turned to face her commander and friend. "On a more serious note, the Major is concerned about the Marines and Rangers on the Fairchild. When Space Fleet Command ordered them along and forced us to place them wherever we could find room, they didn't consider the lifeboats. There simply aren't enough for everyone on Pegasus or Fairchild if it comes to a point where they must abandon ship."

"Any news I might appreciate?' Elie asked.

"I ate Nadia's chocolates," the avatar replied with a straight face.

Elie actually laughed out loud.

"You spent entirely too much time with Coop," she said between hiccups. "His sense of humor rubbed off."

"Funny, I don't think I spent nearly enough time with him," Genna answered.

"I've had thirty years with him, on and off, mostly off, and I don't think I've had enough time with him either," Elie replied. "He can be a pain in the ass with his determination to stay in front and shield others . . . "

"Stupid need to talk out loud about every detail of a plan (Genna) . . . "

"His opinion counts more than everyone's else's (Elie) . . . "

"Telling you what he is going to do when it's too late to stop him (Genna) . . ."

"Deciding it's always up to him to save the universe (Elie) . . ."

"It's like Mags always says," and Elie turned to Genna and together they said, imitating Mags, "Men are stupid."

Both laughed until Genna said, "Kennedy estimates another twenty-hours before he could arrive in the system. Do you believe he thinks Hiro, Mags, and he can take on the Prophet?"

"He has no plans of taking on the Prophet, Genna," Elie said, serious again. "Mags will care for the ship while he and Hiro ghost in, find Soren, kill him, and ghost out again. If they can get aboard the ship Soren is on, he's dead."

Aloud she said, "Kennedy, update, please. Keep it simple."

"Three-hours-fourteen-minutes until within weapons' range of the battlecruisers at AF3 . . . their range. The CVBG's tachyon cannons could engage two hours before that, but would be less likely to cause catastrophic damage. The Mischene destroyers are six hours behind. That will be as close as they can get until we stop. The two-hundred-thirteen mixed armada appears to have taken back control of their systems. They are ten to twelve-hours behind us. The Prophet and his escort have not moved. No additional wormhole activity anywhere in the system. Captain Covane would appreciate speaking with you when you return to the bridge, but said it was not urgent."

"Thank you, Kennedy. As soon as Genna and I get our boots on, we will head to the bridge. Are the other ships in the CVBG holding up?"

"Repairs continue. No one any worse than before, and should be operational for the confrontation at AF3. Except the Fairchild, who will be more functional that operational, but Captain Tal promises the ship will be there to act, and not just for show."

"Captain on the bridge," Sindy Kebede called, rising from the command chair.

"As you were," Elie said, taking the chair and looking around her command. The time surfing the gravity wave allowed shifts to re-settle. She now found Casey Adams on navigation, Michael Cuthbert on communications, Cosoi, looking fresh, at systems, Lesego Ndaba at pilot, Sindy on OPS/TAC, and Genna took her seat at the science station.

"Kennedy, please see if Captain Covane is available."

"This is Captain Covane on AF3," came a female voice over the open coms.

"Captain Casalobos, Captain Covane. First, let me give you my personal thanks for everything you and your people have done to help. Second, we are on an open com on my bridge. Is that okay or do we need privacy?"

"If you trust your bridge crew, we have no need for privacy," The Mischene communications officer said. "It is a pleasure to speak with you, Captain Casalobos. When I was told the officer in charge of your group was female, I was surprised and pleased. Females do not reach that level of command in the Aster system."

"Perhaps that will be one of many things that change when we complete this mission, Captain," Elie replied. "Command doesn't care about a person's sex, religion, or race. Command only requires you are capable of getting the job done. Was there something specific you needed?"

"To tell you we have been broadcasting messages to the people on the battlecruisers you are about to face. Four of the six were commandeered by the Prophet and his people. The vast majority of Mischene aboard were forced into service. We hope that when the time comes, they will mutiny and re-take the ships. It would be a major request on our behalf, but we would appreciate it if you did not fire on the two outer ships on both sides of the line until they fire on you."

"You want us to give them time to take control," Elie said. "That could leave us open to a lot of damage if we give them the time to react, Captain."

"And still I make the request," came the response.

"I'll talk it over with my officers and the other ships' captains," Elie replied. "I cannot make you that promise, but I will try to give a little leeway. You need to impress on potential mutineers the need to act quickly. Anything else?"

"Admiral Nan agrees with Captain Cooper's plan of engagement. However, once the Prophet's officers leading the Zenge on the surface realize what is happening, we will be in grave danger. Our forces are weakened."

"As soon as possible, we will do what we can to assist," Elie promised. "First we have to get through. Then we have to prepare for the destroyers on our tails. Otherwise there will not be anyone available to assist you."

"Understood," Covane responded. "When we receive the signal, we will do our part. That I do promise, Captain Casalobos. I am capable of getting the job done."

"Good show, Captain. And good luck, the John F. Kennedy, out."

Once Elie was sure the coms closed, she said to Kennedy, "Please inform the other ships, and ask they respect the request to not target those four ships until we know for sure they remain hostile."

"I thought you were going to open it to discussion," Cosoi said.

"I'm flag for this group, Dr. Cosoi. That's all the discussion I need."

Two hours and 200,000-miles from AF3, Spirit Team members 2, 3, 4, and 5 left the deck of the Fairchild to fly in formation with the PT-109. Tal remained attached to the deck and remained in command of the carrier from that position.

Paré brought the Pegasus alongside the injured Roosevelt. They would target the enemy cruiser center and starboard their position. The 109 and Spirit squad assigned the enemy ship at center to port. If one of the remaining outside cruisers made an offensive move, Tal and the Fairchild would react.

At 150,000 miles, sixteen tachyon small-beam cannon on the fighters, and four ship-mounted tachyon cannon fired. At the exact moment, five surface-based pulse cannon located at Mischene military bases on Aster Farum 3 also fired on the two Prophet-controlled vessels in the middle of the formation. The result: the atomization of the two ships. The outermost cruiser to the CVBG's starboard released torpedoes and fired its plasma cannon at the on-coming ships.

The Fairchild's operational tachyon cannon responded, as did the gun emplacements on AF3. The ship decimated by the tachyon weapon. Torpedoes from the PT-109 and the PT-99 met and destroyed the enemy torpedoes.

Covane announced the other three ships had been retaken by Mischene still loyal to the traditional military. To prove their intent, all offensive and defensive systems shut down. The three ships drifted in orbit, totally open to incoming fire.

Covane informed Elie Zenge forces on the planet mounted major offensive actions at the bases which fired on the Prophet's space ships.

"Noa, it's Elie. The path is clear. Can you and your engineers put the Fairchild on the ground?" she asked on the personal channel, not wanting the others to know the plan until Tal gave final approval.

"The ship wasn't designed for atmospheric flight," Tal said, knowing Elie knew. "We could use the force field as a heat shield, and enter the upper atmosphere at just the right angle. We'll need a big landing field, and a lot of luck. What the hell. We're not going home in this can. Might as well put it down where we can do some good."

"Genna is sending your Master Chief the location and angle of descent," Elie told her. "Captain Covane is sending the coordinates of a major agricultural farm located five-hundred-miles west of the capital and the military command center. You'll need to disengage your fighter before you hit the atmosphere. You can follow the Fairchild down. I'll meet you on the surface as soon as I'm sure we're solid up here. Elie, out."

"Major Duval, this is Captain Casalobos. Please inform your officers aboard the Fairchild when the carrier comes to rest on the surface be prepped for deployment. They need to protect the ship and crew while you hit the Zenge outside of the command center. Once we have that secure, we'll start making plans for the rest of the planet."

Duval responded, "They'll be good to go. I'll take my best shooters and the two shuttles on Pegasus and head directly for the capital. Once we take out the Mischene officers leading the Zenge it will make it easier to deal with them. Can you ask Spirit wing to strafe the forces outside command until we can get in and set up?"

"Will do," she replied. "We have the game plan we used on Fell. We can use similar tactics on AF3. Biggest difference is the Mischene military is ready for payback and will be able to assist quicker than the Fell resistance. Use Captain Covane on the surface and Colonel Kebede in the air for communications and coordination. Elie, out."

Over the next ninety-minutes everyone in space and those on the surface prepared for the arrival of the Fairchild. The battle carrier was designed to operate in space and use space platforms for refits and relief, not operate within a planet's atmosphere. Once it made it through the upper atmosphere, it would be a semi-controlled fall to the ground. The computer systems were not designed for such an action. The Master Chief and a team of engineers would manually work engines, thrusters, hovers, and anything else they could think of to help guide the fall.

Noa released just before the ship began to heat up from re-entry. Her ship dove down and in front of the Fairchild to provide eyes for the engineers when they came through. Jon-Jon and Trinity soon joined her, while Flamer and Wild Bill headed for the capital and the military command center to begin strafing enemy fighters.

Major Duval and forty-nine Space Fleet Marines exited the Pegasus aboard one shuttle and another fifty aboard the second.

"The three remaining Mischene battlecruisers are providing unrestricted access," Dr. Cosoi told Elie from the Systems console. "I've made sure they cannot maneuver and they cannot fire weapons. You won't have to worry about fanatics re-taking control and stabbing us in the back."

"Surface-mounted cannons are shut down as well," Sindy reported. "The military bases under siege are doing all they can to repel attackers. We have access and control of cannons. You don't have to worry about anyone taking a shot at us from the planet."

"The Fairchild is on course . . . sort of," Genna reported. "We can watch."

She placed video on the SHD screen in front of everyone on the bridge. She accessed the 109's optics, as well as cameras from the surface, and the three Spirit fighters escorting the big ship down.

"She looks like shit," Cuthbert said. "She's going to fly apart when she hits the ground."

"They kept the sub-light engines on and maintain hi-revs to keep the sonic forcefield operating at highest yield," Elie said calmly from the command chair. "They also have the EM force fields up. They are in for a rough landing, but if they don't tumble, they should make it."

Everyone aboard every ship watched monitors. No one talked. Few breathed.

The Fairchild hit a crop field and plowed a good one-hundred-foot depth into the surface layer, surging forward at 1,000mph. The ship plowed through one field after another until it came to rest with a three-mile long furrow behind it.

Cuthbert on coms reported, "Engines shut down. Master Chief Turner is requesting as many docs, nurses, and med personnel as available be dispatched. Reports of people injured and dead on every deck, every level. They took one hell of a ride. The Fleet Ranger commander on board is pulling his people together and headed for exterior exits. Rear hangar doors are above the floor of that furrow the ship created. They will be able to dispatch vehicles and equipment for ground forces. Spirits 1, 3, and 4 are touch-down and crews assisting people exiting the ship. No report of enemy forces nearby."

"Show's over," Elie said to her bridge team. "Have Dr. Singh and techs report to the LBJ with as much medical supplies as they can carry and get them to the Fairchild," she ordered. "Have Sam do the same with his meds on the 99. When Duval is finished using the Pegasus' shuttles to transport the Marines and Rangers, have them ready to provide supplies and personnel to the Fairchild based on whatever Dr. Singh requires."

Elena Casalobos stepped into the role of commander easily. Until someone confirmed Hawks death, or found him alive, she would shoulder the responsibility for those left breathing.

"Michael, tell Noa she commands Spirit in support of surface Marines as she sees fit. Inform Covane and Nan that Major Duval is now ground commander for any and all actions on AF3. If they want us to stay and help, they do what he says or we pick our people up and leave. Sindy, picket the ships to face the vortex and prepare to engage the in-coming destroyers and the armada behind them."

"That last bit isn't necessary," Genna said. "The four destroyers changed course and are headed back to the AF3-AF2 corridor. The Prophet and escort cruiser are also making way for the same corridor. I believe they intend to leave the system and gate to wherever they came from."

"The small mix-matched ships?" Elie asked.

"Still headed this way," Genna replied. "They are ten to twelve hours out, and from Nadia's system scans made during the hack, each one is equipped with a single laser cannon. I don't mean to sound overconfident, but any one of our ships, even hurt, could take out all of them while they are still two hours away from the range needed to use a laser cannon on us."

"The Prophet is sending them to make sure we remain here to keep them away from the planet," Elie said. "He knows now we are free of the vortex. We can outrace his ships to the wormhole gates. We can break up the convoy to send ships after him, or we let him go."

"Are we going to let him escape?" Lesego Ndaba asked. "After all of this, he gets to go home and make plans to do it all again somewhere else."

"We're hurt and we have a lot of dead and injured people," Elie responded. "We need to get AF3 under control and make sure the rest of the system is free of Zenge and Prophet followers. We also need to re-open communications with Space Fleet and Earth, and I do not think that will be pretty. So we let him go."

"What about Captain Cooper?" Casey Adams asked from Navs.

"It might be close, but I don't think Coop, Hiro, and Mags will arrive before the Prophet gates out," Elie said. "Sindy, send our thanks to Fell and tell them they can stand down. We're going to get busy, but nothing they will be able to help with."

"Should we contact Coop directly?" Senait asked.

"Cassandra will monitor communications and know what's going on," Elie said. "Coop is on mission. Unless he breaks silence, don't make contact. I don't think the Prophet's people can eavesdrop on tachyon transmissions, but I don't see a reason to test that theory."

"Will do," Kebede answered. "Elie, you've done a fantastic job. If you had not been in that chair, I'm not sure we would have survived. Ladies and gentlemen, respects."

Col. Senait Kebede stood, faced her commanding officer, snapped to attention and delivered a salute. Everyone on the bridge did the same, holding the position until Elie rose and return the salute, tears in her eyes, pride in her heart.

When she sat down she whispered, but knew she was heard, "Kennedy, I love you. The PT-109 is the finest ship I have ever served on. Good job, girl. Great job."

The Wraith passed over AF3 and into the vortex unnoticed. The combination of stealth, small size, the Lisza Kaugh's new forcefield, and traveling within space-fold meant no one in the system, including their own people, knew Cassandra was minutes from reaching its final destination.

The three aboard monitored all the action over the past few hours. Mags quite entertaining with her on-going commentary regarding everything that happened, good and bad.

As Coop passed within a couple of minutes of his former ship and crew, friends, and fellow soldiers, he said, "Good job."

Now time for him to do his job.

PART 4

Conclusion

Consequences

Rivers eventually end. All the water from all the different origins empty into a larger body. The mouth of a river is often the location civilizations select to build major trading centers. A place of transitions and transportation heading in all directions.

As a consequence, civilization come into contact with other civilizations.

CHAPTER 37

The geniuses at Trent Industries, notably Nathan Trent himself, designed the two-person Wraith for ultimate stealth. No one yet discovered how to truly cloak a vessel, but this ship came damn close.

United Earth Council starships of Space Fleet utilized toned-down space-fold speeds to go from a planet to the outer rim of a system where, once free of the gravity bubble exerted by the system's star and orbital object, could engage full space-fold to journey to another system. The ship reentered natural space before reengaging space-fold at the lower levels to make quick time to the final destination. This often meant it could take as much time traveling from a planet to the system's rim, and the reverse at the other end of the trip, as it took to travel between entire solar systems.

Except for one ship. Cassandra now came equipped with the only force field emitter created by newly discovered and specially cut black diamond crystals. The crystal array enveloped the fighter in a force field nothing could penetrate (and nothing could escape).

On a hunch and a prayer, Daniel Marcel Cooper, employed the force field above the planet Fell and engaged the space-fold array at maximum thrust. The result: a ship able to exit a system without the adverse effects of gravity wells surrounding orbital bodies or the system's star.

Now he and his companions, Hiroshi Kimura (Hiro), and Mary Margaret Moore (Mags) were going to learn if the reverse held true.

Instead of exiting at the Aster system rim and taking the six to eight hours to reach Aster Farum 3 a normal space-fold in-system trek would take, they planned on exiting into natural space three-million-miles beyond AF3. Not only the first test of the combination of force field and space-fold used to exit into natural space inside a solar system, they would be exiting into a gravitational vortex. They would drop into a region producing distortions and disruptions of space and time, and gravity waves capable of moving a small planet or crushing a ship the size of a Wraith.

Mags sat shotgun while Coop piloted the ship from the left seat. Hiro sat at the Communications and Tactical (Com-Tac) console directly behind the cockpit.

"If this doesn't work and we die, I am going to be seriously pissed," she said, watching the navigational heads-up display counting down until exit into natural space.

"Think positive," Coop replied. "It could work perfectly and we could still die from the gravity disruptions in the vortex."

"Or it could work perfectly, we are able to survive the vortex, and the two battlecruisers we are attempting to sneak up on see us and destroy us," Hiro said, checking the location of said battlecruisers relative to their exit point.

"Bite me, both of you," Mags responded, but smiling. "I do have to say I love this ship."

"Thank you, Mags," came a voice with no body attached. The ship's Artificial Intelligence came with an avatar who could materialize through virtual-hologram technology.

Cassie had not yet materialized before Hiro. Coop did not want the distraction of explaining the overtly sexy female form Cassie chose when solid.

"All systems at peak efficiency," Cassie reported. "I loaded the data from the Mischene buoys in the vortex. It should provide sufficient information to allow us to navigate the field's gravitational oddities when we exit."

"Updates on the CVBG?" Coop asked the AI.

"The Carrier is on the surface acting as a shelter and staging area. Spirit Squadron is operating sorties in support of ground forces, or protecting local military and civilian assets. The three remaining ships orbit over AF3. Various levels of damage following the battle. The SFPT-99 reports the most destruction. The destroyer-class Pegasus is in the best shape, and the SFPT-109 somewhere in between."

His long-time friend and one-time living companion, Captain Elena Casalobos, commanded the PT-109. She acted as flag officer for the CVBG. Admiral Stephen Hawks dead, body found pinned within the Fairchild's devastated command bridge.

Hiro reported from com-tac. "The four enemy destroyers that turned away after the battlecruisers orbiting AF3 were destroyed or surrendered continue to make way for a wormhole gate on the AF3-AF2 corridor. They are two-million-miles away and present no danger. The Prophet's battlecruiser and escort are headed toward the same gate location. The fleet of smaller ships remain on course for AF3. Apparently to cover the Prophet's escape."

The Prophet, Atticus Soren, a Mischene racial supremacist and religious zealot believed himself the Sacred Voice of the Tahbita. The religious text of the Mischene race predicted a manifest destiny in which the Mischene ruled the galaxy. The Mischene, in turn, ruled by The Prophet.

Coop faced and fought radical religious extremists in the aftermath of the pandemic on Earth that wiped out half the population. He had first-hand experience with men like the Prophet. People who cared about nothing but personal glory. He decided Soren could not be allowed to leave the Aster system, to return somewhere else later, intent on continuing his war to subjugate the galaxy.

Soren's father initiated the gambit to gain ultimate power by setting his son up as a proxy. Together they were responsible for the death of billions of innocents across multiple worlds.

Atticus Soren ordered his father's execution in his opening salvo to take over the Aster system.

Coop was not going to allow him to escape.

"Five minutes to exit," Mags said. "If these readings are correct, and between that damn force field and the vortex, I cannot guarantee they are, we will exit less than one-hundred-miles behind and below the Prophet's ship. In space distances we call that pretty fucking tight."

Coop and Hiro donned the METS skintight battle suit. The woven kevlar-steel-alloy fit like lycra, but could stop a blade and prevent a laser burst from cutting into them. Of course, the burst would put them on their butts, but better than being dead. They covered the METS in EVA suits with re-breathers, helmets, and mini-hover jets.

The plan called for Mags to pilot Cassandra and place the small ship beneath the Mischene battlecruiser and between the double shafts containing the ship's power plants, weapons armory, and assorted machinery. The site where the vents shunted unwanted gases into space.

A ship, even this specially designed one-of-a-kind might not risk its own destruction by flying into an obviously dangerous, probably insane position. Mags would not think twice about such a maneuver.

Coop and Hiro would transfer from Cassandra to the battle-cruiser by crossing open space.

Coop received a cruiser diagram from Admiral Nan, currently the military commander of the loyalists on AF3. When Coop contacted Nan with a plan to stop the Prophet, he had two requests. The second part included ship diagrams and codes for access points.

The shovel-head craft had an exterior maintenance hatch Coop and Hiro would use to enter the vessel. Nan provided a universal access code they hoped none of the Prophet's people thought to deactivate and recode.

"What happens if the code doesn't work?" Mags asked. "When we discussed the entry and recon, you kind of skipped right by that possibility."

"I send Hiro to the front door to ask who ordered Japanese take-out," Coop replied straight-faced.

"And when they open the fortune cookie, knock-out gas will explode and take out everyone on board," Mags quipped.

"Fortune cookies are not Japanese," the former Japanese Imperial Guardsman said.

"Actually, fortune cookies were invented by a Japanese-American in San Francisco," Coop said. "We could always spike their saki."

"If the codes don't work, you'll make it up as you go," she said more seriously.

"Prepare," Cassie called from embedded speakers. "Exit into natural space in thirty-seconds."

Dr. Nathan Trent was an aeronautics and history buff. When he decided he wanted his own personal fighter-spaceship, he looked back in time and decided to use the Lockheed Martin F-22 Raptor as his design platform.

He did change the pointed nose to a wider, meaner looking front he stole from the Shelby Cobra automobile. The ship sported a sleek profile, delta wings, a raised cockpit, and retractible horizontal and vertical stabilizers in the rear to allow the craft ultimate maneuverability within an atmosphere. Made from next-gen alloys and materials discovered inside the Martian hangar, the components and her low-profile made the ship undetectable by scans and radars.

On a whim, Trent installed an antiquated entrance and egress. The whim about to play a major role in the mission.

Mags handled controls inside the cockpit, sealed off from the rear of the ship. She slipped Cassandra beneath the Mischene battlecruiser and the flagship for the Prophet. Coop and Hiro wore their EVA suits and carried hard-shell carriers holding clothes and equipment they would need once they invaded the enemy vessel. Mags piloted the Wraith, keeping her steady and true in spite of the turbulence from both the vortex in space and the battlecruiser coursing above her. Within feet of the massive cruiser's keel, she opened the hatch.

Coop went up the ladder, his upper body extending into space.

"Mags, I need two-feet forward" he called. She heard and the ship inched forward.

The access door appeared. The alien keypad symbols meant nothing to the human, but Nan instructed him on the sequence, which he entered and waited.

The door popped. Coop's fingers found the edges and slid the cover back to provide an opening large enough for a body. "Keep it steady, Mags. We're about to transfer."

Coop's lean six-one frame flew from the fighter to the cruiser in the weightlessness of space. The access tunnel provided more than enough room, allowing him to turn, take the two cases handed up by Hiro, and then offer his friend a hand. Once Hiro was inside, he said, "We're in Mags. Closing the hatch. Stay close, and stay safe. Coop, out."

Mags placed Cassandra in the rocking chair, matching the cruiser's speed and direction, making sure she maintained clearance on all quarters.

"Cassie," she said. "I'll leave it up to you to warn me of drift."

"Will do," came the reply. "It is impossible to scan the interior of the battlecruiser undetected, but I do have a lock on Captain Cooper and Dr. Kimura's com-trans signals. I imposed them on the schematics for the ship provided by Admiral Nan. I can display on monitors or by hologram."

"I'll just watch the monitors for now, Cassie. If anything important comes across the communications channels, let me know." With that, she sat back in her seat, turned, and propped her feet on the pilot's seat. The wait the hard part now.

Coop and Hiro opened the cases, set out everything on the floor of the maintenance shaft, got out of their EVA suits, and packed them.

Coop strapped two diamond-powered laser pistols onto each thigh using modified latest-generation BlackHawk Tactical Serpa Holsters redesigned on Fell to carry them. He sheathed his rubber-gripped Army Ranger issued Fallkniven A1 knife on the back of his belt.

Hiro wore one laser pistol in a Y-strap holster and carried his katana across his back. Improper for a draw, but easier to transport.

"While the Prophet orbited AF3, the military performed deep penetration scans of the ships," Coop said. "According to Admiral Nan, the Prophet's ship was modified for a space two decks high and several cabins long. We assume this change is a combination throne room and personal chambers. Nan's diagrams indicated we need to climb up six decks and make our way forward a couple of hundred feet."

"Coop, Mags. Can you copy?" Her voice came inside his head via the trans-com.

"Mags, Coop. Keep it short. We don't know if they might detect communications."

"It's important," she replied. "Cassie has been monitoring activity and communications on AF3. Besides the armada of ships heading their way, the sheer number of Zenge soldiers on the surface is too much for them. Even if the Mischene military comes out of hiding, they have been depleted for so long, no one thinks they can put up much of a fight."

"I realize they need help, but we are not currently in a position to do a hell of a lot," Coop responded.

"Maybe we are. A communication between the 109 and AF3 command center says the Zenge still wear their shock collars. If they could get the codes, the computer people could take control. They could shock the Zenge senseless, or even kill them. The only ones in the system with those command codes are the Prophet, and his top general, Trewellan. Both are on board this ship."

"Can't they hack them?" Hiro asked.

"Not since they did it to the battlecruisers baiting the wormhole trap," Mags answered. "They added more security features and limited access to the codes."

"Okay, that is important, and maybe we can do something," Coop said. "I will go after Soren. Hiro will try to find Trewellan and persuade him to provide the codes. Does the diagram Admiral Nan gave us offer any clues as to where Hiro might find the General?"

"Funny you should ask," the pilot said. "The officers' quarters are clearly marked, and include level of available comfort. I believe the General will be in the best one, and that is one deck below the big chamber, amidship. It is directly across from a lift access for added convenience."

"Good call, Mags. Now, unless something equally important comes up, let's try to keep com-silence. Coop, out."

Turning to Hiro he said, "That will be especially true between us. We need to work two missions and try not to communicate until we're ready to evac."

"We'll stay together until we cross the lift shaft," Hiro answered. "I'll get off a floor before you and see if I can verify Trewellan's location. I'll tap the com once if I find him and twice if I need to keep looking."

Coop replied. "If I locate Soren, one tap and two if I'm going to continue looking. Rendezvous will be the maintenance hatch where we re-suit for exit. If all hell breaks loose, fuck being heard. Use coms."

"So we plan on using coms," Hiro said with a smile.

"Guaranteed," Coop answered, and headed up the maintenance shaft wide enough and tall enough for him to walk upright.

He could not read Mischene script, but access panels lined either side the entire corridor. It indicated several of the ship's systems' maintenance, repair, and upgrades occurred right here.

They reached a split in the corridor that wrapped around a service access to an elevator shaft. The shaft went up and down, with rungs attached to one wall. Without comment, Hiro went up first, passing deck access tubes until he reached what should be the officers' quarters level. He looked back at Coop, gave a thumbs-up, and crawled into the tunnel.

Cooper continued climbing for another floor and entered the maintenance tunnel for the level now housing the reconstructed chamber. He lucked up. The tunnel ended with a vented access panel. When contractors reconfigured the floors into one large space, they sheared this tunnel and installed an access vent. The crawl-tunnel began again on the far side of the new space. The vented metal cover provided a view of the chamber.

Whatever Mischene, Zenge, or Prophet time-cycle the ship used, apparently evening occurred now. If the ship was on a war-footing, it did not reach this area. The chamber muted in shadows and quiet.

As he watched, the former sniper allowed sight and hearing to take over. Soon he discerned two soldiers inside the large chamber. Stationed behind a throne at the far end of the room. The two remained on station, indicating they pulled guard duty. Access to private rooms must be behind the throne. All things considered, it probably led to the Prophet. An office or personal quarters requiring more than a simple knock.

Coop pulled soft, collapsible goggles from a pouch on his belt and slipped them on. He extracted a mini-torch next, adjusted it for infrared, and began to examine the vent cover.

Designed for maintenance workers, turn-screws located on his side. Slow and easy, he turned all four to open slot positions. He eased the cover back into the shaft with him. He placed it against the wall, and looked back to make sure the movements went undetected.

After two minutes and no lights or alarms, Coop dropped to the floor, ten-feet below. His landing made no sound, but he remained still until sure the guards did not react.

After short consideration, he decided to walk across the space quickly and quietly. Quick for him equalled way fast for most humans. The reengineering done by the Space Ranger Project increasing his speed along with his strength.

By the time the two Mischene guards realized someone was inside the chamber, he surged left of the throne, both laser pistols pulled. Two quick taps on the triggers and the sentries dropped.

He turned the torch to normal light and revealed a doorway with a security pad. Being squeamish was not in his nature, so taking the hand off one of the guards with the laser pistol did not phase him. He used the pistol instead of his knife to keep blood to a minimum. The laser cauterizing the cut, and reduced the chance he might slip on a wet floor.

He placed the palm against the pad and the door slid into its pocket, revealing a garish bedroom in bright light. As he stepped through the door, he did a quick scan. On his right, a female hung from a wall, lashed at wrists and ankles. Dark, matted hair hanging down across her red face. Sweat covered her body. A metal Zenge shock-collar circled her neck. She was screaming. Unaware he entered, her screams were not a warning.

In front of him, on a double-king bed, another red-hued female lay tied and spread in an x. Also covered in perspiration and sobbing. Another shock collar the only thing she wore.

Next to the bed, wearing an open dark green robe that revealed a scrawny, black body, stood Atticus Soren. His long white hair parted in the center, flowed below his shoulders. In his right hand he held a stick, or baton. The tip glowed red.

Coop noted smoke coming from the girl on the bed's upper right chest. The smell of charred meat in the air.

The woman on the wall stopped screaming at the same time Soren turned towards Coop and yelled, "Who **dares** come into my bed chambers without first being announced **AND** allowed?"

When he saw a human stood there, and not a Mischene or Zenge, he did not act shocked. He did not move to cover himself.

"Who are you and what are you doing in my chambers?" he asked calmly.

Psychopaths tend to focus on the positive. Psychopaths do not take things personally; they don't beat themselves up if things go wrong, even if they are to blame. They remain remarkably cool under pressure.

"I'm Captain Daniel Cooper of the United Earth Space Fleet."

He fired the laser pistol from his hip, without needing to raise and aim. The burst hit the Sacred Voice of the Tahbita, Prophet of the Creator, and Pre-Destined Ruler of the Galaxy under the chin and exited the back of his skull.

Coop walked over to the figure lying in a heap and said, "Just wanted you to know who killed you."

As he walked to the girl lashed to the wall, he unhinged the forward array box and folded it against the barrel of the pistol. He holstered the weapon, single clicked his com to let Hiro know he found the Prophet, and pulled the wicked-looking knife from its sheath.

The girl watched him from beneath wet hair, her face a scowl, but no fear. Bound to wall-mounted metal brackets by straps. He used his knife instead of the pistol to free her. Four quick strokes and she fell loose.

As exhausted as she must have been, she held her hand out until Coop rested the rubber grip of the blade in her palm. She hurried to the bed to free the other girl. After hugging the girl, she picked up two sackcloth shifts lying on the deck, gave Soren's body a good kick, placed one on, and helped the girl into the other. Only then did she turn back to Coop.

"I will keep the knife," she told him. "We will not be taken again." She waited for an argument.

"Makes sense to me," Coop said. "Can you two walk?"

"I can, but my sister is not as strong," she answered. "I will carry her."

Coop was impressed by the tenacity, the pure grit of the young woman. As weak as her sister, she did not back down as he went to them.

"I'll carry and you follow," he said. "Watch our backs and let me know if anyone shows up."

He lifted the small woman, or young girl, he could not honestly tell, across his left shoulder. The other female followed behind until they crossed the throne room to the far side.

Coop placed his load gently on the floor, allowing her to lean against the wall. He asked the other one, "If I throw you up there," he indicated the shaft opening, "will you be able to grab the lip and pull yourself in?"

"I can pull myself in, but how will you throw me ten-feet up?" she asked.

In answer, he turned her to face the wall, grabbed her around her narrow hips, bent and raised up throwing her bodily into the air.

To her credit she made no sound. She grabbed the lower edge of the opening and hoisted herself through. Her head and shoulders emerged. Coop repeated the process. The woman grabbed her sister's arms and using whatever strength she had available, hauled the precious package into the maintenance tunnel. Coop used a short running start, put one foot high on the wall, and finished his leap by grabbing the opening, and entering the tunnel.

He took a moment to put the hatch back, wishing he had taken the time to toss the two guards into the bedroom and close the door, but things were moving rather quickly.

He edged past the two females and told them to follow as he scurried back towards the lift shaft. As he crawled to the elevator, a click came across his com. Hiro located Trewellan.

When they reached the repair shaft for the midship's elevator, he rolled over the edge, grabbed the rungs, and headed to the deck below. He never checked to see if the two women followed, assuming they had little choice. He scurried down another tight shaft for only a few feet, homing in on the light coming from a panel removed in the tunnel's floor and the deck below's ceiling. He popped his head through. The deck corridor dark and empty.

Having to take the chance, but using his personal trans-com and not the tactical com unit, he said, "Hiro, Coop. Sit-rep."

"Coop, Hiro," came the immediate reply. "Location?"

"Over your deck at the panel opening," Coop replied.

"Drop down. I'll have the door open for you," came the reply.

"You two stay here and stay quiet," he told the two women. "Once I drop through, put the panel back in place, but leave a crack so you can see and hear. Open it when I tell you. If anyone else shows up, stay hidden."

He did not wait on a reply, immediately dropping through to the deck below. The door to the cabin directly in front of him opened and he entered.

The officer's cabin was a lot less garish than the Prophet's bed-chambers, and included workspace, a sitting area, and a small kitchen. He guessed the bedroom, head, and other amenities were behind other doors. Hiro stood there. A man with dark skin, white hair, nude from the waist up, and tied to an office-style chair with him.

A dark-skinned, white-haired female sat on the far end of the sofa in the sitting area behind the tied man. Her head buried be-hind pulled-up knees wrapped by her arms. She rocked slowly, but never looked up.

"What is it with men who seem to relate power with sexual perversion?" Coop asked.

"I'm a planetologist, not a psychologist," the Japanese Space Ranger Grad answered. "I'm not a physiologist either, but I have learned many of the pressure points which cause pain for humans are also present on Mischene."

As a martial arts master, Hiro was well acquainted with pres-sure points. The ability to disarm and disable an opponent using accuracy and soft-targets on the body essential skills for men like him and Daniel Cooper.

"I have the codes to the shock collars," he said. "I also have the pass-codes for data-storage files on board this ship. We should be able to learn everything about the Prophet, his father, their plans to dominate the known worlds, the location of the Zenge system, as well as outposts."

"You've been busy," Coop said. "The woman?"

"Trewellan had her taken from AF3 and delivered to him when they first invaded the planet," Hiro said. "She is the daughter of a General Tomas, who was assigned to oversee the Zenge military project until the Prophet killed him, and replaced him with Trewellan."

"My name is Ty Tomas," she said, looking up. "Kasper Trewellan always wanted me, but my Father kept him away. He even transferred Trewellan to the Zenge system when my Father was ordered there. He is a pig. May I get dressed?"

"Of course," Hiro answered. They discreetly looked away as the nude woman rose unsteadily from the sofa, made her way to a door, and through.

"Is it smart to let her out of our sight?" Coop asked.

"Maybe not," Hiro replied, "but it is right."

She returned a few minutes later dressed in a heavy pull-over shirt with long-sleeves, khaki-style slacks, and athletic shoes. Her hair pulled into a pony-tail.

"Are you through with him?" she asked. When Hiro nodded, she asked, "May I kill him?"

Hiro handed her his laser pistol and stepped back. Ty Tomas turned to Trewellan, raised the pistol, forcing him to look directly at the barrel, and said, "For my Father and for the Mischene . . . but mostly for me." She pulled the trigger.

She handed the laser weapon to Hiro. He holstered it, then reached up to her neck, grabbed the metal collar at the clasp, and with genetically enhanced strength, ripped it apart.

She followed Coop and Hiro into the hallway where Coop looked up and called out, "If you're still there, it's okay."

The panel pulled away and a red face peaked out.

"Come down," Coop said.

The smaller girl came first. Caught and placed gently on the deck by Coop. The sister came next.

"I should know by now," Hiro said to him, "that if I find one woman you will find two. How are we going to get them off the ship and onto Cassandra?"

"There are more Hana Kay on board," the one with his knife said. "If we leave they will be tortured and killed when they arrive on Zenge. You must do something for them."

"Do you know where they all are?" he asked. She shook her head in a negative. He looked to the Mischene and asked, "Do you?" She also gave a negative.

"We have to figure a way of getting you three onto our ship without the people on this ship realizing it. That's first, and I honestly haven't a clue," Coop said.

"I do," Ty Tomas said. "The battlecruisers have a docking bay where ships can enter and a vacuum system keeps the pressurization equalized between the bay and space. There's no need to depressurize the compartment. How large a ship do you have?"

"56-feet wide, 72-feet long, and 24-feet tall," Coop answered.

A surprised Tomas said, "That small? How did you manage to fly through the vortex?"

Coop ignored her questions and asked, "Will it fit in the dock?"

"Easily," she said. "It can fly inside the bay. I will be able to command the bay doors to open, but once I do the bridge will be warned. We will have less than ten minutes to get your ship in, get aboard, and get away."

"The crew will know about us then," Hiro said. "I do not care for our odds against the battlecruiser's weapons. Even small and difficult to see, once they know where we are, they will have a good idea where to fire."

"I have an idea how to gain extra time, and maybe do something about the other hostages," Coop said. "Hiro, take Ty and . . . what are your names?" he asked the two Hana Kay.

"I am Ashana Livist Tolnikiton," the red female with the knife answered. "My sister is "Wendapi Arsino Tolnikiton.""

"Ty, show Hiro, Ash, and Wendy to the bay and get ready. When I give the order, you open the doors."

"And you?" Hiro asked.

"We have sticky bombs in our cases, and we need to recover those EVA suits back at the maintenance entrance. Remember that corridor lined with access panels. I think I can create a little havoc. I might damage the ship enough to keep it in the system. The loyal Mischene ships heading this way could convince the crew to surrender the hostages."

Hiro and the women headed for the lift. Katana in the Japanese man's hand, to silence anyone who opposed their trip to the docking bay. Coop climbed up into the maintenance tunnel, and made his way back to the entry point.

Opening the two cases, he removed and placed a dozen explosive grenades with magnets against a dozen panels. He had no idea what each panel hid, but he hoped they were important systems.

He changed into his EVA suit, helmet, and rebreather before saying, "Mags, Coop. You still here, Magpie?"

"About damn time," came the reply. "This wait for the boys to return sucks. You two ready for pick-up?"

"Couple of changes," he said. "Move in to pick me up. We need to fly around a bit to collect Hiro and a couple of extra passengers."

"Of course. Coop?"

"Yes, Mags."

"I win my personal billion-credits self-bet if the extra passengers are female."

"Mags, it isn't on purpose," he said, not smiling. "And Hiro found one of them."

"I'm under you and the hatch is open," she said laughing. "Say, Coop. How many women have said that to you? Get your butt down here and tell me where to go."

Coop directed her up and forward a few feet until he could push the cases into the open hatch and follow. Because the galley space remained weightless, he needed to pull himself down the ladder. Once the area re-pressurized, Mags opened the cockpit door. Coop did not bother taking off the entire EVA suit, just the helmet and rebreather.

"Use Hiro's bracelet to locate him. Don't worry your scan will be detected. We're about to let everyone know we're here."

Mags hit the locator, followed the indicator under the cruiser's port-side power cell housing, and along the side of the vessel until parallel with the signal.

"Hiro, Coop. Open the door," he said.

On the side of the ship a large hangar-style door pulled in and followed tracks until a large hole appeared in the side of the vessel. Mags did not bother to ask. She pushed Cassandra inside sideways, extended landing gear, and settled onto the deck.

Coop opened the rear ramp, and Ty Tomas entered, followed by Ashana, and Hiro carrying Wendapi. He closed the ramp, pushed a button on his wrist-computer, and called out to Mags, "Wheels up and get us distance."

Twelve blasts tore through the maintenance tunnel, effectively cutting off every major operational system within the battlecruiser, just as the bridge crew woke the captain regarding an open dock door.

No more than two-hundred feet into the void of space, Mags initiated the Rys force field bubble and set sub-light drive for Aster Farum 3.

CHAPTER 38

Elena Casalobos sat behind her desk in the Captain's office. She set down the data pad with updates on casualties, after-action reports on surface battles, and demands for information coming from both Space Fleet Command and the United Earth Council back on Earth. She let the tension escape with a long exhale.

This was her office, with her bridge to her right, and her quarters to her left. She dreamed of flying through outer space in command of a beautiful ship with a trusted and valiant crew since she first heard the United Earth Council and the newly formed Space Fleet needed volunteers to create the Space Rangers.

"Coop, you should be sitting here," she mused aloud.

Her communications officer on the bridge interrupted her thoughts.

"Captain, we received a hail by an unidentified ship within the vortex. The pilot said to tell you it was Magpie, and she just stopped by for some girl talk."

Elie smiled, shaking her head in amusement and disbelief. "Put her through," she ordered. "Magpie? This is Loba. It's a little late for Christmas shopping?"

"Hey, Elie," came the voice she heard from the co-pilot seat of fighters for several years. "Actually, I brought you a couple of gifts. I'm on the official channel so I can dump data to you. Kennedy, you eavesdropping?"

"I am directed to monitor all official communications, Lt. Moore," the AI's female voice responded. "I would not characterize it as eavesdropping. I am more of an official busy-body."

Over time the AI developed something of a personality, especially among humans the ship considered as friends.

"I'm sending you a data-dump from the Prophet's battlecruiser," Mags said. "It has all kinds of information on everything Zenge and the plans for galactic domination. It also includes the codes for the Zenge shock collars. I believe they may help with the situation on the surface of AF 3."

Captain Casalobos sat straight up in her chair.

"Madre de Dios, Mags. How in heaven's name did you get those? You shouldn't even be in the system yet. It's too early to have gotten here from Fell based on when you departed."

"Have your Tac-Ops chair check on the two battlecruisers in the vortex," Mags replied. "I'll wait."

Elie immediately called the Tac-Op station.

"The one we believe is the Prophet's ship appears dead in space," Sindy reported. "The other one is making way for the AF3-AF2 corridor and the wormhole gate located there."

Genna broke in to inform the Captain, "The orbital arrangement of the Aster system that creates the vortex has shifted enough for the vortex to begin losing cohesion." In a day or two the region will return to natural space. Captain, the smaller enemy ships are only two hours away. They will be within range to use their laser cannon soon."

"What did you do?" she asked, already knowing part of the answer.

"Hey, I just drove the bus," Mags replied. "A ninja wannabe got the codes and data while some pretty boy offed the Prophet and set his ship on fire."

Mags told her Hiro came along, and Coop, of course, but without using names.

"Soren is dead? Confirmed?" she asked.

"I don't have video, but yes, he's dead. There are hostages on the ship, which is why it was disabled and not destroyed. Hopefully the good guys in the system can find a way to convince the Mischene on board to surrender and return them."

"Anything else?" she asked, almost afraid of the answers.

"We have three of the hostages on board. They are beat up, Elie, and will need medical as soon as I can get Cassandra to you," Mags told her. "In fact, since there are a bunch of nasty boogers between us and you, and I really don't want to fly around them in this crap hole called a gravitational vortex, we're going to start hitting them from the backside. You might want to warn your group. Cassie says they are in range of your weapons now."

"And we might hit you by mistake," Elie said. "Go around, Mags. We have enough firepower to take them on."

"One, I want a shot at them. Two, you should save ammo. You may need it before you get resupplied by Earth. Three, you got no chance of hitting us, hurting us, or even seeing us. Commencing run on the enemy dumb-shits in five minutes. Can you believe they just line up like a marching band on a football pitch? Guess it's good for us these guys just cannot get their heads around the concept of multi-dimensional space. They've only had like five-thousand-years. See you soon, Loba. Magpie, out."

Casalobos headed for the command bridge.

"Kennedy, get pertinent data from Soren's ship to Nadia at systems so she can enter those codes and shut down the Zenge on AF3. Inform Major Duval what is about to happen. Contact the Mischene Command Center and let them know we are going to start disabling the Zenge."

She entered the bridge, still giving orders to the AI. "Tell Pegasus and Roosevelt to begin targeting the incoming enemy ships. Warn them a friendly is in the same space and will be assisting. Tell them not to worry about hitting them. Target fire and not spread. We do need to conserve weapons' stores. Save the tachyon cannons. Railguns and lasers first. Torpedoes or missiles if any of the ships get within 10,000 miles."

She did not wait on or need a response from Kennedy.

"Nadia?" she called, and the systems operator gave her a thumbs up. "Sindy?" she addressed Tactical and Operations.

"Weapons up. CDG ready on your command," Senait responded. Elie took a moment to realize she now commanded a Cruiser Destroyer Group (CDG), the CV of CVBG out of action and sitting on AF3.

"Targeting computers tracking port to starboard with overlaps on all three ships," Sindy told her. "Spirit Squadron is on the ground near the Fairchild and prepared to join if requested. Covane is in touch with Duval and the surface military compounds under siege. She says if you want surface batteries to assist with the incoming armada, release the locks and they will be happy to help. No one within the system detects your friendly ship," she added.

"Nadia. Send the order to the shock collars to disable, not kill. Sindy, tell Covane thanks, but hold surface weapons unless requested. All vessels fire . . . now."

"Commencing run," Coop said aloud. Mags, back at co-pilot, operated weapons' targeting and utilization. Hiro stowed the women into bunks. He offered restraints, but all three paled and denied them. The high-tech gravotonics used on Cassandra should keep them secure, even during the most abrupt maneuvers.

Earlier Coop gave Ashana the sheath to the knife. She kept it close, held her sister beside her in one bunk, and listened to everything happening.

Coming from behind and below, Cassandra passed ship after ship as Mags used the double railguns on either side of the cockpit. The bottom barrel of each gun fired super high-velocity projectiles. She sent four at each target. She timed kinetic bursts from the upper barrels. The kinetic load would pass the projectiles, impact the targeted ship, create an opening in the electro-magnetic force fields, and cause a fair amount of damage inside and outside as the burst blasted the field. Next the projectiles arrived.

At the speeds a railgun created, these relatively small rounds ripped through the spaceships and caused catastrophic damage as they tore through and exited. In spite of construction designed to withstand the rigors of space travel, the projectiles shredded the ships as if made of paper.

"This is almost too easy this close," Mags said, keeping an eye on the heads-up display.

"The Earth ships have engaged," Hiro called from the com-tac console. "The forward enemy ships are destroyed. Remaining ships continue to fire lasers at our ships in orbit. Poor targeting by the enemy. Sonic shields are holding when a laser does make contact. This isn't going to last long," he said.

True to his prediction, Cassandra removed sixty-two enemy ships using 280 of their 500 projectiles. Three of the larger ships required two passes to finish the job. The remaining 151 vessels taken out by Space Fleet fire. In spite of constant requests broadcast for surrender, the Prophet's armada of stolen and repurposed spaceships never responded. Whether crewed by Zenge, Mischene or combinations, they all went down rather than give up.

"Space Fleet vessel PT-dash-109, this is the independent starship Cassandra," Mags called across an open channel. "Permission to use your hangar to land, and we require medical assistance."

"Granted," came the reply. "Hangar is depressurizing. Enter when the doors open. Be warned, we have an Angel-class ship inside. Take care parking your vessel. Medical staff will meet you once we pressurize. 109, out."

"Can you believe that person just told me to be careful," Mags fumed.

"Actually, I'm the pilot, so the warning was for me," Coop said from the left seat.

"Yeah, well he didn't know that," she groused. "I bet he thought since he was talking to a girl driver he better warn me to be careful."

"Or he followed protocol," Coop said, amused at her anger.

"Or whatever," she said and began after-action shut downs, including securing all weapons before pre-landing checks.

"Hanger doors open," she told him, and added, "Please be careful and not scratch Mommy's car."

Coop brought the Wraith in using hovers and thrusters, setting her down on the tripods easy and safe. He gave himself plenty of room on all quarters. While they completed final checks, the hangar pressure returned and Space Fleet personnel made their way to the ship.

Hiro met them at the rear loading ramp, recognizing and shaking hands with three of the five medical corpsmen from the 109. As they entered to assess the three women, Elie Casalobos and Genna Bouvier arrived. Both gave Hiro extended hugs. They separated as a grav-sled emerged carrying the Hana Kay female with more extensive injuries, already hooked to an IV. Her sister walked next to her, paying no attention to anyone but her relative.

"Halt!" came an order from a UEC Ranger, with his hand up and firearm aimed at the thin woman in the drab shift. "That woman has a weapon," he said, pointing at her hand.

"Stand down, Corporal," Elie ordered, and when he hesitated she added, "Now, Corporal." She extended her right hand to the Hana Kay, palm up.

Ashana hesitated before handing the sheathed knife to the Space Fleet officer. Her trembling hand displayed reluctance in the act.

Elie looked over the sheath and blade, gripped the hilt, and pulled the knife out enough to see the black matte blade. As she held the weapon, Coop and Mags walked down the ramp, just behind a Mischene female, and the remaining corpsmen. Elie looked up at Coop, back at the knife, and then to the red-skinned alien. Coop simply nodded.

"Corporal," she said to the Ranger, "please make sure that no one attempts to take the knife away from this lady as long as she is aboard my ship." She handed the weapon back to the shaking female in the thin, sackcloth. When she took the knife, her shakes subsided, and while she did not smile, she did not appear ready to bolt either.

The procession of aliens, medical personnel, and guards left. Genna threw herself into Cooper, and Elie grabbed Mags in a hug that could break bones. The officer and the avatar exchanged people, leaving Genna and Mags laughing together, and Elie close to tears. She never forgot Daniel Cooper was often her rock during difficult times. For the first time in months, holding him and him holding her, she felt secure.

Mags broke through to her when she said, "Elie, if you hold onto him five more seconds that hug will officially have lasted longer than the time it took to wipe out 213 enemy ships."

Before her giggle could escape, a communication came through for her.

"Captain Casalobos, Representative Arcand is calling. He says it is urgent, Captain."

Elie sighed, then replied, "Tell him to give me five minutes to get to my office. Genna will make sure you each get a cabin where you can shower, change, rest, and get something to eat. Let's plan on everyone meeting in my quarters in two hours."

Coop excused himself to the others, needing to do a post-engagement inspection before leaving. He hushed offers of help, and ushered everyone off the hangar.

"Kennedy, I need a couple of favors."

Cassandra set down in the bay of the 99. When informed the hangar secure for exit, he left the ship via the top hatch. When he jumped to the deck, Sam Harrington waited.

"Here to arrest me or kill me?" he asked.

"Ask you a question," Coop replied. "What are your plans now?"

"You know Benny recruited me for the Camarilla Dissolvere."

Coop nodded.

"I wanted UEC destroyed for fucking with my life."

Coop nodded.

"I lost my family."

Coop nodded.

"I was supposed to make sure Space Fleet and the UEC came out of this mission looking bad. Sabotage whatever I needed to in order to make it look as if we had no business in space."

Sam removed his cap, turned it to look at the Space Fleet emblem.

"When Hawks took us into the vortex, I knew he was screwing up, but I stayed quiet. When the attack began, all I could think about was the people of my crew, and the crews on the other ships. I realized I had more than one family, Coop. I did everything I could to keep them safe."

"Will you continue to keep them safe, Sam?"

"Be difficult from prison, but if I ever have the opportunity to serve again, damn straight I will."

"Only a select group of people know about your involvement with the conspiracy. You came in late, you came in angry and hurt, and when the time came, you protected your shipmates. If Admiral Patterson and Governor Arcand believe they owe me anything, you will continue as Captain of the FDR. If you screw up, Sam, I will come for you. I swear."

They assembled in the Captain's cabin. Elie sat in the middle of her sofa with Mags on her left, sitting cross-legged, and Genna on her right, with her legs tucked under her. Hiro sat on the floor, lotus-style. Sindy joined them in the chair to Elie's left. Coop took the chair to the left.

"The UEC is preparing to trash the isolationist ideology," Elie said. "The engagement was reported on by Earth's news networks. When we turned Soren's ambush around and not only defeated his ships, but freed the system from his threat of religious domination and control, it seems the people on Earth took personal pride in our actions."

"How did the news stations get hold of all of this?" Hiro asked. "This trip was known about, but everything handled under classified protocols. The CVBG under Hawks, and then you stopped official communications with Space Fleet Command to concentrate on surviving."

"I don't have proof," Elie said, "but since this was obviously a communications hack, I think there may be blue fingerprints found."

"The Fellens would not know which news stations to contact," Hiro said.

"Nadia Cosoi might," Coop said.

"Earth's news channels received information, and reporters broadcast video and reports of the action. I'm sure they embellished it the way talking heads always do," Sindy added.

"Regardless of how it happened," Elie interjected, "the result is the same population fearing all things bad about alien contact are now cheering our involvement."

Elie stretched out her legs and set her feet on the low coffee table. "Arcand says they will reopen communications with Fell and Rys soon. He expects Earth will renew alliances and trade agreements. Pam Patterson is back as Fleet Admiral, and Singletary is her number one."

Mags mused aloud, "I know that people and politics are fickle, but is the UEC going to change directions with every win or loss Space Fleet experiences?"

"What are the plans for Aster system?" Coop asked, bringing them back to the issue that affected them immediately.

"Aster Farum 3 is under our military rule. Noa Tal is in charge, with newly made Major Covane the liaison. Duval is our ground commander. Combined forces are rounding up Zenge and placing them in POW camps. They are also trying to stop Mischene military and civilians from wholesale slaughter of the captives. Most of the Mischene extremist who worked for the Prophet and led the Zenge have been taken out by Marine and Ranger snipers. The rest will be captured or killed. A few will melt back into the general population. It may take years, or it may never happen that all of those loyal to the Prophet, or those who still believe in Mischene supremacy are identified. The races of Aster have a couple of hundred years of convoluted political intrigue, greed, religious extremism, and racial prejudice they must face and deal with. There is a civilization in turmoil, and a once united system pretty much torn apart."

"That sums up a bleak situation," Coop said. "What are Pam's plans for Space Fleet?"

"Fairchild is lost. We will maintain the hull as a temporary command center for ground forces," she answered. "Spirit Squadron and our ground forces will continue to support the planet's military. Rachelle Paré and the Pegasus will return to the Mars Shipyard and Docks within the week to support the PT-89. We cannot forget several of the Prophet's ships escaped, and there could be untold millions of Zenge warriors and Mischene extremists out there. Our solar system remains a target for them. The 99 needs extensive repairs and Aster system ship builders have volunteered to make them. "

"That leaves the 109 on station as the only space-worthy battleship to cover an entire system of inhabited planets and moons," Sindy said.

"The PT-89 will run re-supply shuttles between Earth and Aster," Elie said. "Once we are sure the Mischene battlecruisers and the system patrol boats are secure and on our side, the 89 will hold station while the 109 returns for repairs and refits."

"Black?" Genna half asked and half spit.

"She's off the 89," Elie replied. "Turns out she was never supposed to captain the boat. She and one Colonel Barnwell will be tracking down a group of conspirators on Earth who tried to destroy the United Earth Council." She looked at Coop who did not respond.

"Tasha and Tista Korr will join our people on the surface. They offered and the Mischene accepted their offer to assist in rebuilding a civilian leadership. Finally, the UEC wants to amend the Space Ranger charter and Arcand asked if I would accept a promotion to Admiral and command all forces in the Aster system until further notice."

After a stunned silence, there came a round of excited congratulations, which Casalobos quickly quelled.

"I said no," she said over the voices. Once quieted, she continued. "I have never wanted that much command. Plus, counting Genna's time in the command chair, the PT-109 has had five Captain's in her short career. I told Arcand I was happy as Captain of the Kennedy, and preferred that role . . . for now. But since the UEC was willing to set aside the ban that prevented Space Ranger graduates from attaining ranks of General or Admiral, I suggested a much more qualified, experienced, and ready candidate. I recommended Senait Kebede."

"Why?" Sindy asked.

"You are smart, a communications expert, the finest tactical and operations officer in Space Fleet, with experience as a ground commander under battle conditions as well as an officer aboard a space ship with battle experience. You have over thirty years of military service, a perfect record, enough commendations and medals to sink a large boat."

Elie smiled at her friend and continued. "Because I like you, trust you, know you, and know you can do the job and do it right."

"Agreed," Coop said from his chair. "Agreed," followed in unison from the others.

"And what did Arcand say?" Sindy asked.

"He has to consult with the other members of the Board of Governors, Admiral Patterson, and the Joint Chiefs," Elie replied. "But he said to find out if you would take the job, because he wasn't going to get turned down twice. He also said if you agreed, to start getting your gear together and plan on reporting to the surface. What say you, Senait Kebede? Are you ready to become the first Space Ranger Grad to make Admiral?"

Sindy hesitated, and then responded, "Yes," to hugs and cheers from those she loved the most.

"Kennedy," Elie said aloud, knowing the AI present as part of the gathering. "Send a message to Representative Guy Arcand of the United Earth Council, and copy to Fleet Admiral Pamela Patterson of Space Fleet Command that Colonel Senait Kebede is prepared to accept the promotion to Admiral when presented."

"Yes, Captain Casalobos. My honor and pleasure," the AI answered.

Soon after people began to leave, Coop the only one remaining with Elie. They sat side-by-side on the sofa, feet up, hips touching.

"What do you do now?" Elie asked.

"Hiro and Mags are going to stay to join Duval and Noa on the planet for a while," he answered. "Hiro can help Duval's people as they assist in the capture of remaining holdouts. Mags will assist Noa by acting as a reserve pilot, giving her people rest. Plus she wants to get her hands on a Spirit-class fighter. It will be like a holiday for her."

"And you? We still haven't addressed the fact that Pam knows you are involved, but the UEC may only suspect it. Hell, no one knows whether you are a deserter, retired, dead, or somewhere in between."

"If I have a choice in the matter, I prefer the somewhere in between," he said smiling. "Until I can work that out with Patterson, I'll stay in the background. I'm going to make a quick trip back to Fell and collect Sky, Storm, and Sparks. Tasha messaged she could use their help for a week setting up new hardware and software on AF3 to facilitate communications on the planet, within the solar system, and across systems. Once we get back, maybe you and Sindy can find me odd jobs to help with."

"I'm sure Sindy will appreciate having a covert agent available, but I have an odd job for you before you go." She stood, pulled her shirt over her head, and unhooked her bra, exposing large, round honey-brown breasts and hard pink nipples.

"Sky and Storm gave me permission to borrow you when needed, and right now I have need." She took his hand, pulled him up and led him, willingly, to her bed.

CHAPTER 39

SOMEWHERE IN BETWEEN

Early next morning he met Elie, Mags, Genna and Hiro in the hangar. Mags and Hiro removing their gear from Cassandra before his departure.

"Sindy's promotion came through," Elie told him. "The vortex is breaking up. Two loyalist Mischene battlecruisers are closing on the Prophet's disabled ship. Everyone hopes they give up peacefully and release the hostages, but they will not take chances. If attacked, I'm afraid they will finish what you started, innocents on board or not."

After good-bye hugs all around, his three friends left the hangar and he entered Cassandra though the rear storage. Cassie became corporeal by the time he closed the storage door and entered the galley. She appeared dressed in khaki cargo pants, tennis shoes, a half shirt displaying under-boob, and her honey-blond hair in a pony tail.

"I like it when you enter from the rear," she said, and licked her lips.

"Don't ever give up, do you?" he laughed as he made his way to the cockpit.

"No reason to give up," she replied, taking the co-pilot's chair. "I have nothing but time, and you are male. Sooner or later I will hit on just the right combination of looks and clothes, or lack of clothes."

"Captain Cooper, the hanger is depressurized and door is open," came the flight control voice. "Good luck and safe flight, Captain."

"Thank you, Control. Cassandra is exiting Kennedy."

The Wraith class fighter eased back and out of the opening into space. Coop used thrusters to drop below the level of the warship before engaging sub-light engines. Cassandra had a course laid in for the nearest system rim. It would take just a few hours to reach a point where he could adjust the array for open space and full speed.

Within the gravity effects of a solar system, the little ship did a remarkable 80,473,995.48 mph. Once they could put the system's effects behind them, the ship would travel 1,000 parsecs (1kpc) in twenty-four hours.

They could cover nineteen-trillion-miles in one day.

The physicists already had a difficult time trying to explain how the laws of physics were more like guidelines in this new age of galactic travel. They offered no clue why every ship with a space-fold array covered open space at the same maximum rate of speed. Whether it was the relatively small Wraith or the PT-109, the same max speed applied . . . 1kpc.

The crystal-laser arrays built large enough for a space-time bubble to form in front of the ship, cover the ship, and then release natural space behind the ship, but size meant nothing to speed.

The trip to the rim passed in comfortable silence. Coop ran different scenarios though his head, trying to decide how the Aster system would begin and proceed through a difficult healing process. Cassandra would fade out from time to time, and return in a slightly different outfit or hairstyle. She never said anything.

"Exiting space fold," her voice informed him. "Resetting navigation for Fell. Re-entering space-fold."

Cassandra coursed for Fell.

"Why didn't you engage the Rys force field and head back to Fell directly from AF3?" Cassie asked.

"Because we don't know how much we tax the systems that way," he replied. "Time was imperative for the trip from Fell to the vortex. If we need to travel that way, we know now we can. Otherwise I don't plan on taking the risk until I know more about the effects. Getting to Fell and then back to AF3 is important, but it isn't imperative." He looked over at the empty co-pilot seat. "Why do you keep materializing and not talking?"

"I'm reading your bio-telemetry," she answered. "I thought I would go about seducing you in a more scientific manner. Each time I appear I gauge the effects of minor changes in my appearance against your biological reactions. I believe that I will be able to create a feminine model you find too striking to resist. I am also beginning to experiment with pheromones. My research indicates human males are often stimulated by olfactory sensations as well as visual appearances."

"You think you can find a combination of looks, dress, and smell that I will be unable to resist? Why do you think that?" he asked.

"My time with Lt. Moore has been as valuable as my time in research," Cassie replied. "Mags said repeatedly men are stupid and easy to manipulate. Human males think with their . . . "

"I know what Mags believes men think with," Coop interrupted. "I also imagine every man has a fantasy woman. I just don't think meeting her will result in a complete meltdown."

When the computer programmers working for Trent Industries were tasked with building an artificial intelligence to operate and maintain systems on the new Wraith, they were also presented with the opportunity of creating the personality for a new holo-avatar. What Trent was not aware of when he gifted the Wraith to Coop, along with the AI and Avatar came a sub-routine within the source codes supposedly deleted before final delivery. A code writer thought it would be fun to have the avatar available as a sex-toy. Stuck on long lonely space flights, it would provide company both intellectual and physical. He wrote a sub-program that would make the avatar sexually attracted to its captain. Too many years of gaming and a computer geek became responsible for the sexual tension between Cassie and Coop. All because Trent took the ship early.

Coop could have the sub-routine deleted. He was not sure if he would or should. He enjoyed Cassie's company, and feared re-programming now might destroy her personality. Still, there were times when she made it difficult not to notice her.

At sixteen hours into the trip, Coop brought the lights down in the cabin and made his way to the bunks. Removing everything but his boxers, ready to climb onto the lowest bunk, he was interrupted by an "Excuse me," from Cassie.

She found the right combination.

Honey-blond hair pulled back into the ponytail he found cute and sexy. The style provided her pretty face full frame, from green almond-shaped eyes, pouty full lips, to the strong chin. Graceful neck. She wore a cut-off white t-shirt to show a lot of tanned, smooth skin, and ripped abs beneath the promise of round, firm full breasts. Her nipples teased through the thin fabric.

Simple white panties hugged the narrow hips of a young, athletic woman. Her legs were long, strong, and also tan. She had on white crew socks and no shoes.

As she moved closer, her breathing raised and lowered the white top. The scent of Caribbean sea and female musk drifted softly across his awareness.

"Your bio-telemetry readings are impressive," she whispered. She pressed a curvy five-foot-nine against his six-foot-one. Her mouth covered his and her tongue worked easily into his mouth. His hands pulled her closer by holding two firm butt cheeks. Her fingers found the front of his shorts.

She pulled away from the kiss and said, "It appears all of your systems are responding perfectly."

Coop did not reply. He lost and he knew it. He pulled her into another kiss and the ship shuddered.

"Is that you?" he asked.

Cassie had a confused look. The ship shuddered again, much more violently. Then it bucked, and in spite of the gravotonics, both were tossed up and then down to the deck, Coop landing on top of the avatar.

"We're under attack," she said, unfazed by his weight thrown atop her or the heavy landing. "I'm unable to . . ." and she dematerialized. Coop dropped the few inches to the deck, caught himself, and pushed straight up.

"Cassie, report," he commanded.

The ship jerked violently. He was thrown backward and into the wall beside the bunks. His head hit and hit hard, knocking him unconscious. As he fell, something yanked his ship out of spacefold and into natural space.

END

8/29/17